# MIXED MESSAGES

## A LOVE STORY...

**Brooklyn Prairie Publishing**



ISBN-13:
ePub - 979-8-9908336-6-1
Paperback - 979-8-9908336-7-8

Love,
South Dakota
Style

# MIXED MESSAGES

A LOVE STORY...

JODI CULLINEY

*For my mom, who read to me, took me to the library, watched as I spent money to buy books, but never questioned or tried to censor anything I read. Thank you, JoAnn, for giving me the freedom to choose.*

# ℗ROLOGUE

Effie, sorry, plane was late getting in. Why did I fly in on the day of the wedding? Good question! Anyway, we are on the way and should be on time for the ceremony.

Happy wedding day!

Of all the days to be late for something, it had to be Josh and Effie's wedding day! Of course, she had been on the verge of not attending at all, so her presence *here* could be considered a minor miracle. Theoretically, she supposed she was on the way "there". Wherever "there" was, Lana considered, gazing out the window of her rental car at the foreign landscape as they cruised down the highway.

"Hey, Earth to Lana," she heard a voice commenting and turned her head toward the handsome man sitting in the driver's seat.

"Sorry, in my own thoughts—what were you saying?" Why couldn't he just give her these two hours (according to Josh, but Effie had told her it was more like an hour and a half) to get herself settled? He was not usually so loquacious (thank you, word-of-the-day calendar), but today he needed to be chatty Cathy?

He laughed as though completely unbothered, which, in all fairness, he probably was. Nothing about this day meant anything to him—even being here (or there), with her. "I just asked if the wedding was going to be weird for you, since you had a 'thing' for the groom?" Out of the side of his blue eye, he shot her a look, before putting both of his eyes back on the road. "Right? Didn't you have the hots for the fancy doctor?"

"Surgeon," Lana corrected him, as her face burned from embarrassment. "Josh is a full-fledged surgeon now, and what we had was more meaningful to me, anyway, than 'the hots'. " Over the last two years, she had done her best to put her past feelings for Josh behind her and loathed being reminded of them, especially since she had become quite close with Effie, his bride-to-be. "Can't you go any faster? I'm afraid we're going to be late."

He grunted as he stepped on the gas pedal. "If you were so worried about it, why didn't we fly in yesterday? And are you sure I look okay? Will I have time to change clothes before we go to the venue?"

"Do you know how expensive tickets were to fly in yesterday?" Lana asked exasperatedly. "I could barely afford these." Lana was now the one to use her side-eye to study him. "You look fine, and anyway, I'm not sure how much of a 'venue' there is…I think it's in the city park or something like that." Smoothing down the skirt to her best dress, Lana regretted her decision to wear it for traveling today, but it had made the most sense when she was packing, as she had wanted to travel as light as possible. However, two plane flights later, plus rushing for their connection and then standing around for hours, had given her a less-than-fresh appearance. She put her ear buds in, knowing her companion would prefer the silence, closed her eyes, and let the sounds of Judy Garland sing her to sleep.

Waking up to a slamming door, just as Judy was belting out "The Man That Got Away", Lana glanced at the clock on the dashboard, stunned to see that she had been asleep for almost an hour.

Opening her car door, he grumpily informed her, "Well, Sleeping

Beauty, it's about time you woke up. According to the invitation you gave me, we are here. Wherever 'here' is. Middle of nowhere, if you ask me." As he took her hand in his to draw her out of the car, she felt his calloused fingers and guilt consumed her as she thought about what it cost him to take this time off from work to be her date.

Now that they were finally "here", all she felt was dread and anxiety. Why had she come? This was a mistake, she told herself, just as a voice screeched out, "OH MY GOD!!! You've finally made it!"

Lana looked to the edge of the open park, and a relieved smile took over her face. Maybe this wouldn't be so bad after all, she told herself, as the butterflies in her stomach settled down, and then responded with a relieved laugh, "Tess! I come all this way and the first person I run into is someone I see on an almost-daily basis."

"Let me look at you—wow, Lana, you look gorgeous! Love this dress! Is it vintage?" If by vintage Tess meant Lana had found it in the back of her mother's closet, then yes, it most definitely was vintage. Lana took a deep breath to answer when Tess quickly fired off a follow-up question. "And who is your date? I don't believe we've met."

With Tess's deep green eyes loaded with insinuations, searching hers for answers, Lana started, "Oh, meet—"and then, as a motion from across the park lawn caught her attention, Lana simply had no more words, for there he was. Tall in his finely pressed jacket she was sure was new for the wedding, he was standing up near the gazebo (of which Lana had heard endless stories about from both Josh and Effie) and was at least half a head taller than the man to whom he was speaking. Chestnut-colored hair glinting in the afternoon sun, she remembered what it felt like under her fingertips, so silky and warm. Knowing it would be unavoidable seeing him, she had come anyway, despite the yearning she knew she would feel (and indeed felt now), as his face turned toward her. The face she had spent the past two years dreaming about: the man that got away.

# CHAPTER
## One

*Lana*

*Two Years Earlier*



Where was she? Squinting one eye open, her location was difficult to tell in the dark, but from the softness of whatever bedding she was lying on, one thing was certain: she was not in her own bed. What time was it? And where was her phone? As her dazed mind began to clear, another question became much more prevalent, and far more horrifying: why was she naked? Followed swiftly by: where were her clothes? Vague and cloudy memories began creeping in then, and she winced as she remembered the shots she had done in quick succession at the bar earlier, and all the licking…and the sucking. And was that…oh no…*tequila* she had downed, like a college kid on spring break in a place with palm trees? Not that she had ever been able to go somewhere so exotic on her spring breaks, in places with palm trees, but she had watched plenty of MTV to know what those breaks must have been like. God, was that tonight, last night, or had she missed an entire day?

Lana Miller reached out her arm beside her in the bed and froze when she encountered another arm—much more hairy, much more solid, and exceedingly more terrifying than her own. With a shocked gasp hissing out of her pursed lips, she rolled over in the opposite direction, seeking an escape from the unknown. And this was why she wouldn't, shouldn't, and couldn't be so reckless, so out of character. She had never done shots, but she had been out with a few girls who, on occasion, liked to do shots, and she had seen some movies where they did that thing she had done at the bar—but licking her own wrist was *one* thing. Licking the wrist of that sexy stranger was something altogether different, she thought, as the events, and her actions, of the night came racing back to her. Was that who she was in bed with now? Too humiliated to look at him, she cast her eyes anywhere but the bed.

Sinking to the floor, as unobtrusively as possible, she searched on her hands and knees for her clothes but came up empty-handed on her side of the bed. Well, almost empty-handed, that is, if she ignored the tiny bottles scattered next to the bed. This had to be the lowest point in her life, right now, in this nameless place. Was it possible she had met a different man last night, after the tequila shots? Whoever was in this room with her, she silently pleaded, let him be hideous, with the kind of face only a mother could love, just as long as he wasn't the man she remembered from the bar. She took a beat as she neared the foot of the bed, then sighed a massive relief as she at last spotted her underwear on the arm of the chair up against the wall. Now that her eyes had adjusted to the darkness, she gradually began to make out certain shapes. Was that…her bra…draped over the lamp on the desk? Already awash in shame, she crept on her knees, doing her best to keep a low profile, snatched her underwear from the chair, and hurriedly slid them on. With some (almost zero, but at least she had a piece of clothing on) dignity, Lana felt she could stand to grab her bra and sling it on. At least she had worn fairly new undergarments for her impromptu and absolutely unplanned evening with a stranger. Wait—was it a stranger? Oh god, please let it be a stranger, she begged, recalling now that hospital staff frequented the bar, which was certainly why Josh had suggested meeting there. Or would knowing the owner of the hairy arm be better?

With her back still to the bed and her underwear now firmly in place, she sidled two steps over and slipped her bra off the lamp and onto her shivering form. A glance into the mirror at her right provided a look at the bed without having to turn around, and the moonlight shining into the room offered sufficient illumination for her to deduce she was, indeed, in a hotel room: the bland yet somewhat tacky art on the walls, the desk she was leaning on for support, and the sterile white of the bedding. Lana averted her gaze from the bed and the seemingly huge form underneath the duvet. She wasn't ready. Taking a deep breath helped her focus her racing thoughts into BT (Before Tequila) and AT (After Tequila) and she felt with a modicum (yesterday's selection from her word-of-the-day calendar—maybe she should be thankful she was now in a position to be able to use it properly) of certainty that there had been no one in the bar last night she had known BT. She didn't need to be Columbo to piece together that being in a hotel room AT meant that was a stranger in the bed.

Now, where were the rest of her clothes? Tiptoeing over to the window, she searched the space between the bed and the air conditioner but found no clothes. Her partner in AT then rolled onto his side, and before she could look away, her eyes took in his face. Okay, definitely not a face only a mother could love (no doubt at least half of the world's female population would, indeed, love this man), and now that she recognized him, everything came flooding back to her. She had been at the bar at the behest of Josh, her office mate and former crush, who had quite cleverly convinced her to meet up with him, a few other surgeons from the hospital, and his cousin. Lana, despite having reports to write concerning the surgical fellowship she had earned six months ago, had recklessly agreed to go for one drink. As she had been waiting for everyone else to arrive, in a sundress she had gleefully unearthed in a secondhand shop on Mulberry Street, the Adonis in the bed had stealthily appeared at her shoulder instead, buying them both tequila shots and beers. His face resembled a cross between Cary Grant and Paul Newman, but his hair was not black-and-white movie material. Even in the pale light of the moonbeams filtering into the room, she could see it was a rich chestnut color, maybe almost mahogany? Lush brown with red undertones. Groaning, she recalled the feel of that head in her hands as she had guided it to certain areas of her body and knew she needed to locate her clothes immediately and get out of this room.

Padding across the room in her bare feet, she studied the couch on the other side of the half-wall but still found no clothes. What the hell? Not even his clothes? And this room was pristine. Why weren't there any items sloppily thrown anywhere? Who was he? A surgeon, like herself? So precise and careful, even in an anonymous hotel room? As she passed an open closet, she looked in and then saw the explosion of clothing, much like the man himself, if she allowed herself to remember last night. Very controlled until he wasn't, but every action timed perfectly for release. Still no sign of her yellow dress, though.

What Lana encountered, instead, was a door in the middle of the wall that was slightly ajar. A quick peek informed her that it was an adjoining room. Oh god, who was in the next room? She thought frantically. Had their activities been noted? If someone was in the other room, she had no choice but to expire in a puddle of mortification. Caught between not wanting to know yet also needing desperately to find out if there was someone in the other room, Lana gathered up her courage, cautiously opening the connecting door further. Pressing her face to the sliver so she could peek in, all she found (much to her relief) was a bed still tightly made, with a suitcase backed up against the foot of the bed. Before shutting the door, she glimpsed an open mini fridge across the other room; after turning, she saw the same item in her own room, whose bare shelves explained the tiny bottles strewn next to the bed. Good lord, how much had they drunk once they got to this room, and had they been so completely addled that they hadn't had the ability to close the refrigerator doors?

A few more steps across the lush carpet in her room brought her to another door, with light glowing from underneath it; upon opening it, Lana almost crumpled with relief as she finally found her dress sitting in a ball on the counter. Grasping the dress in her hand, she startled as two arms dusted with dark brown hairs embraced her from behind and pulled her into a hot and hairy chest. "Where are you going?" whispered his deep voice into her ear, and she was helpless to stop the shiver from running down her body. That voice, she recalled, is what brought her here in the first place, and Lana felt powerless to resist it.

As this man—this fine, delicious man—kissed a line down her neck to her shoulders, Lana forgot herself and leaned her head back against his chest with a deep sigh. The feeling of his hands moving to her hips, though, shot her eyes wide open, and she caught a withering view of herself in the bathroom mirror: a stomach that enjoyed one too many cookies in the afternoon at her desk, thighs that touched each other, dimpled with cellulite, and breasts overflowing the bra she had incorrectly purchased in the size she had worn when she had *last* bought a bra, probably ten years ago, evidently having gone up a size since. Or two. In the harsh bathroom light, with her body's flaws displayed mercilessly, she wrenched out of his arms and then shut the light off to spare herself any extra humiliation.

"Look, it's been fun, and I appreciate how kind you have been, but I really need to leave." She pulled her dress on before he could see anything (hopefully), and then said, "I have to work early in the morning, so I need to be going."

He chuckled, "Fun? Baby, I sincerely hope we had more than 'fun'." Suddenly, her hand was in his and he was pulling her to him. "And Darlin', 'kind' is not the impression I want you to leave with." Then her face was in his hands—the rough, slightly calloused hands that had stroked her thighs and tantalized her flesh. "Now, why don't you stay for a little longer? I have a truck in the lot next door. I can be 'kind' and drive you home after we have some more 'fun'." His lips were on hers then, stealing her breath, her good sense, and every excuse she had in her back pocket to leave.

But she did it—she had to. Lana gently wiggled out of his grasp. "I'm sorry, I can't. I have to go."

He sighed and then handed her a small slip of paper from his left fist. "I wrote this out after I saw you get out of bed. I had a feeling you were going to leave without saying goodbye. It's my number," he explained, as she stared at him in confusion. "Tonight was incredible," he told her as those silvery eyes bored into her own blue ones. "I was thinking that you could meet me again tomorrow night? Just us? No crowded bar?" God, how did anyone ever turn him down? Especially in his far-too-alluring almost-nakedness.

"I don't know," Lana whispered evasively. "This isn't something I do." Yet as she looked into his light gray eyes, there was no doubt she could be easily convinced to do exactly this, with him, whenever and wherever. And that was not something she could afford to pursue.

Pulling her back to him again, he kissed her deeply and then told her, "Now just let me put the rest of my clothes on, and I will drive you home."

As he turned, clad only in his boxers, to grab his clothes out of the bathroom, she snatched her purse dangling on the room door and darted out before he could stop her. With her shoes she had found next to the door clutched in one hand and his number in the other, and she ran down the emergency exit stairs and out into the night of the streets of upper Manhattan.

# CHAPTER
## *Two*

*Liam*



As he drifted in and out of consciousness, buried under the downy bedding, Liam Livingston considered that tonight had possibly been the best night of his entire life, and that was saying something, because he had been gifted in many ways: from looks to personality, parents who loved him, a large and loving extended family, Josh, a cousin who he considered more like a brother, and the means to support the lifestyle he had *occasionally* taken for granted. Not tonight, though: he was not going to take tonight for granted.

Earlier this week, out of the goodness of his heart, Liam had accompanied his cousin, Josh, to New York City, after Josh had spent the last six months back home in South Dakota on some sort of sabbatical/leave from his surgical residency—hating the pain he had seen in his cousin's eyes, Liam had not asked too many questions concerning Josh's reappearance in their home state. Once his cousin had been back home, Josh had begun working in his dad's auto repair shop, and it was there that he had met the woman of his dreams (actually re-met, but that was Josh's story to tell). Now here the two cousins were, staying in a luxurious hotel in upper Manhattan, while Josh figured out how to put the pieces of his life back together. Considering his cousin had suffered one of the biggest betrayals in the romance department (being left at the altar the night before his wedding, and then finding out his best friend from college and his former fiancée had somehow fallen in love) followed entirely too soon by the professional setback, Liam had sweet-talked his mother into letting him take a couple of weeks off from his job so he could support Josh in his life-changing endeavors.

The plan had been for Liam to meet up with Josh and a few doctor colleagues at a country-themed bar on the Upper East side of Manhattan, but when Liam had arrived to find no Josh, he had sauntered through the crowd (as only Liam could) to get a drink while he waited. Not one to get his feathers ruffled over anything, it wasn't a drink he was thirsting for by the time he made it to the bar in the center of the room—oh no, a woman with almost waist-length honey-colored hair had caught his eye, wearing a figure-hugging buttercup-yellow dress that could only be described as what his mother would refer to as "retro", reminiscent of something out of the old black-and-white movies his mom loved. Suddenly he could not wait to lay a little of his Midwestern charm on her, which he had been told he had an abundance of in the thirty-four years since his birth.

Once she had turned her mysterious dark-blue eyes on him, he had been lost—which meant he had done the only thing he knew how to do in any situation in which he felt over his head, and that was to turn the charm up full blast, because he could not let her get away or lose interest before she was completely under his spell. From the way her pupils had dilated, it was obvious she was attracted, and Liam's guide to life was to maintain a woman's physical attraction before she could see any of the cracks that were below his near-perfect exterior. Unfortunately, despite his many outwardly apparent gifts, he was cognizant of what he lacked. He wasn't a genius like his cousin, Josh, or his younger sister, Cait, both of whom were so focused and motivated, each having known what high-pressure careers they had wanted since they were young. Josh the surgeon (once he finally finished his residency) and Cait an environmental lawyer, who had been taking on oil companies for the people in the Gulf of Mexico: until recently, anyway, since she had moved back home to South Dakota a couple of weeks ago to work (like him) for their family's fleet of car dealerships throughout eastern South Dakota. Liam also lacked any particular talents, unlike his cousin Daniel, a talented chef working in a Michelin-starred restaurant in Chicago, or Daniel's brother Felix, an architect designing environmentally friendly housing for lower-income families, particularly those living on reservations in South Dakota. Well aware of how smarmy his vocation of car salesman was, Liam didn't hide it; oh no, he had learned to lean into it, working every room he found himself in, with an ability to talk to anyone, anywhere, regardless of their background.

His mom, Nora, of the long-standing Kinsale family in eastern South Dakota, had always encouraged him to celebrate the gifts that he had been given, and if he had been a disappointment to the family for taking five years to earn his business degree from New York University, well, his mom always smiled, and with a wink declared, "No one had ever looked as good doing it." Of course, it was little known among the family that his parents had threatened to withhold the funds to pay for another year of college, especially at NYU, so he had essentially no choice but to get serious and ace his courses that final year. Liam's problem wasn't that he was not intelligent, no, his problem that he had never had to try for anything. Going to flunk a class? Go flirt with the second-year professor. Need to pass biology lab? Pick a female partner and convince her the only way he could get a decent grade was if she tutored him (and by tutor, obviously he meant: do the work for him). Every transaction had been considered quid pro quo, though, because anyone who had ever helped him in his life had always been on the receiving end of his generosity. Money for the first month's rent on a new apartment? Done. Speeding ticket paid off? Done. Date to the senior prom? He was your man. Men, women, gay, straight, young, old, Liam was a friend to the people. However, more often than not, he felt like the biggest joke in his large extended family.

Before his goddess had gotten out of the bed, Liam felt her delicately manicured nails rake his arm, and his body reacted with anticipation.

Instead of more touching, however, he felt the bed empty out on the opposite side. No—what was she doing? He desperately wondered. He had never had a woman leave his bed; at least, not until she had been resolutely and masterfully loved by him. Unfortunately, despite neither her delectable body nor his not wearing one stitch of clothing, no sex (loving or otherwise) had occurred because this honey-haired beauty had fallen into a deep sleep immediately upon her head hitting the pillow. Yes, they had gotten in some very deeply passionate kisses, and his hands and mouth had journeyed the course of her body when he had disrobed her as soon as they had gotten inside his suite, with their outer clothes thrown into the bathroom and out of their way as they had stumbled deeper into his room. She had whispered, "Any more tequila?" into his ear as her nails had scored the skin of his back, so he had swung open the mini fridge in his room, taken out two tiny bottles of tequila, put them in her hands, and then he had darted into his cousin's room to raid his Cuervo-stash as well. Standing next to the bed, between tossing back the minuscule shots, he had slipped his fingers through the sides of her underwear and dragged them down her body before tossing them over his shoulders. The next round of shots had brought one hand of his behind her back, and with two fingers, he had unclasped her bra. His lustful gaze never left hers as she did the honors of flinging the lacy garment over his head, and he had shuddered as her bare skin touched his. Never more gently had he ever pressed a woman back onto a bed, and something in her face made him want to protect her. As soon as he was next to her in bed, he briskly rolled over to deposit his own boxers next to the bed; when he turned back to her, however, her delicate eyelids had closed.

Under heavy-lidded eyes, he now watched as she searched around for her clothing and felt a punch to his gut each time she was successful. As she crept toward the center of the room, he sat up in bed, and the moonlight shining in brought his attention to the pen and pad of paper next to the lamp on the bedside table. Desperately scratching out his phone number, he panicked in case she redressed before he got to her. Struggling to get his legs into his underwear, he rolled over and landed with what seemed like a tremendous thud sounding throughout the room.

To his immense relief, he found her in the bathroom, her ivory skin illuminated by the normally harsh lighting. She was a siren, and he was powerless to stop his arms from enfolding her still-warm form into his. Studying their reflections in the mirror, he marveled at how perfectly they fit together, with the top of her head not quite reaching his shoulders, but his height over her gave him a definite advantage, he mused lustfully. Her bra seemed almost unable to contain her breasts, and his fingers itched to feel their warmth again.

Suddenly she turned from him, and he found himself practically begging her to stay, offering to drive her home (wherever the hell that was), but she was immune to his pleas. Thankfully, she accepted his phone number with little argument, and he had even gotten what seemed like a tentative agreement for her to meet him again the next night.

After she at last conceded to the lift home, he just reached for his pants on the edge of the tub when he heard the hotel room door click open. No, he thought with a sinking suspicion, why would she be opening the door? Damn, this woman was proving to be difficult, yet something told him the fruits of his labors would be a bountiful payoff. Shockingly, it seemed that she had told him her honest answer when he had first suggested she stay. Swiveling around, with his pants in one fist, Liam swung the bathroom door open, slamming it forcefully into his big toe, while also managing to jam the rest of his foot under the door. "Goddammit!" he swore. "Fuck!" Dragging his mangled foot from underneath the door, he wrenched the door open, hoping he could catch his goddess still in the hallway. One glance in both directions confirmed that she had wasted no time in leaving.

Liam had perfected the art of not taking anything personally, and told himself that he would hear from her, consoling himself as he hobbled his way back to the bed, which he fell onto, landing on his back. Her delicate scent wafted up to him, and turning his head, he saw the pillow she had used still had an indentation from her beautiful head, so he picked it up and breathed her in.

When they had been in the bar earlier, he had pulled out one of his long-standing ice breakers: tequila shots. Not just simple shots of tequila, though; over the years, he had worked it up into an entire routine from which he consistently got rave reviews and excellent results. He had ordered shots for each of them, and then proceeded to lick his wrist, and then hers, watching her eyes widen as he did so. So affected by her response had he been, it had taken his full concentration then to go back to the regime and sprinkle salt on their wrists. Then a nice, slow lick of the salt commenced, after which they each drank their shots, and then sucking the limes ended the practice. Nothing he loved more than watching an attractive woman performing the ritual. However, his companion had taken it up by a million notches when she had then grabbed his arm for the next round of shots to lick *his* wrist for *him*. Not to say that it had never happened before, because it *had*, but never by a woman he had just met. Or, at least, never by the second shot of the night. She was a sorceress, a temptress, a nymph, and he had been out of his mind for her at that moment. And then he had taken her in his arms for an impromptu dance at the bar. His maiden had been soft and curvy, delicate in his arms, and he had felt something with her he had not experienced, maybe ever—sincerity. As he thought of his night with his mystery woman, such a feeling of contentment came over him, and Liam gave himself up to sleep. If he was lucky enough, maybe he would find her again in his dreams.

Hours later, still clutching the pillow he had gone to sleep with, the racket from his cousin's adjoining room awakened him. God, how does one man make so much noise? Knowing Josh, Liam was sure his cousin was trying to deliberately wake him up. He groaned, and with one eye open, studied the pair of water glasses on the bedside table, and he felt the loss of the woman he had brought back to his room the night before. A vibration from his pants caught his attention (not the first time that has occurred, he thought smugly, but he was usually wearing them), and as he grabbed the pants he had attempted to redress in last night, his cell phone slipped out, and he saw all kinds of texts from Josh, Henry (Josh's dad) and Sam (Josh's best friend, or he had been, until Sam had fallen in love with Josh's fiancée a year ago). One night with the woman of his dreams, and the rest of the world suddenly couldn't live without him? That would be a new one, Liam thought.

# CHAPTER
## *Three*

*Lana*



Sighing, Lana leaned her head back against the window of the F train as it made its way south through Manhattan from Lexington Avenue to her stop at 2nd Avenue on the Lower East Side. After she left the hotel, sometime after midnight, she had gotten on the Q train at 72nd Street and then transferred to the F train at Lex and 63rd. What a day this has been, she thought sleepily. Having been awake since five this morning, she had been at the hospital by seven and performed her first procedure of the day at nine. Shaking her head, she chided herself for ever going out to meet up with Josh. Or attempting to, at any rate. Instead of Josh and her familiar hospital colleagues, she had encountered what had to be the sexiest man in all of New York City, and someone she was sure would never have looked at her twice if not for the alcohol he had consumed. Rubbing her eyes, she wondered if it was her contacts making her eyes itch, or if it was the fatigue of the day. Without a doubt, she knew she would have a hangover tomorrow, because she never drank as much as she had tonight. Four bottles of tequila, after doing two shots at the bar? Unheard of for her. Granted, they were those teeny tiny little bottles she had seen people drinking on airplanes, but still. Ugh, she groaned, remembering the beers that had preceded the tequila. What was that saying? Her sisters had always chanted it before an evening out: "Beer before liquor...drunk quicker?" No, that didn't seem right. Maybe "Liquor before beer...have no fear?" Whatever. She had been too young to ever join in with them, and once she *was* old enough, she was in med school, and then preoccupied with her internship and residency, with each of her sisters already raising a family by then.

TEXT FROM GREER

Oh, no you don't, baby sister!

I've already told Ava you have some big secret, so be prepared to spill!

How could she have been so careless, so reckless? she pondered, thinking of her other act of indecency (and by far the most egregious). **Anonymous sex with a stranger.** What was peculiar was how unsatisfied she felt from the main event; compared to everything that had led up to it, the ultimate act of copulation must have been merely formulaic or routine at best. When her sexy stranger had first licked her arm to do that initial shot at the bar, the entire room had flipped upside down from her perspective. Never in her life had she experienced the desire she had felt for him then. Always too centered on school or focused on her studies, Lana had no time for romance or boyfriends as a teenager, not that anyone had shown any interest (aside from Anthony Russo, but since he was her biggest regret, she hated including him). Once in college, the weight of all that her mind and determination promised had fallen heavily on her shoulders, so much so that she had failed to make any friends, really. Of course, it hadn't helped that everyone was older than her. Not by much, mind you, but since she had graduated high school at sixteen, the two-year age gap was enough to set her apart from the rest of her course mates. Especially the students in her pre-med classes who were twenty-one or older, and she was still only nineteen. During the day, her study group would meet at the library or coffee shop, but once darkness rolled around, they all wanted to go to bars and get pitchers of beers while studying. Lana, too serious and solemn, failed to grasp how much learning could be accomplished for biochemistry while they were busy getting drunk. Anyway, joining them was a moot point since not only was she too young, but she also lacked the necessary funds to get the fake ID the older students blithely suggested.

TEXT FROM AVA

What's your big secret? Greer and I are dying of curiosity? Did you finally get a life? Just kidding!!!

Groaning, Lana regretted her impetuous text to her older sister, Greer, who was clearly with Ava, the eldest of the Miller daughters, since she doubted her private life would rank so high with either of them if they were alone. Together, though, Greer and Ava were like two of the witches from *Macbeth*, boiling up trouble in their cauldron of doom and casting spells on unsuspecting innocents. As her train stopped at W 4th St and Washington Square, Lana put her headphones in, pressed play on her phone to "The Boy Next Door" and as she always did, relaxed as soon as she heard Judy Garland's voice. Maybe the song selection wasn't as stellar as she had hoped, though, because it took her mind back to her high school graduation night, and the only sexual experience she could compare tonight to. Lana had skipped two grades when she was in grade school: after kindergarten she had advanced to second grade, and then the summer following third grade, she had gone directly into fifth. Probably part of the reason she had failed to have many friends was that from the time she was nine years old, all her classmates had been two years older. Once she was in high school, at the age of twelve, while other freshmen were knee deep in puberty, Lana had not been—from the outside, anyway. On the inside, she had taken one look at Anthony Russo on her first day at high school, and she had fallen for him. With his shiny black hair and big brown eyes, he possessed a swagger that made her stomach do flips. Anthony, or Tony, as she had heard his friends call him, had arrived at school in a sleek, black BMW, driven by whom she had thought at the time was his dad. Except in Oyster Bay, Long Island, parents did not drive their children, particularly their high schoolers, to school. Oh no, they had drivers to do that menial chore.

Lana had been raised, until she was twelve, in Riverhead, Long Island, New York. Located on the eastern part of the island (many people forget that Long Island is, indeed, an island), Riverhead was where the island forked, and The North Fork was one thing, but the southern fork was *The Hamptons*, with all the glitz and glamour ascribed to it over the years. Not for Lana, however, whose family was neither glitzy nor glamorous. Her father had been a construction worker and her mother a house cleaner (Lana had always thought that house cleaner sounded a step above *maid*); while both jobs usually required traveling the congested roads of Long Island, Lana had considered her mom to have had it worse (still does, to this day) since more often than not, her job required her to travel deep into the Hamptons. Driving her car loaded up with cleaning supplies, and her large vacuum usually in the front seat next to her, Fiona Miller was prompt, dependable, and her fees far too nominal. When she was a teenager, Lana became resentful about how little her mom earned compared to what those people could actually afford—something she had seen up close and personally, since Lana helped her mom during the summers, something her sisters had never been required or expected to do. Her older sisters, Fiona explained, had needed to stay home and take care of Lana, and her brother, the eldest Miller sibling, had always had some form of back-breaking work or another, and once Lana's older siblings were all out of the house, with no one to watch her, Lana had been forced to accompany her mother. She hadn't minded it so much, because she loved to see the sparkling light fixtures, and the gleaming entrances into these grand homes, with some so large Lana had marveled that they didn't break off during a coastal storm and float into the ocean.

Glancing at the time on her phone, Lana groaned when she saw that it read "1:10". Yuck, she thought to herself. She was never out this late at night, unless she was on call at the hospital for emergency surgery. Was this how all sexual encounters were supposed to feel? she wondered. Like nothing had happened? Comparing tonight to her "first time" didn't seem quite fair, because she had been so young and naïve. Lana had no problem remembering that experience in high school with the dashing Anthony, which had been over relatively quickly. She had even managed to spare herself the added mortification she was feeling now because she had even not gotten fully undressed for her tryst with Anthony in the boathouse located on the property of a country club in Montauk. Was the rule: keep your clothes on and you remember everything, but get completely naked and the sex is a blur? Why couldn't she remember going to bed with her sexy nameless stranger? Or could it be that the act of sex in general wasn't as great as the lead-up? Certainly no foreplay had occurred on that night with Anthony fourteen years ago, unlike this evening, which she had *no problem* recalling and would live rent-free in her mind for the foreseeable future. Perhaps it compared to eating an amazing appetizer, like creamy burrata with some salty, tender prosciutto and beautifully toasted crostini, but then your steak arrives and it's overcooked to well-done, so tough that you leave half of it on the plate, but since you're poor you ask for the leftovers to take home in order to dry swallow them the next evening for dinner? Was sex with the mystery man an overcooked steak?

Well, her appetizer tonight had indeed been tantalizing, and Lana had no problem recalling the feel of his large hands on her, roaming her body, or the way he had disposed of her dress once they had been in the hotel room. His shirt had taken two seconds for her to unbutton, so anxious had she been to caress his hot skin. Once they had those garments off, though, she had become nervous, so she had asked if he had anything to drink in the room, and he had indulged her (unfortunately). Stupid Lana, she chided herself. After growing up around the chaos of her family, she had learned through their trial and (many) errors that she could be successful, but only if she kept a tight rein on her impulses and actions. Regardless if some part of her had felt powerful tonight, as she had allowed herself to get caught up in the moment, she still should not have let it happen. No matter how delicious everything had felt (that she remembered).

Her phone pinged with an incoming text as the doors of the train opened, and she stepped out of her car. Dragging her exhausted body up the stairs, she took out her phone as soon as she was on the street and saw that two more messages from her sisters had arrived, each imploring Lana for more details, and chiding her for not answering them yet.

Wait, what was this? A text from Josh, received hours earlier, about not being able to meet up tonight. Well, that explained his absence, and she consoled herself with the fact that at least she had not sunk any further in his estimation of her. Last winter, before Josh had left New York City to take his leave of absence, she had erroneously decided to act on the crush she had developed on him almost from the first day she had been assigned as his office mate two years ago. Now *that* had been a disastrous evening, she consoled herself; unfortunately, it had not stopped her from then proclaiming her undying love for her co-surgical resident in an email she had sent to him soon after he had left New York City. To top it all off, Lana had also inadvertently stolen the coveted fellowship he had counted on receiving. At the time, her only intent had been to help *him* earn that damn fellowship, but on a lark, she had also applied, but only as practice for when it was her time to apply in earnest, in the next couple of years.

What if she had seen his text immediately upon its arrival? How would her night have ended? Although it had been delivered once she was already in the bar, she had no concept of how long she had been there before her hook-up partner had arrived, nor how much time had passed before they had left the establishment together. Her cheeks burned as she cast her memory back to pulling him up against her right outside the doors of Whistling Dixie, and there was no doubt she had been the one to lead the way in her own seduction.

As Lana walked up to her building, key held firmly in her hand to unlock the front door, she wondered if she was more disappointed than relieved at her failure to recall everything that had happened tonight. From the way his lightest touch had made her body tingle, could there be any uncertainty she would have wanted more? Just as Lana inserted the key into the lock on the door, an arm grabbed her around the waist, forcing a scream to pierce the quiet of the evening in the Lower East Side.

# CHAPTER
## Four

## Liam

TEXT TO JOSH

Why do you have so much shit?

Trying to remain focused on my dream girl is impossible when surrounded by your old medical journals.

This had all been his idea, he repeated to himself. From tagging along with Josh to insisting on driving a pickup truck cross-country from South Dakota to New York, Liam had been quite proud of his machinations. Everyone in his family thought he was incapable of planning for the future, yet here he stood, loading up his cousin's past into a rental trailer, making it possible for Josh to instead fly home and begin his future with Euphemie Van Holland, a woman who could fit into anyone's idea of happily ever-after.

When Liam's cousin had returned home to Beverley, South Dakota, six months ago, fresh off a derailed engagement to a woman he had been with for almost twenty years and devastated from his forced leave of absence from the hospital, Liam had been concerned Josh would wallow and sink into a depression (not that he wasn't allowed, of course). Josh had not had an easy life, as he liked to remind Liam whenever his cousin was trying to teach him a "life lesson". After a couple of months of living back home with his dad, Liam had, of course, done the only thing he knew to do in a situation: set Josh up on a blind date. Unbeknownst to Liam, though, Josh had already been reintroduced to the willowy Effie, subject of Josh's early teenage fantasies before meeting the delectable Tess, after he and his dad had moved to Beverley from the smaller town of Clover Lake when Josh was sixteen. Unfortunately, when Josh and Effie had re-met, Josh had been working in his dad's auto shop; hence, Effie had assumed he was a mechanic, not a surgeon, a misconception Josh had not corrected for her until far too late into their burgeoning relationship. That, and the fact that he also hadn't told her his *actual* place of employment happened to be in the biggest city in the United States, had been a dark cloud that had hung over his beloved cousin's head for months had spurred Liam into action. On a Sunday morning not quite two weeks ago, as he had been driving from Sioux Falls back to his own home in the small town of Carlisle, Liam had made a pit stop in Beverley to talk some sense into his cousin in an attempt to urge him into coming clean with Effie. After dropping in at Josh's house, he had only found Henry, Josh's dad. Henry had regaled Liam with the latest news of his cousin making plans to return to New York City to complete his surgical residency, and Liam made a flash decision. Upon procuring Effie's address from Henry, Liam then blew into Effie's house, making sure to cause enough chaos that the entire incident seemed haphazard and unplanned, while managing to drop enough information that would force Josh into confessing the whole truth to the love of his life. The whole scheme had worked perfectly, of course. No one had any idea how much work it took for Liam to maintain his carefully fabricated facade of goofy, carefree, somewhat air-headed, playboy-ish class clown. And that was the way he liked it, because it allowed him the freedom to live his life how *he* wanted to, without any expectations from his nearest and dearest. The downside to his genius was that no one took him seriously. Ever.

When he had met up with his cousin for breakfast this morning, Liam had been bursting to tell Josh about the woman he had met last night, only to have Josh throw it all back in his face once he had begun—mocking his tequila seduction (he supposed it was more of a technique, but last night, everything about it had been sincere). Liam hadn't needed to have a five-hour conversation about open-heart surgery to realize that the woman he had brought back to his hotel suite was intelligent. All he had needed were her big dark-blue eyes staring into his, daring him at every interval to take things one step further last night. Liam hadn't even gotten a chance to explain to Josh how he had danced with her in the bar —something he *never* does, because he has always deemed it too intimate, never wanting to lead any woman on in that way. Intimacy, for Liam, went deeper than the mere sexual.

His breakfast with his cousin had been unsurprisingly interrupted by the appearance of Josh's best friend from college (and current fiancée thief), Sam, who Josh had seemingly forgiven during his Brooklyn excursion to meet up with Tess (stolen former fiancée) and Sam last night. One of the text messages that Liam had woken up to this morning was from Sam:

TEXT FROM SAM

Liam, call me as soon as you get this!

Josh needs our help!

Really need you on your best tmrw.

Be on his best? Liam had scoffed at the message—after all, when was Liam Livingston *not* at his best? Sam had not even said "hello" when he answered the call. Instead, he had immediately begun telling Liam the news about Josh's change in career plans, which involved moving back to South Dakota to finish his residency. Duh, dude, Liam had thought scornfully. Anyone with half a brain would have figured out that plan from a mile away—hence the pickup truck in Manhattan. Despite being annoyed with Josh's "best friend" at knowing this information first, Liam was thrilled for his cousin, though, and excitedly made plans with Sam for the two of them to empty out the storage shed in Brooklyn where all of Josh's treasures had been moved six months ago (probably by the "best friend" himself), when Tess had moved out of the apartment she had shared for five years with Josh. She and Sam had bought a building in Brooklyn that housed their new bakery/bookstore, and the newlywed couple had just purchased a new property in everyone's seemingly favorite borough, a two-family house they were moving into within the next month. Sam had been teeming with information on the phone this morning, further annoying Liam since he had not had any coffee yet, nor had he been allowed to sit with his memories of last night with his dream woman.

Currently, he stood in a storage locker in Industry City, a recently redeveloped area of Brooklyn. He had driven his truck and newly rented trailer over the cobblestone streets, finding a parking spot right in front of the building. The moving team included himself, Sam, Sam's brother, Eric, Eric's boyfriend, Hudson, and Tess. Having known Tess almost as long as Josh had, Liam had been thrilled to see her, and even more so when she supplied them with snacks to help keep up their energy. From the day Josh had introduced him to Tess, probably a few months after they had started dating, he had been charmed by her. Tessa, as Josh had always called her, had always been kind of quiet, but very sweet and warm, super funny, too. Even though Josh and Liam were the same age as Tess's older sister, Ruth, she had always kind of scared him, because if there was anyone in this world who he felt could see through his veneer, it was Ruth. She had an uncanny ability to dig right to the heart of people, pushing all bullshit aside.

"Hey, Tess," he called out to her, "does Josh actually have anything of interest in any of these boxes? I have never been involved in moving anything more boring. Stethoscopes, medical journals, suits. And excuse me, but is this a wok? Are you telling me Josh owned a wok? God, this is bizarre, like when my sister and I had to clean out our grandma's house when she moved into the nursing home. We found all sorts of strange gadgets that hadn't been made in at least a century."

Tess responded with a hearty chuckle. "I am not sure what was up with that wok. All I knew was that it was not mine. I think maybe he got it when he graduated from med school, but we weren't together then, so I never asked about it—sore subject, you know?"

Liam nodded, because his cousin and Tess had broken up the first time when Josh graduated from college and hadn't gotten back together until after he had finished med school. "My cousin—stir fry master. And what is with this random doctor stuff? Why isn't it at his office?"

"I don't know, probably because these were his back-up stethoscopes?" Tess offered with a straight face.

"Seriously…is that a thing?" Liam asked, while everyone in the storage unit laughed at his befuddlement. Once again, he played the part of lovable idiot like a pro—never mind that he could actually see his cousin owning a back-up stethoscope.

"So, Liam, Sam was telling me you met someone last night," Tess said as she handed a medium-sized box to her husband, who then put the box under one arm and hooked the other around his wife, drawing her in for a kiss.

"Oh, did he? What did he tell you?" Liam asked cautiously, desperate for someone to take his evening as seriously as he had, and he hoped Tess and Sam, whose own love story had a somewhat mysterious beginning, would understand.

Tess pulled her long, red hair back into a ponytail and then took off the sweater she had been wearing to tie around her waist. She studied him earnestly and then answered, "He said that while you were waiting for Josh to arrive—sorry about detaining him, by the way—you instead encountered an interesting woman."

Liam had no doubt that Sam, a writer, had used different phrases, but he was essentially right. "That's all he said?"

Tess laughed. "Okay, he said that you guys did some shots. Oh, by the way, did you do that thing where you licked her wrist and then sprinkled the salt?" At his reluctant nod, she gave a small smile and slightly raised an auburn eyebrow. "Wow…I can't believe that still works," Tess remarked, with a slight hint of amazement in her tone. "Although, I must admit, Josh performed your little ritual once, and it was kind of hot." She let out a squeal as Sam wrapped his arms around her from behind and nuzzled her neck.

"Are you two getting any work done over here, or are you too busy comparing seduction schemes?" Sam lightly demanded, with a teasing grin on his rugged face. Liam had known Sam since college, having met him after Josh had joined the same fraternity as Sam. Although the cousins had both attended colleges in New York City, they had gone to different schools; Liam believed that if they had been together, Josh never would have entertained the idea of the fraternity—Josh would have had Liam: his cousin, his best friend for life, with no need for a frat bro. Despite his outward swagger, Liam could not help being slightly intimidated by Sam, author of poetry that had won some awards, and now he had written a bestselling series that he had seen people fawning over at the bookshop near the hotel he and Josh had been staying at while in the city. And where Liam occasionally felt like a fraud when it came to his own confident exterior, he knew Sam had authentic confidence in droves. Liam would also admit, but only to himself, to the smallest amount of jealousy concerning his cousin's friendship with Sam, to whom Josh seemed to confide his deeper issues, leaving only the fluff for Liam. Example: Liam finding out *after* Sam did about Josh moving his life back to South Dakota. Not that he hadn't already suspected that would happen (blatantly obvious to anyone with half a brain), but it had stung none the less hearing it second-hand.

"You know, Sam, if you weren't so concerned with pawing your wife, we could have this place emptied already," called Eric to his older brother, who had already carried out more than his fair share of boxes.

Hudson laughed as he picked up one end of an antique nightstand Liam recognized as having belonged to his paternal grandparents. Sam picked up the other end and the two of them carried it out of storage. Liam's dad, George, and Josh's dad, Henry, were brothers, with only a year in age separating them. Liam and Josh had spent their childhood running after each other in their grandparent's yard in Clover Lake, South Dakota. Their grandpa, William, had owned an auto repair shop that both brothers had ended up working in once they were old enough. Now, George ran the original shop, and Henry had started his own auto shop in Beverley after he and Josh had moved there years ago.

"Okay, Liam, tell us about this woman from last night," prodded Eric, who had taken a seat on a box labeled "anatomy" (yeah, like that wasn't freaky?). "Do you think you will see her again?"

With a deep sigh, Liam confessed, "I hope so, but honestly, I have no idea." Frustratedly, Liam rubbed his hands over his face. "She was like no other woman I have ever met before. Long hair—even longer than yours, Tess, and blonde, but not just 'blonde', more like the color of honey. And she had the darkest, bluest eyes I've ever seen. And she was wearing this dress from, like, the fifties—you know the kind I mean?" Tess and Eric nodded in unison. "She had this vulnerability about her, but also a kind of determination or strength…she was magic, you guys."

Tess whistled. "She sounds like it." She reached into her bag of goodies she had brought and offered them to Eric and Liam. "Peanut butter blossoms, which I'm guessing are now Sam's favorite, judging by the way he devoured about a dozen of them straight from the oven yesterday." Tess was a phenomenal baker and finally had her own bakery, which Josh had raved about at breakfast this morning. "Not for nothing, Liam, but what is her name?"

"This is where it gets tricky…I didn't get her name. Or her number. I know absolutely nothing about her. I know, I know, I am an idiot, which Josh already told me," he told Tess as she shook her head.

"Liam, I have known you since you were sixteen. I have seen you fall for one woman after another. That being said, I have never seen you this bewitched by any of them until now." Tess leaned down and kissed him on the cheek. "You're not an idiot, please. May I remind you that when I met Sam last year, I introduced myself as "Theresa", making it almost impossible for him to find me after he left the train." Sam and Tess had met on a cross-country train ride, fallen in love (never mind the fact that it had been Tess's bachelorette party she had been traveling to, in celebration of her upcoming wedding to Josh, or that Sam had also been traveling to Josh's bachelor party) and gotten separated because of extenuating circumstances. "We also had not traded any phone numbers or personal info."

"Technically, my brother did, though, right?" added Eric. "You just didn't get the letter he left for you."

"Exactly," cried Tess, who snapped her fingers. "That's what I'm trying to say—if it's meant to be, love will find a way, and you are not in the least an idiot for trying to find it."

"The thing is: I gave her my number, right before she left last night." Liam shrugged now, feeling slightly despondent, "but I haven't heard from her, though, so maybe meeting me didn't mean as much to her as it did to me?" Is it possible that he had been wrong to believe last night meant something to both him and his mystery woman?

# CHAPTER
## Five

## Lana



With disbelief, Lana stared at Josh from across the table in the hospital cafeteria. While she was enjoying her ham and cheddar omelet, with a side of two large slices of banana bread (house made in the cafeteria's kitchen and the best in the five boroughs), slathered in butter, the man she held in higher esteem than any other male in her life (with the exception of her older brother Montgomery) had dropped a bombshell on her that she had not seen coming. Way too many surprises had come her way in the last twenty-four hours, and just when she had gotten adjusted to one of them—BOOM! Another one came at her. The first was obviously her drunken hook-up last night, and then as she had been letting herself into her apartment building after her long night, her sister, Greer, had scared the living daylights out of her by grabbing her from behind, which had caused her other sister, Ava, to screech with insane delight.

"What the hell, Greer—you don't grab a woman in the middle of the night outside of her apartment building! What is wrong with you?" she yelled, while holding a hand over her heart.

"God, relax, little sister," laughed Ava, as Greer doubled over in hysterics.

Good god, Lana thought, her sisters were so annoying, especially in the middle of the night. "And what are you two doing hanging outside my apartment, anyway? Don't you have families that need you at home, not skulking around the city?" she admonished her sisters, who, despite both being older than Lana (with Ava nine years older and Greer eight years older) often acted more immature than their "baby" sister (their words, not hers).

"Lana, what is taking so long unlocking this door? I have got to pee desperately." And with that, Greer snatched the key from Lana's hand, unlocked the door, and flew up the four flights of stairs to Lana's apartment.

"Holy hell, girl, I never knew you could move that fast," marveled Ava at Greer's speed, while gasping for her own breath on the landing of the second floor.

"Are you going to tell me what the two of you are doing in Manhattan on a weeknight?" questioned Lana, not that she would get a straight answer out of either of them. Ava and Greer had always been as thick as thieves, too often forgetting when it came to any of their social-izing that they had a younger sister who would like to be included occa-sionally. Unless they needed a place to stay when they were in the city, that is…1…2…3…

"Oh, G and I went to a show tonight—I'm sure we told you about it. Springsteen was playing at the Garden. We figured you'd be working, or we would've gotten you a ticket," Ava explained, doubling over and sucking wind, as they finally reached the fourth floor. In the two years Lana had lived here, she had never walked up those stairs at the snail's pace her sister had set—she always preferred getting the torture of climbing four flights of stairs at the end of her day over as quickly as possible.

Suddenly Greer's face popped out of the door to Lana's studio apartment. "Welcome home, ladies," and she dissolved in a fit of laughter. "I thought you said Lana would be expecting us, A?" Greer asked as she held the door open for her sisters. "And yet, here we were, with no one here to welcome us. By the way, Lana, what was up with that text? Is that why you were home so late?"

God, why had she sent that text to Greer, who had then shared it with Ava almost immediately, she suspected. Between the two of them, they would not stop until they had answers.

"Yeah, baby sis, what have you been doing out all night?" probed Ava.

Trying to distract them, Lana asked, "What happened to the keys I gave each of you? You could have just let yourselves in," she sighed. Trying to keep the hurt out of her voice, she told her sisters, "Anyway, thanks for not inviting me to the show tonight. I could have made it work if you had told me in advance." Imagine, mused Lana, if she *had* gone out with her sisters, instead of hooking up with an anonymous man? Something inside of her, however, refused to feel complete remorse about her evening. Being slighted by her sisters was another matter entirely. Whenever Lana was alone in her apartment, with no one to talk to or go to a movie with, she would think longingly of her sisters, both of whom still lived out on Long Island—a little too far for an impromptu get-together, especially with Lana's schedule. When she began to miss her sisters too much, she then would consider moments like these, when they were all together, yet she still felt alone. That usually cured the longing for the Ava and Greer show.

Greer looked at Lana with a grimace. "Sorry about the key—I lost it somehow." A shrug of Greer's shoulders informed Lana that she had been right in feeling apprehensive about giving her sisters keys to her apartment in the first place. "Anyway, I thought you hated all modern music?" And just like that, it seemed Lana had been successful in making Greer forget all about the cryptic text Lana had sent. Lana stayed silent, unsure of whether to be relieved or disappointed—it shouldn't be so easy for her sisters to forget about her, and that included possibly drunk, post-stranger sex texts.

"I would hardly qualify Springsteen as 'modern', G," Ava mocked. "She's right, though," Ava loftily informed Lana. "You're always going on about your moldy oldies. Besides, we didn't get the tickets until today…oops, I guess technically it was yesterday," she remarked after looking at her watch. "Anyway, Rodney found the key in my purse and accused me of seeing someone else." Ava's husband was long on charm but short on intelligence. Although, to be fair to Rodney, Ava had a rather shifty record concerning her love life, and the men involved.

As usual, neither sister had made an attempt to tell her they were going to be in the city, then, thought Lana bitterly. This meant that after her emotional rollercoaster of an evening, now she had to not only put up with her sisters, each of whom could be insufferably annoying in separate ways, but she would have to sleep on her sofa. Neither Greer nor Ava had said as much yet, but…

"So, you're good with the sofa, right, L?" And there it was—the insinuation that it should be Lana who gave up her comfort. Knowing from past occurrences that it was easier to give in than fight either of them, Lana reluctantly nodded her head. "It's just that, you know, my back and everything…" Ava insinuated. This night kept careening downhill like an out-of-control skier ready to collide with an immense tree at the bottom of that very steep hill. There would be no escaping her sisters in this tiny studio apartment that held no separate room except for the bathroom.

"And Ava and I are just better at sharing a bed, you know?" Greer piped in, already shoving the decorative pillows off the bed. Pillows that Lana had purchased (spending a small fortune on) at the Brooklyn Flea last summer. Finely embroidered butterflies the color of bluebells on the softest linen in a delicate cream color, they were said to have come from the home of an eccentric writer who had lived in The Dakota. The writer, a notorious spinster, had died under mysterious circumstances in the sixties, and, leaving no will or family to claim anything, the tenants of the famous apartment building had divvied up her property as soon as the coroner had hauled the poor woman away. According to the legend, anyway, according to the woman whose stall at the flea market Lana had found the pillows. Lana had been powerless to do anything last night but pick up the pillows her sister had tossed and agree to the sleeping arrangements.

Which explained why, as she stared dumbfounded at Josh now, she could feel the tiniest of tears like needles in her eyes, forcing her to blink them away or have them well up into pools, thus drenching her entire face—she was exhausted, overwhelmed…perhaps a bit lost? "I don't know what to say, Josh. Is this what you really want?" As she looked at his astonished face, realizing she had given the wrong response, Lana rushed on, "I mean, of course, I am so happy for you. It must be nice to look forward to moving back home, I guess." Not that Lana would ever have that feeling if she could help it. Once she had moved to Manhattan, she had vowed to never move back to Long Island—Oyster Bay, Riverhead, the actual town made no difference.

To her relief, Josh smiled at her, assuring her, "Yes, this is what I want, and what I know to be best for me. There's something else I need to tell you, Lana." At his hesitation, she grew uneasy. Looking at his handsome face, into his blue eyes, a flicker of recognition shocked her. Not by Josh, though, but almost like he reminded her of something. He interrupted her thoughts as he said, "My move back to South Dakota is not just professional."

Of course not, Lana mused. Josh was simply too amazing to be single for too long, and she could recognize, finally, that no matter her feelings for him, or the feelings she *thought* she had for him, they would not have worked as a couple. In too many ways, they were far too similar, which was how they had gotten along so well as office mates and surgical residents.

Smiling warmly at Josh from across the cafe table, Lana remarked, genuinely, "I'm happy for you, Josh. Completely and sincerely. You deserve the best, after everything that happened this past year. I hope you know that?"

Lana watched as an unseen weight lifted from his shoulders, and he relaxed visibly for the first time since he had sat down. "I am slowly coming to terms with that, I suppose." He tore off a piece of banana bread from his own plate, moaning as he swallowed it. "Wow, Lana, you were right—this is delicious banana bread. How have I never had it before?"

Lana responded with a laugh, "There are some things I must keep a secret around here. Can't have everyone finding out about this bread. They'll start charging double for it." Although delectable, the banana bread was not a luxury she allowed herself, except once a week. While growing up, Lana had no choice but to learn to keep a close watch on her pocketbook. "Now, tell me about your personal reason for moving back —I assume you met someone?" At Josh's hesitance, she assured him, "Josh, it's fine. You and I are only friends." A relieved look crossed his features, and she prompted him. "Now tell me all about her!"

In awe, she listened to Josh as he told her about knowing Effie as a kid, and then losing Effie, and then encountering her again, and coming close to losing her again. His plans for their future sounded so romantic, and she told him so.

"I hope Effie agrees with you. That's why I couldn't meet up with you last night. I was in Brooklyn with Tess and Sam longer than I thought I would be, and we were brainstorming my return to the prairie. Sorry about that. I hope you didn't end up making a pointless trip over to the bar?" Josh asked.

"Me? No, I just went straight home." The less Josh knew concerning the events of last night, the better. She couldn't bear for him to be disappointed in her in any way. She continued, "So exhausted, you know, with all the paperwork I had to finish up for the fellowship. Plus, I had to be up early again this morning for the appointment with Dr. Gilmore." Dr. Gilmore was the attending surgeon, and since Lana had earned the fellowship last winter, the two of them had a standing meeting at the same time every week.

"Okay, that's good," Josh replied with relief in his voice. "My cousin actually went over there and— " Josh broke off as he looked down at his phone. "This is him now. Sorry, I need to take this in case he needs me— storage unit and everything." Josh rose from the table, and Lana did so as well, dashing over to his side to give him a brief hug. He had already informed her about his cousin and Sam helping him out by moving his stuff out of the unit. He heartily returned her hug, and then grabbed her shoulders, saying, "We'll catch up again sometime?"

She waved him away with assurances, knowing he was planning on leaving in the next hour from the hospital to head to the airport for his flight back. Lana picked up her lunch tray, having eaten every morsel on her plate, and put it on the window near the kitchen. Using the side door for employees only, she let herself out to sit on the paved veranda. Reaching into her bag slung across her body, she took out her book to read in her few remaining minutes as she sat on the bench near the fence that overlooked the East River from on top of the hill the hospital was located.

Although Lana considered herself dedicated to her profession, she had never been able to immerse herself in medical journals the way Josh did. He seemed to have no problem carrying his love of surgery over into his downtime, but Lana needed escape, and currently nothing was better for that than a Gillian Flynn novel. Once Lana discovered an author, she was not satisfied until she had read every book by the author, and she was on the last novel that Flynn had written, which had finally been available for her to pick up last week after a month long wait at her branch of the New York City Public Library. Looking at the title of *Gone Girl*, Lana wondered what it would be like to pretend to be someone different. Just let the world *think* that they knew her, much like the two characters from this book.

As she finished her book, her phone buzzed in her bag. Wondering who was texting her, she reached in and withdrew her phone, staring at the message on the screen:

TEXT FROM UNKNOWN

Sounds good, Baby.

Any time, any place.

Sorry about your phone.

P.S. I had an amazing time last night.

What the actual hell? Oh no, she thought. Nonononononono. Frantically searching her bag for the slip of paper her Hook Up had handed her last night, this morning (whenever the hell it was), she gritted her teeth in frustration when she couldn't find it. Instead, she opened her phone to the message and saw no outgoing message from her. What did he mean "Sorry about your phone"? Throwing her head back, it hit her, and she muttered, "Those bitches."

# CHAPTER
## Six

## Liam



For at least the hundredth time in the last thirty minutes, Liam read the text from his Mystery Woman, still somewhat surprised she would honestly tell him that her phone fell in the toilet. Not many women he knew would admit to that, and last night he had the impression that she was a bit more sophisticated, but Liam tried to have a judgment-free policy. Up until he had received the text, he had been maybe, possibly, the *tiniest* bit worried she would not reach out, but then her text had arrived, easing his mind (and ego). His goddess must have been as desperate to reach him as he was to hear from her, if she couldn't wait to send a text from her own phone, instead using her sister's.

After leaving his cousin's moving crew at the storage unit with the trailer to finish loading everything up properly, Liam drove back into Manhattan to pick up Josh and deliver him to the airport, all while cranking the hits of REO Speedwagon. Cursing his cousin, who had listened to the band almost non-stop during a leg of their journey east, he couldn't fight the feeling anymore that he truly enjoyed some of their songs (of course he would be loath to ever admit this to Josh). Liam had driven over the Brooklyn Bridge to the FDR Drive, and at every stop light or traffic standstill, he glanced at his cell to check to see the message was still there. And, of course, also checking to see if the text he had sent in response had been answered by her yet. Why hadn't she followed up with a reply yet? Was she thinking about him as much as he was about her? Did she remember stroking his chest, after she tore his shirt off, fluttering her fingers through his chest hair? Was she replaying how *she* had been the one to press *him* up against the wall on the outside of the bar, telling him to take her back to his hotel?

Exiting off the FDR onto East 61st Street, he told himself to give her time—she probably had more important things to do than check her phone at minute intervals (like he was doing). Currently, Liam had nothing more important to do than think about the woman from last night, pondering everything about her. For instance, he wondered what she did for a living? Maybe a teacher? Or a nurse? She had given off some heavy nurturing vibes, he mused, as he pulled up to the hospital his cousin had essentially called home for the last five years.

Shaking his head, Liam was still in a slight state of disbelief that Josh was giving all of this up to move back to South Dakota. It wasn't that he didn't love his home state, but Liam had always felt like Josh was bigger than it was…that he could (and would) become, like, the top surgeon in all of New York City. Liam had wanted the same thing for himself, back in college. Not the surgeon part, of course—his grasp of science began and ended with female anatomy; but he had yearned to be a part of something huge, an invaluable link in an integral chain of society. His business degree, for which he had fought hard once he finally buckled down and gotten serious, now seemed like a waste when all he was doing was selling cars for his own family's auto dealerships (and he wasn't even working in the biggest one in the string of Kinsale Autos of eastern South Dakota!). Upon his graduation from NYU, Liam had puttered around the city for a couple of years, first working as a management consultant for a start-up company in Tribeca that had lasted six months. Following that, his second job had been on Wall Street, where a brokerage firm had employed him as an analyst, a job he hadn't expected to like, but had ended up loving. Unfortunately, the stock market had taken a dive, and he had been "let go" after a little over a year, causing him to give up the apartment he had in Battery Park City. Never intending for his move home from New York City to be permanent, he had begrudgingly taken a sales position almost ten years ago, working at the Carlisle branch. Liam had not advanced for six years, until he had finally found himself in charge of the tiny branch. Proving everyone wrong, his family had been forced to admit that the once struggling location had boomed under his management.

A gust of wind flew into his dealership-borrowed truck as Josh opened the door and put two boxes behind the seat before sliding into the front. "Thanks for coming back to take me to the airport, Cuz. Can you take those two boxes yet and put them in the trailer?"

"No problem-o, but you're telling me that five years of working in that hospital and all you have are two boxes of stuff? Is everything going to explode out of them once they are opened?" Liam laughed as he pulled back onto the Queensboro Bridge, with his destination being LaGuardia Airport. Considering how much crap Josh had in storage, though, maybe it wasn't all that surprising everything left in his office *did* fit into two boxes.

Josh responded with a chuckle, saying, "I hope not. I passed on most of my manuals and journals that I accrued over the years to Lana. I never could understand how she never had a subscription to any of the stuff I did. Lucky for me, I guess, that she didn't, because she was happy to inherit everything. I figured if I'm starting over, may as well make it a fresh start, ya know?"

"Maybe she just doesn't like to throw her money away on frivolous science journals, unlike you, who is so economical in almost every other way except your subscriptions. Speaking of Lana, I have to admit that I'm a bit bummed I never did get to meet her. Luscious, luscious Lana. God, what a glorious name—so sexy…right?" Liam nudged his cousin in the arm when there was no response.

"Ouch—what was that for?" Josh exclaimed.

"I was asking about Lana—is she as tantalizing as her name sounds? Yet also classy, right? Maybe sophisticated? I have this image in my head about what she might look like—" Liam stopped abruptly as his cousin vehemently shook his head. "What?"

"Stop with the innocent act and stop envisioning Lana." Josh reached over and turned up the radio when "Much Too Young to Feel this Damn Old" came on, a particular Garth Brooks song favorited by the cousins. As they sang out of tune with each other and the song ended, Josh turned the volume back down before saying, "You know, all these questions about Lana makes me even more thankful that she didn't go to the bar last night to meet up with us. You would've gotten your grubby paws all over her, broken her heart, and then I would never have been able to face her again."

"Speaking of hot women in bars—read this," Liam demanded as he tossed his phone to Josh, pulling onto the BQE, or Brooklyn-Queens Expressway, on their final leg to the airport.

Out of the corner of his eye, he watched as Josh read the messages. "Okay…and?" Liam waited impatiently for his oh-so wise cousin to give him his interpretation of the text message.

"I mean…what's this supposed to prove? 'Hope we can do it again'? What does she mean by 'it'? Like *IT* it, or just the whole meeting up in a *bar* it? And your response: 'sounds good, baby'? Maybe I had to be there, but it's a little…" Josh fluttered his fingers and then stopped speaking.

"Go on—a little what?" Liam prodded his cousin. The thing about his cousin, Liam mused silently, was that Josh didn't have Liam's…experience…with women. Josh didn't understand the flirtation, the innuendos, the insinuations that went along with a night like he had last night.

Josh sighed with what Liam knew could only be exasperation. "Okay, it's a little creepy, maybe."

Liam sputtered in his defense, "Creepy? She's the one who wrote to me saying she wanted to do 'it' again. I was just trying to keep up, return the flirty banter. Honestly, I will admit that I didn't expect it from her, considering the disappearing act she pulled on me."

Josh flashed Liam a surprised look. "What do you mean 'disappearing act'? I thought she was your one true love? Your soul mate? Last time I checked, soul mates and one true loves don't just up and leave. Liam, she didn't even text you from her own phone. Or so she said. That could be her phone, but she wants you to think it isn't, so you don't reply."

"Wow, any other knives you'd like to flay me open with? Maybe you should use one of your precious scalpels? Cuts a little sharper, I've heard." Liam took the exit for LaGuardia Airport and then questioned his cousin, "Why can't you just let me have this experience with this woman? Why does everything have to be black or white with you?"

Liam felt Josh's hand squeeze his shoulder. "Look, you're right. I'm sorry. Maybe I haven't evolved as much as I thought I had concerning my tendency towards pragmatism. Or maybe I have, but only if Effie is with me to temper it. Everyone deserves the chance to be as happy as I am right now, and that goes for you, especially. I just want to make sure you're seeing everything clearly, so you won't get hurt." Did Josh not even know him? Liam never got hurt. "I am curious as to why, if you are so into this mystery woman, you still expressed such dismay at not meeting Lana last night."

"Just always keeping my options open, I guess," Liam explained. "You have to admit, you always were somewhat evasive about introducing me to Lana," he said, trying not to take it personally.

Josh responded, "It wasn't intentional, keeping you two apart, but I *will* admit that you two would never be right for each other. Oh, pull over up there," Josh pointed to the Departures Lane where a car had just pulled away.

Liam pulled up to the curb, parked, grabbed his cousin's suitcase from behind the back of his seat, dashed over to the other side of the truck, and gave Josh a hug. "I know you'll always have my back, just like I'll always have yours. I love you, Cuz," he told him, feeling emotional despite knowing he would see Josh again in only two days.

"Love you, too," Josh returned the hug and the emotion. "You've been my best friend my entire life. I will always look out for you, okay?"

Liam pulled away, patting his cousin's face with one hand. "Enough with this. Get your lucky ass back to South Dakota to be with the woman of your dreams."

Liam wiped away a few tears as he pulled back onto Grand Central

Parkway to head back into the city to his hotel. The plan was to leave the trailer parked overnight in the lot of U-Rent M Storage in Brooklyn, where he would meet Sam tomorrow morning. The two of them would leave bright and early to beat potentially heavy traffic on Staten Island. With the phone in the caddy on the dash again, a green box appeared, showing he had a new text, and he was awash in anticipation. Too much traffic on the road prohibited him from checking it immediately, so Liam did all he could to avoid any red lights to make it back to the hotel parking garage as quickly (and, of course, as safely) as possible.

# CHAPTER
## Seven

## Lana



"What in the world were you two thinking? Do you know how humiliated I feel?" But no, neither of her sisters would have any idea how she felt. Both had confidence for days, and if not, they egged each other on until they were close to insufferable.

Groaning in response, on the other end of the phone, was Greer, having gone back to Long Island this morning, probably long after Lana had been gone. Greer, a yoga instructor, enlisted her husband, Simon, to take their two teenagers to high school every morning on his way to his job at the bank. Greer relished in making her own schedule, leaving plenty of "Greer Time" for herself during the day. Lana could not begrudge her sister this, though, for Greer had worked hard at finding her path after getting into trouble years ago in high school. She and several friends had stolen prescription pills from the elderly clients they cleaned houses for on the weekends, sometimes selling the pills and sometimes using them for their own entertainment. After getting her act together a couple of years out of high school, Greer had attended community college in Suffolk County; just three months shy of earning her accounting degree, however, she had unexpectedly quit altogether. Instead, she had met Simon, her future husband, coincidentally teaching one of the night courses Greer was taking. Simon had been "let go" and gotten a job as a loan officer at a local bank. Greer and Simon had hastily married, had two children in quick succession, and in that time she had tried her hand at catering, landscaping, housekeeping (again, but this time no pill-stealing), and teaching preschool, with no desire for staying at any job for a measurable length of time. Finally, about six years ago, she had taken a yoga class at a community center, and something had sparked in her.

"Lana, the problem with you," oh great, here with go, Lana thought, with a lecture about how to live my life, "is that you are, and always have been, way too serious. You need to lighten up a little or you're never going to find anyone," Greer scolded her younger sister.

Biting her tongue against the hurtful things she could say in retaliation, Lana went instead with, "Did it ever occur to you that I am completely happy being alone? I don't need to be in a relationship to validate my existence," unlike some people, she continued to herself.

"Why so touchy about it? Just laugh it off, then. So we sent your hot dude a text? He must have liked you, right? And wants to see you again, since he texted back? I mean, why did you tell us about it, anyway? You obviously wanted me to know, or you wouldn't have texted me that teaser." Good question, Greer, she silently responded. Why had she texted Greer? she asked herself for the millionth time. And then why had she elaborated and told her sisters everything about last night? Maybe because she thought both of them might be impressed? Lana had been trying her entire life to get her sisters to notice her, and it was just like them to finally pay attention when it was something so startlingly out of character for her. Greer and Ava had not seemed to care that she had graduated from high school at sixteen. Or when she had gotten into med school at nineteen (which she was paying for entirely on her own). Or that, in fact, this surgical residency was her *second* round of residencies, as Lana had already completed three years as a resident in internal medicine. No, her sisters saw that as Lana being "undecided" and unable to make up her mind. On a good day. On other days, Ava and Greer would insinuate that she was putting off joining the "real world" and having to work to make a living. Or that she was "showing off", always having to prove how much smarter she was than everyone else.

Now she told Greer over the phone, "You're right. I shouldn't have told you, and I wouldn't have if you hadn't found that piece of paper with his number on it." Which she had taken out of her bag (after holding it in her hand the entire way home on the subway last night), crumpled it up, and thrown it in her trash, then only seconds later retrieved it *out* of the trash, where she then put it next to her phone on her small dining table. All of which her far-too-observant sisters had taken notice of, immediately darting to the table to look at the paper, squealing with delight once they saw it contained a phone number written in a clearly male handwriting style, and asked her what was going on.

Ava had probably been the most impressed. "Well, well, well, who would have thought that our baby sister would do something so *unseemly* as have a one-night stand with a stranger?" Ava, twice divorced, had married her high school sweetheart the week after graduation. After four years of marriage, and two babies, however, Ava had decided she didn't love him anymore, so had filed for divorce. Lana had been too young to understand that Declan (who young Lana had adored), had been cheating on Ava with Ava's rival from high school, the slut (Ava's words, not Lana's) who had kept Ava from being the head cheerleader for their senior year. Turned out that Ava had *also* been cheating on Declan, though, with the married real estate broker, Crosby, in whose office ·Ava had worked as an administrative assistant: answering phones, filing paperwork, and setting up open houses, while greeting his wife with a smile whenever she came to visit her husband's office. Ava's second marriage had lasted longer than the first, but after one child and six years together, it, too, had ended in divorce. Unfortunately, Ava had gotten her own real estate license while she and Crosby were married, thus freeing up the position of administrative assistant in Crosby's office. Never one to let anyone see her sweat, Ava had not flinched when history had repeated itself; she had, in fact, been preparing for it once she had met the nubile young woman her husband had employed. Fortunately for her, she had just sold a house to an exceedingly charming single man who had never been married but owned a few strip malls around Long Island. Undoubtedly swayed by Ava's prominent assets, Rodney had married her a year later. Perhaps the third time was the charm for her oldest sister, because she had been in wedded bliss for almost ten years now, and the couple had added two more kids to their family.

Sometimes when Lana considered her sisters, though, all she saw was chaos. No, make that **CHAOS**. The multiple careers, marriages, and kids…so many kids. Kids that Lana had been charged with caring for when she had been a preteen and teenager; given the age difference between herself and her sisters, she had been ripe for the picking as a babysitter. And now her sisters had brought their chaos into her life with the thoughtlessly sent text to her Hook Up. She wasn't even sure what to call him in her list of contacts—should she even save his phone number in her phone? Or should she just delete it and forget it had ever happened? After all, he didn't know her name, where she lived or worked. What were the odds she would ever see him or hear from him again? New York City was an enormous place, making it easy to remain anonymous.

No longer able to take any more from her sister, she told Greer, "I've got to go—I have a surgery scheduled this afternoon."

Naturally, Greer despised not having the last word in a conversation, so responded with as much passive aggression as she could, "Go to your fancy surgery, then. God forbid you take five extra minutes to tell me what you plan on doing about meeting up with your sex god tonight. Please, Lana, I'm dying for details here," Greer begged. "Simon and I have hit a dry spell in the bedroom, and I need some inspiration." Lana shuddered, thinking about her sister and her brother-in-law's marital issues. "So, was it the first tequila shot that sealed the deal for you, or did it take the second to fully convince you? I need to know how much to serve Simon tonight." Leaving her sister howling with laughter, Lana hung up the phone.

The honest answer was: she wished she could remember each tantalizing detail from last night. Judging how she had reacted to his tongue on her skin, both in the bar and then later in the hotel room, she couldn't help but believe she could have, maybe, enjoyed herself when they were in bed. And out of bed. Why was everything a blur during the supposed good parts?

As she scrubbed in for her procedure, Lana reflected that it had been her family's messy history that had made Josh so appealing to her. He was calm in the face of a storm: stoic, stable, steady, never flying off the handle or veering off-course. And he had always been prepared, with his manuals, lecture notes, and journals he would share with her—things that she never had the extra funds to purchase or invest in. She had tried to initiate a romantic relationship with Josh at one point, a few months after he had broken up with Tess. Unsure if he had understood at the time that she was, indeed, asking him out, once he had shown up at her apartment with flowers, it mistakenly led her to believe that he, maybe, felt the same for her. Lana had invited him over with the promise of a home-cooked meal, and she had rushed out of the office that day and impatiently ridden the subway from the Upper East Side to the Lower East Side. After visiting the market and buying the ingredients for one of her signature dishes, lasagna, she had simmered the sauce an hour or so, and the casserole was baking once Josh had arrived. Her mouth had gone dry when she had seen his handsome face peeking out from behind the bouquet of flowers that had preceded him into her tiny dwelling. With his tall figure taking up more space than hers did, her apartment had seemed so intimate for the two of them, and she had held her breath all night with the hope that he would kiss her at evening's end. He hadn't, and in fact, the night was never mentioned again. Until last winter, when he had what had appeared to be a panic attack at the hospital before he had been forced to take a leave of absence. All of this had come the morning after he had found out about Sam and Tess being a couple. So devastated had he been, and so lost, that when Lana had tried to comfort him, he had misconstrued her actions and kissed her. At the time, she had wanted nothing more than to become swept up in his embrace, but her always-rational brain had told her it wasn't the right time or place, and she had pulled away. Once he had gone back to South Dakota, she had written him an email in which she poured out her heart to him, confessing all the feelings she had developed for him during the two years they had not only worked together but also shared an office. Writing back to her, he had gently yet absolutely rejected her, and Lana had done her best to not feel mortified. Josh had been the first man she had ever let herself feel anything for, but now she understood that he hadn't been the one. After last night, when she had been consumed with such intense desire for the sexy stranger (even if she didn't remember exactly every dirty detail), Lana realized she had not had the same reaction, ever, to Josh. Instead, she supposed he had reminded her, if she were completely honest with herself, of her big brother, Montgomery.

Montgomery, or Monty (as the family often called him), had been the only stable male in the entirety of her life. Forced into the role of substitute father after their own father had walked out for the last time when Lana was eight, Monty, the oldest Miller sibling, was ten years Lana's senior. Their father had left the family before, though, when the three oldest siblings were young—Monty had been five, Ava had been four, and Greer just three when their father had left their mother for the first time. Thomas Miller, unsatisfied with the wages he had been earning in construction, had gone to get extra work on a friend's fishing boat one day (or so he told his wife), then just never came home, leaving Fiona to care for their young children alone. No forwarding address, no money sent back to the family—he had been a ghost. Fiona had always been a dreamer, trapped, unfortunately, in the harsh reality of being the child of immigrants, and she had wanted grand things for her children (things she had never imagined for herself). As the daughter of Irish immigrants who had come to America in the seventies, seeking a better life for themselves, a twist of fate would have it that conditions for them on the east end of Long Island hadn't been much better than what they had left in Northern Ireland (except for the bombs and terrorism). When Fiona had been growing up, her immigrant parents had fallen under the spell of American culture, Fiona's mother, Nora, especially. Nora would take

Fiona with her to the movies on Saturday afternoon, where they showed classic black-and-white movies from the forties and fifties for a dollar. So imprinted had Fiona been with this experience in her childhood, she, too, had been obsessed with films from that era, and she had named all of her children after movie stars she particularly adored: Montgomery, for example, was named for actor Montgomery Clift, who starred in Fiona's favorite movie *A Place in the Sun;* Ava Gardner, who Fiona had considered the most beautiful actress of all-time, inspired Ava's name; Greer was named after Greer Garson, star of *Pride and Prejudice* with Laurence Olivier (it was well-known had Greer been a boy, she would have been Laurence instead); finally Lana, named in honor of Lana Turner, overall Fiona's favorite actress, yet Lana thought it odd that her mother had saved her favorite for last, because if her father had not returned (likened to a miracle being bestowed on them all, or a prayer having been answered, because of the rosary Fiona prayed every night before bed), then Lana would not exist.

With her surgical procedure finished, Lana stared at the text that had arrived while she had been in the operating room.

TEXT FROM HOOK-UP

In all sincerity, I would love to see you again.

I'm leaving town tmrw, not sure when I'll be back.

Last night was incredible, but no pressure.

Would love to have dinner or even a drink.

Same time, same place? Please?

Baby, I'm willing to beg if that is what it will take...

# CHAPTER
## Eight

## Tess



Tess grinned as she read her sister's message, positive that Ruth would find a way to insert herself into Josh's romantic gesture to ensure Josh had his desired outcome. Ruth was two years older than Tess, and one of Ruth's best traits was reading people. One of Ruth's worst traits was her belief, then, that she always knew what was best for those people. Oh, the yin and the yang of her sister, thought Tess.

As her handsome husband ambled over to her while carrying their two drinks, Tess watched him cross the floor from her seat at a high table in the Whistling Dixie. Overcome with love for him, she was also grateful to her sister, because Ruth had been very instrumental in bringing Sam back to her last year. After meeting by chance on the train, Sam had to get off abruptly due to an urgent family matter unbeknownst to Tess. Left without a goodbye from Sam, Tess had thought (erroneously) that he had just departed without thinking of her at all. Sam *had* left Tess a letter, though, that she unfortunately never received, explaining his need to leave so suddenly. Tess had forged ahead with her wedding to Josh, then, until Sam had shown up at the rehearsal for the wedding. At the urging of Ruth (who had attended a book signing of Sam's to personally deliver a wedding invitation to him), Sam forced Tess to choose with her heart and not her head, even if it meant breaking Josh's heart in the process. Everything had finally worked out for all of them, and now Ruth was helping Josh with the true love of his life.

"God, you are so gorgeous, you know that?" whispered her husband in her ear, as he pushed a lock of wavy red hair behind her ear, and then trailed a single finger down her neck to her throat, where he followed the curve of the tops of her breasts hinted at just below the lace of her dress. "Every man in this place is seething with jealousy because you are going home with me." Sam then slid both hands down to her hips and proceeded to edge her bottom off her barstool and ever so slightly closer to him.

Tess giggled, responding, "Down, boy—save the seduction for when we get back to Brooklyn." She took a sip of the Cosmo he had brought to her, trying to cool down the raging inferno of desire she experienced whenever her husband was within an inch of her.

With one last kiss to her neck, Sam stood up, stretching his long frame as he did so. "Lifting all of those boxes today really did a number on my back—does this mean I'm getting old?" Tess reached up to rub his wide shoulders, and he groaned in response. "I really need to go for a run tomorrow morning, you know, work out all my kinks," he commented with wink to Tess before taking a sip of his Guinness.

"Yeah? You think running is going to work out *all* your kinks? I doubt it," Tess responded, grabbing his hand to pull him down to her level. "It better not, anyway," she told him before she kissed him, savoring the feel of his firm mouth on hers and the way his black curls at the back of his neck felt under her hands.

"Get a room, you two, get a room," the couple heard from behind them. Turning in unison, they saw Liam making his way toward them, holding a pint of Guinness as well. Liam had asked Tess and Sam to meet him at Whistling Dixie for a going-away drink before he and Sam hit the road in the morning. After Liam let it slip that he had invited his mystery woman to meet him again tonight, Tess suspected his invitation to them was more likely so Liam could hopefully introduce them to the woman he had met last night. "Great minds think alike, huh, Sam?" Liam asked as he raised his glass in a toast. "To Josh and Effie," he said.

"To Josh and Effie," Sam and Tess seconded in harmony.

"Tess, what do you think of Josh moving back to South Dakota?" Liam questioned her.

Tess replied honestly, "I must admit, I was a bit taken aback. Your cousin has always been so laser-focused on making a name for himself as a surgeon here in New York, working tirelessly to make it happen." Tess sipped her Cosmo, then continued, "It seems he has finally found that work-life balance that, frankly, he had no interest in before. And I think it's great." Sam had been the catalyst for her to finally end her relationship with Josh, but only after she had honestly admitted to herself that she and Josh were no longer right for each other, after so many years together.

Sam spoke up, "I have had a few conversations with him while he's been back in South Dakota, and I have never heard him that relaxed, or that happy, even back in college."

Liam nodded his head in agreement. "Totally—once he finally admitted to Effie the truth about himself, he was all in. Personally, I am psyched that my cousin is moving back because I will get to see him whenever I want."

"Well, you might want to pump the brakes on that for just a bit," cautioned Sam. "After all, he is going to be in the throes of his newfound love—almost like the honeymoon stage, right, Tess," Sam said, as he kissed the top of Tess's head. Only married for a few months, Tess knew she could happily stay in the honeymoon stage with Sam forever.

"I don't know that I really congratulated you two on getting married. I guess my invitation must have gotten lost in the mail? After all, Tess, I've known you almost as long as Josh has. And Sam, I mean, I thought we were friends?" Though he said this was a grin, Tess thought she could see a sliver of hurt in his eyes. Josh's cousin had always just kind of been there, like an accessory she got used to seeing. He exuded a very carefree demeanor, but Tess often wondered how deep it went. Liam wasn't as seemingly career-motivated the way Josh was, and he wasn't as intense as her husband could be. Often providing comic-relief when situations needed it, Liam never took himself too seriously...which was why Tess never really understood his appeal to so many women. No arguing that he was incredibly attractive, with his reddish-brown hair and those extremely light gray eyes, but whatever he had lurking more deeply below his surface, Tess really had no idea, because far too often, he only chose to let people see his goofy persona, and Tess valued substance.

Sensing Liam needed some reassurance from her now, Tess reached over and squeezed Liam's hand, telling him, "I'm sorry, Liam, we really did have a small ceremony, with only close family and a few friends."

Sam solemnly nodded his head in agreement. "We had enough on our hands getting all four of my brothers there, plus their significant others. You are aware that not even Josh was invited?"

"Obviously, that would have been beyond awkward." Liam gave Tess and Sam a small smile to show them he had no ill feelings about their wedding and then smacked a hand against his forehead. "I'm so stupid! I have something for you back in my room at the hotel. Let me run over there and grab it—I picked it up when I was out walking around earlier," he told Tess, and started to leave their table.

Tess grabbed his hand before he could leave their perimeter. "No, don't go. Just give it to Sam tomorrow when you pick him up."

"No, I want to see your face when you see it. It's all good—the hotel is right around the corner and I shall make haste and be back momentarily," Liam announced with a bow, taking Tess's hand, and gracing the top of it with a kiss.

"'Make haste'? Since when does Liam throw around five-dollar phrases, I wonder?" Sam mused as he took a drink.

Tess poked him in his stomach. "Be nice, now. I know Liam has not always been your favorite person, but you two seemed to really be getting along today."

Sam nodded. "Yeah, it's been kind of weird. Nice, but definitely weird. He has been super chill, which is out of character for Liam. When the two of us are together, I always kind of felt like it had to be the 'Liam show'." Sam provided air quotes for his last statement.

"I know." Tess sighed. "Josh always got the impression that Liam felt like he had to compete with you for attention. Which I get, because you tend to grab the spotlight," she told her husband with a wicked grin.

"Oh, yeah? How about we leave as soon as we can after Liam gets back, so we can spend the rest of the night in bed? I think you'd look incredibly sexy underneath some of that spotlight." Sam slid his hand into her hair and brought her face up to his for a kiss, which Tess lustily returned.

Once they broke apart, and Tess was reaching for her drink, she heard someone from several feet away ask, "Tessa? Is that you?" Stunned, Tess looked up, because only two people ever called her "Tessa"—one of them was Josh, who seemed to have broken himself of that habit, and the other one was Josh's colleague, Lana, who obviously only did so because that was how Josh had introduced her to his office mate when they first met.

Tess hopped off her barstool and hugged Lana, greeting her warmly, "Lana, hi. Wow, what a surprise this is—what are you doing here?" What a coincidence, Tess thought, but considering the hospital was almost literally around the corner, perhaps not completely shocking. Ask any New Yorker and they will tell you that it was not out of the ordinary to randomly run into people you knew no matter where you happened to be in the five boroughs.

Lana seemed not only flustered but also distracted as she responded, "I was just going to ask the same of you. I can't remember the last time I saw you this far uptown. I mean, you almost never visited Josh at the hospital." Another sore subject during Tess's relationship with Josh. Tess couldn't help but laugh, though, because it was true—she had hated traveling to upper Manhattan, where she always had to switch subway lines, especially anywhere on the east side. Not only that, but it frequently proved difficult (before she had her own bakery), having to be up so early to bake in a commercial kitchen and then deliver her baked goods to neighboring delis and cafes. Lucky for her, Tess now had staff to give her a break when she needed one.

Routinely, Tess's sister Ruth would remark that she got the vibe that

Lana had feelings for Josh. "I mean, Tess, they are together almost all day long. That office can't be *that* big, so in a space that small? Ain't no way that woman is *not* crushing on your man," Ruth had even declared once. However, Tess had never believed it. Definitely on Josh's part, she had never detected anything other than professional feelings for Lana, maybe some light friendship, but that was it. And Lana? Tess had only been around the younger woman a few times, but she had always been struck by a certain naiveté that Lana exuded. Although Tess knew Lana to only be a couple of years younger than herself, something about her seemed so innocent and demure. Perhaps it was her wardrobe? Tess had only ever seen her either in scrubs or a doctor's coat at the hospital, except for the one time they had all attended some gala thrown by the hospital to raise funds for the new pediatric unit: Tess had worn an elaborate gown (selected by Josh to ensure she made the right impression of being a surgeon's fiancée), but Lana had worn an A-line dress reminiscent of those worn by actresses from the fifties. Lana had looked fantastic, but unique in a way that Tess had been positive had not been intentional. Looking at Lana now, Tess was taken with her intense, darkly blue eyes and her shining, deeply golden blonde hair falling over her shoulders in waves. That's what was different, Tess thought. She had never seen the other woman with her hair down, and the effect was stunning; even the night of the gala, Lana had worn her hair up, pulled tightly back from her face.

"Actually, we are here meeting up with a friend—Josh's cousin, to be exact. Maybe you met him when Josh was back?" As Lana shook her head "no", Tess could not help but think that was for the best. Tess had seen many women fall under his seductive spell over the years, and she couldn't blame them, because he was so smooth and charismatic, charming and undeniably gorgeous. Unfortunately, Liam apparently had absolutely zero interest in a long-term relationship, and despite his claim from earlier in the day to have met the woman of his dreams last night, Tess doubted it would have ever amounted to anything. "Oh! Where are my manners? Obviously, you never met Sam, right?" Lana shook her head again, so Tess introduced them. "Lana, this is my husband, Sam." Tess couldn't help but give a small giggle. "I'll never get tired of saying that," she told Sam with a smile.

"And Sam, this is Lana—she worked with Josh; in fact, they also shared an office."

Sam held out his hand for Lana to shake. "Oh, this is the famous Lana? I have heard a lot about you over the past couple of years. Josh always talked about his brilliant office mate. You graduated high school at sixteen, am I right? And college at nineteen?" At Lana's blushing nod, Sam whistled. "Unbelievable. Some of us struggled to make it through college in only four years," he laughed.

"Like that was you! Please, only one of us in our party has the claim to fame of taking five years to finish a simple bachelor's degree, and he has evidently abandoned us because he forgot something. Typical Liam," Tess chuckled.

Lana looked around the bar as if she was scanning the room for someone in particular. Tess realized Lana had never said why she was in the bar tonight—is it possible that she *was* meeting someone here? Channeling her inner-Ruth (who never failed to get answers out of anyone), Tess asked her, "So, Lana, what are you doing here? Back for another round?" Lana flashed Tess a shocked look, and Tess could have sworn she heard her gasp. Well, this was interesting. Why was she so jumpy? "I was just teasing you. I heard we prevented Josh from attending his own going away party last night. Sorry about that."

"Oh, um, actually, I didn't get over here last night. You know, with the fellowship and everything, I had so much paperwork. I didn't leave my office until later than I meant to, and then I was exhausted, so I just went home." As Lana was frantically speaking, her eyes kept glancing toward the front, almost as if expecting someone. Tess couldn't help but think she seemed disappointed every time she looked back at their table.

Tess tapped on the seat next to her, indicating Lana should take it, but her offer was met with a polite refusal. "Actually, I need to go." Lana looked down at her watch, but so briefly that Tess didn't believe she had truly registered what time it was. "So nice seeing you, Tessa, and meeting you, Sam. You both seem very in love. Sorry, I just realized I'm late for something. Take care." And with that, Lana turned abruptly and darted to the front entrance.

"Is it me, or was that weird?" asked Sam. "I mean, obviously I have never met Lana before, but she seemed…"

"No, that was not the Lana I have known. She was severely distracted, and kind of on edge. Never in a million years would I have recognized her, either, with her hair down like that," Tess confessed.

"Yeah, whenever Josh talked about her, he painted her as, like, hair pulled back kind of look, like your average scientist. Unassuming, I guess, is the description I got. Good thing Liam wasn't here," Sam laughed.

Tess nodded in agreement. "He would have eaten her alive." Watching as Lana rushed out the front doors, Tess couldn't help but think that something had been off about the encounter with Lana. No doubt Lana had been trying to meet someone in here tonight, but who could it have been? Someone from the hospital that Tess also knew, and that was why she had acted so strangely?

# CHAPTER
## Nine

## Liam



Liam breezed back into the Whistling Dixie to the sound of a Garth Brooks song he loved. Hell, he loved all of them and would be hard-pressed to name his absolute favorite. This was part of his problem—Liam favored many things, but gave them all the same credence, which diminished their meaning over time. Like the women he had dated in the past, each relationship had ended on good terms (relatively speaking), and while in those relationships, he had felt genuine, honest affection for the women. Looking back, however, he realized that general affection was all he would have ever felt for them—never love.

Speaking of love, Liam walked up to the table to be the third wheel in the love fest that seemed to consume Tess and Sam endlessly. Thanks to Sam's words of caution earlier, Liam now worried about the future closeness he had been looking forward to sharing with Josh once he was settled back in South Dakota. Dawning on Liam was the realization that Josh would be busy finishing his residency up at Beverley General, and then he would be an on-staff surgeon there. Josh and Effie would probably be engaged by the time Liam saw his cousin again (at the rate their relationship had already gone), so goodbye to the cousins enjoying a night out at Shorty's to shoot some pool or heading to Lake Shelley on a slow afternoon for a swim during the remaining weeks of summer. Or just hanging out with Josh and his dad, Henry, maybe even Liam's dad, George, as they all worked on the car that Josh and Henry had begun restoring last winter, a '72 Dodge Dart.

While Liam had been back in his hotel room, he had texted his Mystery Woman, hoping to hear from her before he returned to the bar, but there was still no response. "All right, you two, get decent," he told Tess and Sam, making it a point to inject his words with a humorous tone he was not necessarily feeling. Sam was sitting on a bar stool and tiny Tess stood behind him, massaging his bulky shoulders. Feeling a tightness in his own back, Liam considered that he, too, possibly pulled a muscle today while hauling out his cousin's treasures. How inappropriate would it be to ask Tess to give his shoulders a go when she was done with Sam? Giving the idea a second thought, Liam decided it was best not to press his luck with Sam (who had four younger brothers and could probably take him in a fight), especially when the two of them had been getting along so well all day. Both men were tall, standing around six feet, but Sam probably had an inch or two over him. Not only that, he knew Sam ran every day (something obscene, like five miles). Back in high school, Liam had been a sprinter on the track team, and while those days were long gone, he did some weight lifting in his home gym, since appearances were important when selling cars. Liam tried to work out every day, and in the summer played baseball on the local amateur team for the Carlisle Canaries. To keep up with the younger guys in their twenties, he often went to the batting cages in Beverley and hit some balls, taking out any aggression he had pent up after a long week of sales. If his Mystery Woman failed to show up tonight, he would have even more reasons to swing a bat at some balls once he got home to South Dakota.

Tess finally finished seducing her husband in public, allowing Liam to hand her the small bag he had retrieved from his hotel room. "I saw this down in Midtown when I was walking around earlier this evening and thought of you guys."

Watching Tess's emerald eyes light up as she pulled out the "Our First Christmas" ornament out of the bag, he knew he had been right in running back to the hotel to get the small gift. "Oh, Liam, this is so sweet," she said, turning over the ornament of a small couple, one with red hair and one with black hair, to see the date on the back was the date of their wedding. She swiped at tears in her glowing green eyes, and she gave him a hug. "Thank you," she whispered to him. Liam had been teasing Tess earlier about not being invited to her wedding to Sam (how awkward would *that* have been?), yet something twisted in him, knowing he probably hadn't even been considered.

Even Sam looked impressed as he took the ornament Tess was handing him. "Very thoughtful, Liam. I have to say, I am down with this new side you are showing," grinning as a barmaid appeared at their table with a fresh round of drinks, to whom Liam handed several bills.

"What? I have always been considered generous," Liam countered, slightly offended at any insinuation to the opposite.

"Yes," Tess agreed, "but primarily to single women. Ooh, by the way, you missed a good one just now," she informed him, nodding to a tall, brown-haired woman leaving the bar.

Sipping his Guinness, he studied Tess over the rim. When Tess had called off the wedding to Josh, Liam had been stunned. The couple had seemed made for each other, and one of the few pairs he knew whose relationship had started in high school and lasted not just through college, but after. Well, he guessed there had been the time that Josh had broken things off with Tess just as he graduated from college, but Liam had always chalked that up to "the grass is always greener" thinking, since Tess was two years younger. Liam had assumed his cousin would sow his wild oats, but Josh had just proceeded to have two back-to-back semi-serious relationships, thus negating his theory. Funny, Liam thought to himself, Josh's shortest relationship lasted longer than any of Liam's ever had. Not that he was a commitment-phobe, as one ex had once accused him; Liam was terrified that once a woman got through his outer layer, she would find nothing of substance to keep her interested.

Watching Tess with Sam earlier this morning at the storage unit and now tonight at the bar, he couldn't help but envy their closeness, and that short-hand communication style that really great couples perfected. With just a look, Sam seemed to anticipate Tess's needs, and more than once, Liam had noticed a casual touch from Tess to Sam that had nothing to do with desire (he thought), but more about wanting to connect. Would he ever find that? Did he want to? Something about his night with his Mystery Woman made him believe so. His parents have been happily married for over thirty-seven years, and together for almost forty. And though there had been minor quibbles or disagreements between them, they always seemed happy and in love. Yet here he was, almost thirty-five years old, no partner, not even sure if working at the auto dealership could be considered a "career". Though he certainly made enough money to get his own place, Liam didn't see any need to and was content living with an old buddy of his (one of his baseball teammates) in Carlisle.

Frustratingly enough, now that his sister, Caitriona, was back home, though, she had already started looking for a place to buy (so she could move out of their parents' house) and every Sunday family dinner was peppered with her comments about how immature he was, how irre-sponsible he could be (which was really rich coming from her), how pathetic his personal life was. Two years his junior, Cait had attended college down in New Orleans, at Tulane University, with the under-standing that she would return to South Dakota to earn her law degree at the University of South Dakota. Had she done that? No, she had stayed down there for law school and then continued to live and work down in the Gulf area for five more years. Until a few months ago, when she had moved back home under a shroud of secrecy.

"Oh, yeah?" he now asked Tess. "You think I missed meeting the woman of my dreams while I was gone for ten minutes?"

Tess shrugged and told him, "You never know, Liam—that could have been her walking out the door. You need to remain open if you want to find love."

Clearly, Tess didn't believe that what he had shared with his Mystery Woman last night was meaningful, any more than Josh had. He said doubtfully, "She'd have to be pretty phenomenal to compare to the woman I met last night." Maybe they were all right thinking he was a fool, once again, and he gave a rueful laugh. "At least she'd be here, though, and not in the wind like my Mystery Woman seems to be." Feeling dejected, now that he had not heard back from her, he faced the reality that his multiple texts to her would all remain unanswered. None of this had made sense, he thought. She had been undeniably into him last night, as much as he was into her. Doubts crept into his mind, suggesting that maybe she had expected more? Had he unknowingly disappointed her in some way? Perhaps the truth was that he had not made as much of an impact on her as she had on him.

He felt Tess's warm fingers on his hand and smiled at her. "I'm sorry, Liam. I know you were really looking forward to seeing her again."

"Did she say definitely that she would meet you?" asked Sam. "If it was all up in the air, it's possible that something came up." Great—now Sam, the fiction writer, was creating a story for Liam, a sign that he was as pathetic as he was beginning to suspect.

"No, she didn't, but she didn't tell me to go to hell, either." Desperately needing to be alone to drown his sorrows, Liam told them, "Listen, it has been great hanging out with you guys, and I appreciate you coming all the way uptown, but it's getting late. I know you have to be up early, Tess, to start baking in the morning." He looked at Tess, and then at Sam, and continued, "And you and I want to be on the road at dawn, so maybe we should call it a night?"

"Well, if you're sure?" Tess questioned, her green eyes relaying her empathy for his lost cause.

"We don't mind staying for a little longer," Sam reassured him, looking as if he was getting ready to order another round of drinks from the bar.

"No, get home, you two." Liam stood now, indicating to them that he was fine with them leaving. "Besides, I'm sure you two want to spend some time together before you leave, Sam." Liam hugged each of them and watched forlornly as they left the bar.

TEXT TO JOSH

Good luck with everything, Josh!

Love you, cousin

Shaking his head, Liam wondered why he was feeling so morose? Just because a woman had rejected him (which had never happened before) didn't mean the world was ending. Was it more than that? Needing to put a pin in this evening, he sent another text. Maybe this would be the invitation she'd need, he hoped.

TEXT TO MYSTERY WOMAN

Guess it wasn't meant to be for us?

I'm still at the bar.

I'll wait around a while longer, if you decide to stop by.

I'd love to see you.

No sooner had he sent the text than a woman in her mid-twenties approached his table. "Hi, mind if I join you?" Well, was this a new low for him? Now women ten years younger than him thought he was fair game? Looking at her fresh face, he had to admit that she was attractive, but he doubted they would have much in common.

"Umm, sure," he responded. "I'm meeting someone, though, so…"

She responded by sliding her hand up his arm, "Well, maybe we could keep each other company until they show up?" As she took a sip of whatever concoction required an umbrella in her glass, his phone rang.

He answered it with a half-frown on his face to the stranger at his table, hoping it showed his half-hearted regret at having to answer his phone. Then, because of the increased volume in the darkening bar, he quickly ducked outside to take the phone call.

"Josh, miss me already?" he teased his cousin.

"Absolutely. I can't live, if living is without you, you know," Josh responded.

"If you're quoting seventies rock, that must mean you're with your dad on the way home to Beverley. How was your flight?" Flying to South Dakota from New York meant Josh had to make a connecting flight in Minneapolis. More often than they would have liked when they had been college students traveling home, one or both legs of their flights home would be delayed (at best) or cancelled (at worst).

Josh laughed, "Actually, the song was my choice, but the Mariah Carey version, so it's nineties pop. The flight was fantastic—I got the last seat in business class so I could just relax in the air on the flight to Minneapolis. Listen, I wanted to just call to say thanks so much for everything. I was an absolute idiot half the time when I first was back home, but you put up with me. Not only that, you helped me get out of my funk, even if I didn't always seem to appreciate it. I want you to know that I did and I do, always."

Liam sat in a stunned silence on the other end of the phone; his cousin was not the most verbally effusive man, so to hear him now say this had to be an indication of how content and happy he was to be going home to connect with Effie.

He assured Josh, "I know you do, without ever having to say it. I have to admit, though, it's nice hearing it occasionally. I invited Tess and Sam up to the bar from last night to have a couple of drinks and they just left. You really dodged a bullet there, dude. Those two are head over heels in love, and it would have been awkward if she had ended up marrying you, you know."

The cousins laughed, and then Josh asked, "Can I assume that you are still there—maybe hoping that your dream woman will show up again?"

"Well, I must admit that was my plan, but it's looking prognosis negative right now. I've sent her a few texts but haven't heard anything in response. Probably for the best, I know, since I'm leaving tomorrow. You were right," Liam sighed. Fewer things in life killed him more than having to admit his cousin was right about something.

"Look, no one has confidence like you do, Liam. It might do you some good to take a few knocks. I mean, have you ever had a woman turn you down?" Nothing Liam could do with his cousin's question but remain silent. "Exactly—there's my answer. Go back to the hotel room, chill out, and get to bed early. You don't know what is up with this woman, and this time it may be *YOU* that dodged the bullet." His sensible cousin always had all the answers—the problem was, Liam didn't always appreciate it.

"Okay, that's my exit. You're right, just this once! See you in a couple of days, and keep me updated on your plans for the big romantic Effie gesture, okay?" Liam hung up the phone and still had his head down when he turned around to walk past the entrance of the bar. A flurry of commotion busted through the doors and forced him to take two steps back or be trampled. Holding out his hands to steady himself and whoever it was that had barged outside, he looked down to see the top of a honey-blonde head. As the head tilted back, he was swallowed up by an enormous pair of dark-blue eyes, which widened in surprise once his face was registered.

"I thought you weren't coming," they whispered to each other, almost in unison.

# CHAPTER
## Ten

## Lana



Lana flushed from head to toe the moment his hands were on her. Without even having to see his face, she recognized his touch, and his scent, as she caught the light aroma of his aftershave wafting around her. As she tipped her head back, her gaze kept traveling up and up. Wow—was he taller than last night, or was there something about him making him appear larger?

As a rush of people flowed around them to get into the bar, Lana and her sexy stranger stood immobile, blocking one of the bar's double doors. "I didn't think I was," Lana finally found she could answer.

"What?" his deep voice inquired, and his gorgeous chestnut eyebrows (why was everything about this man so attractive?) drew together, as if confused. He wasn't alone in that state of mind, though. All that was registering to her now was the fact that his hands were still on her, cupping her elbows; she had not moved out of touching range—could not move, to be honest. He pulled her infinitesimally closer, enough so she could feel his breath on the top of her head, see the pounding of his heart in the open neck of his shirt, and smell the citrusy cologne on his skin—that golden, rough skin that she longed to put her tongue to, and the thought jarred her, and a memory came back to her from last night of her doing the just that.

Lana licked her lips and saw the gray of his irises overtaken by his widening pupils. "Tonight. I didn't think I was coming here, either," she explained. "But I'm finding you very hard to resist."

Now one of his rugged eyebrows raised, an act that made her knees sink ever so slightly. "Oh, really? I'm glad you changed your mind." And then he grinned, reminding her of how she had woken up naked in his bed. Which definitely would not happen again. Definitely. She was positive, until he leaned down to her ear, whispering, "I don't even try to resist you."

Shivering in response to his warm breath on her neck, she was helpless to stop herself from sliding a hand up his chest, telling him, "I was worried I had missed you…that maybe you got tired of waiting for me."

"Baby, I would wait forever for you—I was pretty sure I made that clear last night," he breathed into her ear, while leaning fully into her. How was she to resist him? Why should she? She knew her sisters wouldn't because they had been text bombing her phone all day long. In her spare time today, she had done nothing but fantasize about going back to his hotel room again tonight. Lana hesitated…should she suggest it? It seemed like something one would do in this situation, but she didn't want him to think she was a brazen hussy. I mean, she thought rationally, we can't stand almost in this doorway the whole night. She could just suggest, "Maybe we could go somewhere a little…quieter? I was just inside, and it was getting busy. That's why I was surprised to see you out here. I went in and you weren't there. Actually, you weren't there before, either, and I wasn't sure— " stop rambling, she scolded herself.

Lana was a mass of conflicting emotions, both anticipating yet dreading a kiss from the way he was staring down at her—what if it wasn't as good as it had been last night? What if she wasn't what he remembered? She was then slightly disappointed when one of his fingers reached for her and only stroked her cheek. "Why don't we go back to my hotel?" At his words, Lana experienced a flash of panic, which must have shown up on her face, because he continued as if to reassure her, "There's a little coffee shop right off the lobby," he explained. "No pressure, I promise. It's right inside the entrance. Very cozy, quiet, intimate… they make a mean latte, if that's your thing?" Was it her thing? She had no idea and could not concentrate, as his finger was sliding down her check and then her neck…so slowly, so deliberately, and Lana leaned into his tall frame. *This* seemed to be her thing—his touch, his gaze, his heat that radiated through their clothes.

Should she do this? she wondered. Follow a nameless man to his hotel (again)? For the second time in as many days, she breathily told her sexy stranger, "Lead the way." Reaching down, he laced his long fingers through her smaller ones. After waiting for what seemed like hours at a stoplight, he led her across First Avenue, both of them silent as they walked up the avenue to Sixty-Fifth Street. The doorman standing in front of Hotel Delacroix tipped his hat at the couple and opened the door for them before stepping out onto the curb to hail a taxi for a very distinguished-looking woman carrying a briefcase.

Emitting a tiny gasp as they entered the grand lobby, Lana remembered nothing about the elegance of this hotel from last night. Hotel Delacroix was the most stunningly beautiful building she had ever been in, including some of the homes she had visited as a child, and she could not help but feel slightly out of place. Despite spending her summers in the Hamptons with her mother, where she helped her clean houses for the very wealthy, extremely wealthy, and the obscenely wealthy, Lana always felt unsure and awkward in places of elegance. Constantly marveling that the homes her mom cleaned didn't already have a staff doing it daily, her mom had explained to her at an early age that some of the more ostentatious estates did, but the "old rich" (always the air quotes with her mom) reveled in their ability to show *less* of their moneyed lives. These affluent families had summered in homes out in towns called Sag Harbor, Quogue, Sagaponack, Montauk, and, of course, the collection of Hamptons: Southampton, East Hampton, and Bridge-hampton, for over a century. Living for three months in shingle-sided homes tucked between sand dunes, so close to the ocean that sea spray was unavoidable, some of the moneyed people complained about it, but Lana had loved opportunities to breathe in salt-tinged air. Not *every* home her mom cleaned was so adjacent to the water (they were never far from the water, though, just usually minutes by foot), but the ones that were had always seemed more magical. As a girl, Lana would step out onto whatever deck or patio was available and watch as the waves broke in the distance, huge swaths of water capped with foamy tops, looking to overtake anything floating in its way. Occasionally, she could break away from her mom (and her own duties as co-house cleaner) and walk down to the beach, running her hands across the waving beach grass that brushed her shoulders. No matter the weather, Lana would then slip off whatever footwear that she had worn, sinking her toes into the gritty sand the moment she had reached the beach. Something about the way the ocean water would rush in with the tide, cascading over her bare feet, always exhilarated her, and then when it went back out to sea, she would feel a pang of loss. Always the loss, an unavoidable feeling she had learned at an early age out in the Hamptons.

As he held out a chair for her to slide into, her sexy stranger inquired, "Can I get you a mocha or a latte from the cafe? Or would you prefer something else, maybe a cappuccino? Unless coffee isn't your thing—maybe a tea?" Where was her suave seducer from last night? Could he be as nervous as her? Lana watched him pull out the chair across from her, moving it closer to Lana. Was this a date? Were they really going to have coffee? She would bring Josh a coffee when they worked together, if she knew he was going to arrive at the hospital earlier than herself, and he had would do the same for her, something that had initiated when he had brought her a coffee on her second day of sharing an office with him. Not wanting to appear ungrateful, she had then brought him a coffee the next day, and their tradition had lasted until he had left last winter for

South Dakota. A tradition, if she were honest, had proved difficult to afford on such a regular basis, especially towards the end of every month. Confiding to her sisters once of her spending conundrum, they had been incredulous, assuming that since she was a doctor, she could easily afford it, but she had medical school to pay for, along with rent on her apartment. What she did not tell them was how much money she put in savings to ensure that she would always feel secure.

Lana, intending to be as nonchalant as possible, smiled appreciatively up at his handsome face. "Oh, nothing fancy for me. Whatever is easiest." Reaching for her wallet in the bag that crossed her front, Lana then did the mental math, realizing that she had spent her last ten dollars in cash at the hospital cafeteria an hour ago. When she had run into Tess and Sam earlier at the Whistling Dixie, Lana had played it cool as long as she could, but had been terrified her sexy stranger would show up while she was with the couple. How would she have introduced him? She didn't even know his name! And how would she have explained how she knew this man? The fact that she had even showed up at the bar in the first place still stupefied her, after swearing to herself all day that she would not meet up with him. Yet, with each text he had sent, something melted in her—something about them spoke to her, like there was so much hope when he wrote them, that his words reached to her heart. Upon arriving at the bar and seeing Tess, as beautiful as the last time Lana had seen her, she had been stunned. Tess, so confident in who she was and what she wanted, falling in love with one man while engaged to another, and starting her own business. And here was Lana, on her second residency, still unsure of what path (general medicine or surgery) she was going to take when she finally finished. Lana had been relieved to leave the bar before HE arrived, sparing her any awkward introductions. Once outside the bar, reluctant to get on the subway to head home, for whatever reason, Lana had instead walked back to the hospital, going to the cafeteria for the second time in one day, where she had gotten a bowl of matzoh ball soup and another slice of banana bread. All during her dinner, she chastised herself for sticking around. What was the point? She was not interested in a repeat of last night's performance, nor was she looking to make a fool of herself once more in this man's presence. Then she had received the text from him saying he was still in the bar—and she had done her best to not respond to it in any way. Instead, she had finished her meal, now reading a couple of chapters from her dog-eared copy of the Lisa Kleypas romance novel she always carried with her, preferring the steamy romance over the psychological thriller she had read from earlier. The thought of her Hook Up waiting alone for her to arrive to meet him at the bar compelled Lana to walk by Whistling Dixie *just one more time* before heading downtown to her apartment, even though it was in the opposite direction of the subway. Surely by then he would be gone, but no harm in just *checking*, right? she had asked herself. Once there, though, she had to go in and make sure he wasn't sitting forlornly in a corner somewhere, even if it meant running into Tess and Sam again. To her relief, they were not still there, but to her dismay, neither was he. Lana had been the forlorn one, then, walking through the establishment, not finding him there. Made sense, because what was so special about her worth waiting for? She was positive he had found another woman to occupy his time and attention.

"Darlin'," he said in a sultry tone, "never in a million years would I let a woman I am with pay for anything. Whatever you want, I am happy to provide," he whispered into her ear. God, he had to stop doing that, because it made her feel tingly in every inch of her body. He unfolded his body to his full height and kissed the hand he had held while they walked to the hotel. "Now, I can see from their menu board that their special is a S'mores flavored latte—how does that sound?"

Lana loved anything s'mores, almost as much as she was beginning to love his lips on her skin, his breath in her ear, or his hand in hers, so she simply nodded, telling him, "Thank you." Admiring the way he sauntered into the coffee shop, she saw the head of almost every woman in the place turn to watch him, and knew they held the same appreciation for him. He had an alluring, graceful way about him, and she was reminded of the breathless way he had made her feel last night, with his hands stroking her bare skin and his hair between her fingers. God, what was she doing? She should be heading home, she mused, as she read a text from Ava, dropping her head back to rest on her chair.

No word from you yet—can we assume this is good news? Don't stay out too late, though. We're expecting you!

Tomorrow morning, she was due to take the train out to Long Island for Sunday dinner with her family, as she was expected to do any Sunday she had off: it usually ended with one of her nieces crying, her oldest nephew stealing a car (okay, that had only happened once), or her sisters fighting. Meanwhile, their mom, Fiona, beloved family matriarch, often looked too tired to stand (after probably working at least a sixty-hour week) yet often cooked an elaborate meal, making something rich and hearty, determined to show her family how much she loved them. When Lana went tomorrow, she would try to take over the cooking, urging her mom to sit down. Her sisters would float in, using their own children as excuses about why they could not possibly help their mom, and Montgomery would more than likely be working on some issue with their mom's house, yard, or car—all chores that everyone acknowledged had fallen on his shoulders at the age of eighteen, once their dad had finally left for the second (and *last)* time. In truth, the responsibilities of his family had become Monty's at the age of five, the *first* time their dad had left.

"I got you a surprise," a husky voice announced, just before he put down a tray laden with steaming coffees, both topped with whipped cream, and enormous slices of the richest looking chocolate cake Lana had ever seen. Ugh, she thought, not chocolate—her ultimate weakness. At least, it had been until she had met this man, whose white shirt, stretching tightly across his chest, should have been tawdry, but instead was ever so sexily appealing.

"I can't stay," Lana impulsively, and emphatically, told him as he was sitting down. And she couldn't, really. Not only that, she shouldn't. He was far too tempting as he scooted his chair closer to hers. When Lana first sat in the buttery-smooth leather-bound chair, the experience was as if sinking into a deep cloud, and the finish rivaled the deep reddish undertones of the hair of the sexiest man alive. Sitting across from her, his silvery eyes pinned her into place. He had left open the top few buttons of his oxford shirt, and as he got closer to her, she could see his silky chest hairs, which she had been working so hard on ignoring. Or trying to. Swallowing proved difficult as she remembered, quite clearly, running her hands across his chest, reveling in the feel of his maleness. So unlike her first and only encounter at sixteen—Anthony's chest, at eighteen, had been smooth, and his frame, which she had considered quite broad back then, would be scrawny next to the Adonis who was currently brushing a hand through her hair. She shivered in response, proving why she needed to leave *posthaste*. How did he do it? Did he study to make himself so tantalizing, or did it come naturally?

"Don't leave yet," he murmured to her, "you haven't eaten your cake." Taking one of the forks, he handed it to her, then picked up the other one and proceeded to take a huge bite of his slice of cake, catching the crumbs with his finger before then putting the same finger in his mouth. This man was far more tempting than any baked good she had ever encountered, and more than likely twice as bad for her, and her mouth watered in response.

Licking her lips, she glimpsed her cake in the corner of her eye, and it looked undeniably delicious. As a child, she had learned to cook and bake, chores that were hers after school when she was old enough to be at the stove. Since her mom was usually home quite late, and her sisters had whatever odd jobs they were doing, or bits of college they were attending, and her dear brother frequently popped in between the two full-time jobs he always held, Lana was expected to have dinner started as soon as she got home from school. Knowing her brother had a sweet tooth as demanding as her own, she would bake him cookies or snack cakes, sometimes a pie, rewarded with a bear hug from him when he tasted the results of her efforts. Her sisters were typically on one diet or another, to keep themselves appealing to the opposite sex, despite being in relationships (or possibly because of those relationships). Finally, once her family was well fed, she was free to study and do her homework, sometimes staying up until far into the night. Occasionally, she would still be awake when her mom rose before the sun was up to set off for work the following morning, so she would brew her mom coffee and make Fiona a quick breakfast to take with her. Her mom would ask about her schoolwork, what she was studying, declaring it was over her own head, but Lana knew that to be untrue. Her mom was brilliant but had made the mistake of falling in love with the wrong man at an early age and staying in love, despite his failure to love her back. Fiona had sacrificed her life to his love, then gave up her dreams for her children, which was something Lana had vowed to herself she would never do.

Giving into temptation, she cut a chunk of cake, noticing how he smiled as she started eating. Ignoring the fact that she was in a hotel that never in a million years would Lana ever be able to afford (she was a charlatan for even sitting in the lobby), she settled into her chair, relishing her cake (which was luscious), drinking her coffee (licking some of the sweetened whipped cream from the top), and enjoying the view of her sexy stranger. As he took a drink, a bit of the cream smeared under his lips. Lips that were full and firm, and she recalled how they had roamed her body last night, traveling across her bare stomach, down her legs. Okay, enough cake and enough lusting after this sexy man, Lana decided, still in a state of disbelief that he had ever desired her in the first place. In a dark bar last night was one thing, and even in the hotel room after several drinks was understandable, but here in this glamorous hotel—why would he? Also, she wondered how was he able to afford to stay here? Lana could not think of many people she knew that would ever have enough money to even cross the threshold of the gilded age entrance of this place. Not only that, but what about that adjoining room from last night? Who was staying there? Where were they now? Suddenly panicked with these questions in her head, Lana stood up abruptly, nearly spilling her coffee in the process. "I'm sorry, but I need to leave. I have to be on a train to Long Island in the morning, so I—"

He stood also and, as if by some magnetic force, she fell into him. Once her body had contact with his, Lana was powerless, as she had feared would be the case. Stroking her hand across his shoulder, feeling the feathery curls of his hair at the nape of his neck, she stared into his eyes—mesmerizing, spellbinding eyes. "Tell me what you want, baby," he told her as his hands cupped her face. "I am all yours," and with those words (words that should not work so well on her, but did), he gently brushed his mouth across hers. Her mouth opened willingly and eagerly under his, and she seized the opportunity to deepen the kiss, causing his hands to slide down her back, settling on the curve of her waist. Careful to avoid a public spectacle (because who knows how she had behaved last night?), she took his hand in hers and tugged it, leading them as discreetly as possible toward the elevator. Hmm, she silently mused, she must not have been as out of it last night as she had thought, though, because she seemed to know the exact location of the elevator.

As one of the multiple elevators opened, it was Lana who led the way in, and he followed, embracing her from behind as the doors closed, finally. He was a giant towering over her, so when she turned in his arms and backed them into a corner, he had to bend close to her to hear her whispered words, and he groaned in response as she brought his head determinedly down to hers.

TEXT FROM GREER

Can we assume that you are with him now?

You can thank us tomorrow.

# CHAPTER
## Eleven

*Liam*



Liam had been stunned into silence (a condition he rarely, if ever, experienced) when his Mystery Woman had knocked into him outside of the bar. Every message to her had gone unanswered, so to physically and literally run into her outside Whistling Dixie? Liam was not a praying man, but he had been sending his pleas out into the universe, and they had manifested abundantly. Other forces had to have been at play, because what would have happened if he had left with Tess and Sam? If he hadn't still been here when she had arrived? Would she have gone home, thinking he had stood her up, or would she have sent him an urgent text, begging him to meet her?

Instead, he was the one willing to do the begging, enclosed within this elevator; in the reflective walls, he studied their blurry image, mesmerized by the sight of her body tucked into his. In his arms, lushly filling them, her hair fell over her shoulders and covered his hands, and her eyes were two dark blue pools, so inviting as he stared into them. Speechless again when she pulled them into a far corner of the elevator, he was also without the ability to breathe when she started their kiss, just as she had done the night before. As he lifted his mouth from hers, the elevator made a stop, and a family of four got on. Damn, he cursed to himself. Had people never heard of taking the stairs? His body was thrumming with electricity as they stood together, still in each other's arms, despite the parents casting withering stares their way.

When they had first entered the hotel earlier, Liam had stolen a look down at her as he guided them to a small table outside the luxurious coffee shop tucked into the corner of the sumptuous lobby. Something about her expression made him view the hotel in a new way, and he didn't see the chandeliers that hung from the ceiling as elegant, but instead garish. The silver-encrusted features of the front desk shined too brightly. He had chosen this hotel because of its location near Josh's hospital, for his cousin's convenience, but had never stayed here before, instead always preferring to stay in Brooklyn whenever he would visit Tess and Josh over the past five years. When she had reached her dainty hand into her bag just before he approached the barista for their order, Liam pondered what could be going through that adorable head of hers. Was she reaching for money? Did she really think he would accept money from her to pay for a cup of coffee? There was something so innocent about her that brought out an urge to protect her—yet there were other things about her that brought out many, many different feelings for her, all of which he was currently experiencing. When he had left her at the table to get their refreshments, he had noticed she had her phone in her hand and kept glancing toward the entrance; as the barista rang up their beverages, he impulsively added two slices of chocolate pound cake to their order, hopefully enticing her to stay. Born with an insatiable sweet tooth, as Liam carried their treats to the table, he noted that his Mystery Woman looked far more delicious than the cake he couldn't wait to taste. Makeup free, her cheeks blushed the most charming shade of pink, making her look good enough to eat. He had been afraid, though, that she was too close to darting off. With her teeth biting her bottom lip, it plumped up more every time, as if daring him to press his own mouth to hers, so his own teeth could bite those delectable lips. He had told himself that he wouldn't, though…not without her asking him to. Maybe even convincing her to kiss him first? As the strands of her honey-gold locks trapped the glistening light from the chandeliers above, she had been glowing, and Liam was mesmerized. Until she had abruptly stood up, declaring her intention to depart—then he had been panicked. Liam, usually so smooth with any woman, regardless of his intentions toward her, had been failing with this one, or so he had agonized. She had been only an exhalation away from hitting the front door of the hotel, which they had been sitting far too close to, he recognized in retrospect. Underneath the sparkling lights, she looked so delicate, almost fragile, and then they had each stood up, almost simultaneously, tumbling into each other. Thank god, for that had brought about their insanely and intensely passionate kiss.

At the next stop on the elevator, the family got out, and the kids, who were probably preteens, each glanced back before the doors closed, giggling. Alone once again inside their steel love shack, their kiss escalated, and Liam brought her body in blissful contact with his, but a little voice in his head began lecturing him that this was not what he had intended to happen tonight. He did not want a night of forgettable sex with this woman (although Liam firmly believed that every woman he had ever been with had *never* forgotten a moment of his magic), and he definitely did not want just drunken foreplay, either, like last night. Wanting to *connect* with her on a deeper level, making it possible to begin something significant before he went back home, had been his reason for inviting her to meet him again. Was he deranged, though? Here she was, his Mystery Woman, so soft and supple, clearly attracted to him, judging from the way her hands were fluttering all over his chest and shoulders, slipping her fingers into his hair and tugging.

"Thirteenth floor" announced the recording in the elevator, as they finally arrived. Regretting the need to physically separate from his Mystery Woman, he took her hand in his, with the small, slender fingers he had been intrigued by as they had wrapped around her coffee downstairs. No acrylics or polish for her, but she needed no adornment in any area. With their fingers laced tightly together, their pace could not have been quicker as they strode down the hall. Liam slowed slightly when it seemed she was running more than walking—he had always considered Tess and her sister Ruth to be on the short side, but his Mystery Woman was an inch or two shorter than them, and he shivered at the memory of her shorter but oh, so sexy legs entwined with his on his bed last night. Before the tequila she had drunk had finally kicked in, causing sleep to overtake her, much to his disappointment.

Willing his hand to stop quivering as he opened his door, he was thankful when it successfully granted him entry on the first try. The moment the door shut behind them, his Mystery Woman had backed him up against it, her hands pressed firmly on his chest as they made their way up to his head and curled into his hair. Growing up, he had been self-conscious about the color, the same shade of deep auburn both he and his sister shared, inheriting it from their mother, who had always referred to it as "chestnut". No boy wants red hair growing up, no matter if it is called "chestnut", "auburn", or the general "dark red". "Such an attractive boy—too bad his hair isn't blond, like his dad. It would go so well with those eyes. But really, his eyes are so light. What are they? Not quite blue, are they, dear? It's unfortunate he didn't inherit your green eyes," Liam had heard his grandma Kinsale announce to her daughter, Nora, one afternoon when Liam had been about five. The endless inner soundtrack had played over and over in his head during his roughest patches in puberty. A scrawny thirteen-year-old, not as smart as his cousins Josh and Felix. And though he had also played football in middle school, he had not been nearly as fearless as his cousin Daniel. On the other side of puberty, though, Liam had come out shining, determined to highlight the attributes he *knew* he had: chiseled features, muscles he had worked on during endless hours in the gym, hair that, despite its red tint, had some curls at the back that females simply could not resist digging their fingers into, and his laid-back, carefree attitude that let everyone know he wasn't bothered by any insensitive comments finding him lacking when compared to his cousins or even his sister.

The woman in his arms didn't seem to have any complaints concerning him, as far as he could tell, even if he had been concerned that she would not meet up with him, and after she had been a breath away from leaving him downstairs. Now that they had made it to his room, he was comfortable enough to take the seduction more slowly, allowing them to savor the rest of the night. "Baby," he whispered, "how about we slow things down a bit?" His hands framed her delicate face, and he watched as her eyebrows drew together in a frown.

"Slow things down?" she repeated. "What do you mean?"

His thumbs touched the dark circles he noticed now under her eyes, thanks to the bathroom light across from them. "I just wanted to see you again…we don't want to rush anything."

His Mystery Woman leaned up to kiss him again, and this time her fingers began unbuttoning his shirt. Who was he to argue with her? Wait — no—he could have casual, meaningless sex with any woman, but with this woman here, he longed for her to mean something to him, so he stilled her hands with his, bringing her fingers up to his mouth, kissing each one, and then led her over to the bed. As he sat down, he leaned over to get her the ornament he had picked up for her earlier. Intending to choose something truly meaningful, he had found hers at Tiffany's on Fifth Avenue, not at the Christmas Shop on Seventh Avenue, where he had purchased the one for Tess and Sam. His Mystery Woman's token needed to be special, more thoughtful. With his small token in his hand, he turned back to her to find that she had opened the front of her striped dress, revealing her matching lingerie underneath. His mouth was the desert as he attempted to swallow, but the task proved impossible. God, she was more than his Mystery Woman now—she was a temptress, a goddess, and her curves were on full display as the dress hung at her sides.

Pushing Liam back, she straddled him on the bed and bent to kiss him, and he was cognizant enough to know that if her lips made contact with his, his good reason would leave this room entirely. "Baby," he moaned, "what's the rush? We have all night to get to know each other," he told her, running his fingers up her legs.

His Mystery Woman sat back on her heals. "What's wrong?" Her golden brows furrowed in concern. "Do you need something to drink? Maybe they restocked the bar from last night? I mean, I know some people need alcohol to perform—I'm sorry, I guess I should have realized after last night…" her voice drifted off, and Liam waited for her to finish.

"After last night…what?" Liam struggled to sit up with her still on top of him, certain that she could not *possibly* be putting him into this category of needing to be hammered to have sex??? Could she???

Her honey-colored hair tumbled down her back as she lifted her leg over his prone form to dismount onto the bed, and he was too shocked to stop her as she hustled over to the fridge and opened it. Grabbing two tiny tequila bottles, she brought them to him, thrusting them in his face. She opened one up and handed it to him. "Drink up," she demanded.

"Baby, I can assure you that not only do I NOT need to be drunk to be able to 'perform' as you put it," he informed her, using air quotes while he gently brushed aside the hand shoving the tequila in his face, "but I was not even close to being drunk last night." Liam grabbed the sides of her dress together as he brought her closer to him.

"But," she protested, "what about all of the bottles that were on the floor when I woke up?" she asked, pointing to the floor, which had been cleaned quite thoroughly by housekeeping sometime today.

Liam shook his head, laughing. "You drank two bottles when we got here last night, and so did I. Anything not resembling tequila was tossed by you after you raided both refrigerators. You told me you had some kind of track record with tequila, and who was I to argue with someone as beautiful as you?" Thinking maybe now was a perfect time to show her how much he had thought about her all day, and what their night together last night had meant to him (even without having fulfilled his sexual fantasies with her), he reached over to grab his little gift for her, again, which he had dropped after seeing her displayed in only her extremely alluring underwear.

Visibly distraught, she sat next to him on the bed and put her face in her hands. "Ugh, god, I must have been so out of it." Lifting her head, she opened her dark-blue eyes, so serious in the ambient streetlights from the city outside the window. "I never drink—not really, anyway, so my tolerance is pretty low. I guess that explains why I don't remember…"

Once again, he waited for her to finish, and when she left him hanging for the second time, he prodded her. "Don't remember what?"

She shifted a lock of moonlit hair behind her ear and whispered, "Us. I don't remember us last night, I'm sorry. I'm sure you were great, and I have no doubt I was in complete agreement with everything that happened," she assured him, so earnest that he could do nothing but laugh in response. "Was I not...you know...good?" She clutched her dress tightly to her body after she asked him this.

Wait? Was she inferring what he dreaded? Could she be thinking that they had sex last night? Liam responded emphatically to correct her. "Let's get one thing straight, right now: we did not do *anything* last night besides drink some tequila and sleep. A generous amount of foreplay occurred between drinking and sleeping, but nothing else more... ahem...intimate." Finally, she looked him in the eyes again, as relief dawned on her expressive face.

"I remember that," she said. "I remember the...umm...foreplay. Very well," she told him as she began leaning into him.

Well, at least that made an impression, because otherwise he would have been forced to give up the "world's best lover" title he had bestowed upon himself many years ago. The idea that all day long she had thought they had actually *had sex* but couldn't remember was enough to torture him for the rest of his days. And to think she would believe he would *ever* be that intimate with a woman who had been as drunk, tired, incapacitated, whatever, as she had been last night?

Liam reached out his hand and cupped her cheek, stroking back her hair from her face—she really had the most amazingly gorgeous hair. As he wrapped a fistful around his hand, he lowered his lips to her ear. "Baby, I can assure you that when we are finally, fully intimate, you will remember it. Completely, totally, absolutely. And I won't need anything but the scent of you, or the sight of you, or just the sound of you, to 'perform', because you have had me tied up in knots since I first saw you last night." His other hand traced the line of her lips just before he kissed her. And then he kissed her again, more deeply. Liam felt her hands slide up his chest, until she had burrowed them under his shirt, pushing him back on the bed once again, the ornament he had painstakingly chosen for her dropping to the side of the bed, forgotten once more.

# CHAPTER
## *Twelve*

## *Lana*



With his intense gaze following her early morning departure from the hotel room last night, Lana had walked to the subway and headed home, her emotions tossed between feeling elated and forlorn. Receiving his text while she had climbed up the stairs of the subway, with the sun just rising, had sent a shock of longing through her, and she cradled the small package he had given her just before she left, wondering what she was supposed to think of it. Her hook-up had told her that he had thought about the gift for her while he was getting something for newlywed friends of his at a little Christmas shop on Seventh Avenue, and she was fairly certain it was the one close to Carnegie Hall. On her days off, Lana loved to wander the streets of Manhattan, especially those near Carnegie Hall, The Metropolitan Museum of Art, or Lincoln Center, especially when the opera or the ballet was performing. Never having been able to afford a ticket to such opulent productions, she would sit by the fountain and see the polished people dressed up in their finest (or those that did, anyway). Lana was always hugely disappointed when she saw people wearing jeans or, god forbid, *shorts* to such a decadent event. Lana supposed she could afford a ticket to a performance now, but she still saw herself as the girl who grew up poor, doing her best not to look like it.

Listening to *Judy at Carnegie Hall* as she stood under the steaming spray in her own studio apartment, she thought back to the times spent watching people with exceedingly high taste. Replaying the events of last night over and over in her mind, Lana believed that it possibly could have been the most amazing night of her life, while also knowing she would more than likely never see him again, despite his text to the contrary. Perhaps there was a chance he would come to New York again, but she knew absolutely *nothing* about him, like where he lived or even his name! And yet, she pondered with an unusual grin (one bordering on *wicked*, her sisters would probably say), there was something very freeing about her entire situation. No baggage concerning her family and their chaos, no talk of her career and what medical career avenue she had to choose to take in just a couple of years, and certainly no talk about how smart she was, how she had graduated early from high school and college and med school, how driven she was with her career, blah, blah, blah. Instead, *she* had seduced *him* last night, pushing aside his inclination to "get to know each other better". Nothing had ever made her feel more powerful, more alive, or more alluring than maneuvering him back on his bed and straddling him. How she had *ever* thought of that move perplexed her, but Lana had read each emotion crossing his handsome features, and even if she still had no idea what attracted a man like him to someone like her, she had still reveled in the knowledge that he had, indeed, desired her.

Now, as her train on the Long Island Railroad pulled into the station at Riverhead, she grabbed her overnight bag from the overhead rack, trying to temper her emotions to the best of her ability: put as much pep in her step as she could, because if she displayed even the slightest lack of enthusiasm, she would face the family drilling squad and their endless barrage of questions; not too much pep, though, or she would be pestered non-stop about *why* she was so giddy. Her family was always one wild card away from screaming, either from exasperation or exhilaration, and Lana usually tried to find comfort in remaining as neutral as possible, a seemingly impossible task where her family was concerned.

Exiting the station, Lana was immediately grabbed from behind in a bear hug (why was her family so insistent on this mode of affection—it never failed to scare the life out of her!) and a voice in her ear said, "I missed you, Auntie Lana," and she relaxed in the still clamped arms of her niece, Julia. Born when Lana was just ten, Julia was the oldest of Ava's children (her father was Ava's first husband, Simon), and thus the eldest of all the nieces and nephews. Currently, Julia was studying to be a nurse at one of the state universities, and Lana remained hopeful that Julia could stay her course to finish her degree. Lana turned around to look at her niece, her personal favorite (although she would *never* admit that to any of the others), yet also a painful reminder of the responsibilities Lana had to bear from a young age. Julia had been the end, essentially, to Lana's childhood; Lana had to pivot from being the baby of her family to taking care of the new baby, and the transition had not been smooth or welcome.

The spitting image of her mother, Ava, Julia's black hair and dark blue eyes (the one trait all Miller siblings had inherited, for better or worse, from their mostly absentee father), made her so insanely gorgeous. Perhaps it had been her mother's multiple marriages, or Lana's own attitudes toward relationships, but Julia, at the age of twenty, was wary of relationships herself, instead focused on finishing her nursing degree so she could live independently, without the need for any man.

"So, Auntie, Mom tells me you hooked up with some hot stud?" Lana shut her eyes, embarrassed that all of them already knew her business, with her family finding it hard to believe it was even possible—they all believed her to be some sort of nineteenth century spinster.

Oh god, Lana inwardly groaned, here we go, and braced herself to face the family assault. "How does she know he was a 'hot stud'?" Lana hated reducing her Hook Up (as she had taken to calling him in her mind) down to his appearance alone (although she could admit, at least to herself, that he was, indeed, a hot stud), but it wasn't like she had loads of evidence to counter with about his personality or intelligence. Unless, of course, Lana considered their "date" last night, when he treated her to coffee and cake. Or the way his breathtaking silvery eyes sparkled when he touched her? Or the gift he had chosen (specifically for her, he told her)? Still wrapped in tissue paper, crinkling in its plush velvet bag when she put her hand in her purse to stroke it comfortingly.

Julia stopped at a light and then turned her face to study her aunt. "Well, I'm guessing he must have been pretty incredible, considering the way your face is flushing," she teased. "Seriously, though, is he *just* a hook-up, or is it more, since you guys had another date or something last night? You are *clearly* interested in him."

TEXT FROM HOOK UP

I have never felt this way about any woman before you. You take my breath away, you steal my sense, you make me burn.

I want you even now.

Tingling as she read his message, Lana tried not to be too obvious, and sighed, frustrated that now it seemed her entire family was going to be up in her personal business. "It wasn't a date, necessarily, and honestly, I wish I had never even said anything to your mom and Greer. I'm going to blame it on the tequila." Yet there had been no tequila last night to explain away her actions, and the more she thought about how she had all but thrown herself at him, doubts began to overcome her concerning the events of last night. Maybe he had only wanted to "get to know her" because he didn't want to have sex with her, initially? And yet, his eyes on her…and his gift to her…those things meant something

—didn't they? "I'm sure my sisters are getting a kick out of all of this, anyway," she muttered, staring out the window, seeing the faint image of her face reflected in the glass. Her Hook Up had been quite...ummm... excited, when removing her clothing last night, and he had been an intensely involved participant all throughout the evening, but what choice had he had when she had all but bodily attacked him? Was he having any doubts this morning, despite his messages? "They must think it's hilarious seeing me humiliated, anyway."

"What? No, it's not like that, Lana," Julia emphatically corrected her. "Why would you say that? And why would you be humiliated?" questioned her niece.

Deciding to admit some of the truth, Lana said, "God, Julia, if you saw him, you would understand. He is so far out of my league, and between you and me, yes, he was 'hot'. Gorgeous, actually, which begs the question of why he would be interested in me." Lana stole another glance at her phone to quell her doubts concerning proof of his interest. "I don't want to talk about my hook-up anymore. He's irrelevant, especially since he left for parts unknown this morning, and I am not likely to see him ever again. I'm not exactly memorable—never been the life of the party, like my sisters, nor do I look like either of them, both of whom won some kind of genetic lottery. Like you," Lana nudged Julia. "You know, your mom is 'the hot one', Greer is 'the fun one' and I am 'the smart one'. I know my place." The sad part was that Ava was *also* the fun one, and likewise Greer the hot one. Only Lana was stuck in her lane, but at least she had that. And now she had last night.

"And what about Uncle Montgomery? What is his title?" Julia cocked her head to the side. "I guess," she continued, answering her own question, "he's all of them, right?"

Lana nodded in agreement, because her brother definitely was—he could be the family comedian, there to lighten the mood when the estrogen levels in the house threatened to bring the entire place down. Also extremely serious, the family could count on Monty to be the primary system of support for any of his sisters—herself, in particular, she had always believed.

As Julia pulled into the driveway of the home her mother had lived in for almost fifty years, Lana heard a soft ping from her purse. Telling her niece that she needed to make a work call and would be in soon, Lana watched as Julia bounded up the stairs to the small house, immediately bringing her phone out and looked at the screen.

TEXT FROM HOOK UP

Can't stop thinking about you.

Tell me you feel the same.

Lana flushed, holding her phone next to her heart. Should she respond? She wanted to…desperately, but had restrained herself from answering his previous texts. Last night was meant to be casual, a onetime deal. On the other hand, she had no idea where he was, and responding to him could be kind of interesting. Like having a pen pal of sorts, she imagined. A very sexy pen pal, she smiled to herself, who had ever so gently helped her redress this morning before she left his hotel room. Gathering up her clothing at some point while she was sleeping under the downy duvet, he had dragged a chair next to the bed, so everything she needed was there for her, especially her beloved blue wrap dress, thrifted from Housing Works in SoHo one afternoon this past summer. The multi-pierced clerk named Jeffrey confided that it had only been brought in that very morning by a woman reeking of gin, who had proclaimed to him that she had been roommates with Grace Kelly when they both had attended drama school in the late forties—Grace had owned the dress but had unintentionally left it behind after moving out. Once Lana had tried on the dress, which fit her perfectly, she had doubted the story, since she was sure Grace Kelly had to have been at the *minimum* several dress sizes smaller. At least.

Lana reread his texts again, her fingers stroking the screen as if she could reach through and touch him again. Before she could stop herself with what was left of her good sense, she typed:

TEXT TO HOOK UP

Can't stop thing about you, either.

Wish you were here now.

Would give anything to kiss you.

Have your body on mine.

And then, without giving herself more time to ponder, Lana sent the text, and her heart hammered in her chest. She was reeling from last night, steeped in the way he had made her feel. A noise from inside the house caught her attention then, and she looked up at her childhood home. What would her Hook Up think of all of this? Lana thought, studying the bordering-on-dilapidated (no matter how many times Montgomery tried to repair them) steps leading up to the small house she had grown up in until she was thirteen. From the driveway, she could see the chipping paint on the front of the house, where the blue gave way to the yellow underneath. When Lana had been twelve, she and her siblings had spent two weeks repainting the house. They had grown tired of the pale yellow of their home, and one Sunday dinner when their mom had stated wistfully that she had always wanted the house to be blue (but their dad had painted it yellow instead), Montgomery had immediately gone to the hardware store in town and gotten at least a dozen blue paint samples. After the opulence of the hotel she had spent the night in, the run-down appearance of this house stood in stark comparison. Lana looked further up the house, at the window screens, where every single one had some scratches (varying in size) caused by the rescue cats Fiona could not resist saving. Currently, her mom owned four cats, but she usually fostered one or two as well for a local animal rescue.

"Auntie, Auntie, come see grandma's new kittens," her nephew Leo rushed out of the house, grabbed on her leg and began tugging her up the stairs, his black hair gleaming in the sun. Lana lifted the four-year-old, Ava's son, with her third (and current) husband, kissing him on his cherubic cheeks until he squirmed to be let down. Looking up at his aunt, Leo informed her, "She has two new kittens! Kittens, Auntie, not *cats*. Mommy said I have to be gentle. Come on, Auntie, come see them." Leo was nothing if not persuasive, so Lana sighed slightly, letting Leo lead her by the hand to the front door, dreading having to walk into the house to face everyone who knew her business. She heard her phone ping once more, and the notification left her short of panting, desperate to be alone.

"Just a minute, Sweetie. Auntie will be right in, okay?" Lana ushered Leo through the door, and then turned to sit on the porch railing, feeling it give slightly. Not good—she had better mention it to her brother (as if he already didn't have a million other small chores to do around this house).

TEXT FROM HOOK UP

I can still smell you on me.

With her heart racing, she reached into her purse to touch his gift to her, which she had not yet taken out of the bag. Lana had always (until last night) been more of a believer in making something last—no instant gratification for her. Once she opened that velvet bag, it would be over. No more looking forward to opening it, no more anticipation, no more wondering what it could be. Instead, she feared she would be left with disappointment once she finally revealed the contents.

TEXT FROM HOOK UP

I can still feel you in my hands.

Suddenly, two more nieces busted out of the house and raced over to hug her: Allie, fourteen, and nineteen-year-old Amelia. Lana dropped her phone inside her purse, intent on putting him out of her mind.

"Who's your boyfriend?"

"Did you go on a date?"

"What's he look like?"

"You said you'd never have a boyfriend!"

TEXT FROM HOOK UP

I can still taste you on my tongue

Her nieces questioned her, speaking over each other, leaving no time for Lana to answer either of them, thankfully. Each one grabbed a hand of hers, yanking her to the front door. Shutting her eyes briefly, she sent her Hook Up a mental reply, asking him to turn around from wherever he was headed and come back to New York. Raised voices from inside the house broke her out of her reverie, and she put one foot inside the door, knowing it was going to be a long day.

TEXT TO HOOK UP

You were right—I completely,

totally, absolutely remember it.

Every moment.

# CHAPTER
## *Thirteen*

## *Liam*

*Three months later*

TEXT FROM MYSTERY WOMAN

Happy Thanksgiving!!!

Walked by Whistling Dixie last night, And, as usual, thought of you, as I do every time. Needed to meet my family on the West Side for the traditional blowing up of the balloons for the big parade today. We do that every year since… never mind. Anyway, I can't believe it's already Thanksgiving. And I can't believe it's been three months since meeting you. Sometimes your messages are all that keep me focused during the day.

TEXT TO MYSTERY WOMAN

You beat me, Mystery Woman—you are my first
Thanksgiving greeting of the day! As far as time
passing—wow! For me, it seems longer than
three months that we met, because you are all I
think about every night before I go to bed, when
I get out of bed, and every minute I am in my
bed. My cold, lonely bed, where I dream of you
being in my arms, or on top of me, or under me.
Now how is it I still don't know what you
call me?

It must be something really bad…

TEXT FROM MYSTERY WOMAN

Haha—not bad, just embarrassing. Don't know if
I can truly admit to it yet, but keep in mind, it
was something my sisters called you, so it's how
I saved your number when I thought we had…
you know…before I passed out in your room.
You know, I'm still wondering who was in that
adjoining room??? Oh, I'm at my subway stop.

P.S. I think about you when I'm in bed, too.

TEXT TO MYSTERY WOMAN

I never told you who was in the next room
because you forbade any personal information! I
will give you a small hint: it was someone I am
very close with. Anyway, the person almost
caught us that first night, especially since you
left the door wide open on your liquor hunt.

TEXT FROM MYSTERY WOMAN

Hey! I thought we agreed not to discuss how
much I drank that night! My nerves were all
tangled up that night. I don't normally pick up
strange men in bars and make them take me
back to their hotel rooms.

Just you.

TEXT TO MYSTERY WOMAN

Just me, huh? Baby, I wouldn't have had it any other way. It's a bummer you have to work on Thanksgiving, though, but it makes me wonder. If I were to start guessing about any of your personal information, I'd probably start there, like what kind of occupation do you have requiring you to work on a national holiday?

TEXT FROM MYSTERY WOMAN

Well, there could be any manner of things I could do for a living, and I admit that I kind of like that you are thinking about it so much. I like knowing I am on your mind, because I feel the same. My thoughts are consumed with memories of you. Of us. I miss you.

TEXT FROM MYSTERY WOMAN

Did I say the wrong thing?

I'm sorry if I went too far, especially since I am the one nagging to keep whatever this is from being too serious. Let's go back to just talking about Thanksgiving dinner. I usually load up on sides, but am really feeling a turkey craving this year. This morning I heard a rumor that the place where I'm going to eat may run out of the good stuff before I get a chance to eat dinner.

TEXT TO MYSTERY WOMAN

I'm going to be worried all day that you won't get any turkey to eat. Meanwhile, I am going to be with my extremely loud, extremely crazy family.

P.S. Saying you miss me is never too much.

I miss you every day, and not a day goes by that you are not on my mind. Hell, if I'm honest, not a minute goes by. I have to reel myself in from showing how serious I am about this.

TEXT FROM MYSTERY WOMAN

I've decided I will be okay with no turkey. As long as there is still pecan pie. And stuffing. Do you say stuffing or dressing? Enjoy your holiday!

P.S. I'm pretty serious about you, too.

TEXT TO MYSTERY WOMAN

Dressing…always dressing.

And I am a chocolate cream pie man.

You know, you never did tell me what you call me in your phone? Guess it must be pretty bad, huh?

Oh, I bet I'm listed as something like "Hot Stud" or "Sex God"—am I right? Especially if your sisters are involved.

TEXT FROM MYSTERY WOMAN

Oh, your family holidays sound like mine.

I see what you did there, pointing out my sisters.

I should never have told you about them!

I knew you'd use them against me ;)

Liam sat down to dinner at the home of his grandparents in Clover Lake, seated in between his cousin, Josh, and his sister, Cait. Thanksgiving dinner always started promptly at noon, with just enough time for dessert, some card games, an afternoon stroll if the weather permitted (it was South Dakota, so it could be snowing or it could be sweltering), and then a follow-up supper feast promptly at five p.m.—Grandma Livingston's orders, without fail, every year Liam could remember.

"Josh, I figured you and Effie would be gracing the Van Holland table today, since it's your first Thanksgiving together?" Tossing Effie a wink, Liam continued, "Isn't that what couples have to do? Share the holidays with the in-laws?" Effie's face lit up and her tawny-colored eyes sparkled at the talk about couples, in-laws, and holidays.

Josh laced his fingers with Effie's, kissed her hand, and nodded, "Well, we are going to walk over there this afternoon, after I beat you in a game of cards. Toss me a dinner roll, will you, Dad?" Josh called to his father, Henry, who was seated across the table next to Liam's dad, George.

Liam's mom, Nora, walked behind Henry just as he picked up a dinner roll, and she snatched it out of his hand before he could throw it across the table. "Absolutely no throwing! Cait and I did not spend the entire morning putting out the fine china to have you two behave like teenagers. And Henry, you should know better! Effie, honestly, how do you manage? I know Liam has been spending a lot of time at your house these past couple of months, and for that, you have my sympathies." Everyone at the table laughed, knowing Nora loved every moment of the foolish behavior.

Effie responded with a giggle, "Actually, Liam has been great, never mind the fact that we never have any leftovers when he comes to the house for supper, nor can I ever manage to find the television remote once he is gone."

The entire table responded with laughter, and one by one, members of the family added their own personal grievances concerning Liam, who smiled and graciously let everyone have their turn, but squirmed in discomfort when they began a second round. His mom, always so good at reading him and then rescuing him when she needed to, broke in with, "And could someone tell me again about the myth of families splitting the holiday? Last time I checked, we spent every Thanksgiving with the Livingston family...not that I'm complaining," and Nora smiled her smile—the one both her son and daughter had inherited, and Liam's dad reached over and squeezed her hand.

"Sure, Mom, make Grandma Livingston feel bad, now, knowing she is deprived of us at Christmas," Liam teased his mom, grateful to her for changing the subject from him, while winking across the table to his beloved grandmother, Catherine, the matriarch of the Livingston family. Liam and his parents, along with Cait (if she graced the family with her presence for the holiday), always spent Christmas with the Kinsale family, while Thanksgiving was always the Livingston holiday; this year, however, they were missing his Aunt Beatrice's family. Sister to George and Henry, Beatrice and her husband Brian, long with his cousin Felix, had all gone to Chicago to spend the week with Liam's cousin Daniel, an accomplished chef working in one of the top-rated restaurants in the Windy City.

"Liam," his dad, George, began, "how is it working in Beverley? It seems like since you started at the dealership there, I never see you." Completely untrue, Liam thought, but both of his parents had shown a flair for drama over the course of his life—and they wondered why he acted the way he did???

"Seriously, Dad? We see each other every weekend at Uncle Henry's!" The four of them, Henry, Josh, George, and Liam, had been restoring a '72 Dodge Dart for most of the past six months. Work on the classic car had progressed more slowly since Josh had begun at Beverley General to finish his surgical residency. When they had first started the labor of love, Josh had been working with his dad at Check Care Auto in Beverley. Liam's dad (and grandpa, occasionally) ran the auto shop in its original location in Clover Lake.

Liam continued, "If you really want to know, I am starting to feel more at home in Beverley—so much so that this seems like the perfect time to make an announcement." Liam waited for his family members to settle down around the table to announce: "The big news is that I think I've found a house to buy, and it's just a few blocks from Effie's!"

Unexpected silence followed, which was not the reaction Liam had been expecting to his proof of maturity. An "Oh, Liam, wow, what a commitment you're making," would have been nice to hear. Or: "Congratulations, you are finally an adult," even if made with sarcasm, would have been the acknowledgement from his family that they saw his progress he'd made in his personal and professional lives. About a month after Liam had returned home from New York City, his mom had announced that it was time for her son to run one of their more prominent locations for Kinsale Autos, in Beverley. For years, Liam had waffled between grateful and resentful concerning his placement of his rung on the Kinsale leadership ladder. At the small location in Carlisle, Liam was able to essentially come and go as he pleased, flirt with the single women who stopped into the shop (many of whom came in for that particular purpose, in many cases), take off whatever time he needed for the array of bachelor parties he was so often invited to (and more often than not put in charge of), or spend his time in his office on the internet, in search of any other job that seemed to be his calling more than that of car salesman (no matter how good he was at it). No one in the Kinsale family could deny that he had made a success out of the formerly struggling Carlisle location, though. Although it was the smallest in the dealership chain, Liam had made it the most profitable for its inventory size. Finally rewarded with a move up to the larger town of Beverley, after so many years of being stuck in the sticks in Carlisle (although lovely, it was much too small for Liam's taste). Now in charge of the Beverley branch, his job was proving to be a bit more of a challenge than the one he left behind in Carlisle, and not a challenge he necessarily wanted. Unfortunately, the move also meant that his sister could keep a close eye on him, since she not only also lived in Beverley (after her return home about six months ago) but worked there, as well. As the head of legal and business affairs for Kinsale Autos, her office was in downtown Beverley, located above the popular coffeehouse, Mr. Beans (fortunately for Liam, it was on the opposite end of Main Street from the dealership).

As he took the bowl of stuffing from Josh, Liam felt his phone buzz in his pocket. He had put it on silent just in case his Mystery Woman responded to any of his texts, which she had done rapidly, until she had to go to work. He longed to know everything there was to know about her, but she had stubbornly insisted on anonymity between them after their last delicious night together. Immensely satisfied that night, he had fallen asleep with her lush body in his arms, only to be awakened by her slipping out of them (again) late into the evening—or early in the morning, depending on perspective. That time, though, he had held on firmly, unwilling to let her leave the bed just yet. "No, baby, don't go," he had whispered huskily into her ear. "I spent all day wanting you so badly. We need more time."

She had turned in his arms, her hair falling in waves over the pillows, on his arms, and her scent was everywhere. She had plunged her hand into the hair at the back of his head, an action that made him shiver each time she did it, performing the act countless times that night. "More time for what?" she had asked, with a small smile making her face light up.

Because the hotel was so far east in upper Manhattan, it towered above any surrounding buildings, allowing abundant starlight to stream in the large windows, bathing her ivory skin in the glow.

"For anything. For everything," Liam had replied earnestly.

She had responded to his pleas with deep kisses, stroking his chest, running her short nails through the hair she had moaned about at one point during the night, telling him how sexy the color was as she licked the spot on his neck where tendrils touched. Just as he slid his mouth across her stomach, she brought his face back to hers. "I never do this... one-night stands." She drew in a shaky breath before continuing, "In fact, other than a terrible experience in high school, you are the only man, really, I have ever been with." Her honest confession had stilled him, and Liam leaned up so he could kiss her gently.

Gradually, the truth had sunk into his addled brain. "That's why last night..."

Her golden eyelashes had fluttered as she nodded, and pink flooded her cheeks. "I must seem terribly naïve, I'm sure."

"Never, baby, never," Liam had desperately reassured her, finally understanding how special she truly was. Her fists had clenched the blanket as she started to cover her body, and his body had covered hers, instead, as he told her, "I wish you had told me, though—" Her small finger pressed on his lips, preventing him from speaking.

"I just wanted you to know that this means something to me, too." Liam had given her a relieved smile and sighed, but cut it short when she had continued, "But I have too much going on in my life and goals I am so close to accomplishing, so I can't have any distractions. I don't *want* any distractions." She put her arms around him then, telling him, "And you, with your sexy voice, your enchanting eyes, this hair I am wild for, and all the words that you always seem to know what exactly to say to me...you would be a distraction. So, I don't want you to tell me any personal details. Personal becomes too...complicated..." and then all talk had ceased, as she had shown him again exactly what she wanted from him, and he had happily acquiesced.

Over the past few months, though, mixed messages abounded, because despite his Mystery Woman claiming she did not want to form anything deeper with him, she always responded to his texts to her.

Although direct questions went unanswered, she still kept the communication open. As casually as he could now, in full view of his family at their holiday table, he slid his phone out to read what he was sure was a text from her. And he was not disappointed.

TEXT FROM MYSTERY WOMAN

HOOK UP.

That's how I saved you in my phone.

Although you are a hot stud. ;)

And now I am mortified that not only did I call you

that in the first place, but that I just admitted it to you.

Or was he disappointed—just a tiny bit? Her last text, sent after she had hours to think about it while at work, was not exactly the revelation he had been hoping for on the holiday, and he was somewhat disconcerted that she had not given him a new name, following months of communication.

"What's got your attention, Liam?" Liam raised his head to see the entire table studying him, and he wasn't entirely sure who had asked him the question.

"What? Oh, nothing," he responded, super cool, super casual, a total Liam delivery. He hoped.

Josh peered across Liam's arm and spied the phone he was still holding. "Oh, I see—is it the love of your life?" he teased. Liam's face grew serious, and the expression on Josh's face became mischievous, and his tone teasing. "She finally texted you back, huh?" Liam had told no one about the texts he and his Mystery Woman had been exchanging the past three months, not wanting anyone to dismiss his growing feelings for her or to diminish the meaning he gave each and every message that she sent, even if a large part of him would have preferred the ones sent by her to carry more personal insight into her life. Of course, he had no one to blame but himself, since every time he texted with her, he honored her request from those many months ago to not get complicated.

"What is he talking about, Liam?" his mom asked. "Or should I say, who is he talking about? Have you met someone? Oh, Liam, why didn't you ask her to join you today?" He could murder Josh for starting this.

His grandma Catherine chimed in, "You know we would love to meet your young lady! I have been praying that one of my grandchildren would give me great grandbabies before I leave this earth! Josh has Effie, so that's a start, and now you have someone, too? Oh, praise the Lord! All those nights I spent with my rosary clutched in my arthritic fingers, asking God to shine down on my precious angels: Daniel, Joshua, William, Felix, Caitriona. I ask Him to please lead the way for them. Let them find love, make a family, practice the faith…"

And on and on his grandmother went, with each of her "precious angels" silently begging her to stop, because no eating could begin until she had finished—they had learned the hard way, in the past, receiving stern looks from their grandpa William, who, according to family legend, had never interrupted his wife during their almost-sixty years of marriage. Liam seized the opportunity to hurriedly, under the cover of the tablecloth, send a text.

TEXT TO MYSTERY WOMAN

I am open to hearing every admission you have.

He then gave his cousin a hard nudge underneath the table, letting him know that *he* had been the one to open this particular can of worms. He hoped his cousin was stewing right now, because Josh was the one in the hot seat with their beloved grandma, since he was the only one of her grandchildren truly in a meaningful relationship. Grandma Catherine had voiced some concern about Josh and Effie, though, "living in sin" (grandma's words, not Liam's). It mattered not that Josh had lived with Tess for five years without the blessed sacrament of marriage, because that had been an "out of sight, out of mind" scenario for their grandma, since they had lived in Brooklyn. Back in South Dakota, under the wide swath of Grandma Livingston, he knew his cousin had to be feeling some of that Catholic guilt they had been steeped in while growing up.

As another ping came from the phone he still held in his hand, and Liam cast his eyes down to look at it, as discreetly as possible.

TEXT FROM MYSTERY WOMAN

How was your dinner? I am stuffed!

Don't worry, I got plenty of turkey to eat today.

The stuffing was extra yummy this year ;) I had two pieces of pie--pumpkin and, in honor of you, Chocolate cream. Today I am most thankful for having one of the greatest nights of my life with you.

As I was eating, I tried to imagine you surrounded by your family, and what your holiday was like. A coworker used to talk about all of his cousins, and how one of them was more like a brother, and I was in awe of that familial closeness, since I don't have any cousins.

Happy Thanksgiving, Hook Up.

Beside him, Liam heard his sister say, "Texting an anonymous woman during Thanksgiving Day dinner? How very Liam-coded." Well, he couldn't argue with that, except that she was not some "anonymous woman", despite not knowing her name. No, she was his Mystery Woman, and he had never felt closer to any woman, emotionally or physically.

Josh then added, "Oh, we all know Liam. He'll be with someone new by the time Valentine's Day rolls around." Ignoring them, he got up from the table and began clearing away the remains of dessert, and once in the quiet of the kitchen, he took advantage of his solace and messaged back.

TEXT TO MYSTERY WOMAN

Only one of the greatest nights in your life?

I accept that challenge. The question is: are you ready for more? BTW, I had three pieces of pie: pecan, chocolate, and pumpkin.

How's that for Thanksgiving, Mystery Woman?

P.S. I have cousins, and they can be a pain in the ass.

# CHAPTER
## *Fourteen*

## *Tess*

TEXT FROM JOSH

If you're sure it won't be a hassle, Effie and I would love to stay with you and Sam!

Can't wait for you to meet her!

TEXT TO JOSH

Yay! I can't wait to meet Effie! I have been so jealous that Ruth has already become such good friends with her!

TEXT FROM SAM

Can you come up to my office?

Need to discuss something urgently!

With only two weeks before Christmas, Tess was singing along with *It's Beginning to Look a Lot Like Christmas*, and was up to her elbows in flour, sugar, and butter, filling all of her holiday cookie orders, along with baking the usual treats for her customers in her bakery, The Cookie Jar. She and Sam had spent Thanksgiving Day hosting the Charles family: his parents, his four brothers, their partners, and his toddler niece, all of whom were visiting from Boston (except for his brother Eric, who lived in New York City). Tess's in-laws had assisted in taking down the autumnal decor in the bakery and then putting up Christmas. Each time someone asked her if they were done, Tess's response was, "Almost." In Tess's world, too much holiday decor was never enough, and luckily, whatever she wanted was what Sam wanted as well.

After they had purchased the coffeeshop last spring, their original intention had been to convert the top two floors of the building into their home. Instead, Sam had suggested they make the second floor a bookstore, and outfit the top floor with an office/writing room for him, with a separate apartment for visiting family. As luck would have it, a two-family home had been for sale just down the block from the bakery and since Sam's three novels were all bestsellers, he had gotten a very sweet advance for the next novel in the series, making it possible for Tess and Sam to offer more than asking price on the house. The wood-frame house was a dream, with exposed brick on the main floor, along with an open plan for the kitchen and living area. The charming blue and white house also had a basement, a second floor with two large bedrooms, and a separate apartment on the top floor, which would provide extra income to the newlywed couple. While their house purchase was closing, they had lived briefly on the top floor above the bakery, and the arrangement proved cozy for the lovebirds, with neither one in a rush to move. Tess and Sam eventually moved into their house in the early fall. Soon after, both businesses were up and running, with all renovations to the bakery and bookstore completed. At last updated and now ready to rent out, the remaining issue had been the apartment on the top floor of Tess and Sam's new house.

Tess sighed as she considered her husband, a true partner in every sense of the word. Although the pair had only connected a year and a half ago, they had clicked instantly. With Josh, self-doubt and uncertainty had routinely plagued Tess, too often making her believe she wasn't good enough for him; then Sam had rolled up into her life on that fateful train trip—desiring her, wanting her, valuing her, and believing in her, leaving no room for anything but the strong, unrelenting force of his love. Looking back on her years with Josh with gratitude, Tess was cognizant that their history helped make her into who she now was. Last night, Josh had called Sam, telling him he wanted to bring Effie to New York City for the week between Christmas and New Year's. Eager to meet Effie, Tess had heard nothing but rave reviews concerning Effie from her sister, Ruth, who could be a little too judgmental when she first met someone, so the high praise held a lot of weight.

Wondering what her husband needed to discuss so urgently (his words) with her, Tess asked Marisol to cover the front of the bakery while she ran upstairs. Marisol had been the very first employee Tess had hired eight months ago, right after she opened the doors. Originally from Puerto Rico, Marisol's parents had moved to Brooklyn as newly-weds, and lived one street over from Tess and Sam. Not only was she enthusiastic about learning Tess's recipes, she was absolute amazing with customers, and the young woman worked as close to full-time as she could, while also taking classes at Brooklyn College.

Walking past the bookstore on the second floor, Tess waved to Isaac who was right inside the entrance. A college student also, Isaac lived in Borough Park, a neighborhood with a large Hasidic community that bordered Greenwood Heights. Although Isaac was Jewish, his family was not Orthodox, so even though it was a Saturday, he was working on inventory for Sam. "Hi, Isaac, how's everything going?" Tess asked him.

"Business has been great today. Submitting an order for more of the new Kristin Hannah—Sam mentioned that you hadn't gotten your copy yet," Isaac answered.

"Oh, good. No, I haven't, but make sure to save one for me, okay?" With the rush of holiday baking, Tess had not gotten as much time to herself to read as she would have liked, but she had been considering trying out some audiobooks to listen to while she baked.

"Will do. So...is Marisol still downstairs?" Ahh, Tess thought. She knew she had been right about the young employees! Just yesterday, she had remarked to Sam that the two of them seemed attracted to each other. Wouldn't it be nice if they started dating? Tess had mentioned, before her husband reminded her to not meddle in the personal lives of their employees, and then suggested she stop commenting on the mistletoe (she had discreetly placed throughout the building) when they were around.

Tess smiled at Isaac, telling him, "Yes, she is. You're about done up here, right? Make sure to stop in and get a box of cookies before you go. I left one for you on the counter." What harm was there in a little gentle nudging where the heart was concerned?

At her husband's office door, she knocked before entering, looking forward to giving the owner of her heart a quick, fierce and not so gentle nudge. Sam looked up as the door opened, with a smile lighting up his very handsome, very serious face. Pushing his glasses up his nose, he unfolded his tall body and stood up from behind his desk. "Working hard?" Tess asked her husband.

"Why don't you come over here and find out?" Sam responded with a wink to her. Tess sauntered over to him, and he met her eagerly at the front of his desk, pulling her into his arms. "God, I've missed you," he muttered before devouring her mouth with his. Immediately, his hands untied the apron she had neglected to take off before leaving the bakery, and pulling it aside, he complained, "Why are you wearing so many clothes?"

Chuckling, Tess slid her hands over his sexy, strong forearms, where he had rolled up his long sleeves. "Did you lock the door behind you?" Sam whispered.

"I did—we don't need anyone interrupting our serious discussion, now do we?" Leading him to the sofa on the other side of the door, Tess gently pushed down on her husband's shoulders, and when he was sitting, sat astride his lap. "I knew this couch would be the best piece of furniture in the place," she said, while unbuttoning his shirt, stopping herself from ripping it open.

"MMM," Sam agreed, tugging on her hips as he kissed her neck. Then those big, firm hands moved from the generous curve of her hips, spanning her waist, before cupping her breasts. "My luscious wife," he groaned, as her own lips sucked a line from his ear down to his chest, "always knows best."

Much later, Tess smiled to herself as the bell jingled above the front door to The Cookie Jar. She looked up from behind the counter where she was putting the finishing touches on some cookie gift boxes for a customer, the landscape manager at Green-Wood Cemetery, who would pick them up tomorrow morning. Tess had become friends with Sara after several chance meetings during the daily walks she and Sam took, and the woman was a loyal consumer of her baked goods. Almost closing time, Marisol had gone home for the day, accompanied by Isaac, who Tess had found clearly lingering in the bakery when she had come back down after her afternoon delight. Tess had wanted to get the bows added to the gift boxes before she closed for the day, and had suggested the young people go for an early dinner down at Industry City.

"Hi, how can I help you?" Tess asked the customer walking up to the counter as she came around the display case, only to stop in her tracks at the unexpected sight of the woman in front of her. "Wow—Lana. Hi, how are you?" Tess reached out to bring the younger woman in for a hug. What in the world was Lana doing in Brooklyn? Tess wondered.

Lana chuckled and said, "I'm good, thanks. Is this what heaven smells like, because I think I could die pretty happy here." Standing in front of the display case, Lana asked, "My god, Tess, did you bake everything?"

Tess proudly laughed, "Yes, and what you're seeing are the end results of baked goods ravaged by customers since seven this morning. Here, have a seat." Tess, mystified about what could have brought Lana to Brooklyn on a late winter afternoon, indicated a small table near the entrance that was also next to the Christmas tree. "Can I get you some coffee and some peanut butter blossoms?"

"Has anyone ever said 'no' to that offer? If they have, they need their head examined!" Tess watched as Lana took a seat and checked her phone, smiling at whatever she read on it, which was a gorgeous sight. In the few times Tess had seen Lana at the hospital when she visited Josh at work, she had never seen the other woman even remotely light-hearted. Lana had, instead, always presented as quietly serious. "Cream and sugar?" she called out to Lana, who didn't seem to be able to tear her gaze from her phone.

Lana lifted her flushed face, saying, "Yes, please, both." Hmm, mused Tess, what could be putting that look on Lana's face? Both secretive and revealing, Tess recognized it as similar to the one she herself must have worn after meeting Sam on the train.

Tess brought over a tray of the peanut butter cookies, each topped with a chocolate kiss, and two coffees. "So, what brings you to Brooklyn, Lana? It's not exactly around the corner from the hospital. Not that I'm complaining, mind you. It's always so nice to see a familiar face, especially this time of year." Tess sipped her coffee and then remarked, "I really enjoyed the night that we saw you in the bar. I left wishing that I had given you my phone number." Tess regretted not making a greater effort with Lana when she had worked with Josh, thinking that it may have been a missed opportunity for the two women to be friends. Truthfully, it hadn't been easy, though, when so much of Josh's life had been consumed with his work at the hospital, leaving Tess resentful of everyone there who saw more of her fiancé than she did; and Ruth, despite never having met Lana (but having heard stories from Tess), had been convinced that Lana had harbored stronger feelings than friendship for Josh. Tess had never held that against Lana (if it was even true at all), and she could certainly understand how working together, spending hours in the small office they shared, would have been conducive to the development of any feelings. After all, look at what had happened between Tess and Sam within the confines of the train—a much larger space than a mere office.

"Let me lock the door so we don't get interrupted by any late sugar-seekers," Tess announced, hopping off her chair. On the way back to Lana, Tess grabbed several more of the peanut butter blossoms for the table. "Here, I brought you more of these," she told Lana, and put the plate in front of her companion.

Lana smiled up at her and said, "I really shouldn't, but these cookies are so delicious, Tess. Josh always used to brag about what a fantastic baker you are, and I can see now that he wasn't wrong." Lana sipped her coffee and then said, "He called me this morning saying that he and Effie are coming for a visit."

Well, this was strange, Tess thought. Did Lana come all the way to Brooklyn to discuss Josh? The trip from the hospital was about an hour by subway, but Tess then remembered Josh mentioning that Lana's apartment was downtown in Manhattan somewhere, so maybe she had come from home? Either way, Tess's bakery was most definitely not on the way to or from either place. Tess nodded and told Lana, "Yes, they are staying with us, actually."

"That's kind of why I am here." Lana took another drink of her coffee and then hesitated before continuing, "The thing is, Josh mentioned that you and Sam have an apartment for rent, and I was kind of wondering about it? My lease is up next month and even though the rent is stabilized, I need to find a different place."

"You do know, Lana, that your commute will almost double living here, right?" A faint sound came from the table, and Tess looked over to see Lana's phone had lit up with a message, and the notification held Lana's attention for a moment. How interesting. Lana was clearly caught up in whoever was on the other end of those messages.

Okay, now Tess was officially surprised, but she still didn't know why the other woman appeared so nervous, until Lana said, "And the sooner I can move, the better."

She waited for Lana to look up and then continued, "Yes, we do have an apartment for rent, on the top floor of our house. We just finished some minor renovations, so it is move-in ready, theoretically, but if I can be nosy—why the rush? And why the move?" Tess watched Lana glance down at her phone before she lifted her face back up, with a wide grin having taken over her beautiful features. Lana really was stunning, and now that she had removed her coat, Tess saw she was wearing a navy woolen dress with big brass buttons down the front, almost like something out of a black and white movie from the forties. Tess could picture her with a jaunty hat on top of her wavy, honey-blonde head. "I love your dress. You have unique tastes when it comes to clothing, I've noticed. Very stylish, very demure."

Lana blushed and thanked Tess. "I got it at Housing Works—have you ever been there?" Tess shook her head "no" in response. "People bring in some really amazing vintage items, and occasionally I get lucky and find something in my size, which can be kind of difficult when you're not, well, skinny."

Tess knew that feeling well, and nodded in agreement, having struggled with her weight most of her life until giving up the fight. Now, she focused on making healthy choices and being as active as possible, not always easy with her rigorous schedule, but she and Sam made dinner together every night and took a vigorous walk together in the neighboring cemetery at some point every day. Her husband certainly had no complaints about her figure, though, never managing to keep his hands to himself when they were together. "Well, you clearly happened to be there at the right time. It's gorgeous."

Lana blushed and thanked Tess. "I guess I should explain about the move," Lana said with a small laugh. "I am finishing my residency in the city next spring and then I am starting a new rotation in Brooklyn, at the hospital in Park Slope, in pediatric surgery, and figured I'd get a jump on looking for new housing."

Okay, now Tess was officially surprised, and thought back to how she had asked Josh to consider moving his residency to a closer hospital, making more time for them as a couple. Lana told Tess, "The sooner I can move, the better, because it's not just about the commute. The truth is that I've been kind of lonely, and my mom is fostering two older cats that desperately need a home, but my current landlord is super picky about pets. I guess I should ask if cats are okay?"

Tess's ears perked up at the mention of cats. Tess and Sam had a pet policy, alright: the more cats, the merrier, with their three indoor-only cats, the colony of four that had amassed outside of their new home within a matter of days after moving in, and the volunteer work they did with a local rescue group. Sam often joked that any rental income they made would go toward feeding every cat in the neighborhood.

Tess started to respond to Lana's inquiry about pets, but before she could, Lana said, "I'm getting ahead of myself. Obviously, this is an informal meeting, and I will pay a pet deposit or whatever." Lana gave a small shake of her head before continuing, "Maybe I should have started by asking how much the rent would be?" Now Lana finally hesitated, as if dreading the answer. Tess wasn't sure what Lana's current financial situation was, but she knew surgical interns made a fairly decent income.

Josh had once mentioned that Lana had gone to a state university out on Long Island for her undergraduate and her medical degree, whereas Josh had attended Columbia. Even though residents were compensated, if Lana grew up in a struggling household, as Tess guessed, she would still have a hard time believing she could afford certain things, and Tess presumed Lana's love of thrifting had as much to do with personal style as well as money management.

"Well, to be honest, Sam and I haven't worked out the numbers for the rent yet. To be fair," Tess laughed, "the apartment rental is more Sam's area. I can assure you, though, it would make it worth our while to have someone in the apartment that we already trust and have a rapport with. The apartment does have a unique set-up with the layout but is perfect for a single person. There is a lovely bedroom space and fairly large kitchen, especially by New York City standards, with plenty of built-in closets and shelves. Best of all, the view at the front overlooks the cemetery, which is gorgeous." Tess suddenly realized she had made a generalization about Lana and tried to correct it. "I'm being presumptuous, assuming it is just you. I'm sorry."

After a glance down at her phone once again, Lana confirmed with a nod, "Yes, just me. I don't have time for anything else. I can't afford to get distracted; plus, I've never been good at relationships." Interesting, Tess thought. Who was Lana trying to convince? Well, whatever was going on with that phone of hers was certainly taking up plenty of Lana's time and attention, and despite her words to the contrary, she seemed quite pleased about the messaging relationship she had been maintaining since being in the bakery. "My current apartment is a studio, anyway, so anything else would be a palace, probably," she chuckled.

"Why don't I take you over there so you can have a look at the apartment? I can shoot Sam a text and see if he has any idea about rent, okay? That way you have more information to go on," Tess offered, and stole a glance at Lana's coat, which was frayed around the edges, probably from having been worn well for many winters.

TEXT TO SAM

Hey, Babe, Lana is here about renting the apartment.

Said you could give her an idea about rent?

I don't think she can afford much.

XOXO

TEXT FROM SAM

Here we go—we will be the bleeding-heart landlords.

Always happy to pass on our good fortune to people who need it.

Having someone we trust in the place will be huge, though. Meet you there in five?

Just feeding our lords and masters.

Love you.

"Okay, Lana, I texted Sam—he's at the house already, so will meet us upstairs. Want to take your coffee and the rest of the cookies to go?" Tess dashed behind the counter to shut off the coffeemaker, and filled up a large to go cup, leaving room for Lana's cream and sugar, and then added a ham and cheese croissant, blueberry streusel muffin, and an assortment of Christmas cookies to a bakery box. She had everything ready before Lana could refuse any of the offerings. Still, the other woman tried.

"Tess, this is too much. Let me pay you for this, please," Lana insisted.

"No way—I have to discount it anyway tomorrow, or force feed Sam, and he says he is eating too many carbs while he is writing. Silly man, jogs every morning, walks with me every afternoon, and has a disgustingly high metabolism. I would hate him if I didn't love him so much," Tess declared lovingly. Holding the door open for Lana, she wondered if whomever was on the other end of her phone had anything to do with whom Lana had been expecting the night Tess and Sam had seen her at Whistling Dixie. Then again, Tess thought, that was months ago, and Tess knew from experience how much could change in that amount of time. Probably just a coincidence that Lana was as flustered now as she had been back then.

# CHAPTER
## Fifteen

*Lana*

TEXT FROM HOOK UP

I hope you are ready—

I have a surprise for you!

TEXT TO HOOK UP

What do you mean?

TEXT FROM HOOK UP

I have a Christmas present

I think you're going to like :)

TEXT TO HOOK UP

Ooh—interesting. You're such a tease.

But I haven't opened the first gift you gave me last summer.

TEXT FROM HOOK UP

And why is that?

Are you a delayed gratification kind of woman?

TEXT TO HOOK UP

Haha, I don't know about that. Remember how I
had my hands all over you?

I have told you I am saving that present until I
get my Christmas tree!

TEXT FROM HOOK UP

Aww, Baby, this gift is bigger than that

TEXT TO HOOK UP

I like bigger…

TEXT FROM HOOK UP

Oh, do you? Baby, I will give you bigger in a
matter of weeks.

What would you say if I told you

That your surprise is having my hands

All over your body?

Lana flushed at least sixty shades of red, never having considered, in a million years, that she would be making tawdry sexual references to perhaps the world's sexiest man, yet here she was. Casually reading and replying, making all attempts to not appear flustered in the least. As she sat across from Tess, she wondered if Tess had noticed her change in complexion. Tess gave no sign she did, so Lana must be playing it much cooler than her racing heart indicated. What could his surprise be? Lana wondered, as she felt her body tingle. He had asked her—well, not asked, more like hinted—about wanting to know where she lived and for at least a hint about her occupation. He would text things like:

If I knew your address, I could send you flowers

Or:

Every business I pass by, I think to myself,
"maybe my Mystery Woman works at some
place like that"

Lately he had been a bit more persistent in trying to get his answers, but there was something to be said for this cloak of anonymity she had draped over their relationship, if one could even call it that. Lana could be anything with him: seductress, enchantress, mysterious (all adjectives he often called her) and not just the "smart" girl, who constantly had people reminding her of the major accomplishments she'd had so far in her thirty years of life. No one except her mom had ever called her beautiful, and certainly no one had ever referred to her as sexy. Lana was a misfit nerd, not fitting in with her sisters, having no close friends, and her Hook Up did not know about any of it. As she grew more comfortable conversing with him through texting, the less she felt inclined to answer his personal queries. Why couldn't he just be happy with what they already had established, little by little?

Looking around at the festive holiday decorations of the bakery while she hummed along to "Last Christmas", Lana remarked to herself how warm Tess was, how giving, especially after giving her a box of goodies to take home. Josh used to go on and on about how great his "Tessa" was, routinely causing Lana some feelings of inadequacy. As she watched Tess lock up her bakery, Lana turned her hand slightly so she could hurriedly type,

TEXT TO HOOK UP

I'd say I could already feel you

taste you

smell you.

I remember everything

Lana pressed "send" and then panicked at her impulsive reply to him. Oh god, she thought, did she just send a sext??? Was that a sext? Maybe she was overthinking things.

"Ready?" Tess asked before Lana could send a follow-up text downplaying her previous words to him. Reluctantly, Lana tucked her phone in her pocket.

Lana nodded her head and followed Tess across Fourth Avenue. Under the twinkling street lights, with snow lightly falling, Lana pondered how vastly different this neighborhood was from both her current working and living environs. Here, in this part of Brooklyn, the buildings were not as tall as those found in other areas of the city, most of them only two or three stories, and as they walked up the block to Tess's house, Lana noted that either brick or wood-framed houses lined the entire street except for a couple of taller apartment buildings near the end of the block toward Fifth Avenue.

Surveying the street they were walking up, Lana noted the black iron fence that lined the opposite side of the street. "Is that part of the cemetery I saw when I got out of the subway at Thirty-Sixth Street, Tess?"

Tess responded, "Yes. Sorry, I should be giving you more of a tour—how remiss of me. After living here for five years, I guess I am so used to seeing our neighbors that I forget to point it out. That is all part of Green-Wood Cemetery."

"Does it ever seem a little spooky living next to a cemetery?" Lana hesitantly asked Tess. Ever since she watched *The Exorcist* with her brother at the impressionable age of eleven, Lana had been terrified of anything even slightly supernatural.

As the women stood under the snowflakes drifting down from above, Tess cocked her head to the side, considering Lana's question seriously. "At first, it maybe seemed a bit strange, I guess, but we never have to complain about our neighbors being too loud," and both women laughed. "Honestly, having that space almost in our backyard is unbelievable. All the trees and plants and flowers changing with the seasons during the year, the walking paths that wind up and down the hills, Green-Wood is a refuge for Sam and I. You'll see once you live here," Tess assured Lana.

"Is this your house?" Lana gasped as they stopped outside a charming three-story house trimmed with Christmas lights. Green garland adorned the fence separating it from the sidewalk, and red bows surrounded the lamppost in front of the house. Looking up, Lana marveled at the garland and lights decorating each window; there were also wreaths on the door at the top of the steps leading to the second floor and the door under the same set of stairs. "Tess, this is stunning, and I love how you can see your Christmas tree inside your windows." Lana had always loved Christmas, and despite her mom never having quite enough money to buy any of her children expensive presents, Fiona would spend the few hours she had in the evening knitting beautiful sweaters, scarves, or hats for all of them, which were much more attractive than anything she could ever buy.

Tess giggled. "Too much, do you think? I wondered what my neighbors would say, but I could not restrain myself from going all out. I have wanted to decorate the house like this since we bought it, and Sam only kept urging me on." Tess led the way up the stairs outside and told Lana, "This would be your entrance."

After unlocking the door, they walked through another set of sturdy wooden doors. Just inside the narrow hall, Tess pointed out a small closet to the left of the staircase in front of them, saying, "After we moved in, Sam built a closet down here for the tenant upstairs. The door right here," Tess pointed to the door immediately to her left, "also leads to our house, but we never use it, unless we need access to the apartment upstairs for any maintenance reasons. It will always be locked, and we would let you know if we needed anything." Walking up the stairs, which creaked slightly under their feet, Lana ran her hand over the wooden banister and imagined the people who had walked up these same sets of stairs during the last century.

As Lana and Tess reached the door on the third floor, Lana remarked, "This beats the walk up to my current apartment. My sisters about died of a heart attack the last time they visited."

"Oh, you have sisters? Aren't they the best? I can't imagine my life without my sister. She has been my best friend my entire life." Silently groaning, Lana held back from confessing to Tess that her sisters were far from her best friends and indeed were too often more of a burden to Lana. As Tess pulled a key out to unlock the door, it opened spontaneously, and Sam greeted them with a grin.

In the four months since Lana had seen Sam, she had almost forgotten how attractive he was, with his black hair and dark brown eyes, and his expression as he looked at Tess led Lana to believe that he would probably prefer to be alone with his wife right now rather than showing an apartment to her. Nevertheless, he was genial when he greeted her. "Hi, Lana, it's nice to see you again," he told her as he held out a hand to shake hers. "Tess says you're moving?"

Lana crossed the threshold as she nodded her head. "Well, nothing is decided yet, but I'm completing the last year of my residency at the hospital in Park Slope. Since my rent is increasing at the beginning of next year anyway, I thought it would be a good idea to consider my options and find something closer to my new hospital?" Lana looked from Sam to Tess, both of whom were smiling from ear to ear.

"Before we get distracted, Lana, you had asked about our pet policy?" Tess asked Lana. "I'd say it's that we insist on pets, especially cats. You mentioned possibly adopting a couple of cats your mom is fostering?" Lana nodded, and Tess continued, "I apologize that I never answered your question about this over in the bakery, but we jumped from one topic to another," Tess laughed. "Your kitties would have a place here, rest assured. Why don't you take a look around, Lana? Sam and I will give you some space." Lana watched as Tess took Sam by the hand, entwining their fingers, and pulled him into the kitchen area.

Although it was difficult to see since it was dark outside, Lana imagined the three large windows at the front of the apartment let in ample light during the day and combined with the windows she had glimpsed at the back of the apartment in the kitchen, she imagined a nice cross-breeze blowing in if the windows were open. Walking to the front, she saw almost what looked like an alcove, but much larger, to the side, where her queen-sized bed would fit perfectly. Not a bedroom, per se, because there was no door, but so much space she was positive she could fit the antique bureau currently in her apartment and possibly the matching dressing table with a mirror her mom kept safe at the house in Riverhead. Her bedroom furniture came from a set she had inherited from her grandparents when they had passed away a few years ago. Her mother's parents had been a love story for the ages, married for fifty years, and then her grandma Frannie had gotten dementia, and the family made the decision to move her to an assisted living facility. Not wanting to be separated from his beloved wife, her grandpa Edwin had chosen to live there with her, despite being hale and hearty enough to continue living on his own. Grandma Frannie would fluctuate between good and bad days of recognizing her daughter and grandchildren, but her one constant had always been knowing her husband—until the day she had a stroke, wiping her memory almost entirely. Yet even though she did not call him by his name, her hand would always lift when Grandpa Edwin came to her side, almost as if to touch his face as he bent it close to hers. Two months after her stroke, she passed during the night, held in Edwin's arms, as the two had slept every night of their marriage. Her grandpa had been completely bereft and grieved the loss of his love inconsolably. Family members would try to remind him that he had lost her, in truth, months ago…years ago…but Edwin maintained Frannie had still known who he was even as she passed. Lana never argued with her grandfather, because she had, on occasion, seen what could only be described as a flicker of recognition cross her grandmother's beautifully lined face upon seeing her grandfather. In college at the time, Lana would take the bus from campus, making the hour-long journey to visit the assisted living residence as often as she could, as frequently as four or five times a week. With her books balanced on her lap, or her second-hand laptop seated beside her, she would read, make notes, write papers, all while rolling along, oblivious to Long Island passing by outside, usually while also listening to one of Judy Garland's greatest hits compilations. Once she got to the room her grandparents shared, she would read to her grandma from copies of her dog-eared novels of Danielle Steel, Rosamunde Pilcher, and Sidney Sheldon, while her grandpa brushed her grandma's hair or painted her fingernails. Her grandpa would tell Lana stories of how radiant her grandma had been when they had met, and how she always liked her hair and makeup done—that she had always been the most beautiful girl in the world. Sadly, but unsurprisingly, her grandpa had not even lasted a week after his wife had passed. Over the course of four days, he simply stopped eating, despite the family pleading with him. Lana knew that without his wife (his reason for living, he often told her), her grandfather would not last long. Sure enough, on the fifth day, they got the call from the home that Edwin had passed overnight, holding Frannie's hairbrush in his hands, almost as if he had been using it when he died. Lana had claimed their bedroom furniture as her own, getting no argument from her sisters (both of whom declared the items as dusty relics) or brother (who would never deny his youngest sister anything). The pieces were magnificent: solid oak in a dark brown stain, and every time she touched them, they reminded her of her grandparents.

Overcome with the memory of her grandparents, Lana wiped away a few tears as she stood looking out the front windows into the darkness, barely able to make out the black iron fence of the cemetery across the street through the falling snow. Certainly, more peaceful than the location of her current apartment on the Lower East Side, which bustled with activity almost all hours of the day and night, in true New York City style. Here in Greenwood Heights, with a pizza place on the corner, several bodegas lining the avenue, taco trucks on the street above the subway stop, not to mention Tess's bakery and Sam's bookstore, she would have every convenience she desired within a block or two. Lana also recalled seeing a Chinese takeout place across the avenue near the subway.

Feeling her phone buzz against her hip, she reached into her cross-body bag and pulled it out.

TEXT FROM HOOK UP

Darlin', you make me crazy.

Get ready, because I am coming back to you the week between Christmas and New Year's.

Want to ring in the new year with me?

Practically hyperventilating now, Lana dropped her phone back in her bag, then touched the cold glass of the windowpane in an effort to bring her back to reality. What was happening? Somehow, the universe had moved the pieces of her life into place without her help at all, a completely foreign experience for her, especially if she now had found a new apartment. Flushing from head to toe with anticipation, Lana walked in a daze through the middle of the apartment, doing her best to concentrate on admiring the built-in shelves and the gleaming caramel-colored hardwood floors and not imagining how she would welcome him back to New York. If indeed she would see him, of course. How could she not? But then again, she thought nervously, how could she? Sending and responding to flirty, meaningless texts was one thing, but carrying that intensity back into her real life? Lana was worried she could not handle it. Furthermore, was the entire idea of seeing him again ridiculous…even fruitless? What would possibly come from it?

Opening the door to the bathroom, Lana forced her sexy pen pal to the back of her mind and gasped upon seeing the freestanding claw-foot tub (a luxury she had always dreamed about), noting the space inside the room was at least twice as large as the bathroom in her studio apartment. The bathroom tiles were a multi-colored mosaic pattern, and the fixtures all sparkled as if brand new. How could she possibly afford such decadence? Lana considered the salary her surgical residence brought in, and while she knew she made enough, her brain still computed everything in terms of the poverty she had spent much of her childhood experiencing. Trying to avoid ever living that way again was one of her primary motivations for becoming a doctor—job security, financial stability, and the opportunity to work long hours in a profession that meant something had all been factors in her decision.

Approaching the kitchen now, she hesitated at the doorway once she saw Tess and Sam embracing. The couple was so openly intimate yet stopped short of being vulgar. She remembered several times, when Tess and Josh were still together, that Josh would comment on his friend from college, newly divorced and visiting from Boston, and what a match Josh thought Sam would make with Lana, suggesting that the four of them double date. Shaking her head, she couldn't believe it had even occurred to Josh to set them up. Nothing about her would have attracted Sam to her—she still had a hard time believing that her Hook Up was interested enough to maintain long-distance communication with her for four months. Lana knew she could be categorized as reasonably attractive, but nothing about her was spectacular, except maybe her intelligence, and that was the one thing she took pains to hide so people didn't make such a fuss. Knowing that this nameless man desired her was a thrill she had never experienced before, such a hormonal rush, and it was titillating to get these secret messages from him, making it seem like they were the only ones in their electronic world.

Breaking away from Sam, Tess smiled at Lana, who was still in the doorway. "I'm sorry, Lana—there's no excuse for us, except to say that we are newlyweds." Lana noticed Sam give his wife an appreciative grin as she walked away from him.

"It's all my fault, actually," Sam laughed. "If I had insisted she marry me the minute we met, we would be an old married couple by now." The three of them chuckled, and the way the sound filled the empty space charmed Lana. Vintage cabinets, attractively painted a light gray, filled the kitchen; the color reminded her of her Hook Up's eyes. Surveying the rest of the kitchen, her imagination took over as she envisioned his tall body at the stove, the two of them making dinner together. He had confessed to her in a text a couple of weeks ago that he loved to cook, but no one in his family knew it.

TEXT FROM HOOK UP

Have you ever felt invisible?

Or that the people who love you don't really know you? Growing up, I felt like no one took me seriously. Hell, they still don't.

Can't blame them, really. I do my damndest to hide the things about me that are meaningful. Like how I took cooking classes at the college last year. I just did it to impress a woman I was dating, but ended up loving it. She didn't last (nor was she impressed), but now I make a mean Beef Bourguignon.

If my family knew, I know they would tease the hell out of me.

"So, Lana, what do you think? I know that cabinets are a bit old-fashioned, but we take that into consideration with what we will charge for the rent," Sam informed her.

"No, I love them. Everything about this apartment is perfect, honestly." In a rush of spontaneity, she surprised each person in the room by saying, "When can I move in?"

# CHAPTER
## Sixteen

*Liam*



Walking across the peanut shell-lined floor of the Cattleman's Club Steakhouse in Beverley, Liam greeted various employees of Kinsale Autos, some of whom he had known since he was a child. Both of his parents had flourished in their respective family automobile businesses, and Liam had tried, as a teenager, to work alongside his dad, grandpa, uncle, and cousin at the repair shop in Clover Lake, but he had hated getting dirty, in all honesty, and he never enjoyed the puzzle of diagnosing any issue when it came to servicing cars. Instead, Liam gravitated toward the dealership and its sales division. Even as a small boy, he loved running his hands across the smooth leather interiors or plush upholstery in the new vehicles. Inhaling that infamous "new car" smell got him almost high, and yet there had been something uniquely satisfying when he would have to clean up a used car for resale. Even though they required more polish and cleaning, Liam always found it particularly rewarding when he accomplished making the used cars as attractive to a buyer as the ones directly from the factory. During the hours he spent doctoring up the second-hand cars, he would imagine the life the car had held previously: parents bringing home their newborns from the hospital, newlyweds leaving their wedding reception heading to their honeymoon, grandparents visiting their children and grandchildren at Christmas. His sister, Cait, had often tried to nudge him out of the dealership and into the repair shop, especially after his uncle Henry had left the Clover Lake location to start up his own shop in Beverley. "Dad needs you now, Liam. You have to grow up and work with him and Grandpa," had been on repeat, but had fallen on deaf ears. Cait considered the dealership hers to inherit, even as she stayed down in the Gulf after graduating from college, and then law school, in New Orleans.

Tonight, Kinsale Autos was hosting its annual Christmas party, and this year his mom had relinquished the honor of planning the holiday extravaganza to him, after much needling and coercion on his part. Renting out the steakhouse for this Monday night (always the slowest night in the restaurant world, his cousin Daniel often told him), Liam congratulated himself on curating the perfect holiday playlist for the party as Bruce Springsteen's live version of *Santa Claus Is Comin' to Town* caused the partygoers to start moving to the beat of the holiday classic. Just nine days until Christmas, which meant ten days until he got what he wanted (more than any gift sitting under the ten-foot-tall tree at his parents' house), and that was his Mystery Woman in his arms again. Liam went from confident to concerned regarding her, based on her texts to him. Sometimes she was clearly as filled with anticipation as he was, and other times she seemed reserved and unsure. He tried his best to keep up his facade of bravado and assuredness, but her fluctuations left him perplexed and anxious, feelings he was unaccustomed to experiencing when it came to women. His previous relationships, such that they were, had been easy and mutually agreed upon: casual dating, no deep feelings, and when it needed to end, both he and his partner separated amicably. Not counting the woman he had dated in college (for obvious reasons) who had slashed open a stuffed bunny and then poured red dye in the open cavity, in some kind of sick homage to *Fatal Attraction*. When he had showed the poor thing to his cousin back then, Josh had pointed out (in that factual, no-nonsense, and annoying way he had) that the bunny in the movie had been boiled and not transected. He supposed he should also consider the flight attendant he had met one night when he had been in Sioux Falls for a concert: their romance had been hot and heavy for a few months until he just got bored having to travel two hours every time he wanted to see her. So, he had broken things off with her as gently as he could, yet he had discovered that while he had been waiting to pay the bill for their breakfast, she had been busy slashing the tires of his loaner car from the dealership.

Certainly, his Mystery Woman did not come across as someone who cut up bunnies or tires, but he would like to be certain that she was as interested in him as he was in her. When he had brunch with Josh and Effie yesterday, the three of them had discussed their upcoming trip to New York City, and Josh had brought up how ironic it was that Liam could not maintain a relationship with a woman two hours away, yet here he was traveling halfway across the country for a woman. "Liam, seriously, what are you hoping to gain from this? I mean, do you plan on moving there? Do you even know any personal things about her yet?" His cousin had questioned him last night.

He had responded, "I guess I should remind you that you started up…whatever that was between you and Effie…before you had a clue what you were doing. I seem to recall you had one foot out the door back to New York, and you hadn't even told her that you were a surgeon." Josh had some gall, admonishing Liam for his interest in a long-distance romance, he thought.

Thankfully, Effie had laughed, keeping any tension between the cousins at bay. "He's right, Josh. Besides, I kind of think it's romantic. Especially with all of the texting that you and your Mystery Woman are doing, it's like that movie with Meg Ryan and Tom Hanks."

"*Sleepless in Seattle?*" asked Josh last night.

"No, the one after that…*You've Got Mail!*" Effie had exclaimed and sighed, "I love that movie. Both of them, actually."

Liam had nodded. "Both are good movies, but I like to think my situation is more like *The Shop Around the Corner*. Despite what some people think, I've always seen myself as more of a Jimmy Stewart than Tom Hanks."

Josh had thrown his cousin a skeptical look. "Jimmy Stewart, really? And I have never once heard anyone compare you to Tom Hanks."

"Okay, okay, I agree. I mean, one of my exes said I reminded her of that actor from *Outlander*." Liam had looked to Effie to back him up, and she had nodded with no hesitancy at all.

"Ooh," Effie had said, "yes, I can totally see that. Although, his hair isn't as dark as yours, but with the height and especially since you've been working out more? Yep." She reached over to Josh and slid her hand up his arm over his long-sleeved shirt. "Babe," she had told Josh, more than likely attempting to soothe his ego, "I've always seen you as more of a Brad Pitt or the guy from that TV show about the half-brothers who play basketball."

"What?" scoffed Liam then. "No way. You have definitely got love goggles on, Effie. Brad Pitt?" Looking at his cousin, Liam had asked, "You do realize she's just saying that since she complimented my body, right? She has to make you feel good, too."

"Okay," countered Josh last night, "and what about that malarkey about the actors your 'exes' compared you to?" Josh had supplemented his question with air quotes, something he knew Liam could not stand.

Thinking about the conversation now at the holiday party, Liam was still somewhat perturbed about Josh throwing in that comment about his exes, which he did essentially to point out that Liam had no exes, since he had never been in a relationship long enough to make a true commitment to anyone, a long-standing joke by everyone about Liam. Who was Josh to throw shade at him, anyway? It wasn't as if he was an expert on the subject, only having seriously dated two women, Tess and Effie, and casually dated *maybe* two more. At least Liam had experience with women overall.

Nearing a table that held appetizers, he was now approached by a woman who worked in the dealership in Carlisle, where Liam had also worked until a few months ago. He nodded to her as she stood in front of him. "Hey, Candace, how are you? I see you made some amazing sales last month! Any new gossip since I left?" Recently divorced when she first began working there two years ago, Candace was a few years older than him. When they had worked together, he had noticed that she was a woman with a very free spirit, and someone he would have been interested in as recently as the past summer. Until he met his Mystery Woman. When he had been her boss, she had been off-limits. Looking at her tonight, in her tight-fitting dress with the plunging neckline, Liam wondered if maybe she had come tonight in pursuit of someone? Or something?

Candace looked him up and down and then leaned into him. "Liam, I was hoping to get a chance to talk to you tonight." Her hand reached out and slid up his chest, and she moved closer with her glass of wine held precariously in her other hand. "The kids are with their dad tonight," she whispered into his ear, and judging by her breath, she had somehow gotten around the two-drink maximum his mom had insisted on. "Just in case you were feeling in the mood to celebrate," she told him, practically devouring Liam with her eyes.

Part of him wanted to take her up on her offer—after all, he had to admit that Josh was right concerning whatever this was he had going on with his Mystery Woman. What did he really know about her? He had tried, with numerous texts, to elicit personal information from her, but she stonewalled him at every turn.

TEXT TO MYSTERY WOMAN

Finally, I get to plan our company's Christmas party!

Do you have anything like this lined up over the holidays?

TEXT FROM MYSTERY WOMAN

Not really—far too busy for that.

Might have drinks with my supervisor.

OR

TEXT TO MYSTERY WOMAN

Had dinner with my parents tonight, and I told them about my upcoming trip. Mentioned you, but just a little bit. I am open to meeting any family while I am there, since it is over the holidays. I understand how difficult it can be to take time away from your family.

TEXT FROM MYSTERY WOMAN

Don't worry—no family in the city! You would be terrified, anyway. Way too many of them.

Vague responses only from her, yet here he was, making plans to travel halfway across the country to see her. To what end? Maybe part of the allure with her *was* the fact that they knew nothing about each other. But, on the other hand, what did he need to know about her? Would knowing her name make him feel differently? Would her occupation make her more appealing, less appealing, or have no impact? Admittedly, anonymity allowed him the ability to keep the parts of himself he was less proud of private, as well. With his Mystery Woman, he could be whatever or whoever he wanted, without having to admit his slightly sad reality of selling cars for a living. For his family's company, no less. When he thought in stark facts about himself, perhaps the most shaming aspect for him was the fact that he had earned nothing based on his own merit or skills. Yes, he had performed exceedingly well with the dealership in Carlisle, thus being rewarded with the Beverley location, and he had earned it through long days and many nights working long after everyone else had gone home. His career was built on getting people to say "yes" when they were thinking "no", but the only way he got his foot in the door in the first place was because of his mother, and his sister seemed to take immense pleasure in pointing this out to him. Never mind that Cait had returned to South Dakota during the cover of night, refusing to talk to anyone about why, after living in New Orleans, Louisiana, and then Mobile, Alabama (supposedly loving it so much down there she rarely even visited), she suddenly wanted to move home? For all her bluster, she, too, was working for the family company, yet somehow it was only Liam who took advantage of his mother's generosity.

As Candace took advantage of his silence by pressing her body against his, Liam's watched buzzed on his wrist. Candace heard the noise and took his arm to read the display. "Oh, this is interesting—who is 'Mystery Woman'?" she asked as she threw him a pouty look. "Hopefully not my competition," Candace said into his ear. "Why don't you come home with me tonight? I'll make you forget all about this 'mystery woman'…" and as her offer stagnated in the air between them, Liam was rescued by his sister, and he had never seen a more reluctant savior.

"Liam, can I talk to you for a minute? Sorry for interrupting whatever…this…is?" Cait gave him one of her signature withering looks, and he responded with a beaming smile, something sure to annoy her even further.

Beginning to pull out of range of Candace, who looked disappointed at being interrupted in her seduction, he bade her farewell. "Sorry, Candace, duty calls. I hope you have a nice rest of your evening." Liam hated leaving a woman unsatisfied, but it was bound to happen at some point with her, because he had absolutely no interest in any other woman. Especially now that he was so close to seeing his Mystery Woman again.

"So what was all that about?" Cait asked Liam, looking pointedly back at Candace, whose eyes had trailed Liam as he walked away with his sister to stand by the bar. "I hope I don't need to remind you that sexually fraternizing with subordinates in the workplace is frowned upon, even if you are the owner's son," his sister needlessly mentioned, with a raised eyebrow for emphasis.

Liam recoiled, "'Sexually fraternizing'? God, Cait, you need to read something other than the employee handbook in your spare time," he told her as he ordered a Manhattan from the bartender. "Do you want a drink?" Liam asked Cait.

"No, and how many drinks does that make for you tonight? You realize you need to be setting an example, especially now that you are managing the Beverley location? And can we get back to what was going on with that woman back there?" Liam stared in stunned silence at his younger sister, who he had been fairly close to, until she had gone away to college, becoming cold and distant, barely recognizable as the warm and fun-loving little sister she had once been. As he thanked the bartender for his drink, he wondered again why Caitriona was suddenly back home, with no word about what had happened leading to her decision. He and his sister both shared the same dark red hair and light gray eyes. It was a shame she was so guarded, because he constantly had male friends asking if she was single—not that he would ever set any of them up with her, afraid she would nag them to death. Now that he thought about it, though, the number of single, male friends had dwindled, with few remaining. In the past year, he had two friends get married (three if he counted Sam, but since he hadn't been invited to the wedding, he probably shouldn't), three friends got engaged, and none of those numbers even included his cousin, Josh, who had been engaged, dumped, and was now living with his new girlfriend.

Liam sighed and decided that maybe answering his sister's rather pointed questions would be a way to share some Christmas spirit. "For your information, 'that woman' you're referring to? Yes, she was trying to entice me into some after-work activities, but I turned her down. Or I would have, if you hadn't come up to us. Her name is Candace, which you should have already learned by now since you've been working for the company for four months. Also, she works at the Carlisle location, so is not a direct 'subordinate'. None of that matters, though," Liam rushed to tell his sister, "because I have zero interest in her, or anyone else employed by Kinsale Auto. Also," he added as he raised his drink, "this is the first drink I've had tonight with alcohol and will probably be my only drink with alcohol. I realize that I have painted myself as a careless playboy in the past, but I take my position in Beverley seriously. And even though it has been a topic of ridicule in the family, I also am quite serious about the woman I am going to New York to visit." He had been the subject of joke after joke about his relationship with a woman he knew nothing about, except the way she made him feel when he thought about her or texted her or read one of her texts to him. For now, that was enough.

"Okay, fine, but I'm glad you brought up your trip. You are aware that if you were a regular employee, you would not be able to just take time off whenever you wanted, right? Your job is not there based on your whims, William, and there is scheduled time off for a reason." Now she was calling him by his legal name? What in the hell had gotten into her? Was she deliberately trying to annoy him, or was her entire personality completely disagreeable?

Liam hotly responded, "The last time I checked, you were not my boss. I'm not sure what right you think you have to be away for so many years only to come back and start implementing rules and regulations that, as far as I can tell, only have to do with me. I checked with Mom before planning any of this, and I don't think I need to check with the company *lawyer* about my personal life. Now, if you will excuse me, I am going to go out and mingle with employees of Kinsale Auto, all of whom I know by name, including the names of their significant others, their children, if they have any, and even their pets, when applicable. You should do yourself a favor and try to get to know some of them, too, if you are so interested in their welfare." With that, he turned on his heel, finally able to check his phone with the text that had arrived when he was with Candace.

TEXT FROM MYSTERY WOMAN

I am overwhelmed by your gift. Just unwrapped it and put it on my tree.

It is truly the most beautiful ornament I have ever seen. Thank you..

XOXO

With a relieved smile, Liam ducked outside through the door that led to the patio that overlooked Lake Shelley. As he walked to the raised fence, he remembered choosing the gift for her. Upon entering Tiffany & Company, Liam had peered into several glass cases before he landed upon the perfect gift for his Mystery Woman: a crystal ornament with clear etchings of birds, snowflakes, and garland. It was classy, simple, and beautiful, just like his Mystery Woman. When he had given her the aquamarine-colored velvet bag, he assumed she would recognize the signature Tiffany color and be impressed, but she had given no indication, then or now, that she knew it, and he wasn't sure how he felt about that. Used to making women swoon, Liam was experiencing difficulty processing subtle appreciation.

Just as he was feeling too chilled standing outside in the December air of South Dakota, his phone rang. A shiver ran through him that was not caused by the temperature, but by reading the name of the incoming caller: Mystery Woman.

# CHAPTER
## Seventeen

## Montgomery

*Group Text with Ava and Greer*

Text to Ava and Greer

You're sure she's planning on meeting up with this loser again?

FROM AVA

How can he be a loser when he has such great taste as our sister?

Settle down, Monty. Just remember: you're not her father.

FROM GREER

Yeah! What A said!

Besides, if you heard the description of the hotel room, you would reconsider your definition of loser.

FROM AVA

And who are you to talk? Are you and Megan even remotely committed to each other? I mean, you still live apart, after how many years together???

When was the last time you guys spent the night together? Hahaha

FROM GREER

Totally! Maybe you should take a note from this guy!

He sounds so hot, though.

Makes me think I should have gotten Simon a gym membership for Xmas…

FROM AVA

Wow, G—a little harsh even for you?

Simon still has some definition.

Not even Rodney can come close to the bod Lana said her hook up had, and he works out every day!

TEXT TO AVA AND GREER

Don't you two have anything else to do? This is why I hate group texts.

Two people in the group go off on a tangent and then I get annoyed by the constant updates.

FROM GREER

Who's going to tell him that he started it???

It was the morning of Christmas Eve, and Montgomery Miller pulled into the train station in Riverhead to pick up his baby sister. No matter how old they each got, he could never believe that the tiny little baby his mom had brought home from the hospital when he was ten years old was now a fully grown adult. Not only that, when he considered how accomplished she already was, and how much more was ahead of her, his pride had no bounds. Lana meant so much to the entire family, but no one was prouder of her than her big brother.

Montgomery scratched his chin at the beard he had grown, finding it gave his face some added definition, while also providing protection from the salt air that came in from the ocean when he was outside working. Ladies appeared to appreciate it, also, except for his girlfriend, who was threatening to break up with him if he didn't shave. Considering they had been dating for almost six years, her threat did not particularly bother Montgomery. They had developed a mutual understanding concerning their relationship, and he took solace in the fact that although they were committed to each other, they didn't feel the need to spend every holiday together (or even live together, for that matter): Megan had her life, and he had his. Boundaries were at the top of his list of priorities and had been since he was five years old (otherwise known as the first time his father had walked out on his family). Montgomery had shouldered so much responsibility at such a young age, having to comfort his sisters Ava and Greer and his mother, Fiona, as well. Only a kindergartner at the time, he had not known why his dad hadn't been there to take him to Tee Ball that spring, like the other fathers. For Montgomery, there had been no Tee Ball, because his mom worked too much to take him, and his grandparents had enough on their plate watching his sisters (only four and three at the time). With no explanation, his dad just didn't come home one day after work. When Thomas had lived with his family, their mother hadn't worked during the winter off-season, but once she only had one income, she began cleaning the "winter" homes of her clients, with some locations taking Fiona hours to commute to, making many nights difficult for Montgomery, who had been used to having his mom read him bedtime stories until he fell asleep.

Smiling at Lana as she opened the door to his truck, he turned down the volume to his favorite Christmas song, "Hard Candy Christmas", by Dolly Parton. One of the lines from the chorus always struck him as bleak but beautiful: "I'm barely getting through tomorrow, but still I won't let sorrow bring me way down". Almost a chorus from his own life.

"Hey, Baby Sis, I'm glad we finally get you here for a holiday," he told Lana as he wrapped his arm around her shoulder and hugged her. Since her residency started a few years ago, the family rarely saw her on a holiday.

Lana responded with a laugh. "What are you talking about? I saw you on Thanksgiving!" Montgomery looked at her without blinking, and she amended her statement, "Okay, it was the night before, but we still had fun watching the balloons being blown up in the city, right? Love the beard, big brother—you look very dashing! Whew! That was like a train ride from another world. I swear I had at least three drunken Santas ask me what I wanted for Christmas. Anyway, I know what you meant—I'm so excited to spend Christmas with you guys. I think the last time I had Christmas Day off was when I was still in med school." Lots of talk from his sister, who usually kept things close to her chest.

As Montgomery listened to Lana list everything she was going to help their mom make for the holiday meal, he marveled at her ability to still be somewhat naïve where the world was concerned. Certain that the Santas on the train, drunk or not, had wanted more from his sister than her gift list, he was relieved that they had not harassed her more. Montgomery had failed to protect his sister a few times in her young life, and he had vowed to himself he would never fail again.

When Montgomery was eight, his dad had miraculously reappeared back in their lives, with no one explaining just where Thomas had been for three years. During that time, Montgomery had gotten used to doing little things to make his mom happy, like picking wildflowers when he went with his grandpa to work. Edwin, a general contractor, worked on Saturdays, and he claimed it as "their" day together to make his grandson feel less neglected or abandoned, while trying to fill the role of father left vacant by Thomas. Or reading bedtime stories to Ava and Greer when they cried at night. Because his grandma, Frannie, had knee surgery in both knees when he was seven, and neither his grandpa nor his mom got home before dinnertime, Montgomery had learned to cook, guided by his grandma, who would read aloud recipes from a kitchen chair, tutoring her grandson from across the kitchen island. "Turn the heat down—your water is going to boil over", "Monty, you need to make sure to cut the vegetables smaller so your sisters won't choke", or "Sweetie, the one thing you can do for your food is to season it, always, with salt and pepper. The rest will follow." Montgomery made pot roast (his mom's favorite), spaghetti Bolognese (Ava's favorite), and chicken and dumplings (Greer's favorite) while also mastering brownies (his grandpa's favorite) and chocolate chip cookies (his grandma's favorite). Once his dad returned, that had ended Montgomery's job as chef—Thomas had insisted on Fiona cutting back with her cleaning jobs so she could make him his favorites. His sisters had clung to their daddy, wanting nothing to do with their brother reading to them at night anymore. And his mother had been the recipient of store-bought flower bouquets. The family had continued to live with his grandparents, though, because despite his dad having money to burn on frivolities, he had none to pay the rent. After Fiona had become pregnant with Lana two years later, Grandpa Edwin, the former employer of his son-in-law, had hired him again, tired of watching Thomas reap the benefits of everyone else's hard work.

During the ten-minute drive to their mom's house, Montgomery saw Lana check her phone, smile, respond with flying fingers, smile again, and repeat this process in a cycle. He could only assume that she was communicating with this mystery man, or "hook up" as his sisters annoyingly insisted on calling the nameless stranger. He shuddered, thinking about what kind of creep would take advantage of a young woman in a state of inebriation. Ava and Greer had advised him to chill out and not make a big deal about things to Lana, but that wasn't saying much for them. Lana was the only one in the family to rise above her raising, and he would be damned if he would let some idiot from nowhere come in and ruin her dreams and aspirations. "So, who are you texting, Lana? Seems to be pretty important, since you can't seem to stop looking at your phone."

Lana immediately put her phone in the pocket of her red wool coat. "What?" She blinked the Miller dark blue eyes that all the siblings had inherited at him and used her innocent expression to try to dissuade him from asking any more.

Montgomery pulled into the parking lot of Friendly's so he could get some answers now, because once they got to their mom's house, and all the assorted children belonging to his other sisters came streaming out of the house, hopped up on candy canes and eggnog, he wouldn't get a chance to elicit any answers from his youngest sister.

"Monty, what are you doing? Mom is expecting us—she said Christmas Eve Mass is at five this afternoon, and I told her I'd make the pies when I got there. Plus, there's the chili and clam chowder to make for dinner tonight yet. It's already eleven, and I am starving, but I don't want to eat at Friendly's—" Lana stopped talking as Montgomery put the car in park and turned to her with a scowl on his face.

"So, who is this Neanderthal you have been texting?" Montgomery demanded.

"What? What are you talking about? Why are you calling him that?" Lana asked, and with the car in park and the music turned off, they both heard the ping sound for an incoming text.

"That! That is who I mean! What else am I supposed to call him? Your "hook up"?" Heavy emphasis on the air quotes here. "Like everyone else does?"

"What?" Lana gasped. "How do you know that?" Lana, with her honey-blonde hair and fair complexion flushed brighter than her coat.

"Despite what our sisters think, they are not exactly great at keeping a secret, especially since Julia and Amelia also know, and I'm pretty sure Allie does, too." He informed her.

"But she's only fourteen—" Lana protested.

"And? She's around her older cousins, and her mom and her aunt, who are always talking about some sexy dude their auntie Lana sees whenever he's in town. Lana, you should be ashamed of yourself," he admonished her. "I thought you were better than this. This is the kind of crap Ava and Greer used to pull, but you need to be above it."

Lana put her face in her hands and then ran her fingers through her shining hair as she started to braid it. "Okay, first of all, I am mortified to be discussing this with you, but I have to clarify: it's nobody's business but mine what I am doing. I'm hardly seeing him every time he's in town, because he hasn't been here since the first time I met him, and I only saw him twice then. For your information, I could have gotten his name anytime I wanted since then, and he has asked me for personal information, but for the first time in my life, I am taking a chance and being impulsive, or secretive, or whatever I am doing, and I like it. I'm not doing anything to be ashamed of, for your information, so you need to back off, and I say that as your adoring little sister."

Montgomery clutched the steering wheel as he listened to her voice speak more sternly to him now than she ever had, which caused him to remind her, "The first time in your life? Are you forgetting the last time that you acted rashly? Or do I need to remind you how I rescued you that time? How you called me, so hoarse from crying that I could barely understand you? How I found you in that boathouse?" He had never been more terrified in his life when she had called him, on the night she graduated from high school, only sixteen years old. He had no idea what had happened to her—only that his sister was in tears.

"This is nothing like that—he's not some rich kid sleeping with the maid's daughter." Lana shook her head. "I hate that you still see me as a victim from that whole incident. Whatever I did with Anthony that night was because I wanted to—I thought I loved him. So, yes, I was distraught when I realized what a lie it was. But this is not that. I am an adult now, just having fun—easy, no strings!"

Montgomery studied Lana, wondering if she was trying so hard to convince him or herself. "Well, I hope you know what you're doing. And whatever it is, I hope it is not a distraction from finishing your residency."

Lana gave a sigh that sounded like it was tinged with annoyance, something he rarely heard from his youngest sister. "Monty, please. My residency is going to be wrapped up with a big bow in two years, as planned. My fellowship is going strong and will end right before I transfer to the hospital in Brooklyn." He felt her smaller hand pry his fingers from the steering wheel. "Now, can we please go to Mom's? Word on the street is that she made those fantastic sausage rolls with the puff pastry, and have I mentioned that I am starving?"

Montgomery gave up on talking some sense into his sister about this no-name man, but he would try again, and he grimaced when she immediately brought her phone out to smile at it while she tapped ferociously. What kind of man was content with some pseudo-relationship where the participants didn't even know each other's names? Ignoring the fact that he was forty, never married, and still living alone was easy to do when every one of his sisters, including Lana now, created enough chaos to keep his private life in the dark.

# CHAPTER
## Eighteen

*Lana*

TEXT FROM HOOK UP

Counting down the days now.

I have been walking around at work looking like a madman, I am sure, smiling at everyone. My sister accused me of flirting, but nothing could be further from the truth. I only have eyes for you.

TEXT TO HOOK UP

I have never felt this level of anticipation before.

It's like every part of me is tingling.

Honestly, I don't know what to think if you were flirting, because I have no right to be jealous or upset. But I know I don't like what I feel in my stomach when I think about it. Ugh—I know I am the one who said casual.

TEXT FROM HOOK UP

Please know, in all sincerity, that you have been the only woman I have eyes for since that night we met. You said casual, but my thoughts have been anything but casual. You consume me, even when I am asleep, every dream is of you. I'm going to make one confession to you: my family has never taken me seriously, probably for good reason most times. I dicked around during college, dated non-exclusively, never charted my own career path. But you and I—I take us seriously, more than anything ever before. Sorry, that's not casual…

You know, your voice on the phone caused me to lose sleep for the entire night—I was a complete mess at work the next day.

TEXT TO HOOK UP

Not sure how to respond to that.

Other than my career, I have never thought about anything as consistently as I think of you. I guess we are kind of the opposite, because I have been accused of being too serious, too staid. Too ruminative (word of the day calendar). My family has a lot of expectations of me, and the weight from them overwhelms me.

Your voice made me remember your touch on my skin.

TEXT FROM JOSH

Merry Christmas, Lana!

I hope we'll be able to see you when we're in the city?

Effie would love to meet you.

On the first train back to Manhattan the day after Christmas, Lana's nerves were as jittery as if she had drunk five cups of coffee, brewed by Ava. Her sister loved her coffee the stronger the better (like my men, she loved to proclaim, but having met her "men", Lana tended to disagree with her statement). Anticipation had filled every blood cell in her body since her Hook Up had told her he was coming to New York. In a stroke of good fortune, since Lana had worked on Thanksgiving and the days that followed, she had Christmas Eve, Christmas, and the day after off. Lana had switched two of her "on" days with two other residents, one of whom, Amara, was from India and more than happy to fill in one of the days; the other resident was a divorced dad, Gregory, who had approached Lana first, telling her that his ex-wife and her new husband planned on taking his kids to Montreal over the holiday break, and he needed to keep busy. Now Lana had off every day but one during the week her Hook Up would be in town, and she smiled every time she thought about it.

TEXT TO JOSH

I would love that, too, but I just don't know if I can get away. You know how the hospital is on the holidays.

Was she outright lying to Josh? She wanted to meet Effie, but splitting her time between her Hook Up and the man who was once the focus of a girlish crush and his girlfriend was, frankly, not as enticing, especially when Lana remembered how her Hook Up had sounded on the phone when she had called him last week. Something had possessed her, and before she could have a second thought, she was pressing his number to call. What was it about him that made her so impetuous and carefree? And then the way he had answered her phone call? "Hey, Darlin', I was just thinking of you." Whether or not it was true, his words had thrilled her, and she had asked, "Really?" The words had struck her to her core. Everything about him should have screamed at her to run the other way if she didn't want her heart broken, but her head was the last organ involved in any decision concerning her Hook Up. A devout consumer of romance novels since she was twelve, her Hook Up personified the "Rake" description in each one. Even after confirming her suspicions about his dating history, her heart would not be swayed, because his words sounded so sincere when he told her that she was the only woman he was thinking of.

Love you, Aunt Lana! Thanks so much for the cardigan!

It's so cozy XOXO



Love you, too!

Sorry I had to leave so early this morning, but I'll see you for NYE, right?

You and Amelia are coming into the city?

Her nieces staying the night at her apartment was the only glitch for her week with her Hook Up, but Lana figured it should be easy enough to at least tear herself away from him to meet up with them briefly before they were off to whatever concert it was they were seeing at the Bowery Ballroom, a few blocks away from her apartment on the Lower East Side. She had already told them they could stay the night there, since she had plans to be in upper Manhattan that night. With him.



All I want is for you to be all that you can be.

You've always been the best of all of us.

Until the other day, Lana had never brushed off her brother's advice on anything in her life. She had gone to him so often during her life for his sage wisdom and practical way of looking at the world. Never in a million years did she think he would ever bring up the biggest mistake in her life (so far, anyway)—Anthony Russo.

As Lana listened to perhaps the most melancholic of Christmas songs, "Have Yourself a Merry Little Christmas", she couldn't help but become emotional as she thought about that sad, pathetic time in her life. When she should have been teeming with pride from excelling at her studies in high school and graduating early, instead she had been awash in despair from the treatment by her father and the discovery that the boy she thought she had loved had only been using her.

When Thomas Miller left his family the second time, Lana was eight years old. Though the rest of the family seemed to expect it (had, in fact, known it would happen eventually), his actions had completely blind-sided Lana. Her doting father, the man who took her to school and then picked her up, who bought ice cream for her even when it was cold outside, the man who helped her learn every song from *The Wizard of Oz,* was gone from her life without even a goodbye. Unconsolable, Lana sobbed herself to sleep every night, rejecting her mother's offer of cuddles, kisses, and even cookies. Her sisters had seemed, mostly, unaffected by their father's disappearance—teenage girls wrapped up in themselves. Of course, it explained Greer's trouble with the law and Ava's trouble with men. Montgomery had stepped up, once again, to be a father figure to his youngest sister, almost as if no time had passed when he had done it for Ava and Greer the first time. Music had been Lana's only salvation, when her brother began playing songs for her. Montgomery was a fan of classic rock and country, and he would strum a guitar he had garbage-picked one afternoon on the way home from school. Sitting on his bed, plucking along to the Nitty Gritty Dirt Band's "Fishin' in the Dark", with Lana nestled in an enormous, Barbie-pink bean bag Monty had procured somehow with whatever funds he made working with their grandpa on the weekends and after school. Lana sang along to Patsy Cline's "Walkin' after Midnight", "Feelin' Alright" by Joe Cocker, and "Thinkin' about You" by the singer who became one of her favorites, Trisha Yearwood. "Some of the best songs drop the "g" and add an apostrophe, baby Sis", Monty told her, and who was she to disagree, having those prime examples?

The summer after Lana turned thirteen, having finished eighth grade two years ahead of the kids she had begun kindergarten with originally, Thomas resurfaced again, somehow having gleaned the news about his youngest child's intelligence. "She needs to go to a high school that understands her brilliance," he insisted to her mother. "I can give her that." The man who had been in and out of her mother's life for twenty years, dragging Fiona around emotionally, was at last ready to disengage himself permanently and was seeking a divorce. Thomas wanted to move on with the other woman in his life, a woman he had met years ago, when he had worked for his father-in-law. A woman who Thomas had lived with when he wasn't living with Fiona. The woman's husband had died (finally), leaving in his wake a rich, but not-so-grieving, widow. What could her mother do? Refuse the opportunity for her youngest child to receive the premier education that she deserved? Though it pained Fiona to send her child away, she had done it selflessly. Lana had tested ridiculously high in the placement tests for the collection of private schools in Oyster Bay, chosen by her father. For three years, Lana lived with her father and his new wife during the week for the school year, attending the school that Thomas ultimately deemed suitable for his brilliant daughter. Living with her dad hadn't been easy, and being subjected to her stepmother's various rules and regulations concerning Lana's diet and exercise regime (or lack thereof, according to the wicked witch) made it worse. On the weekends and every school break, Lana went back to Riverhead and her family, but there were times she felt like she hadn't belonged there, either.

Mixed emotions had plagued Lana when she left her family the first time at thirteen—she missed her mom, her grandparents, and her siblings terribly, yet, she could not stop herself from being excited at the thought of starting high school (all of her knowledge about high school had come from Judy Blume novels) and attending the advanced science classes in which she excelled. School was not a challenge, but making friends had been a constant struggle, which was made worse when Lana tested out of most of her freshman classes, advancing then to junior and senior levels. What seventeen-year-old wants to be friends with a fourteen-year-old? Until Anthony Russo had breezed into her life…

TEXT FROM AVA

> At least you have something sexy for your hottie hook up to unwrap.

Still unsure if she was happy she had confided in her sisters about her Hook Up coming to New York, Lana had at least gotten the benefit of their stylish generosity. Separately, each sister had gifted Lana with some clothing to celebrate her reunion with her Hook Up. Never before had Lana put as much thought into her wardrobe (or lack of wardrobe) as she had since her Hook Up had told her he was coming to New York. Ava had given her a gorgeous green velvety dress she said she had found in a thrift shop out in East Hampton. Back in high school, after having to relinquish control over her daily wardrobe because of the private school's uniform policy, Lana had been desperate to express herself in a way completely her own, so she had begun wearing primarily dresses. While some may consider her style outdated, it always made her feel closer to her own mother, recalling their love of movies and television shows from the forties and fifties and the glamour of the era.

Greer's gift had been a lacy, red pajama set that at first glance looked demure, but when Lana had tried it on last night before going to bed at her mom's house, she had gasped after seeing herself in the mirror. Not entirely positive she would have the courage to wear it in front of her Hook Up, the outfit had at least given a boost to her self-esteem, which Lana had been slowly rebuilding for years after having it ground into dust as a young teenager upon her move to Oyster Bay. Considering this bit of self-reflection, Lana put her head back on her seat and wondered if that was what she loved most about whatever she had going on with her Hook Up—she finally felt seen and desired for simply being HER.

TEXT FROM GREER

No matter what Monty said, and I know he gave you some lame ass lecture in the car the other day, you are free to have fun, L. You don't owe this family anything except to be yourself.

Lana held her phone close to her heart at seeing her sister address her as "L". She had always envied the easy way Greer and Ava had with each other, but now they included Lana in the shorthand.

TEXT FROM HOOK UP

Hey, Darlin', just got into JFK.

Can't wait to see you.

I've done nothing but think of you since we met.

TEXT TO HOOK UP

I'm on the train heading back from my mom's house.

You take my breath away when you say things like that.

And she couldn't wait to see him again, absolutely true, but also: she couldn't breathe when he told her things she had only ever dreamed of hearing…couldn't believe he was thinking of her as often as she thought of him…but most importantly, she couldn't let herself blur the lines between want and need. She needed to have fun, and she wanted to have fun with him, but Lana was going to ensure that her want for her Hook Up did not turn into need.

What's this? she thought as she read another incoming text from him. Oh no, oh no, oh no. Scrolling up the messages, Lana saw that she had mistakenly sent the reply intended for her niece, Julia, to him instead.

TEXT FROM HOOK UP

# CHAPTER
## Nineteen

*Liam*



If I squint hard enough, I imagine I can see you on the train. You said it was cold! This is nothing compared to where I'm from—oops, almost gave it away! Can't have that, now, can we? See you soon, Mystery Woman

Having had no reply from the text he had sent his Mystery Woman, in which he had jokingly said that he loved her, he was worried that he had gone too far…that she hadn't understood he had only been kidding. Immediately upon reading her text concerning whoever Amelia was, he knew she had sent it by mistake to him but wanted to have fun. The only problem was typing those words of love (even in jest) came all too easily for him, and she was more than likely able to read through the lines and see his vulnerability. Now he anxiously waited to see hers.

"There's Sam—he's coming up this lane. Everybody ready to hop in as soon as he gets here?" Josh asked Effie and Liam as they waited to be picked up at the airport.

Liam responded sarcastically, "Yes, Dad, we're ready to go. Any more instructions on how to deal with life?" Liam rolled his eyes at Effie, who smiled in response while she rubbed Josh's shoulders. Effie never seemed to get annoyed with Josh and his verging-on-nagging demeanor, but Liam intended to put a stop to it now, before they made it out of JFK. "God, Josh, you'd think I've never been picked up at the airport before. Since when did you become such a mother hen? Maybe you should just concern yourself with Effie here and leave me be." And with that, Liam hoisted his duffel bag up onto one shoulder, thankful that he had put so much effort into working out religiously for the past four months since the weight of the bag only made him pause to adjust it ever so slightly, doing his best not to attract the notice of his companions, who were far too interested in his workout regime as it was. Not only did he feel he was at his peak strength-wise, but he wanted to impress his Mystery Woman, make himself unforgettable in this enormous city of hers, surrounded by all kinds of men he was sure were waiting to get a chance with her. "And I told you, Cuz, I can get my own ride into Manhattan— there was no need to include me in this pick up. Doesn't Sam have enough to do? He's an author, he's a landlord, he's a newlywed! Oh, I forgot—he's a business owner now, too." After having spent so many years harboring a small grudge against his cousin's best friend, it was hard to let it go now that Josh had moved back to South Dakota, where Liam could see him on an almost-daily basis. When both he and Josh had decided to attend college in New York City, Liam had a fantasy of the two of them hanging out on the weekends; once Josh had joined that damn fraternity and met Sam, though, his fantasy had been shattered. Just once, Liam wanted to be someone's first choice, not the back-up plan.

Effie murmured to Liam, "Settle down. You are way too wound up." A slight nod in response earned a smile from Effie, who was very skilled at getting the cousins to relax in tense situations. Liam was trying his best to be grateful, but all he wanted was to beeline it into Manhattan.

Josh, who had taken charge of both his and Effie's luggage, raised an eyebrow at his cousin. "Man, you'd think since you are so close to finally seeing your mystery woman again that you'd not be so tense—oh, here's Sam," Josh announced as Sam pulled up in a black Lexus SUV only a few years old.

Whistling to himself, Liam could see by the evidence that Sam not only was busy but also prosperous, another reason to hold a grudge. As he opened the front door to the vehicle, he got another reason: Sam's handsome bearded face grinning over at him. God, Liam silently groaned, does this man have any flaws? Despite Sam being over-the-moon happy with his beautiful wife, Tess, Liam still wasn't thrilled at having to invite him to the group dinner he was planning, so everyone could finally meet his Mystery Woman. The last thing he wanted to do was introduce her to Sam and Josh, both of whom were successful and brilliant, but it had to be done at some point if he wanted this relationship to progress. "Hey, Sam, you really don't need to take me into the city—I'm more than happy to get a cab there."

Sam waved aside Liam's protest as Effie and Josh hopped into the backseat. Over the obnoxious sound of the whistle being blown by the man outside trying to keep the traffic moving, Josh yelled, "Just get in the damn car, Liam." Knowing his cousin only used foul language under extreme stress or annoyance, Liam got in and slammed the car door at the same time as the man in the orange reflective vest pounded on the hood, directing them to leave.

As the group pulled up to a red light before getting on the Van Wick Expressway, Sam glanced at Liam and told him, "It's no bother to drive you in to the city, Liam. I love driving in New York, despite whatever traffic there is—it is still more chill than driving in Boston. Once you've experienced driving in Massachusetts, you have no fear; we're notoriously terrible drivers up there. I used to get defensive whenever anyone brought up the topic, but now that I've lived down here for almost a year, I can't deny it anymore," he laughed.

Liam nodded, ready now to be gracious instead of prickly. "I've heard that about your people. Anyway, thanks for giving me a lift."

"Well, I also figured that it would be a chance for Effie to see the city skyline at dusk, which is always an amazing sight," Sam said. "Effie, it's a pleasure to see you again. Tess is thrilled to play hostess to you guys and show off the house. She really went all out decorating it—it's by far the house with the most holiday cheer on the block!"

"I can't wait to meet her," Effie answered, "but I must admit I am intimidated by the description of her cooking. I consider myself to be a pretty good cook, but Tess's food always sounds so yummy, and her pictures on social media make me hungry no matter what time of the day it is."

Josh responded assuringly, "Effie, your delicious cooking is why I have gained ten pounds since I moved in." Lifting her hand to his mouth, Josh kissed it tenderly. The action used to be rather out of character for him, but since Effie, he had grown more publicly affectionate. "Not that I didn't need it. I was getting a little too thin last winter."

Everyone in the car remained silent, since the reason for Josh's loss of weight had been his break-up with Tess, combined with his career almost coming off the rails. Liam broke the silence by asking Sam, "I assume you know that I'm staying at Hotel Delacroix again?"

Sam nodded as Josh asked, "Why *are* you staying all the way up there, if you don't mind my asking?"

Liam shrugged, "Why wouldn't I? The location is great—offers a magnificent view of the city, but we're away from most of the tourists. Plus, it was obviously convenient for my Mystery Woman to get to, so maybe it's close to her apartment or her job? Anyway, she didn't give me any indication to *not* get a room there."

"Any idea where she does work, Liam? Or what her occupation is?" Sam asked.

"No. We both agreed to keep it casual and fun," Liam responded as lightly as possible. "No personal info."

Effie inquired, "Where is Hotel Delacroix, Liam?"

As much as Effie had been the topic of conversation the last time Liam, Josh, and Sam had been in New York together, it was hard to remember that she actually hadn't *been* there. "It's on the Upper East Side," Liam told her as he turned around in his front seat to answer, watching her golden eyes widen. Effie was half Native American, Lakota specifically, and her features told of her heritage, from her sleek black hair to her tawny skin. She was on the taller side, for a female, and whenever Liam saw her long legs, he remembered how swift she was back in high school, competing at track meets.

Effie raised an eyebrow, asking Josh, "Isn't that where your hospital was?"

Josh, who had been watching out the window, probably to ensure

Sam didn't crash into anyone, replied distractedly, "Umm, yeah, but lots of things are there."

"Wouldn't it be wild if that was where she worked?" Effie queried the men, who all looked at her as if she were out of her mind. "What?" she demanded. "You're telling me it never occurred to any of you that this mystery woman could work in the hospital, possibly be a doctor there, or a nurse or something? Hospitals employ hundreds of people, maybe even thousands, here in New York, so the odds are that if she works in the area, it could very well be there." Again, instead of agreement from the men, she was met with silence. "Sam," she implored, "help me out here—you're a writer, who, presumably, has an imagination, unlike these two. Wouldn't it be so romantic if Liam's mystery woman ended up being someone from the hospital that Josh knows? It would be like destiny," Effie said dreamily.

Sam nodded his head. "Well, to be fair, what were the odds that Tess and I would have taken the same train last year? You never know who you are going to bump into or who is walking around on the street tied, somehow, to someone you know, somewhere."

Liam laughed, "Okay, first, I take offense to your comment implying I have no imagination. Second, say you're right?" Liam half-turned in the front passenger seat to look back at Effie. "Who is my mystery woman?"

"Well, I don't know who she could be, specifically," Effie shrugged, "just that you might know her tangentially."

"I know," Sam announced to the car as he merged onto the Long Island Expressway, "what about Lana?"

Josh grimaced. "What about Lana?"

"Ooh, yeah, Josh, what about Lana?" Liam now looked at his cousin. As Josh shook his head, Liam nudged Sam in the arm. "He always does this when it comes to Lana."

"I always do what?" Josh demanded.

"You always refuse to tell me anything about her, just like you've always refused to introduce me to her." As Josh now glared at Liam, Liam followed up, "How many times, when I visited you in New York, did I ask to meet her?" Then Liam waved his finger at Josh. "Yet every time, you always had some excuse, like she was busy, or she wasn't my type. Honestly, if I didn't know any better, I would have thought you were keeping her to yourself."

Now Effie raised her eyebrows at Josh. "Oh, really? Is that what you were doing? And here I thought Lana was completely harmless—no competition at all." Effie giggled and then put her hand on Josh's cheek and brought his face to hers to kiss. "Just kidding," she hurriedly told him before he could get upset. "I know you said that everything that happened with her was a miscommunication."

Sam nodded in agreement. "From what you told me, Josh, I can understand how it all happened."

Liam's head felt like it was exploding—what were they talking about? How did he know nothing about what had, or hadn't, occurred with Lana? "Why am I the only one in this vehicle who doesn't know what the hell is going on? Please, for the love of god, what happened with Lana?"

"Settle down, Cuz." Josh sighed, and Liam knew this information was probably causing his cousin some angst, since Josh preferred to not really speak about anything too personal. "Okay, after Tess and I broke up, Lana offered to cook me dinner one night, which I accepted because we worked closely together, and she knew how I had been struggling."

"You mean you talked to a female co-worker about your relationship?" whistled Liam. "Huge mistake, Dude—you made her your work wife, which is one of the biggest no-nos in the workplace. Am I right, Sam?" Liam looked to Sam for support.

"Honestly, I wouldn't know about that, considering my work wife *is* my wife, and before that, I had no co-workers, what with being a writer and all." Sam deftly weaved his car around a car in the far passing lane, since it was going more slowly than appropriate for the flow of traffic.

"Okay, okay, I see your point. Effie? What about you? Have you ever been a work wife?" Liam looked in the mirror on the visor at Effie and caught her eye.

"Umm, not to be sexist, but librarians are mostly female, especially those that work in public libraries. Now, I have had a couple of lesbian librarians talk some crap about their partners," she laughed.

"*Anyway*," Josh interrupted their banter, "I will admit that yes, talking to Lana about any issues Tess and I were having was a mistake, and one that I apologized to Lana about last spring."

Josh quit speaking then, so Liam prodded him, "Okay, she invited you for dinner—did you go?"

Josh reluctantly nodded, saying, "Yes, I did, and then, because I am a gentleman—"

"One of the greatest, in my opinion," Effie interrupted him, and brought his face to hers again and kissed him.

"Okay, okay, my cousin—the gentleman. God, get a room, you two. You're as bad as Tess and Sam. Can't keep your hands to yourselves." Could he have this kind of demonstrative affection with his Mystery Woman?

"So, because I am a gentleman, I stopped at the bodega on the corner of her block and bought some flowers, because when I was with Tess, she always insisted on buying flowers for people who invited us for dinner."

Effie sighed, "Aww, that was sweet."

"I thought you heard this story before, Effie?" Liam questioned.

"I have," she confirmed with a nod. "I just love hearing how thoughtful my man is, you know?"

Rolling his eyes, Liam said, "Well, can you not interrupt, then, and let him finish?" Muttering under his breath, Liam said, "Now I've heard everything—he's a gentleman, he's sweet…he's a pain in my ass."

"I can hear you, you know," Josh admonished him as Sam and Effie laughed. "In hindsight, I think buying the flowers intimated to Lana that things were a bit more…personal between us than they actually were—"

"Ya think?" Liam interrupted, amazed that his cousin had made such an idiotic decision. "Single man brings flowers to a single woman? I just know this is going to get awkward."

"Nothing more happened with her, though," Josh insisted, "until I was forced to take my leave of absence. I got drunk after Tess and Sam told me the truth about them, as you know," and Liam nodded. "After I got the news, then, at the hospital, about losing the fellowship, I was… shell shocked, for lack of a better term, and Lana was being so kind to me…that I kissed her."

Liam's jaw dropped to the floor of Sam's car. "YOU WHAT? How am I just hearing this now? My god, all the other stuff you told me, but never this?" Liam could not believe that his closest family member…his best friend from practically birth…had not told him any of this. Yet, the friend who betrayed Josh, and the woman he had only been dating since the summer…both of them knew? What stung more was Josh's absolute refusal to introduce him to Lana, every time Liam asked, always insisting that she didn't date, that she was married to her work, that she wasn't his type. What it sounded like, now, in Liam's head, was that Josh didn't think that his cousin was good enough for his office mate, because clearly, she had been good enough for Josh to hit on. And she wasn't too married to her work to make dinner for Josh. Josh may have thought that Liam was only joking whenever Liam had raised the idea of meeting Lana, but he hadn't been. Josh had always spoken of her in a flattering way: she was brilliant (which intimidated him slightly) but also that she was kind and thoughtful, bringing him coffee or treats when they both worked together. He also made references to her personal life, making Liam think that she was lonely, maybe, without many friends, and that struck a chord in him. Despite having more friends than he could keep up with, Liam only really had Josh he could count on, along with his other cousins, Daniel and Felix. Sometimes his sister, Cait—when she wasn't being a pain in his butt.

Josh responded to Liam's previous questions with a shrug. "I was trying to downplay everything, and when I got back to South Dakota, I just wanted to forget any of it had happened. You're the best at helping me do that, Liam." Was his cousin trying to soothe him now? "Sometimes I want to live in your world where everything is easy and casual, but I'm way too uptight for that, but you let me visit your world, and that always helps."

Casual, easy—Liam wished people, especially Josh, could see the hidden depths he had, but again, he had no one to blame but himself. What was it Dolly Parton always said—"It takes a lot of money to look this cheap?" Well, it took a lot of concerted efforts to make the world believe he had no worries.

As they crossed the Queensboro Bridge into Manhattan, Sam said, "Not for nothing, but you tried to set me up with Lana a couple of times. Can you imagine?" Sam chuckled and then added, "She's fantastic, by the way, now that I finally had a chance to meet her."

Oh, so Lana was good enough for *Sam*? Why did that come as no surprise? I guess everyone was good enough for her except me, Liam thought sullenly, tuning everyone out as a dark cloud formed over him. Until, finally, like a beacon of light, a text pinged on his phone.

TEXT FROM MYSTERY WOMAN

Just got back into the city.

Heading to my apartment to grab some things, and then I'll be up to meet you.

Still at the hotel? Can't wait...

Here was someone who he *was* good enough for; too bad she knew absolutely nothing about him. Liam couldn't help but wonder what she would think of him if she *really* knew him...

# CHAPTER
## Twenty

*Lana*



"Marshmallow World" greeted Lana as she walked through the revolving doors of Hotel Delacroix, and her breath caught in her throat as she listened to Dean Martin. Growing up, she had seen Christmas opulence at its finest when she joined her mother to help her clean the stately (some purely ostentatious) homes out in the

Hamptons during the holiday. Huge Christmas trees, all lit up in glowing white lights, decorated in monochromatic themes. Here, in the hotel lobby, there were trees in every window, with every color of the rainbow shining from them: the one directly to her left had strings of red and white, decorated with candy canes and bows striped with the same pattern. Next to it, Lana saw a tree shining with blue and white lights, shimmering snowflakes, and snowmen strategically placed underneath. Festooned with multi-colored lights adorning it, the next tree Lana noticed to her right had two huge nutcrackers flanking it, and as Lana got closer, she could see ornaments from the ballet: a mouse king in his bright red uniform; Clara, with golden ringlets, in her baby blue night-gown; sugar plum fairies in purple fluttery tutus; and more nutcrackers in green, blue, and yellow. When she was fifteen, her dad had taken her to a performance of *The Nutcracker* ballet during Christmas, and it was just the two of them, making it extra special for Lana. Dressed in her best dress, Lana had felt like a princess attending the ballet on the arm of her father. The year before, her mom had given her a secondhand dress one of Fiona's clients no longer wanted. Red and white with a tulle overlay on the skirt, Fiona had sewn shut a rip in the back of the dress. Aside from that flaw, it was perfect, much like that evening she had spent with her father. Unlike the rest of her siblings, living with Thomas afforded Lana opportunities to spend quality time with him. She had been so young when he had left, and his reappearance in her life five years later, when she was thirteen, had been perfectly timed. Firmly entrenched in adolescence, Lana remembered bickering with her mom constantly and feeling smothered by her grandparents. She now understood the relent-less attention from her grandparents was overcompensation for an absent father and a mother who worked too much; at the time, however, it only made her long for more freedom. Well, when her father had whisked her away to his posher lifestyle, she had gotten her freedom. While living with him, she had rarely seen her dad except fleetingly during the week, usually when he carved a night out for just the two of them: they would go to the movies, have pizza at the place her step-mother "would not set one foot in", or bring home Chinese food to eat in front of the TV (another act frowned upon by the wicked witch) as they watched reruns of *Seinfeld*.

Lana gently touched one of the nutcrackers on his head as she thought about those times with her dad, and melancholy began to take hold, when suddenly a deep voice whispered in her ear, "Merry Christmas, Baby," and the husky tone of voice combined with the warm breath on her neck nearly brought her to her knees, overshadowing any despondency. Closing her eyes, she thought about all the lonely nights she had spent since she had last seen her Hook Up, and how, just when she was almost asleep, her phone would ping with a text, always from him, as if a string connected them from wherever he was in the world to where she lay in her bed. Strong arms now enfolded her from behind, and his body heat warmed her even through her bulky winter coat. "I've been watching you since you came through the doors. You're so damn beautiful," he told her as one of his hands swept her honey waves aside to kiss her neck. At work, Lana wore her hair firmly restrained in a bun or braid (a loose ponytail was as close as she normally got to having her hair down in public), but when she got ready this morning, her memory reminded her how she loved the way his hands slid into her long hair when it was loose. And then there had been his texts:

TEXT FROM HOOK UP

Sometimes I look down at my hands and still see long, silky waves of your hair wrapped around my fingers.

TEXT FROM HOOK UP

Did I ever tell you that when the moonlight was shining through the hotel window, it hit your hair as it cascaded down your back, making your hair shine, and the glow made me breathless every time?

TEXT FROM HOOK UP

I'm going to spend the entire week watching the way your hair falls across my chest as I'm holding you. I will memorize every individual strand, I will inhale the aroma that is all you. You know, I smelled every shampoo in the store just so I could smell you again. Nothing came close.

Her Hook Up had completely bewitched her, so Lana had cautioned herself multiple times on the train ride home to do her best to remain steady—to not fall any more under his beguiling spell than she already had. Wishing for a close girl friend more than she ever had in her life, and knowing her sisters were viewing this as a game (mostly Lana's fault, having downplayed her emotions to them), all she had was her brother to talk to, so when he had sent his last text, only wishing for her happiness, she had confided:

TEXT TO MONTGOMERY

I'm afraid of falling in love.

TEXT FROM MONTGOMERY

I'm afraid you already have.

He was wrong, of course, because you don't fall in love with someone after spending only two nights with them (one of them drunken). But, her little-Lana voice inside whispered, what about all of those texts? Some so intimate, so filled with personal details (despite her admonishments), while giving nothing away as a clue to his identity?

TEXT FROM HOOK UP

Haha, yes, I have a job! I'm actually quite successful! I also just bought a new house a couple of months ago. Haven't lived with my mommy for seventeen years.

Want to know something, though?

I still feel like I didn't earn any of it.

Other family members of mine are out of this world amazing, so much so, that most of the time when I'm with them I feel like a fraud.

He had written that text to her a couple of weeks ago, one night while she was working an overnight on-call shift, and she was so wired she couldn't sleep in her downtime, even though one of the mantras of being an on-call surgeon was: Sleep when you can. He was sleepless as well, he wrote, filled with the anticipation of seeing her again. She had jokingly asked him (for peace of mind) if he was employed or if he spent all night partying and all day sleeping, while living in his mother's basement. His earnest response, and his vulnerability, had kept her company during the entirety of her shift. So much of the sense of loneliness she got from him matched how she felt most days.

Now, in the festive lobby of this grand hotel, surrounded by more Christmas trees than she had undoubtedly ever seen in her life, she released her hold on the handle of her suitcase to turn in his arms, which was not easy to do when wearing bulky outerwear. Inwardly gasping when she saw him, her eyes took in the black sweater he wore, which emphasized the light gray of his sparkling eyes. His hair, gleaming deep chestnut, as if freshly washed, seemed a tad longer than she remembered, and her fingers itched to touch it—apparently, she was as obsessed with his hair as he was with hers, she mused, recalling his earlier words to her. "Hi," she said to him, suddenly overcome, not knowing how to speak to him now that he was so close. Was it her imagination or was he even better looking now than he was four months ago? Did his shoulders seem wider? His lips fuller? Helpless to stop herself, her hand reached out and touched his chest, registering the shiver that ran through him. "Merry Christmas," Lana told him.

Her Hook Up reached down and grabbed her suitcase with his left hand and with his other hand he clasped one of hers, steering them to the doorframe of the coffee shop where they had their second unofficial date, she supposed. After letting go of the suitcase, he then pointed above their heads, and Lana saw the mistletoe hanging over them. She grinned just as both of his hands cupped her face ever so gently, as if she were made of glass. His thumbs stroked her cheeks, and leaning down to her, he murmured, "I missed you." Finally, his lips met hers, and she closed her eyes, savoring the taste of him—candy canes and coffee. Her mouth opened under his, just as a bell clanged—was that in her head? He pulled back suddenly, looking around, so she assumed he heard it, too. Laughter rang out, then, from within the coffee shop, where on the other side stood an older woman, probably late sixties, holding a silver bell in her hand.

The barista behind the counter, wearing a red Santa hat, leaned around the cash register, calling out, "We ring the bell for anyone who kisses under the mistletoe."

"Oh, really?" asked her Hook Up. "How many have you gotten today?"

The woman who had rung the bell came over to them and replied, "You are the first couple today! It's been kind of slow, but now that it is dark, everyone will be out looking at the Christmas lights, so they'll need a hot beverage." Looking at her Hook Up, the woman's eyes took him in from head to toe, then said to Lana, "You definitely have all you need—he's hot enough to keep you warm, I imagine." Lana blushed in response, and with a wink at them both, the woman turned back to the counter.

Placing another lingering kiss on her lips, her Hook Up queried, "Do you want a hot beverage?" Lana shook her head no, and he asked with a grin, "Or am I hot enough for you?" Bell ringing ensued once more as Lana melted into him and they finally, but reluctantly, broke apart.

Breathing heavily, he pressed his forehead against hers, asking, "Are you ready to see our room?"

"Yes," she whispered, shuddering in his arms, unable to believe how easy it was to fall into him. After so many months apart, they were in sync with each other, as if no time had passed at all.

Taking her suitcase again in one hand, and one of her hands in his other, he led them to the elevator. With a key card, he accessed the top floor of the hotel. Bewildered, Lana watched as he pressed the button for the penthouse floor. Why were they going up there? she wondered, unable to believe that was where their room was located. Her brain found it impossible to process the cost of a regular room in this hotel, let alone anything on the penthouse floor.

TEXT FROM HOOK UP

I'm going to get us a room again at Hotel Delacroix. I hear it is all decorated this time of year. Plus, it's away from the too-touristy areas, and we can still walk to Central Park and down to Midtown if we want.

TEXT TO HOOK UP

Isn't that place super expensive?

We don't need to stay there.

It's too much…

TEXT FROM HOOK UP

Don't worry, Darlin'.

I got a good deal through a travel site.

Besides, nothing is too much for you.

She seemed to recall he had mentioned his work the last time he stayed here, so maybe whatever company he worked for paid for it? Was he going to "write it off", as they say? Not that she had any clue what that meant. Even though she dodged any of his questions about her own career, she could not keep herself from speculating about his, imagining he was some kind of businessman, maybe an executive? Possibly a salesman of some kind? Or maybe a lawyer? He certainly had a way with words, easily swaying her his way every time, that was for sure.

The elevator doors opened, and Lana followed him out and over to the door to their right. "Ready for this?" he asked her. Maybe? she thought, not entirely sure now that she was faced with the reality of the hotel room door but nodded her head and then gasped after he opened it.

A Christmas tree stood inside, about halfway into the room, with multi-colored lights shining from its boughs. Strung around the room were the same lights, with green garland adorning the doorway to the bathroom and the archway leading to the far end of the room, where Lana assumed the bed was located. Over to her right was a deep jacuzzi tub, and Lana marveled that this front area alone was almost larger than her studio apartment, bathroom included.

In a daze, Lana walked over to the tree and tentatively touched one of the branches; after realizing it was an actual tree, she squeezed the needle-covered branch between her fingers, then brought her hand up to her face. Inhaling the pine scent deeply into her nose, she closed her eyes in bliss. Before her dad had left her family, they had always had a real tree, and Lana remembered several Christmases when the whole family had driven to a Christmas tree farm out on Long Island, on the North Fork, to pick out their tree. The Christmas after Thomas had left, there had been no tree at all, because no one had been in the mood to celebrate (except young Lana), but the following year, her grandpa had come home with an artificial tree that her mom still used today. Even though Lana had gotten a real tree this year, it was tiny, and sadly the smell had faded after one day, with the needles shedding almost immediately after.

Feeling his arms pull her close, he rested his chin on the top of her head. "Do you like it? You mentioned that you preferred colored lights, so when I arranged all this, I made sure only colored lights were used. I have to say, you are right: colored lights definitely give everything a more festive feel. As pretty as they are, though, they are nothing compared to you." Lana's eyes filled with tears, unable to remember the last time anyone had gone out of their way to create something so spectacular for just her. He then reached down, still behind her, and unbuttoned her red wool peacoat, gently slipping it down her arms when he finished. Lana watched as he carefully hung up the coat in the closet next to a leather bomber-style coat that she knew he would look so handsome in.

"Did you bring it?" Lana nodded at his question and reached into the pocket of her skirt.

TEXT TO HOOK UP

Do you think there will be somewhere in the hotel room I can hang the ornament you got me? It's so beautiful and I want to be able to see it when I'm with you next week.

Every night since she had put her treasured ornament on her tree, she watched it twinkle in the lights. Hoping to convey in her text to him how much his present meant to her, she had been delighted at his response.

TEXT FROM HOOK UP

Baby, I will make sure to find the perfect place for it. No matter how beautiful it is, though, I am warning you that I will only have eyes for you.

"Now," her Hook Up said, "where should we hang it?" Placing his hands on her waist, he drew her close and kissed her forehead.

Holding the precious ornament between two fingers, she walked around to the side of the tree that she was sure they would pass by every time they went out the door or to the bathroom—it also happened to be in line of sight from the jacuzzi, and she had a flash in her mind of the two of them together, immersed in bubbles, staring at the tree with the gorgeous ornament in view. Because the tree was tall (taller than him, so she imagined it had to be at least seven feet tall) with so many branches, Lana giggled as she tried to hang the heart on a top branch. "Right here," she declared, changing her mind, and delicately placed it on a branch eye-level with her.

Lana turned to see what he thought and found him staring down at her. "I was right," he told her. "Everything in this room pales in comparison to you." As he drew her into his arms, he told her, "I need you to understand that I have never felt this way about anybody."

With his mouth just a kiss away, she whispered, "No? Not anyone?"

"Not anyone," he confirmed, and then, as if unable to wait a second longer, he wrapped his arms around her back, cupping her bottom to bring her flush to him. Her hands did what she had been craving, plunging into his hair at the nape of his neck, followed immediately by bringing her mouth up to meet his.

"Baby," he moaned against her mouth, "I made seven o'clock reservations for us. We'll never make it if we get started now."

Lana traced his back with her hands and then slid them around to the front of his jeans. "I hear the room service here is phenomenal."

# CHAPTER
## Twenty-One

*Liam*



Coming in to Union Square to show Effie the Christmas market, maybe we will hit up the one in Bryant Park, also. Want to meet up with us with your Mystery Woman?

TEXT TO JOSH

Not sure—just woke up, but she's still sleeping.
We have plans tonight for The Nutcracker.
Maybe you guys could get tickets???

Holding a steaming cup of coffee in his hands as he stood out on the balcony, Liam surveyed the city as the sun rose. Wrapped up in one of the oversized, fluffy white robes that were courtesy of the hotel, he was as warm on the inside as he was on the outside. Last night had been beyond anything he could have dreamt about. Too excited to wait for her alone in their room, he had been pacing in the lobby for almost an hour before she showed up, looking tastier than any Christmas cookie. Her red coat was cinched at her waist, the hem ending at the luscious curve of her hips. He then saw that whatever skirt she was wearing came to just above her knees—

shorter than anything he had previously seen her wear so far, with the sight of her legs sheathed in black tights making his mouth water. Despite the Christmas carols echoing through the lobby, the beating of his own heart was the only music he could hear as he approached her and wrapped her in his arms.

Now Liam peered back into the room, making sure his Mystery Woman was still sleeping. Not entirely sure at what time he had awakened, he had stayed in bed, savoring the weight of her body curled atop his and relishing the gentle snores she elicited every so often. It had been torture leaving her in the bed, but he knew if he stayed another minute, she would not, in fact, be sleeping any longer. All of this—the trip to New York, the expense of this hotel room—was worth it just watching her face last night each time she saw something that took her breath away (not even counting what had happened between the two of them that had also stolen *his* breath time after time last night). He had known, the minute he had booked this room, that he wanted to surprise her with their own Christmas tree in the room, and once she had hung the ornament on the tree, he practically fell to his knees with the significance it had for him. Was this what it was like to be in love? Finally, after so many years, and the insignificant relationships he had been involved in, his Mystery Woman fit together with him as if she were the missing piece to his seemingly uncomplicated puzzle. Seeing most of his friends and Josh finding their soulmates left him feeling like there was something wrong with him. Why couldn't he find that? What was it about him that made it impossible for him to fall in love? Lord knows, he had tried, multiple times, to convince himself that various "shes" could be the one. Hell, Josh had managed to have two different soulmates in the same amount of time Liam had none.

Sipping his coffee, Liam saw, out of the corner of his eye, movement from the bed. Not wanting her to wake up alone in a strange place, he rushed back in, being careful not to make too much noise in case she wasn't actually waking up yet. Once he had gently extricated himself from the bed this morning, he had ordered up a coffee service to their room. Always starving in the morning, a full breakfast service tempted him, but didn't want to make a heavy-handed decision in case she wanted to go out for breakfast (or brunch, depending on how long it took them to leave the room). Instead, he had ordered a few croissants to tide them over—two chocolate and two ham and cheese, which remained under the gleaming silver cloches on the tray next to the Christmas tree.

Standing next to the bed, Liam looked down at her sleeping form tucked under snowy white piles of downy comforter. To say she looked like an angel would be an understatement. Also, not quite believable, considering the night they had just experienced, he thought with a smile. Shrugging out of his robe, he slid back into bed, and immediately she rolled over and tucked herself into him. With awe, he stroked her hair back from her cheek, struck by how perfect she seemed for him, along with the unrelenting and ever-growing need to know more about HER. Every question posed by Josh, Effie, and Sam had gotten him wondering what her truth was. Where did she work? The hospital seemed like a potential choice, considering she had to work on Thanksgiving, and she had mentioned needing coworkers to cover a couple of shifts for this week. One of his primary goals was to convince her to open up about aspects of her personal life.

Liam ran his hand down his Mystery Woman's back, recalling the lingerie that had buckled his knees last night. Once he had lifted her sweater over her head, the devastating sight of her wearing the sheer, black bustier had him thanking whatever fate had put her in his path the night they had met. Surprisingly, she had been the one to suggest they run the water for the jacuzzi (something he had assumed they would work up to in a few nights). Between long, sensual kisses, Liam had delicately removed her intimate clothing, relishing the sight of it carefully placed next to the jeans he had almost torn off his own body.

Surrounded by the foamy bubbles in the jacuzzi, as the lights from the tree illuminated the room, and with her back pressed against his chest, he had asked her what her best Christmas memory was. As she stroked his thighs under the water, she told him, "When I was seven, my parents got me a bicycle. A pink and purple Schwinn. We were all so happy, or so I thought…"

Liam had paused with his very concerted effort of massaging her silky shoulders. "Or so you thought? What do you mean?" Those same shoulders rose and fell under his hands with her shrug.

"Nothing…sorry. Anyway, my brother spent the next day helping me learn how to balance on it. We didn't have any snow that Christmas, and I remember being outside with only my Christmas sweater on."

Liam had reached out a hand to skip a Christmas song he loathed, wondering why it had been her brother who had taught her how to ride her bike and not her dad, when he heard her whisper, "He left a few months later."

She said nothing more as "Merry Christmas, Baby" by Bon Jovi played softly from his phone. He wrapped his arms around her, pulling her more tightly against him, asking, "Who left?"

"My dad. He just left us one day. It's okay though," she said hurriedly, before he could respond or act in any way. "My mom is amazing. And my brother. My sisters are so-so," she chuckled, turning in his arms. "Now it's your turn to tell me—what's your best Christmas?"

With her soft breasts caressing his chest, he responded huskily, "Now, absolutely, unequivocally, this Christmas is promising to go down in the record books as one of the best." From that point, all conversation had ceased entirely.

From his bedside table, he heard his phone ping with a text, and a glance at his Apple Watch read:

TEXT FROM JOSH

No tix for tonight, it's sold out

The four of us are going—

Nope, Liam told himself as he read only the preview on his watch face; whatever his cousin wanted could wait until much later, as he felt her soft hand on his stomach, followed by her plump lips on his neck. "Mmm, this is definitely a nice way to wake up," he heard her whisper into his ear, and her fingers swirled through the hair on his chest. "You have no idea the fantasies I had about your chest hair," his Mystery Woman said.

He chuckled. "Really? I think we will definitely need to discuss every fantasy of yours in great detail," he responded. "But showing is much more satisfying than telling."

Slowly moving her hand from one side of his chest to the other, she commented, "I'm sure all women have found your chest very, very appealing."

Wanting to keep his past escapades behind him, Liam laughed, hoping to deflect, then decided to admit one of his more painful memories in an effort to be more vulnerable with her. "Once, just after I had moved back home from college, I began dating a waitress, Patti, who worked in a cafe in town; she kept bugging me to shave my chest—complained it was too hairy for her. Like an idiot, I agreed. What people don't tell you is how much that hair itches when it grows back!"

With her shoulders shaking with laughter, she cried, "Oh no! This is terrible! I can't imagine asking someone to change their physical appearance for me," she told him, as her supple lips kissed a line from his ear down his neck, all of which caused him to quake. "So, what happened with her?" How could she form a coherent sentence while seducing him all too easily? Liam wondered. His own fingers traced the silky skin on her back, and he forced himself to carry on the conversation, placing more value on talking to her than ravishing her (for now).

"Well, it turned out that wasn't her only complaint about me," he admitted. "Mainly, she hated that I didn't spend enough money on her, and that I worked too much." Even though he worked for his family's dealership, he did not have free rein over the family "fortune", despite what Patti had erroneously thought. While aware that his job at the dealership could seem frivolous, he earned every dollar he made there, through long hours and many weekend shifts. After three months of dating, he had broken up with her after a set of silver candlesticks had gone missing from his parents' house: Liam and Patti had been to dinner there the previous night, so when his mother called frantically saying her heirloom candlesticks were missing, Liam had, of course, defended his girlfriend against the insinuation. Two days later, she had cancelled a date with him, saying she was under the weather. Liam dropped in at Patti's house with a quart of chicken noodle soup, one of the cafe's specialties. Patti's roommate had let him into the house, telling him that Patti was still sleeping. Taking the soup into the kitchen to put it in the fridge for her, Liam had seen the candlesticks, tossed haphazardly on her kitchen counter. Liam relayed the story to his Mystery Woman, unable to stop the shame from flooding his body. He admitted, "The relationship wasn't that deep, honestly, but she humiliated me. I brought her into my parents' home, and then to have her steal something? She made me feel worthless…used." Liam had never admitted that aloud to anyone, preferring to remember instead the countless relationships that had ended amicably and drama-free.

His Mystery Woman stopped stroking his chest and leaned up on her elbow to look him fully in the face. "I'm sorry that happened to you. I know what it's like to feel like you're not enough." She kissed him softly on the lips, and he felt her smile against his mouth. Then she said, "For the record, I don't have any complaints about you."

"Oh, no? Not a single one?" Liam questioned, as he rolled her over and slipped off the sheer and very short scarlet nightie she had slipped into sometime during the night, which was a shame, really, because even though the minuscule garment was sexy as hell, the sight of her in absolutely nothing was far more…gratifying.

"Do you know how sexy you are?" she whispered in his ear. "I've done almost nothing these past months except think of you." Putting her hand in his hair, she told him, "I dreamed about the way your hair felt against the insides of my thighs," and he was helpless to stop the moan from escaping his lips, since he had spent many sleepless nights reliving the same images. "And then I fantasized about how strong your arms were when you held me up in the shower the last morning we were together," she confessed, her fingertips fluttering over his biceps. Oh god, Liam thought: the shower, when her skin was hot and wet and slick. "Most of all, I've been imagining the way your mouth would kiss my—" and Liam swallowed whatever she had been about to say, as he kissed her, deeply. Over the years, he had countless woman say provocative things to him, but her words were the only ones he would ever want to remember.

Waking up much later to the sound of "I don't care about the presents underneath my Christmas tree" being sung from the bathroom, Liam grinned. Her voice was as amazing as everything else about her. He rubbed his belly, starving now that they were both awake (for food this time), and then the smell of coffee hit him. Looking at the bedside table, he saw two cups of coffee, emanating steam, and two of the croissants, and was struck by her thoughtfulness.

"Hey, Mariah, I hope you're not going to make me eat breakfast by myself," he joked.

A flurry of white robe came rushing at him, then, and Liam was marginally disappointed to see that she had changed out of her nightie and into the robe, until she bent over and he appreciated how well she filled out the robe. She exclaimed, "Oh, perfect—you're finally awake! I'm starving!" She brought her face down to kiss him, and he registered that she was wearing glasses, a sight which was almost more erotic than that of her in the robe, with its deep V giving him an ample view of her cleavage.

"I didn't know you wore glasses," he remarked as he stroked the seam of her lips with his thumb casually, doing his damndest to restrain himself from pulling her under the duvet once again.

"Oh, I just showered and took my contacts out. I'll put them back in," and she started to get up to go back to the bathroom, but he grabbed her wrist.

"No, don't. God, you're so beautiful," he whispered, sitting up and pulling her into his lap. "I have never felt so at ease with anyone before —I want you to know that. Glasses, no glasses; hair in a ponytail, hair down; wearing this robe or wearing next to nothing," he winked at her, thrilled to see her responding blush. "I want to see every aspect of you this week—no pretenses, no secrets." As her body began pulling away from his, he rushed on, "What I mean is that I want us to just be *US* this week." He took a breath, trying to explain, "Baby, that doesn't mean we have to tell each other our names...*yet*. I just am trying to say, I guess, that I am going to let down any walls I have with you and be all in." Liam stared into her dark blue eyes while he laced one of his hands with hers, bringing it up to his mouth to kiss her fingertips.

As her other hand grazed his cheek that was desperate for a shave, she replied softly, "Me, too. I just want to be present with you, in this time with you, not thinking of anything else. No work, no family, nothing but me and you and this city." Her mouth descended on his, followed by her pushing his shoulders back onto the bed. Wet strands of her long hair fell all around him while she leaned over him. His last coherent thought was telling her to keep her glasses on, again, as he unbelted her robe. So much for breakfast...

# CHAPTER
## Twenty-Two

## Lana

TEXT FROM AVA

Update, please! You have been radio silent for almost 24 hours!

Do we need to send in a rescue party :)

TEXT FROM GREER

Why are you keeping the dirty details from us? You must have had a few minutes to yourself to give us an update! Is your Hook Up still as smoking hot as you remember? I can't believe you're staying in such a fancy place again—he must be loaded! L, what if he is, like, some oil baron from the south? Or like a lawyer from California? You can't move away! Mom would be broken-hearted! All joking aside (except the Mom part)

Monty is, like, completely mental about all of this. Mother Hen is worried sick about his baby chick.

Lana's first thought that morning was one of regret—letting the small detail about her personal life slip while talking about her favorite memory. That bicycle had been a complete surprise, and the only thing she had requested that year as a gift. Unfortunately, once her dad left, she had hated it, until her brother convinced her how happy her mom was when she watched Lana riding it. From that moment on, Lana rode her bike until she grew too big for it.

After finally emerging from the confines of downy comforter and fluffy robes, the two of them had been starving. While they waited for two orders of eggs Benedict to be delivered to their room, plus a fresh pot of coffee, along with tiny pitchers of cream, the duo ate every croissant he had ordered earlier. To her delight, once the food arrived, Lana discovered that her Hook Up had also ordered two cups of warm eggnog (suggested by the seasonal menu), and it proved to be more decadent than anything she had ever had to drink in her life—creamy, with fresh nutmeg grated on top, and the slightest ribbon of steam rising from the pot. Lana's eyes widened when she found the side of Chantilly cream that accompanied the eggnog, and her Hook Up spooned pillows of it on top of their seasonal drink. Laughing, they had taken turns wiping off whipped cream mustaches from one another after drinking the eggnog.

Once she showered and put on her clothes for the day (a long black wool skirt and red and white striped sweater), she had been ready to face the world shortly after noon. Her Hook Up had dressed in a dark blue turtleneck that was so soft it had to be cashmere, and a pair of dark blue jeans that fit him so well her mouth watered every time she looked at him. "Where are we going?" Lana asked, but he refused to give anything away. Taking her hand upon leaving the hotel, he guided her as they walked several blocks downtown, passing by Serendipity 3, home of the famous frozen hot chocolate. For Lana's thirtieth birthday last summer, her mom and sisters had come into the city and the four of them had gone to the restaurant after Lana's shift at the hospital. The food had been pretty good, if a little spendy, but the interior decor had been worth the extravagance. Finally turning east, they ended up at the Roosevelt Island Tram. Lana gasped, "The tram? Are you sure?"

Wrapping his arm around one shoulder, he had pulled her close to him, nuzzling her ear. "Have you ever taken it?"

"Absolutely not! I'm terrified of dangling over the river, trapped in a car with twenty strangers," she replied vehemently.

He whispered in her ear, "Come on, Baby—it'll be fun. Plus, it's something neither one of us has done before, and I want to experience new things with you." As much as she knew that the independent woman in her should loathe him calling her "Baby", his words thrilled her each time he said it; maybe it was the fact that it was so unlike the reverence everyone else used when addressing her in her daily life when she was working, or it could be that when he said it (as with everything else he did), he put his complete focus into it. His breath on her neck caused her to shiver as he kissed her behind her ear, then gently sucked on the tender flesh of her earlobe, making her gasp in response. "I'll catch you if we fall," he promised almost solemnly. Who was this creature he had created, allowing such public displays of erotic affection?

How could she deny him anything when he was just *so* charming? Eagerly, the two of them hopped on the tram, which took them over the East River, from Manhattan to Roosevelt Island. Suspended in the air, he insisted they take a picture together with the cityscape behind them. Not sure what the point was, since she assumed a casual affair didn't include encapsulating it with a photo, Lana resisted, even though part of her wanted the physical reminder of this moment. However, another couple on the tram, who had just had their photo taken by a stranger, approached them, offering to take their picture. Regardless of common sense making her wary, Lana smiled broadly for the photo. With her Hook Up's arms encircling her waist, and his chin resting on the top of her head, she relaxed into him. Using her Hook Up's phone for the photo op, the woman told them, "You guys look so happy." Lana felt a kiss on the top of her head.

As he took back his phone, he pulled her to him and asked, "Are you happy?"

Smiling in response, she nodded, wondering if she had ever been happier. He pulled her close to him, kissing her on her forehead, and whispered, "Me, too."

Walking hand in hand, they headed south down the island after getting off the tram, passing the spooky remains of a smallpox hospital that had opened in the 1800s, back when the island had been called

Blackwell's Island. Reading the signs outside the landmark, her Hook Up told her, "One of my cousins was obsessed with the history of this place back when we were in college. He used to go on and on about the fact that despite the availability of the vaccine, so many people were still contracting the disease."

Astonished, Lana turned to him and exclaimed, "Wow! I had a co-worker who used to bring up the same topic. Even though I had never visited here, I had read up on the history of the place, and I was always more fascinated by its history as a charity hospital, you know. The fact that it was used to treat the poor and anyone society deemed unstable really disturbed me." Lana grew silent, thinking of the women whose husbands or fathers sent to the island's "insane asylum", sometimes for depression or "loose morals", and sometimes simply because those men couldn't "handle" or "control" them. Having been at the mercy of her father, who refused to pay for medical school to teach her to be "financially independent", her sympathy for these misunderstood women brought a tear to her eye.

"Hey." His hand raised up her chin. "You okay?"

Lana drew a wobbly breath and explained to him the upsetting details of the hospital, and his face grew solemn. "I feel so uneducated—I never knew any of that. Come here," he whispered, hugging her to him. "You're not going to like this, but I'm figuring out that you are incredibly empathetic. Can't go back now," he teased, placing a gentle kiss on her lips.

Her Hook Up added, "When I get home, I will have to have a serious talk with my cousin, and how short-sighted he was, only going on and on about the disease; although, I guess he *is* a doctor now, so that may have explained his interest in it." Lana laughed, letting his lighthearted tone lift her spirits. "I still have an issue with him about this place."

Lana noted his heated tone, asking, "Really? Why?"

"He came here several times back then, but only with his fraternity brothers—he never invited me along, even after I'd asked him about coming here several times."

Something about his tone sounded so sad to her ears, knowing from experience what it meant to be on the outside, watching other people having fun. "Were you guys close?" she asked, immediately adding, "I guess you must have been, if you went to the same college."

He nodded his gorgeous head, almost reverently. "We were…still are, actually. Best friends who are more like brothers than cousins. Although sometimes I wonder if he isn't ashamed of me just a little bit," he confessed. Lana squeezed his hand in comfort, having also been on the receiving end of not feeling in sync with her own family. He continued, "We didn't go to the same schools, though. He went to Col-" he stopped abruptly, looking down at her and grinning. "Are you trying to get to know me, Mystery Woman? I warned you how irresistible I can be," he stated, before pulling her into his arms again, kissing her within an inch of her life. Being with him was so freeing, so easy, that he did, in all honesty, make her want to get to know him, despite every warning bell in her body trying to signal her otherwise. How could she resist, though, when so many of their experiences mirrored each other's?

They continued strolling further south on the island, toward the Franklin D. Roosevelt Four Seasons State Park with breathtaking views of Manhattan, Queens, and Brooklyn. Lana waited until they sat down on one of the benches before asking him, "Do you want to know a secret?" she asked him, with a flirtatious lilt to her voice, wanting to share some of her own news with him.

"Baby, if I haven't said it before, I want to know everything about you," came his response, and once again he bridged the gap between casual and sincere with his light tone of voice speaking words that struck such a chord in her. It was his eyes, though, that shot her in the heart, followed by his mouth on hers, warming her from the cool breeze on the narrow island. His finger traced the curve of her cheek, and he brushed a lock of hair behind her ear.

Taking a deep breath, before she talked herself out of it, she confided in him, "Okay, then, here it is: I'm actually moving to Brooklyn next month; somewhere over there, I think," as she pointed across the East River, past one of the highest points she could see in Brooklyn: the clock tower. "I'm a little nervous," she admitted, surprising herself with the relief she felt at sharing this with him. Lana had been doing her best to ignore the butterflies in her stomach anytime she thought not only about moving, but also about changing hospitals. It wasn't that she was nervous about living or working someplace new, but that loss had always accompanied life changes for her, and she was bracing herself for whatever that could be, unfortunately. "Here's another secret about me: I am also going to be working there as well." Oh no, she thought frantically, what had she done? Her only intention had been to tell him about her change in living quarters, knowing his optimism would soothe her worries. Now he was likely to follow up by asking her more personal questions, and she wasn't sure she had the inner strength to not answer them.

"Congratulations," he told her, then said, "maybe I'll have to come back to help you move, now that I'm an expert at it."

Was he joking, Lana wondered, or was he serious? Unsure, she responded lightly, "That's right—you moved recently, as well. How do you like your new place?"

He chuckled and told her, "I love it. Starting to put down some roots and make the place my own. But don't try to distract me—I have two new breadcrumbs dropped by my Mystery Woman," he stated, his arms sliding around to keep her close. "Currently, you do not live or work in Brooklyn. Or does that count as one large breadcrumb instead?" He must have felt her tense up in his arms, bracing for more questions. "God, you're amazing," he said as he looked into her eyes, the intensity cutting out the rest of the world as he kissed her deeply. "Thank you for sharing that news with me. Now, do you want to head up toward the lighthouse?"

They walked hand in hand for a few feet before she heard him say, "You know, lighthouses have always fascinated me. Beckoning to anyone needing help out in the sea." She felt his eyes on her as he asked, "How about you?"

Lana tensed, thinking of the heartbreak that had occurred for her as a teenager out at the lighthouse in Montauk. Thankfully, she was spared having to answer, as an icy breeze had picked up over the water, causing her to pull her hat out of her coat pocket and put it on.

"Want to get on the shuttle and warm up?" he asked as he helped her arrange her hat. "Damn, you are adorable," he told her. Then he nodded to the approaching shuttle, grabbed her hand, and the couple raced to catch it.

Riding the shuttle north in companionable silence, with her hand still in his, his thumb began rubbing the inside of her palm, and she found the gesture helped block out her painful memory of Anthony and the lighthouse. Lana sighed contentedly then, soaking in the perfection that had been the past twenty-four hours, and quelled the urge to pinch herself to make sure she wasn't dreaming. Right now, her life was like a movie—one that she wanted on repeat, and she told him just that when he asked what she was thinking about.

"I just had a thought—have you ever seen that movie *Meet Me in St. Louis?*"

Joyfully, Lana responded, "It's one of my favorites—I watch it every Christmas!"

"Me, too! I usually watch it a couple of times. My mom caught it one year on tv when I was in middle school and ever since, we have watched it together. Here's my thought: do you think this could count as a trolley?"

"What? A trolley?" She shrugged her shoulders as she pondered his question seriously. "I guess I don't see why not—at least a modern day one." Suddenly, he then made a sound with his mouth that sounded like bells ringing. "What are you doing?"

Then he responded by singing softly into her ear: "Clang, clang, clang went the trolley. Ding, ding, ding went the bell," and then he abruptly stopped. Lana shot him a surprised look, wanting him to continue, but he said, "Sorry, is this too much? I have occasionally been accused of being too spontaneous."

Surprising herself with her own spontaneity then, Lana sang, "Zing, zing, zing went my heartstrings. From the moment I saw him, I fell." And it was true, she thought. Too true, especially now that he was referencing one of her favorite movies of all time. "I love *Meet Me in St. Louis* so much. I started watching it when I was young, too."

"Oh, really? Another thing we have in common, huh?"

"It seems like it…actually, I was even younger than you. Probably a couple of years after I got my bike. My siblings were out of the house, so it was just mom and me, and my grandparents. My mom is a big fan of old movies. Personally, I love anything with Judy Garland in it. Growing up, I used to wish I had been named Judy instead of—,"

Lana stopped in the nick of time before she accidentally revealed her name.

"What was that?" Her Hook Up asked before leaning down to whisper in her ear. "Did you almost tell me your name, Mystery Woman?" Kissing the tender skin just behind her ear, he assured her, "Don't worry, Darlin', your secret is safe with me." Oh, how she loved it when he called her "darlin'".

"Oh yeah?" She laughed, trying to make him forget she almost told him her name. "How do I know I can trust you?" She glanced over at him in the seat next to her, and then down to where their thighs were touching and seeing his blue jean-clad leg next to her skirt-covered one made her feel content, cared for…wanted.

Then he said, "You can trust me with all of your secrets," and as he kissed the fingers on each hand, she wondered at the dangerous emotional game she was playing with herself.

Intent on lightening the mood, even as electrical currents coursed between them on the shuttle, she confessed, "I have to be honest—I'm still kind of shocked that you know *Meet Me in St. Louis*." Lana had never met anyone her own age who even knew that movie, let alone loved it as much as she did.

"Don't let this pretty face fool you—I'm not as shallow as most people think," he said lightly. Was that what he thought? He was proving to be many things—spontaneous, generous, thoughtful, and kind, but never shallow. Wistfully, he told her, "It really is a perfect movie—for one thing, many people consider it a Christmas classic, but it really covers all the bases for a year-round movie." Lana nodded as he continued, "And then the Grandpa character? God, I thought he was the funniest one, even as a kid. My grandpa is kind of like him—always with the wisecracks but sticking up for his grandkids whenever possible."

"The part that always gets me is when Judy's character sings 'Have Yourself a Merry Little Christmas'. Such melancholy." Just thinking about the scene made her eyes well with tears. Or perhaps it was this moment between the two of them, discussing a movie she held so dearly in her heart, with a man she had never expected to connect so deeply with. He continued to add layers, when she had been expecting him that very first night to be (oh no, she groaned inwardly) as shallow as possible. He had been right, she thought regretfully. Before she could say any more, the shuttle pulled up to the last stop: Blackwell Island Lighthouse, and the pair exited.

Lana watched his face light up with awe as he took in the red and white striped lighthouse, wishing she could view it as a beacon of hope, the way he did. Walking to the lighthouse, her Hook Up confessed, "It's so impressive. Coming from a land-locked state, I've always had a thing for lighthouses, and they never cease to amaze me." As he took out his phone to take some pictures, he grinned down at Lana. "Not too much information about me, is it? Still keeping it casual, right?"

Lana told him seriously, "I am finding you to be absolutely fascinating, no matter what you tell me, regardless of your state's access to an ocean." The pair laughed and shared a kiss.

"What about you, Mystery Woman? What are your feelings on lighthouses? You never did tell me. You're likely used to them, living on the East Coast."

She pondered her own feelings for lighthouses, which were more mixed, and thought about what to tell him. "Yeah, they are beautiful," she agreed somewhat reluctantly. "I spent my childhood staring at the one out in Montauk in the Hamptons…do you know it?" At his nod of affirmation, Lana decided to wade deeper into her waters of truth, telling him, "My mom cleans houses for a living out there, in the Hamptons." Lana paused to study him, looking for signs of judgement on his face, or any hint of distaste. Could she trust him? She wasn't sure yet, but she yearned to, so she ventured on, "When I was growing up, I had to go with her to work. Not so much to help her, but because she couldn't afford a babysitter. Sometimes while my mom was working, I would go outside and run around on the private beaches." Feeling melancholy herself now, Lana was thankful for the low light of the late afternoon as tears welled in her eyes once again as she thought of her mom. What did her Hook Up think of her now? He must have some kind of wealth, considering he was able to pay for such a decadent hotel room, or go into a store like Tiffany & Company without a care? Learning she was the daughter of a servant, essentially, had to make him think twice about who he was entertaining this week. Unable to keep a touch of bitterness from lacing her voice, Lana added, "You know, my mom never took the time to walk outside to see the view. Always stuck inside, cleaning. Still, to this day." Her mom, never getting to enjoy any of the fruits of her labor. What would *she* have thought of the hotel room her daughter was staying in? Afraid to look at his face in case she could read any distaste or see judgement, Lana kept her eyes on the lighthouse, recalling the last time she had been with a man...no, a boy, really...out near one. When something she had loved became a symbol of her pain, when her humiliation had known no bounds.

"Hey," he said softly, tipping her chin up so he could see her face. "It sounds to me like you have an amazing mom who raised one hell of a daughter. I'm sure you must see me as some kind of rich playboy, considering all of this. But I'm not. Maybe I was, in another lifetime. A lifetime not so long ago, admittedly. But there's more to me than that," he insisted. "I come from a line of manual laborers as well. My dad is an auto mechanic who works with his dad. If I had been any good at it, that's what I would do, too. I'm not, though. What I am good at is charming people for a living." He grinned a sexy, lopsided grin at her, asking her, "How am I doing so far?" Heaven help her, she could do nothing but approve of his performance, with a kiss under the shadow of this lighthouse.

When the arrival of a city bus interrupted their kiss, they broke apart reluctantly and hopped on. Her Hook Up brought one of her hands to his mouth and kissed it, telling her, "Thanks for trusting me back there. You are so incredible, I want you to know that." He laced his fingers with hers, then, and she put her head on his shoulder until they reached the subway station on Roosevelt Island, each of them apparently deep in their own thoughts. Lana had never considered how her own misconceptions about him would make him feel. Hearing the pain in his voice made her regret any assumptions she had made concerning him.

Once on the F train back to Manhattan, Lana finally had a moment to check her phone, seeing the texts that had come in from her sisters. She refrained from answering either of them yet, knowing the breezy answers they expected would diminish the effort the man beside had obviously put into their time together so far, not to mention her growing feelings toward him, despite every instinct reminding her to not fall for him.

Upon exiting the subway at Lexington Avenue and 63$^{rd}$ Street, her Hook Up told her cryptically, "I have something planned for tonight, but we need to go to the hotel first." What could he have planned now? Lana mused on the walk back to the hotel. As far as Lana was concerned, the day had been perfect, and she would be content to spend the rest of it in their room, shrouded beneath the warm comforter, with his body next to, on top of, or under hers.

"You know, we don't have to do anything tonight—I don't need to be entertained or have an elaborate evening out," Lana informed him gently after they entered the hotel elevator, needing him to understand that she did not require any money being spent on her—that just being with him was enough…he was enough.

With his powerful arms around her once again, he stared into her eyes as he said, "I don't *need* or *have* to do anything. What I *want* is for us to have an amazing week together, filled with surprises and holiday cheer. And sex, of course," he informed her, with a straight face, as he began to unbutton her coat on the elevator. "Lots," he kissed her neck, "and lots," he kissed her collarbone, "of endless," he unbuttoned the top two buttons of her sweater, "satisfying," he kissed the tops of her breasts after he unbuttoned another button of her sweater, "sex." The elevator doors opened on their floor, and he closed her coat before stepping out. "You'll see," he winked at her. "Don't think that you seducing me is going to make me spoil it for you, though."

Lana laughed and denied his claim as he unlocked their door. "I believe you were the one undressing me in that elevator." Shrugging out of her coat to toss it into a nearby chair, she followed up with, "After all, I believe your buttons are all still firmly intact."

"Darlin', just being in your presence is seduction," he told her, and finished unbuttoning her sweater. Lana pushed his coat from his body, then, not caring where it dropped. Sliding her hands under his turtle-neck, she raked her nails across his chest before he pulled it off himself. Her bra fell off along the way, along with her skirt, as she led him to the bed, where she tried various methods of coercion to make him confess about their evening plans. No amount of kissing or stroking or whispering to him of all the ways she could make him reveal his surprise could sway him, though.

Once they had been satiated, her Hook Up announced, "Okay, enough lallygagging around! Time to get ready!" Practically springing from their love cocoon, he slipped on some shorts, and walked over to grab his coat from the floor. Lana sat up when he draped the coat around her before offering her a hand. After she stood, he reached into one of his coat pockets, bringing out a small paper bag. "Here's a little something I picked up for you this afternoon," he told her, smiling as he handed it to her. "You may sense a theme."

Opening the bag, she reached in and took out an ornament, this time a small replica of the lighthouse on Roosevelt Island. "Where did you get this?" Lana gasped.

"A gentleman never reveals his secrets," her Hook Up playfully responded. Lana thought back to the only time they had been apart on the island—when they had first arrived. He had gone ahead to get a map at the information center just down the hill from the tram while Lana used the restroom. "Go ahead," he urged her, "hang it up on our tree." Our tree—the phrase made her heart skip a beat, bringing along with it the beginning of a sense of belonging.

After hanging it near the heart ornament, Lana threw her arms around him, thanking him with kisses, moved, once again, by his thoughtfulness. Finally, with a groan, he told her, "You are way too sexy wearing only my coat, so now I need you to look in the closet before I do something rash like cancel our plans for the night." Following his instruction, Lana saw her green velvet dress hanging up in a new dry-cleaning bag. In a move she was beginning to be particularly fond of, his arms wrapped around her from behind. After he kissed the side of her neck, he asked, "I hope you don't mind? I saw you had this dress hanging up in here, so I asked the concierge to arrange for it to be pressed, along with my suit. It's gorgeous, but only half as much as you are," he informed her, before turning her around, and she gazed into his enchanting silver eyes. "I can't wait to see you in it tonight—you're going to dazzle everyone."

TEXT FROM JOSH

Coming into the city tmrw to show Effie my old stomping ground.

Are you able to meet for lunch?

Coming into the city tmrw to show Effie my old stomping ground.

# CHAPTER
## Twenty-Three

## Liam



Beginning to think that your Mystery Woman doesn't exist! Effie said to tell you that we want to meet her and won't take no for an answer! Let's have dinner tonight? All six of us. Come to Brooklyn unless you have other plans?

Groaning, Liam knew he shouldn't have opened his messages first thing in the morning. Now Josh would see that he had read the text, pestering him until he answered.



No can do today, Cuz. Taking my Mystery Woman to see the Rockettes at Radio City this afternoon, and don't want to plan around that. Does tomorrow work for all of you?

His Mystery Woman made a soft snore as she turned in bed, tossing an arm across his bare stomach. Wrapping honeyed tendrils of her hair around his fingers, he wondered at her ability to look absolutely angelic while sleeping, considering the magically sinful acts she had performed with him last night. His surprise for her had been fourth row orchestra seats to the ballet, in the dead center. When he had escorted her up the stairs that led from the sidewalk to the theatre at Lincoln Center, she had pulled back once they got to the top. Almost frozen in place, she had asked, "What are we doing here?"

He had gently drawn her to him and responded, "Your surprise this evening is *The Nutcracker*! Have you ever seen it?" Hesitating for a brief second, she shook her head "no". "That's what I was hoping. There was a part of me earlier today that was nervous that maybe you wouldn't want to come to a ballet. I bought these tickets right after I planned my trip, so I have been looking forward to tonight for a month. I never imagined myself as a 'ballet' kind of guy, but they say the right woman will inspire a man to do almost anything." Liam, prior to that babbling moment with his Mystery Woman, had always prided himself on saying exactly the right thing, and keeping cool if he couldn't, but something about her silence had unsettled him.

He had been about to continue with his stream of consciousness when he heard her murmur, "Thank you." Looking down at her, he could have sworn she had tears in her eyes as she said more audibly, "Thank you. So much. This is truly one of the most thoughtful things anyone has ever done." Then she had smiled broadly at him, with the tiniest of tears escaping the corner of her eye, and told him, "I can't wait to see it."

Prouder than any other moment in his life (including *finally* graduating from NYU), he had held the door for her to walk through into the theatre. She was an ethereal goddess, oblivious to the looks other men cast her way. Based on throwaway comments he had heard her make since the first night he had spent with her, he knew she didn't understand or appreciate her own sexual power. Although she tried to hide it, he could see the haunting vulnerability lurking just beneath her surface. Having been with enough women to recognize how chaste she was, her lack of artifice floored him, and her tender yet enthusiastic touches electrified his body in ways he had never experienced until her. Humbling him was the knowledge that she wanted to spend not just her nights, but also her days, with him.

After *The Nutcracker* had ended, with her cheeks pink from exhilaration, he escorted his Mystery Woman across the avenues to Central Park, where he had made reservations at Tavern on the Green for dinner following the show. Another gasp from her once they had stepped inside the restaurant had convinced him he had made the correct choice. "Have you ever been here?" he had inquired. When he had been in college, he had met many students whose families lived in or close to the city yet had not availed themselves of all there was to do here, so Liam had vowed to make no assumptions concerning his Mystery Woman.

With a small laugh, she had answered, "Definitely not. I've walked by it during the day a few times, when I've been in the park, but this is beyond anything I could have imagined." Passing an enormous Christmas tree as their hostess took them to their table outside, his date stopped for a second to marvel at it. "Oh, my—this is so beautiful," she had announced with what sounded like awe. What was beautiful, in Liam's eyes, was her wonder with the world and everything she encountered. Threading his fingers tightly with hers, he patiently waited for her to soak it all in.

After the hostess had seated them at a table near an outdoor heater, Liam had stood up to help her out of her coat, draping it around her shoulders in case she was chilled. "Are you comfortable here? I can check to see if they have any tables inside." Fervently hoping she would decline his courteous offer, the sight of her illuminated by the shining lights stole his breath. Outshining even the Christmas tree, it dumbfounded him that she had been alone in that bar the first time he had seen her. What kind of idiot stood up a woman like her?

"No, I'm fine," she assured him with a smile. "I feel so awkward right now, though."

"Why? You are clearly the most stunning woman alive tonight," Liam told her, with more sincerity than he had ever used in his thirty-five years. Reaching across their table, he laced her fingers with his, bringing her hands up to his mouth so he could bestow kisses across her knuckles.

With her eyes sparkling, she responded, "No, I just question what I have done to deserve all of this, when I don't even know your name. I know I'm the one who keeps insisting on keeping it anonymous, but after everything you've done...your kindness and generosity, I—"

"Hey," he interrupted, "names would never make this more special. Who cares what my name is? I know a couple who fell in love without knowing each other's names. Now they're married and conquering the world together—or at least their own slice of Brooklyn." He was ready, though—ready to divulge every single thing about himself to her. Ready to move to New York, if he needed; ready to start over, using his business degree in a different way than just selling cars back home. Or, if she was interested in a change of location, ready to welcome her to his house in Beverley. "Just say the word and I will lasso the moon for you, nameless or not." And he would—he would do absolutely anything for this woman.

"That's not fair," she whispered, "you can't quote *It's a Wonderful Life* to me while also telling me about a real-life love story. Especially not on top of taking me to the ballet and now here for dinner." She clenched his hands in hers and looked lost for the moment. "I want to be with you, to tell you my name, but I'm just afraid to upset this delicate balance. I know that's stupid."

Shaking his head, Liam assured her, "I understand, and it's not stupid. What we have right now? It's magical, for both of us. And there's no rush for anything. Baby, all I need to know for now is that you are coming back to our hotel room with me tonight." Discreetly interrupting them, their server had approached their table for a drink order, and their dinner had deliciously progressed from there, as they shared a grilled octopus appetizer in a roasted lemon vinaigrette. Liam ordered the caramelized lamb chops for his entrée, and his enticing companion had chosen the Merlot-braised beef short ribs.

After dinner, the couple strolled arm in arm down to Columbus Circle, where horse-drawn carriages awaited passengers for rides through Central Park. Inspired, Liam approached a coachman, and after a back-and-forth between the two men, Liam whisked his Mystery Woman up into an emerald-green coach. Giving a surprised giggle, she asked, "What are you doing?"

Fervently, Liam responded, "Sweeping you off your feet, Darlin'. James is going to drive us back to the hotel in style."

Her large, dark blue eyes grew wider as she admitted, "No one's ever done this—swept me off my feet or granted me a carriage ride. I feel like a princess," she told him, softly.

"Not a princess—Baby, you are a queen." Kissing the hand he clasped in his, then drawing her to him, he covered them with the tartan blanket provided by James. Once Liam tucked them in, he slung his arm around her, sharing his body heat. Along the way back to their hotel, James attempted to point out landmarks, but gave up after realizing his efforts were fruitless since the couple only had eyes for each other. Liam heard him mutter "Lovers" and then he played "I'll Be Home for Christmas".

Curled under his arm, he heard a sigh and then she asked, "Okay, I'm not asking for specifics, but where *do* you live? Just give me a broad, general answer. Like I will tell you that my apartment is in lower Manhattan. There, I did it—volunteered personal information!" Stunned, Liam sat in silence, unable to believe that *she* had been the one to initiate this topic of conversation.

Breathing steadily, afraid she would change her mind and tell him to remain silent, he quietly answered, "The Midwest. I'm from the Midwest."

Smiling beguilingly, she leaned up, dove her hands into his hair and told him, "I was totally thinking California," before she kissed him.

"Really?" Liam asked her, perplexed she had picked up on a California vibe from him. If anything, he preferred the densely packed east coast if he considered living anywhere other than South Dakota, especially after going to college here in New York.

"Oh, yeah," she smiled at him. "Total surfer material."

Once back at the hotel, Liam lifted his Mystery Woman down from the carriage, keeping his hands on her hips as his lips brushed over hers. Moaning in response, she murmured, "Let's go to our room." After hanging up the ornament they had chosen together at the merchandise table in the theatre's lobby, a dancing Clara (in her nightgown, awaiting the arrival of her prince), Liam stroked the soft cheek of the woman who was making all of his dreams come true, and on a blanket made by their coats, he showed her how much she meant to him already. Later, looking up from underneath the tree, Liam envisioned it being decorated in five days with ornaments the two of them had picked out all over the city, in remembrance of their time together.

Reveling this morning in the feel of her body as she curled up on top of his chest, his Mystery Woman shifted in his arms, and he could not keep his hands from caressing her lush curves or stop his mouth from tasting her sweet skin. Seeing her in that green dress last night had almost undone him—the way the fabric draped, enhancing her womanly figure. He hadn't been exaggerating when he had told her she was stunning, but more than that, it was her cautious way of looking at the world that was drawing her into his heart. On more than one occasion, a family member or friend had accused Liam of being reckless, careless, too quick to jump into questionable scenarios or circumstances. Being with her, experiencing how she measured the world before acting, only highlighted how well the two of them fit together.

Fluttering fingertips flitted over his chest let him know his Mystery Woman had woken up. Liam shifted so his face was level with hers. "Hey, I wasn't done caressing your chest," she complained.

"No? Well, neither was I last night before you—" and with her mouth on his, she silenced the rest of his words, which was completely fine with him, because it afforded him the opportunity to begin skimming her thighs, and her answering moans told him of her approval. Would he ever get enough of her? Even now, after two days together? However, with just four days remaining, his impending departure loomed just beyond his current bliss.

Ensconced in their fluffy robes later that morning, they were lounging on the sofa near the Christmas tree. With room service coffee and everything bagels on the small coffee table in front of them, his Mystery Woman said, "I have a confession to make," as she spread jalapeno cream cheese on half of a bagel, "I wasn't completely honest last night."

Startled, Liam studied her flawless face, free from any guile as usual, asking her as lightly as possible, "What do you mean?" He reached for the other half of her bagel to stop himself from studying her.

"When you asked me if I had ever seen *The Nutcracker* before, and I told you no. It wasn't true." She hesitated now, as if caught between wanting to tell him more but not being sure how to, so he just gave her space and whatever time she might need. Slowly, she brought her coffee to her mouth and took a sip; Liam saw a small smile cross her face when she tasted it. He had prepared her coffee the way he liked his—sweet and with a heavy splash of cream. "My father took me once, when I was fifteen."

Putting his bagel back on the table, Liam held her as she told him about the history with her father, filling in the blanks from the Christmas present story she had told him two days ago. Having grown up watching his parents be outwardly affectionate with each other, clearly still in love after almost forty years of marriage (according to his mom, she still fell more in love every day), it pained Liam to hear her words laced with the pain she undoubtedly continued to feel. Experiencing that genuine commitment in his life was likely the biggest reason Liam remained chronically single (Josh's words, not Liam's). What he wanted was a love that knew no distance, no time, no boundaries. Often, Liam's dad would come home from being nowhere fantastic, yet somehow always managing to find some small gift to surprise his mom with; seeing her eyes light up with joy at his dad's thoughtfulness had made Liam (at six, or ten, or seventeen) consider what it was like to be truly happy with a partner. And it wasn't just his dad, either—no, his mom, somehow knowing when George had had a particularly stressful day at the auto shop, would make him his favorite supper, treating him after he finally washed off the grime and grease from his manual labor. Or Nora would plan date nights for the two of them, arranging for Liam and Cait, when they were young, to stay at a cousin's house or with their grandparents. Small tokens or grand gestures, his parents were unashamed to show their love.

Of course, while he had seen true devotion from his parents and his grandparents, he had been cognizant that not every family was a happy one, with his cousin Josh as a prime example. He and his cousin had always been close, and watching the devastation that Josh's mom had wreaked when she had left Josh and his dad had shattered Liam.

"Even though I was living with my dad and his new wife, there were so many times I could tell that she didn't want me there," his Mystery Woman confessed, her words and the angst behind them kicking him in his gut. Who could not want this ray of sunshine around? Her smile lit up every room she entered. "He must have felt it, too, or known it, because he started doing little things for just the two of us and taking me to *The Nutcracker* was one of those special moments. I remember, though, when we got home that night, my stepmom was upset at how late we were and clearly annoyed at how much money my dad had spent on the tickets. You see, even though my dad earned his money working in construction, she never had to work for hers—her money came from being a rich widow."

Liam's heart ached for the girl who, it sounded like, had wanted the unconditional love only her father could give her. "She sounds like a head case, if you want my opinion. I'm sorry you had to go through that, Darlin'. I'm sure it wasn't easy being away from your own mom." As she shook her head no, he shifted on the sofa, stretching out his long legs, and then scooted her back to nestle her against his chest, doing his best to lend her his strength so she could tell him whatever she wanted.

Relaxing into him, he heard her say softly, "It was hard being away, but honestly, it was my sisters and my brother I felt sorry for, though, even when I hated living with my stepmom. None of them got to experience what I did with my dad—they only saw him as someone who had abandoned them not once, but twice. My brother bore the brunt of it, though. My dad criticized everything he did, and to me, my brother was my hero. Has always been my hero. Monty works so hard—he's always had, like, four jobs at a time. If anyone needs anything, he is there to help them, no matter who it is. And he's so smart, but he wasn't given the chance to go to college. And the way he can fix everything?" She gave a small laugh and told Liam, "I told you how I am moving soon? Well, Monty has already figured out which truck he is going to bring, and he's lined up a bunch of his buddies to help. He always takes care of every-thing." So relaxed was she that she hadn't even realized she had used her brother's name, and Liam grew warmer.

Compared to her brother, who sounded like a paragon of virtue, the more he thought of it, Liam found himself to be inadequate once again. Would his own sister ever speak of him with such reverence? Feeling the need to distract her and draw her mind back to him, Liam said boldly, "Baby, I'm here now, ready to take on all of your needs." And his hands found the tie to her robe and slowly unknotted it. Just before it opened, she twisted in his arms, pressing her soft curves into his chest.

She pulled her knees up to straddle him on the sofa and, as her dark blue eyes glittered with desire, she asked, "You know what I need right now?"

Liam groaned as he stroked her hips, thinking of at least fifty needs he had, all of them requiring her to be divested of the robe she still wore. She kissed him passionately, then licked his neck before putting her lips to his ear. "I need to be in that tub again, with you, covered in bubbles, getting clean and then getting dirty and then—"

TEXT FROM EFFIE

Ignoring us while we are all in NYC together? So Liam-coded…

# CHAPTER
## Twenty-Four

*Effie*



TEXT FROM HAMILTON

Hey, Sis, I know Mom called you last night about Dad. Don't worry, he's doing better today. Drs say it was just angina, but they will keep him in the hospital overnight. Mom wants you to stay and have fun in NYC. Tell Josh I installed that basketball hoop at your place and am ready to take him on when you guys get back. Peace out

TEXT TO MOM

Hi, Mom, tried calling you earlier but I guess you're at the hospital. Ham texted and gave me an update. Are you sure we shouldn't just come home? Love you. Give Burnie a hug from me.

Until her mom had called last night about Effie's stepdad, Burnside Van Holland, Effie and Josh had been having a wonderful time exploring New York City for the past two days. Diadema always held tight control over her emotions, so when Effie heard her mom so upset on the phone, frantic and in tears, she had almost become hysterical as well. Luckily, Josh had been right beside Effie to speak with the cardiologist concerning Burnside's condition. Apparently, he had been having chest pains all day, and Diadema had finally convinced her husband to go to the emergency room in the small hospital in their hometown of Clover Lake; from there, an ambulance had transported Burnside to the cardiac hospital in Sioux Falls. Coincidentally, Josh had just finished a three-month rotation at the cardiac hospital, where he had worked closely with the cardiologist treating Burnside. Driving two hours every day from Beverley to Sioux Falls, Effie had worried about Josh being on the road in inclement weather, but now she was so thankful for the time he spent with, and the care he gave to, his patients, and his exquisite attention to detail. However, she was anticipating this spring, when he would finish his residency altogether and work only at the hospital in Beverley.

"Effie, are you sure you don't want to head back to Sioux Falls? I can see how worried you are about your mom." Her love...her Josh. His long, powerful arms drew her to him and held her close as they stood in the spare bedroom at Tess and Sam's house in Brooklyn. Immediately after the phone call last night, Josh had insisted they return home, desperate to do anything to alleviate any anxiety Effie was feeling. Simultaneously, Josh had also reassured her that Burnside was in the best hands with his care team in Sioux Falls, telling her the angina was not life-threatening, and by the time they made it back home, her stepdad would already be out of the hospital and back to his regular life.

"Speaking of my mom, she just sent me this text." Effie held her phone out for Josh to read.

TEXT FROM MOM

Darling Euphemie, please don't worry yourself. Burnside is getting the best treatment here, probably because Joshua is so important! You would not believe how people respond when I tell them that my daughter is practically married to the brilliant surgeon, Dr. Joshua Livingston. Anyway, your brother has been a saint, bringing me coffee and food.

"Brilliant, huh?" Josh stroked the sides of her neck with his graceful surgeon's fingers, as he tilted her face up to his, kissing her until she was breathless. "I'm relieved to see your mom write about me in such high esteem, although in the next sentence she does refer to your brother as a saint, so there goes her credibility." With her hands framing his face—the caring face that had first drawn her in as a teenager—she then kissed him, returning every ounce of love she had in her body for him.

"You're forgetting 'important' as well, my love," she pointed out to him, undoing the top button of his shirt.

"Diadema does make another good point: 'practically married'. When are we going to take care of that bit?" Josh teased her as he tossed her phone onto the bed behind him. Last spring, after fleeing her broken marriage in Denver, Effie had moved back to South Dakota, humiliated and her spirit broken. Leaving everything behind—husband, friends, apartment, and librarian job—she had found all she was seeking back in her home state. Although she and Josh were living together in the house Effie had bought last summer, that was as far as their commitment to each other had gone, and that was enough for both of them. For the time being. Neither Effie nor Josh was eager to rush the progression of the relationship, yet it was openly acknowledged, by everyone in *and* out of their immediate circle, that they would, indeed, be married someday.

Effie's hands traveled the length of his torso, aware that Tess and Sam were out of the house and working, which meant she could get as loud as she wanted with Josh right now. And she loved to scream the house down when she was with him, because he was so *very* thorough in giving her what she wanted. As she unhurriedly unbuttoned the remaining buttons of his sky-blue Oxford shirt, she murmured, "Have I ever told you how sexy I think you are in these shirts?" She kissed his chest after opening each button. "So professional, so doctor-y, so much more complicated than wearing a simple pull-on shirt," she breathed over his skin as her nails raked his chest. "How you stand there—half dressed, half undressed with your shirt open, Dr. Livingston. All you're missing is a tie, because then I could—"

Suddenly she found herself lifted, with his strong, desirable hands cupping her bottom, bringing her flush with his body. Wrapping her legs around his waist, twining her fingers in his hair (hair that he had grown out a bit after Effie commented on the attractive waves of blond that curled around his ears), she moaned into his mouth—growled would probably be a more precise term for her sound, though. So many people thought of Josh as staid or uptight (even he had declared himself boring on more than one occasion), but Effie didn't agree with any of those adjectives. Instead of staid, he was reliable; instead of uptight, he was intelligent; and instead of boring, he was exciting, caring, thoughtful, resourceful. And he was just so fucking hot.

Josh carefully lowered her to the bed, and she protested as he separated himself from her, but only to remove his clothing, and then he was back on top of her, slipping her ugly Christmas sweater from her prone body. "Careful with that..I *am* wearing it later," she warned him, laughing at the grimace on his face. Effie had chosen the neon-green sweater, with its large pink Christmas tree front and center, right between her breasts, because she knew it would drive him crazy for two reasons: 1—the tackiness of the sewn-on ornaments that hung limply from an inch of thread, and 2—he had to focus on her breasts whenever he looked at her. Well, he wouldn't *have* to, but she knew her man well enough to know that he would not resist. Her jeans were the next item he removed, skillfully done with his mouth—Josh had gotten quite good at removing her clothes without using his hands at all. Really, he should get some kind of award for his dedication and precision, she thought with a giggle.

"Really?" he asked, making eye contact with her as his mouth kissed a line from her ankles to her waist. "You're laughing at a time like this? I guess I need to try a little harder to get you to be serious," and then she added "determined" to the list of things she loved about him, and stared at his hands against her thighs, the difference in their skin tones making her burn even more. Josh had the paler skin his blond hair and sky-blue eyes belied, whereas Effie's half-Lakota heritage gave her flesh a golden-brown hue. Her neck arched then, causing her straight-black tresses to fly across the pillow, and she closed her tawny eyes and gave herself over to Josh completely.

When Effie woke up with her head on Josh's solid chest sometime later, her thoughts went back to her mom and stepdad, whose marriage Effie had always seen as safe and rather unexciting, until a few months ago when her mom had opened up to her about it. Diadema had confided in her daughter how meeting Burnside had helped her heal from the incredible loss she suffered after Effie's beloved biological father, Nathaniel, had died. Taken from his wife and young daughter too soon, Nathaniel, a member of the Grass Valley Lakota tribe, had perished in a car accident when Effie was only five years old, and she only had a few treasured memories of him from her childhood. Effie's relationship with her stepfather had not always been an easy one, but as she had gotten older, he had become a better father to her, and over the past year, during which she had faced her toughest challenges, he had proven to be a vital thread in her support system.

Feeling Josh stir underneath her, she knew she needed to get dressed again or they would never make it into Manhattan. Yesterday, their plan had been to go to Union Square and possibly Bryant Park to the Christmas markets at each place, but after a morning spent in bed, they only made it as far as exploring Green-Wood Cemetery with Sam. They had watched red-tailed hawks soaring in the blue skies above the barren trees and walked up to Battle Hill, the highest natural point in Brooklyn. Standing on the hill beside the statue of her sister, Minerva, they had waved to the Statue of Liberty in the harbor. Later in the day, once Tess had closed the bakery, the foursome had driven over to Dyker Heights, a neighborhood in Brooklyn known for their over-the-top Christmas lights and decorations. Effie had seen nothing quite like the festive displays, as they had strolled with the massive crowd down the streets, carrying their hot cocoas purchased from ice cream trucks, repurposed for the winter season. From there, the two couples had gone to L&B Spumoni Gardens, located in Gravesend, a different Brooklyn neighborhood. Baked clams, so buttery and garlicky, with perfectly crisp breadcrumbs on top had been the appetizer, followed by square slices of Sicilian pizza, with the most mouth-watering tomato sauce Effie had ever eaten in her life topping the thick slices of pizza covered in mozzarella. For dessert, she and Tess had chosen the spumoni, an Italian ice cream with three flavors: chocolate, cherry, and pistachio, while Sam and Josh had each ordered lemon Italian ice, that was so tartly delicious she almost ordered a serving for herself after finishing her spumoni.

Listening to Coldplay's "Christmas Lights" while they redressed—

Effie in her jeans and Christmas sweater and Josh in his dress shirt and khakis—he asked her, "Do you think Liam is deliberately avoiding us while we're here?"

"What?" Effie looked at Josh, wondering about his question. "What makes you think that?"

"Well, one of my texts yesterday went completely unanswered, when I asked him about going to Dyker Heights, and then this morning, I asked him to come to Brooklyn for dinner tonight, but he claims they're going to the Rockettes at some vague time this afternoon that he refused to be specific about. So what if it's this afternoon? They could still come for dinner, couldn't they?" Josh tossed a pair of socks into the corner, his tone of voice startling Effie —almost like he was offended by Liam. While the cousins could butt heads occasionally, she knew how much they adored each other. At times, though, they could be *too* much in each other's business, particularly Josh, who tended to "want the best for Liam", which could come across as controlling. Sometimes.

"Sweetie," she told Josh, walking over to pick up his socks, "I don't know why you are taking any of this personally. He clearly came to New York to shack up for the week with his mystery woman. Who knows what the hell they're up to, but if it's anything like us," she winked at Josh as he looked up at her approach, "all they are seeing is the inside of the hotel room. We had a lot on our agenda yesterday, but didn't get out of this house until later in the afternoon. And look at us today—it's almost eleven and here we are: putting our clothes on for the second time this morning."

Josh sighed and agreed. "I guess you're right. I just have a weird feeling about his 'Mystery Woman'. It's almost as if he's hiding her— what is there to hide? Or maybe she is the one hiding something?"

Effie laughed, "Oh, really, Mr. I Share Everything?" Effie bent over to kiss his cheek and handed him his socks. "I just think that if he is as crazy for her as he has said he is for the past four months, then he only wants to be with her while he is here. Look, his whole situation is very Liam-coded. He wants what he wants, and clearly what he wants is this woman. Just let Liam do Liam. After all, they only have this week together, so it makes sense they would hole up in whatever posh hotel room he treated her to."

Josh rose to his feet and grabbed Effie to him. "Is that a jab at me for staying here for free with our friends?" And he wiggled his eyebrows at her to show her he was joking, and she chuckled.

"Correction: we're staying with your college frat brother and your ex-fiancée. Although Sam is phenomenal and I can totally see why Tess fell in love—" and Effie squealed when Josh picked her up and tossed her back on the bed. "I must admit that Tess clearly has good taste. Not much sense as far as I can tell, though."

"Oh, no?" Josh questioned.

"Look what she tossed aside, and for that I am forever in her debt," Effie told Josh, framing his face in her hands, completely earnest now. She and Ruth, Tess's sister, had struck up a wonderful friendship since Ruth had moved back to Beverley; because of that (and since Tess was Josh's ex), Effie had been eager to get to know Tess. Over the past couple of days, she could now count Tess as a friend. Some people may think it odd that here they were—all staying in the same house, but to Effie, it all made perfect sense. Unlike what Tess had told her yesterday: that Lana, Josh's ex co-worker, was moving in to the apartment next month. From the little Josh had told her, she had gotten the idea that Lana had not really cared for Tess, undoubtedly because she had feelings for Josh.

Helping Effie into her coat, Josh said, "The thing about Liam is that I have seen him in all kinds of relationships, but what he's doing right now? This is new, and frankly, I'm concerned for him. What if he gets his heart broken?"

"You really think that is going to happen?" Effie asked. "I guess my only reference for Liam in a relationship is from high school, when I would see him with you at the pool or around Clover Lake. He always had some girl he was flirting with, or who was hanging all over him. When was the last time he had a girlfriend? He hasn't even dated anyone since we've been together, right?"

Josh shook his head and slid his arms into his own wool coat. "That's what I'm talking about! Liam loves having a girlfriend, even if they don't last beyond a few months—so for him to not have even *dated* since his last visit here? I don't know if that's a sign of growth or a cause for concern."

TEXT TO LIAM

Can you manage to break away from your love nest to meet up with us? Your cousin is worried about you! Also, guess who might meet the famous Lana tomorrow? That's right—me! Josh is trying to set something up with her at the hospital—I guess she has to work. Rumor has it that it's right around the corner from you…. I might need you to distract her attention from Josh.

TEXT FROM LIAM

Calm down there, the big guy is all yours! As for getting together, I just texted your man and we will come to Brooklyn tmrw night!

I just used the most !!! In my life!

Until then, I may potentially be free during the day tmrw. I think my Mystery Woman has to work.

# CHAPTER
## Twenty-Five

*Lana*



Reluctantly, Lana crawled out of bed minutes before her alarm went off at five in the morning, cursing her shortsightedness in believing that she would be fine working this one day in the middle of her week off. How had she *ever* imagined she would welcome a break from him, or that they would embrace the time apart today? After blindly stumbling to the hotel bathroom, she stood under the hot spray from the shower, letting the pellets of water try their hardest to wake her up. Mere seconds later, firm hands surprised her by slicking over her wet skin.

"You didn't think I was going to let you leave me this morning without saying goodbye, did you?" His husky voice nearly buckling her knees as he breathed into her ear. He then braced her between his tall form and the tiled wall of the walk-in shower, thus saving from collapsing. Turning in his arms, she placed her own hands on his biceps, wondering if they had gotten their girth from lifting weights or some form of manual labor requiring him to lift heavy objects frequently. Ever in awe of the power he exuded, sexually, she thrilled at how different he was from every other man she had ever been attracted to. Granted, she had never been in a serious relationship with anyone, or even exclusively dated, but the types of men she *had* casually dated were more like, say, Josh: intense, intelligent, introspective. This man, her Hook Up, was expressive, energetic, ebullient. Nothing seemed complicated when she was with him, and that was part of her attraction to him.

Yesterday had been another magnificent day with her Hook Up, beginning with waking up in his arms under the Christmas tree, and then sharing the bagel breakfast, when she had trusted him enough to tell him about her dad. The temptation to be vulnerable with him was proving relentless, and she was gradually becoming more relaxed about it. Seeing the Rockettes at Radio City Music Hall fulfilled a lifetime wish for her. Almost her entire life, living on Long Island, she had heard other kids talking about seeing the Christmas Spectacular; when she had lived with her dad, she had begged him to take her, but he saw it as "common" and refused her pleas—the night at *The Nutcracker* had been his way of compromising. Finally, though, her dream had come true, because of her Hook Up. Gasping when they stepped inside Radio City, it had been Lana's first time inside the landmark theatre. Filled with the glamour of a bygone era (much how Lana usually saw herself), the Art Deco building was spectacular, from the sweeping mural in the high-ceilinged foyer to the grand staircase. The chandeliers and the marble were breathtaking, and Lana had almost given herself whiplash as she tried to take it all in. Together, they had chosen their ornament for their hotel tree, and it depicted the Rockettes in their famous Parade of the Wooden Soldiers. Lana had been giddy at the performance, never more so than when her Hook Up had reached over to lace his fingers with hers. His thumb grazed across her knuckles before smoothing the skin on the inside of her palm, causing her to shiver every time. Lana had become too warm at one point, and when she had tried to shrug her arms out of her cardigan, he had leaned over to help her, draping it around her shoulders once her arms were free, whispering in her ear then: "Nothing I love more than getting you out of your clothes, Darlin'." Heaven help her, if he had suggested they leave the performance early (despite how much she was enjoying it), she would have led the way.

Following their show, they had walked around the block to Rockefeller Center to see the famous Christmas tree, along with about a million other people, but unlike most New Yorkers, she hadn't minded the crowd. Every year since she had lived in the city, Lana made it a point to visit the tree, usually when one, some, or all, of her family members were in town. Even as a child, once her brother got his driver's license, he would drive at least Lana and their mom into the city one night during the holiday season; after parking the car, they would walk to the tree, visit St. Patrick's Cathedral, watch the light display on the outside facade of the Saks Fifth Avenue building, and then meander down to Thirty-Fourth Street and Sixth Avenue to Macy's at Herald Square. Occasionally, one or both of Lana's sisters would join them, until Ava's daughters were born, making it impossible for everyone to fit inside Monty's vehicle.

Traveling the same path with her Hook Up as she had with her family, they stopped to watch the light show at Saks Fifth Avenue. Somehow managing to wedge them up to the front of the barricades lining Fifth Avenue, he stood behind her, engulfing her in his arms, and the heat from his body warmed her so she barely felt the frigid air. Their tour of Midtown had ended, or so Lana believed, until he had directed them from Macy's up to Keen's, one of the oldest steakhouses in New York City, a place Lana had never eaten, but her brother had. When Monty had graduated from high school, their father had taken him to dinner there, a tradition Thomas claimed he would do with each of his children upon their graduations, but that had been the only time, because the following week, Thomas deserted his family.

Despite of the bad feelings the restaurant could have stirred up in her, Lana refused to let it. Instead, her dinner at Keen's had been nothing short of gastronomic perfection, as the couple feasted on oysters, clams, Caesar salad, and chateaubriand steak for two, plus a bottle of red wine. Too stuffed for dessert, Lana had taken his hand to lead him out of the restaurant. Once outside, she drew him around the corner of the restaurant, pulled down on the lapels of his jacket, and fused her mouth with his. "Do you know how much I want you?" Lana had murmured to him sultrily, both desire and wine making her words bold. In the dark, her hands had unzipped his jacket and slipped inside, untucking his shirt so she could caress his honed chest. Relishing in the feel of his hot skin and the way his chest hair tickled her fingers, she grinned when he shivered from her touch.

Groaning, he had muttered, "Baby, if it's half as much as I want you, we're both in trouble." Hastily, he had hailed a cab, and they climbed into the back. Unable to control herself, Lana had passionately kissed him as soon as her Hook Up had given the hotel address to the driver, then twisted her body so her chest had pressed firmly against his. Not long after, she had been aware of the hem of her knee-length skirt being raised, and one of his large hands stroking the outside of her thigh through her wool tights. Mindless to anything but her own sensual craving for him, when he had pulled her onto his lap, she straddled him. Over and over, her mouth had devoured his, until her lips kissed a line down his sexy throat. His cheeks and chin had grown rough with a beard that late in the day, and as the bristles had scraped against her own sensitive skin, she gripped the curls at the back of his head. When Lana moaned into his mouth, both of his hands had moved so his fingers feathered over the insides of her thighs.

Unaware of the cab stopping, the pair had continued kissing, until a voice called urgently, "EXCUSE ME!", followed by a loud clearing of the driver's throat.

"Oh my god, kill me now," she had groaned, sliding off onto the seat next to her and burying her head in her hands. What had come over her? Before this week, she would never have imagined she would be astride him, ready to do almost anything in the back of that cab. Her Hook Up had handed the driver a wad of bills, clearly too impatient to run his credit card through the machine, and Lana wondered if he knew or even cared how much money the ride had cost. Opening the door to the cab, she had heard the driver remark to them as they exited, "That was one of the best shows I've seen in a long time—I wish every couple I picked up was as in love as you two."

Lana had looked at her Hook Up, unsure if he was as uneasy with the man's words as she was, but she had found him smiling down at her before he had ushered them through the hotel lobby and swiftly into the elevator.

The memories of last night were making it exceedingly difficult to concentrate on preparing to leave him for the day, but as she twisted her hair into a French braid, Lana transformed from the "Mystery Woman" he knew her to be into the exacting surgeon she actually was. She slipped into a simple navy dress, and in the reflection of the mirror, he stared at her from behind. Turning her to face him, he told her, "You're so beautiful," as he cupped her cheeks in his hands. "Even with only the Christmas lights on, I can see how the color of your dress matches your eyes." She covered his hands with her own, opening her mouth as his lips met hers. "How will I survive the city without you today?"

"I should be back around five, okay? Then I'm all yours again," she said as she reluctantly broke away to put on her shoes.

He snapped his fingers, then said, "Speaking of five, I forgot to mention that my cousin wants to get together tonight for dinner. He has asked me every day since we've been here, but I keep putting him off. I think he's beginning to think I made you up," he said with a small laugh. At her silence, he added, "Remember, I told you I was traveling with my cousin and his girlfriend?"

All Lana had focused on was only his arrival since he had announced he was coming to New York, but she somewhat vaguely recalled him mentioning a cousin would also be in New York. "Umm, I'm not sure," she responded hesitantly. Why was he pushing for this? The last thing Lana wanted was to share him this evening, especially after being away from him all day.

Pulling her to him, he asked playfully, "Not sure I told you about them or not sure about dinner?"

With a small laugh, she kissed him on the cheek, rougher than it had been last night, and said distractedly, "Both?" At his crestfallen look, she added, "I'm sorry. I know you told me about your cousin, but I just think I might be too tired tonight." Not entirely true, as she was always completely energized at the end of a shift, but he was flipping their script on her—meeting with family? This had not been what they had talked about.

"No problem, I understand." He didn't sound as if he understood, though...he sounded as if he was disappointed. Then he raised his gorgeous eyebrows at her (really, it was a crime he had such perfect brows) and said, "Maybe I could have them meet up for lunch instead? You must get a lunch break, right? We could join you somewhere."

How could she meet him for lunch? That would require telling him she worked at the hospital, which he may have already narrowed down. Not only that, but she was already planning on meeting Josh during her break, and there was no way she was going to introduce these two men. Lana had already sacrificed her dignity at the altar of Josh too many times. Why couldn't he be happy with just the two of them? Why was he asking for more? He had to have known this would be uncomfortable for her—what if she were to ask *him* to go out to Long Island and have a meal with *her* family? Now she stood here, being evasive, inventing reasons she could not meet for lunch or dinner with his cousin. Part of her wished she *could* have lunch with everyone—this man in her arms, Josh, and his girlfriend. Breaking out of his hold as delicately as she could, she then told him, "I'm meeting up with an old coworker today. I'm sorry."

Taking one last look in the mirror, she smoothed her hands down her braid, making sure no hairs were escaping. Her Hook Up sighed then. "I get it. You're too busy for lunch." Was it her imagination, or did she glimpse hurt in his eyes as she met them in the mirror? Had she gotten this all wrong? "I will just have to spend the day alone with every fantasy I have about you." Watching in the mirror as he wrapped his arms around her from behind, she stood mesmerized as his head dropped and his tongue traced her pounding pulse on her neck. "Are you sure about dinner, though? We can make it an early evening, take the subway out to Brooklyn, eat a slice of pizza or whatever they had planned?" His hands spanned up her chest as her head dropped back, and she fell under his intoxicating tone. "Please?" He nuzzled her earlobe now. "My cousin's girlfriend texted me saying he was bummed, and trust me when I tell you that he can be a bit of a downer, anyway. Let's show them how much fun we're having—easy, breezy, no strings fun." At her dazed nod of agreement, he added, "They don't expect much more from me, anyway."

And there was something in his tone, more so than the words, that made her turn to him and agree to his request for the evening. "Okay, I will gladly go with you and have dinner with your cousin and his girlfriend." Seeing the relief cross his handsome face, and the devilish grin that came after, she surmised it was possible he had just played her, knowing all along that he would use his very considerable wiles to get her to agree to this plan of his. "Brooklyn, though?"

He shrugged nonchalantly and said, "Didn't you say that you were moving there? This'll be good for you—like a practice run," and then kissed her on the forehead.

TEXT FROM JOSH

Excellent! We will see you there!

# CHAPTER
## Twenty-Six

## Josh



I hope you two are enjoying your trip. You deserve a vacation, son.

Any news about Burnside?

I feel terrible for Effie. She deserves nothing but the best.

Give her my love, would you? I've been thinking of her mother, wondering if I should give her a call?



I'll tell Effie all of the above. Having a wonderful time. Tess and Sam are doing great. I'm thrilled for both of them. I guess things always work out like they should. Yeah, terrible about Burnside, but he's doing really well. He'll be going home tomorrow and only in overnight for observation. Love from Effie. And from me.

Should he feel awkward walking into his old stomping grounds, Lenox Hill Hospital? Josh pondered. Just a couple months shy of a year since he had imploded, it was a bit surreal to be here now, he admitted to himself. When everything had blown up back then: his relationship with Tess, his relationship with Sam, his relationship with Lana, and his relationship with his career. Josh could never have imagined he would regain all the losses in his life and be a better person because of them. Sure, those relationships had changed and morphed in ways he could never have imagined, but Josh would argue they were for the better, for everyone involved. Including his career trajectory. Moving back to South Dakota enabled him to forge a new direction for his future in surgery while also living a more balanced life. Admittedly, he had been the problem back then, not the hospital or his career, lacking both balance and focus with both. Looking to his right, down at the hand holding his, he saw his guiding angel, his reason for calm, the love of his life. With Effie by his side, her support and belief in him overshadowed any difficulties he experienced. Knowing Henry and Diadema had some history that went all the way back to high school, Josh decided not to encourage his dad to call Effie's mom.

TEXT FROM DAD

In other news, I have been thinking of putting myself out there, maybe joining a dating service? It's so hard to meet someone when you're my age. Maybe I shouldn't have waited so long.

Love, Dad

After getting into the hospital elevator, Josh showed Effie the texts from his dad. "Oh, wow, you go, Henry!" Effie laughed. "Your dad should date again! He is quite a catch for any woman—so considerate and soft-spoken. Not to mention *still* so good-looking. Makes me look forward to how you will look in twenty years," she told Josh as her soft lips kissed his cheek. "Send him my love. It's so sweet he is thinking about my mom—I'm sure she would love to hear from him. Hmm, I may have an idea for your dad. There's a high school teacher who's been coming to the library—her name is Charlotte. She teaches English, and I get the vibe from her that she would be perfect for Henry. Ooh, I should text Ruth, see if she knows her." Heaven help his dad if not only Effie was interested in his dad's love life, but now Ruth? The two women were unstoppable.

TEXT TO DAD

What about that woman who brought her Jeep in? You said she stopped in another time, too? You kind of hinted there could be something there.

Or, Effie says she could fix you up with the high school English teacher…

Pocketing his phone as the hospital elevator opened on the cafeteria level, he chuckled when Effie commented, "Wow, smells good up here. I can't wait to hear all the stories about getting together with the gang after some tough surgery, hashing out everything that could have gone sideways but didn't." Josh flinched, since he actually *had* performed one of those surgeries that could have gone terribly wrong, and it was still a sore point for him. Effie, ever-observant while also being stunning, gasped, "Oh, Babe—I'm sorry. Thoughtless comment while I'm trying to be funny." She tugged on his hand and pulled him to the side of the entrance to the cafe. "Forgive me?" Her tawny eyes stared into his from just a few inches lower.

"Always," he responded seriously, knowing she would never intentionally hurt him. Months ago, he had convinced himself to see his error in the operating room as a learning moment instead of one to be ashamed of. After he kissed her on her smooth forehead, he told her, "You've been watching too much *Grey's Anatomy*, though."

Effie gasped, responding, "Shut your mouth! All my tv doctor knowledge comes from ER—I'll take Dr. Mark Greene any day of the week."

And her response was exactly why he loved this woman with every breath in his body. "For that answer, I will let you in on a little secret about this cafe: they purportedly have the best banana bread in the city."

Effie's eyebrows raised, and Josh knew her well enough to know she would have some of that banana bread—she loved bananas, and she loved trying any food deemed "best of". "Ooh, come to mama, then, because I am starving. Should we find a seat or get our food?" Effie hummed along to "Home for the Holidays" while she scanned the crowded dining room of the cafe. "Do you see Lana?" He knew Effie was excited to meet Lana, since Josh had told her about their past friendship. Josh held Lana in high regard, had even felt protective of her during her first year of residency. Being a surgical resident was one of the most high-pressure positions in a teaching hospital, and he had recognized her natural gift for medicine and care towards every patient as something to preserve. During his five years at the hospital, he had witnessed a dozen surgical residents either change to another focus or drop out of the program entirely, and he hadn't wanted that outcome for Lana. His younger colleague had a vulnerability that she had tried to mask with guarded comments about her personal life, but Josh knew that Effie would be gentle with Lana, because the woman holding his hand had a way with people—she was trustworthy and sincere, completely without guile.

Instead of seeing Lana, a second glance around the room offered up a different familiar face, sitting in the far corner of the cafeteria—that of his friend, Cal. Josh and Cal had gone to med school together, and the man had been a lifesaver after he and Tess had broken up a year ago. Cal, recently divorced last year and sharing custody of his daughter with his wife, had allowed Josh to stay in his second bedroom after Josh had moved out of his shared apartment with Tess. Overstaying his welcome last year, Josh had almost messed up that friendship. Cal had forgiven all since then, so after Josh pointed him out to Lana, the two of them approached his table.

Doing a double take as Josh greeted him, Cal exclaimed, "Oh, my god —Josh Livingston!" Leaping out of his seat to hug him, Cal followed it with heartily patting him on the back. "What the hell? Last time I heard from you, you weren't sure if you were going to make it up here while you were in town." Cal looked over to Effie and surmised, "And this has to be the enchanting Effie?"

Effie reached out to Cal for a hug after he simply offered her his hand. "Cal, it's so nice to meet you. Josh has told me so much about you —all good things, I promise," Effie joked, earning a laugh from each of the men. "I hear you have a completely gorgeous daughter, Cal."

Nothing Cal loved to talk more about than his daughter, so Josh wasn't surprised when Cal pulled up some recent photos on his phone to flash around. "I'm forgetting my manners—please, sit. Here, Josh, let me grab a chair from that table over there," Cal insisted, since there were only two chairs at his table.

Effie whispered to Josh as Cal borrowed a chair from the neighboring table, "You were right, he's very nice." Cal returned with the chair and held it out for Effie to sit in. "Thanks so much, Cal."

Cal shook his head, remarking, "I can't believe you're here, Josh. After you left last summer, I wasn't sure if I would ever see you again. What brings you to the hospital today?" Josh didn't answer immediately, because he was checking his phone for any communication from Lana, who he hadn't heard from since before six that morning. He heard Cal say excitedly, "Don't tell me you came here because you're moving back?"

Startled, Josh looked at his friend and burst out laughing. "Sorry to disappoint you, Cal, but no, I am not moving back." With a wink at Effie, Josh told Cal, "We're more than happy in Beverley—you should come visit sometime. Actually, we are supposed to be meeting with Lana."

"Oh, I thought I saw her just before you guys came over. Guess maybe she was looking for you because she just kind of breezed through here without saying anything to me," Cal told Josh with a shrug. "I always thought she was a bit of an odd duck, to be honest. Other than her taste in men, that is," Cal stated with a leering look at Josh.

Oh, no, Josh thought, not this. While Cal was generous and kind-hearted, he could also be a bit immature, a trait he had withheld from Effie. "What are you talking about?" he groaned, hoping Cal didn't say anything that would lead to Effie reevaluate Josh's taste in friends.

"Josh, seriously, remember how I warned you to not be alone with her in that office too much? I could tell from the moment you introduced me to her that she already had a thing for you." While speaking, Cal poked Josh in the arm, as if his statement needed any emphasis.

"Stop," Josh protested, worried that Lana could walk up at any minute. "It was never like that—we were always simply just friends and absolute professionals." Only Effie and a few other people knew about Lana's invitation to her apartment last year for dinner, or that Josh had stupidly tried to kiss her a few days after that. "Please never infer anything like that to Lana. She would be mortified."

"Of course not. She's a good kid. A little too eager sometimes, and a bit of a know-it-all, but what surgeon isn't?" Cal, a pediatrics resident, had always ribbed Josh about how surgeons thought they were gods. "Anyway, I need to be getting back," Cal stated as he rose from the table. "Effie, it was really great meeting you." This time, he initiated the hug with Effie. "Josh, please let me know next time you're back here," he told Josh, before he gave him, too, an energetic hug. As Cal pulled back, he exclaimed, "Oh, I almost forgot to mention that Sadie and I are seeing each other again!"

"What? That's amazing!" Josh had always wondered what had come between the couple, because they had always seemed madly in love. When Josh met Cal in med school, he and Sadie had already been married.

Now Cal appeared sheepish. "It is amazing, and I am not taking a second chance with her for granted. I'll keep you posted on any developments," he told Josh with a huge grin. "Next time, maybe the four of us could all get together, huh?"

"Let's plan on it. Take care, Cal, and give the family my best," he directed his friend before he left, shooting him a parting wave as Cal looked back at Josh and Effie before leaving the cafeteria.

"Well, that must have been a surprise to hear about Cal and his wife getting back together, huh? He's really sweet, Josh. I mean, I don't like what he said about Lana. I've never met her, but that was unnecessary information, in my opinion," Effie remarked. "Has she sent you a text or anything?"

"No," Josh replied, "and that is so unlike her. Let me text her again and see if something came up."

"Ok, I'm going to get some coffee and some of that famous banana bread—do you want some, too, Honey?" Effie inquired, while she smoothed his hair back from his temple. When he was with Effie, regardless if they were alone or in a crowded hospital cafeteria, Josh felt wrapped up in a cocoon of love. Meeting up with her at his dad's auto shop had been part of what saved him last year, and he would spend the rest of their lives doing whatever he could to make her as happy as she made him.

Taking her hand as she stood up, Josh kissed it while staring into her enchanting eyes, so gold and glittery. "I'll take anything you're offering, my love." Then he watched her walk over to the coffee area. Reaching into his pocket to check his phone, he saw a missed text from Lana:

> Sorry, Josh, can't meet you after all. Something came up, and I need to meet last minute with an upcoming patient. Was looking forward to meeting Effie, but maybe next time?

> Take care.

"What's up?" Effie asked as she returned to their table, placing a tray in front of Josh. "Any word from Lana?"

Josh drew his eyebrows together in a frown and shook his head. "It's weird, look," and he showed Effie the text. "Unless there's an emergency, we don't 'meet last minute' with a patient." Shrugging, he threw a helpless look at Effie. "Something just doesn't feel right."

"Plus, isn't the timing questionable? Look," she told Josh, pointing at his phone, "that text came in as we have been here. Plus, Cal said he thought he saw her before we got here. How far away is your office?"

"Just the next floor up," Josh answered, scratching his head. "Maybe she was here looking for us to tell us she couldn't stay?"

Effie asked hesitantly, "You don't think she heard what Cal said, do you?"

"What?" Josh asked, shaking his head again. "I would have seen her if she was that close, I would imagine."

"Babe, look around—it's crowded in here, and you are sitting with your back to the dining room. I don't know what she looks like, other than 'small blonde'" Effie told him, using air quotes for the description Josh had given her about Lana. How else was he supposed to describe the woman he had foolishly tried kiss to the woman he was madly in love with?

Josh answered, "But Cal would have seen her again, don't you think?"

Effie gave him a doubting look. "We were all wrapped up in looking at pictures of his kid and talking about his reconciliation with his wife. All I'm saying is that it is possible she was here, heard what Cal said, and then left. In which case, she's probably embarrassed."

Josh groaned then, "Ugh. This sucks if that is what happened. I wanted you guys to meet, and I don't want to leave here on a bad note."

"Here's a suggestion: why don't we get this stuff to go, get something for Lana, and take it up to her office? That way, if she really is too busy working, we can still see her for a minute or two. Worst-case scenario, if she *did* happen to overhear anything Cal said, we can smooth it over or just act like he's an idiot." Effie sipped some of her coffee then and added, "Which he is, bless him."

# CHAPTER
## Twenty-Seven

*Liam*



Are you around? Done at the hospital, so thought we would pop into the hotel. Effie is dying to see the place.



Just come on up when you get here.

Room 1211.



Hey, Darlin', I have a surprise for you when you get here. Missed you all day. Can't wait to see you. Xo

"Is this what you do with the company's money? Throw it around without a care for what it costs the bottom line? God, Liam, when will you grow up and at least try to behave responsibly? I didn't come back home to clean up your messes, big brother," Liam heard his sister say scornfully, having called him, she claimed, to discuss some of the bonuses he had given out at his dealership for the top salespeople.

"Well, since you brought that up, why don't you come clean about why, exactly, you did come back? Seems to me you love pointing out all the frivolous reasons—your words, not mine—you *didn't* come back home, yet you have not once given a genuine explanation as to why you *did*. I'm sure it wasn't to be on my ass every chance you get." Liam drew in a deep breath, knowing losing his temper would not get him anywhere. His sister was like a robot, and her ability to remain stone cold in the face of intense emotions was impressive, and more than likely, what had made her a killer environmental attorney. Unable to help himself, he fired back. "I was told by Mom and Grandpa Kinsale to treat employees accordingly, and I think I did that."

"And 'accordingly', to you, means giving a bonus to every single employee in Beverley? How do you think that makes the employees at the rest of the locations feel, *William*?" Oh, so now Cait was using his proper name, knowing full well, since they were kids, how much it pissed him off.

"Christ, *Caitriona*," he vehemently responded, using her full name, the Irish version of Catherine that she had always complained was too old-fashioned and stuffy. Right, because the woman herself just exuded such an easygoing demeanor. "Well, I'm not positive how employees at the other locations will feel—perhaps like their managers shouldn't have such a stick up their ass? Oh, wait, but *you* approved the bonus proposals in the other locations. When I send the company memo, I'll make sure to give you a proper shout out."

"God, this is so you—what is it that Effie says? Oh, right, this is 'so Liam-coded'—all flash and flair to make yourself look good, meanwhile never mind who you put down in the process. Does your 'Mystery Woman' know how shallow you are yet? Or have you managed to keep up your supposedly interesting facade in the few days you've spent together? You realize there is a reason she hasn't told you her name, right? Everyone is laughing at you behind your back, you know," his sister told him, more nasty words hitting Liam where he had always been the most vulnerable. What had changed with her? When they had been kids, they had been close, and she had idolized him as her big brother—for years, he could go nowhere without Cait tagging along. After Josh's mom had left, Liam and his cousin had grown very close. Was that when he and his sister had begun to grow apart? Liam and Josh had been twelve, and Cait was eleven. When he became a single dad, Henry had brought Josh to work with him at the family's auto shop in Clover Lake. Although Josh had been far more interested in learning how to fix cars than Liam, when Liam then started accompanying his dad to the shop, he would convince Josh to play instead of apprentice, and the two would bike around town, go to the swimming pool, or hang out in the park. All while leaving Cait alone at home.

"Why are you doing this? Why call me now, in the middle of my trip, to read me the riot act? How small is your life that this is what you are doing in your downtime? Nothing can come from it and certainly could have waited until I got back." Stumped, Liam wondered what was causing his sister to freak out like this. After her blow up at him at the company Christmas party, she had apologized, and they had been getting along, but he now assumed that had more to do with family politics than his sister's giving nature.

"Right—because no one should ruin your good time, Liam. Do you know how sick I am of having to hear about how fun you are? 'Oh Liam, he is just *SUCH* a good time'. No one talks about how hard I work, or how stressful it has been for me to move back to South Dakota, leaving everything I've known for a decade down in the Gulf. Where I was truly doing work that *mattered*, not selling cars to drunk cowboys and desperate farmers." His sister's voice, filled with such venom, that deep inside, Liam knew had nothing to do with him, not really, but her words were bullets, firing into the fragile ego he had concerning his career and his finely tuned persona. She was right, though, undeniably so: her work had mattered. Cait was brilliant, an environmental lawyer who sued big oil companies for spills, polluting groundwater, and once an exploding rig that killed a dozen men. Sure, all Liam did was sell cars, but so many times it was more than that: he had, on more than one occasion, used his own money to buy a used car to donate it to someone in need: a single mom who was a nurse lived fifteen miles out in the country but worked in Beverley. After she had failed to make car payments (struggling because her ex-husband, working off the books as a farm hand, wasn't paying child support), the bank had seized her car. Liam had secretly paid down the balance, telling her the dealership needed the space for inventory. There had also been the young grandson, recently out of college, who had moved in with his grandpa after his grandma died. Struggling to find a job in his small town, he had needed a reliable car to take his grandpa to and from doctor appointments in Sioux Falls, an hour's drive each way. Liam found odd jobs for the young man, allowing him to pay for the car on an extended "loan", at a pace that enabled him to put his grandfather first.

Not bothering to defend himself, since he wanted to save his energy for his Mystery Woman, and knowing his words would fall on deaf ears, Liam remained silent. When Cait offered no more of her verbal virulent attack, Liam said, "So…we done here?"

Cait sighed on the other end of the phone, "Whatever," but remained on the line, so he waited. Finally, she added, "Look, I'm sorry. You're right—this probably could have held until you got back. But you need to start being more responsible, Liam. Your actions have consequences, and I'm sorry if Mom and Dad have let you off Scott-free—"

He interrupted her, "Okay, yep, we're done. Bye Cait. Love you." And he hung up.

Why did his sister have to call today, of all days? And why had he answered? He should have known better than to think she was calling to check on his trip or ask about his Mystery Woman, both of which were evidently a big joke to her, and everyone else as well.

Following his dreadful conversation with his sister, he had taken advantage of the hotel's fitness room to burn off her bad vibes. After he lifted weights and ran five miles on the treadmill, Liam was reading *The Brief Wondrous Life of Oscar Wao* (for the third time, yet the flow of the prose still kept him engaged), when the text from Josh had come in. Thinking it would be nice to have Josh and Effie meet his Mystery Woman (and hopefully put her more at ease) before they had dinner tonight, Liam was fantasizing about the three couples all out for the evening. He had never done that—gone on a double date (or triple date, in this case). His world had expanded during this time he had with his Mystery Woman, and he had vowed to himself that he would know her name before the end of this evening. By tomorrow morning, the two of them could be planning a future filled with endless possibilities.

The buzzing on his wrist indicated a text had come in, and Liam swiped his watch to read the incoming message from Josh.

TEXT FROM JOSH

We're here…heading up now

A quick glance around the hotel room assured Liam that it looked presentable enough for his cousin, who could be a bit of a neat freak. Spotting the robes he and his Mystery Woman had discarded in the early dawn this morning, Liam grabbed them and shoved them onto hangers in the closet. His senses flashed back to this morning: the touch of his hands on her soft honey-colored curls, so pure and delicate; the scent of her body wash in the shower, filling his nostrils in the steam; tasting her mouth, minty fresh from her toothpaste as he licked her lips; her moans rising over the pounding in his head; and, of course, the sight of her ripe, voluptuous body when she first left him in the bed, illuminated by the Christmas lights as she walked to the bathroom to get ready for her day. More importantly, his heart was consumed with who she had shown herself to be over the course of the past few days—caring, if the money he had seen her give to Salvation Army bell ringers twice in one day was an example; tender, if the way she cried when they had watched *The Shop around the Corner* late one night was any indication; intelligent, judging by the way she had finished the *New York Times* crossword puzzle one morning after breakfast; brave, if the way she was spending the week with him was a sign; and cautious, an attribute he discovered he was particularly fond of, especially considering his tendency to be impulsive.

His day hadn't been limited to only staying in the hotel, though, and before he shut the door to the closet, his hand couldn't help but pat the pocket of his coat to ensure that his latest purchase was still safely tucked away. A knock on the hotel door meant his cousin had finally arrived, and Liam hurriedly walked the few steps to it and opened it. "Welcome, dear family," he greeted Josh and Effie.

"Is that…Mariah Carey I hear? I thought you hated this song," Josh told him, peering into the room with a bewildered look on his face as he stepped to the side to let Effie in the room first.

"What? I never said that," Liam denied vehemently—he had chosen this song in anticipation of his Mystery Woman's arrival, thinking of her singing it in the shower the other morning. "I may have, back in the day of my misspent youth, inferred that this song was a *bit* overplayed."

Effie whistled as she stepped into the room. "Oh my god, Liam, was the tree your idea?" She walked over to get a closer look, reaching out a hand and gingerly touching one of the ornaments dangling from the branch. "How beautiful—is this a Tiffany heart?" she asked, with a touch of what he thought was awe in her voice.

"Yeah," he answered. "I got that for her the last time I was here, the day after we met. I had her bring it along when I surprised her with the tree."

"Oh, Josh, look at this Clara ornament. We'll have to get one like that when we see the matinee tomorrow." Josh went to stand behind Effie, and Liam saw how reverently his cousin's hands touched her shining hair, so dark it was almost raven black. Josh's eyelids closed as he kissed the top of Effie's head, and though the gesture was completely chaste, it was also filled with such intimacy that Liam wondered if he should step out of the room and give them some privacy. Liam had been around his cousin and Tess during the entirety of their almost twenty-year relationship and had assumed he had seen his cousin in love, but nothing during those years had compared to what Josh and Effie shared, and witnessing them together made Liam certain he had been right to wait so many years before committing to any woman. He and his Mystery Woman could have what Josh and Effie had. What he had seen Tess and Sam have the day they had cleaned out Josh's storage unit. What Ruth, Tess's sister, and her husband, Sean, had. And what his mom and dad had for almost forty years. Hell, what both sets of his grandparents had for sixty-plus years.

"Anything you want, my angel, shall be yours," Josh murmured to Effie. Then he turned to Liam and said, "This is all amazing. I mean, everything you have done here—from the tree to every experience you have made possible for your Mystery Woman, including this hotel room. I should never have doubted your feelings for her." Josh clapped a hand on Liam's shoulder, and Liam reeled him in for a hug, which Josh heartily returned.

"Josh is right," Effie agreed, with tears shining in her tawny-colored eyes. "Your Mystery Woman must be over the moon for you, Sweetie." She stood and lifted her head to kiss Liam on the cheek. "She is very lucky to have you, you know." Liam and Effie had gotten quite close since he had moved to Beverley. He wondered if Effie had figured out that he had deliberately nudged his cousin into action the day Liam had inadvertently let slip about the truth Josh had been keeping from her.

"Enough about me," Liam demurred, probably for the first time in his life. "How has your trip to New York been? You guys went to the hospital today to see the old 'gang'?" Liam asked, using air quotes.

"Well, that's what we intended. We ran into Cal, completely by accident, in the cafeteria. Oh, thanks," Josh told Liam, when he handed his cousin a Heineken from the bar. After Effie nodded, Liam poured her a glass of white wine from the bottle he held up for her. Grabbing a beer for himself also, he gestured to the sofa for the two of them to sit as he pulled over an armchair from the other side of the room.

"Oh, really? What's he up to these days?" Aware that Cal had been a good friend to his cousin, especially after he and Tess had broken up, he nevertheless believed that Cal considered himself to be better than other people, Liam in particular.

"Being judgmental, if you ask me. He was kind of a dick," Effie informed Liam emphatically. One of the things Liam appreciated about her was her ability to be not only candid, but very frank; with anyone else, Josh could be a little too formal, but Effie brought out an edge in him that he had denied for years. Or she tried to, anyway.

"Nothing new there, then," Liam responded, wondering how his cousin was going to defend his friend. "You have to admit that Cal has a tendency to lord it over people."

Josh drank his beer and then put it down on the coffee table. "I wouldn't say that he was being a dick, as Effie put it." He laced his fingers with Effie's and kissed the fingertips. "Although since she tends to be right most of the time, I will admit that he was a bit of a cad, I guess, for lack of a better term."

"God," Liam wailed, "the suspense of this story is killing me, and if it is anything short of him sending nude photos to each of you, I will be disappointed—just warning you now."

Effie chuckled, "Well, sorry, Liam, but it's not that. We were supposed to meet Lana there but found Cal instead. And when we mentioned to him we were meeting her, he went off on how Lana had a crush on Josh—"

Josh interrupted, "Lana only *thought* she had a crush on me, by the way. Probably more like a hero complex than anything else." Liam stared at his cousin, perplexed if he was being serious or self-deprecating.

He raised an eyebrow at Josh. "'Hero complex'? Really? Didn't she graduate high school early, and then finish college *and* medical school in six years, and then earn that fellowship-thingy you also applied for?"

"Well, sure, but I am older and *somewhat* more experienced," Josh defended himself while Effie and Liam laughed.

"Anyway, cut to the chase—what did you think of Lana, Effie? At least you got to meet her after less than a year of being with Josh, meanwhile here I sit, never having met her, despite a plethora of opportunities." He said, glaring at his cousin, who glared back at him.

"And I asked you if you wanted to come along today—" Josh started.

Liam broke in, "A lot of good that does me now! I don't need to meet any woman now that I have my Mystery Woman! Besides, all I wanted to know was Effie's impression."

"Effie's impression is zip—I didn't get to meet her. She didn't show up. Technically, I guess she did, because Cal saw her there before we arrived, but she left." Effie drank the last of her wine. "We are afraid she may have overheard Cal talking about her, because she sent Josh a text saying she had some work thing."

"Oh, wow—that sucks." Liam imagined how she must have felt, listening to Cal make fun of her to Josh and Effie, especially if she had feelings at one time for his cousin. Having been on the receiving end of playing the fool, he could understand if she had been embarrassed.

"Yeah," Josh shrugged, "we took some coffee up to the office to see if we could talk to her there, but she wasn't in."

A jiggle of the door handle caught Liam's attention, and he sprang up from his chair. "Oh, that must be my Mystery Woman," he told his guests, as he bolted to the door to welcome her.

# CHAPTER
## Twenty-Eight

## Lana and Liam



Just FYI, my cousin and his girlfriend were in the area and came up to our room. Can't wait to introduce you to them.



Okay. I'll be there soon. Might not go to Brooklyn tonight. My day was not great. Sorry.

Lana rested her forehead against the door to the hotel room before entering, hearing the cacophony of voices from within. What she longed for was to spend the rest of the day wrapped up in the strong, sexy arms of her Hook Up, but clearly that would have to wait. Perhaps if she had gotten his text before leaving the hospital, she could have justified a reason to spend more time in her office, in order to avoid meeting his cousin and the girlfriend. Her head had been pounding all day, made worse by her attempt to meet up with Josh and Effie. At least she had gotten a glimpse of the goddess herself; Lana had never felt more wanting after seeing Effie in real life—tall, just a few inches shorter than Josh, from what she had seen from a few feet away, and stunning, with her golden skin and sleek, shoulder-length black hair that sparkled under the fluorescent lights of the cafeteria. How did she manage that? Lana mused, never actually having seen anyone's hair sparkle before, outside of a shampoo commercial.

Upon finishing her scheduled surgery earlier that day, Lana had taken a quick shower before heading to the hospital cafeteria to meet up with Josh and Effie yet still arrived a few minutes before two that afternoon. Instead of finding Josh, however, she had spotted Cal. After locking eyes with her, he had given a quick wave before looking away. Okay, she got the hint—don't try sitting at his table. When she had shared the office with Josh, Cal never invited Lana whenever he popped in to ask Josh to go for lunch or a cup of coffee. Since both men were older and had a previous friendship that predated working at the hospital, Lana was on the outside looking in when they were together and today proved that point. When she circled back around the cafeteria with her banana bread and Yorkshire Gold tea, she found Josh at Cal's table, accompanied by the woman she could only assume was Effie. So intimidating had the scene been to Lana that she crept (for lack of a better term) up to the table, stopping dead in her tracks when she heard her name being mentioned. After learning just how *desperate* and *pathetic the other doctors viewed her*, Lana could not bear to see the pity in the faces of Josh (a sight she was already too familiar with) and the glamorous Effie, so she had swiftly turned around and taken her tea and bread back to her office, where she had texted Josh, promptly canceling their reunion. Luckily, Lana had managed to avoid further awkward interactions by being in the restroom when Effie and Josh had attempted to seek her out at her office. As she was coming around the corner by the elevator bank, intending to return to her office, she heard Josh's voice coming from down the hall. Swiftly, she had turned to catch the elevator to a different floor—it hadn't mattered which one—and she had found herself summoned down to the third level, where the chapel was. Although she had been raised Catholic, Lana was not a religious woman and hadn't been to church since her confirmation, but she found herself sitting in a pew. A small choir was at the front, singing "Oh Holy Night", Lana's favorite religious Christmas carol, and she found herself unable to stop the flow of tears. Surrounded by stained glass and poinsettias, Lana wondered what she had gotten herself into. What should have been a casual, fun, sexy adventure with her Hook Up had taken a turn, becoming more serious, and she wasn't exactly sure when it had happened. Maybe when he had her dress pressed and ready for their night out at *The Nutcracker*, maybe when she saw the hotel room he had taken such care in choosing and preparing for her, maybe when she had finally opened up her first ornament from him back in the solitude of her apartment, or maybe as far back as when she met him all of those months ago—when she had acted completely unlike herself and had given herself up to the pleasure he had promised and delivered. Had she truly not been herself that night, or had she ultimately discovered her true self, after so many years denying who she could really be? Did questioning the when and why even matter? The end result was that she was in over her head, drowning, in love with a man whose name she didn't even know.

On the other side of the door, Liam reached for the handle, only to find himself having to take a step back as his Mystery Woman filled the doorway. Exhaling heavily (he hadn't been aware he had been holding his breath), he could breathe again now that she was here. Unfortunately, her previous text insinuated, even proved, that she would always be one step away from canceling on him, and the realization made him anxious, disappointed, also, because he had hoped they were beyond that. Reaching for her, he scanned her face for signs of the bad day mentioned in the text and found traces in her enchanting dark-blue eyes. Worry made the corners of her eyes turn down, and after he pulled her into his arms, he placed gentle kisses on each tender eyelid. "I missed you," he whispered in her ear, before he then kissed the top of her honey-blonde head. "Do you need a minute to decompress?" She shook her beautiful head 'no', and he saw the tight braid she had pulled her waves into this morning had loosened, leaving wisps of her hair framing her face. "We're having some drinks in the living area—can I get you something to drink, Darlin'?"

Smiling up at him, Lana replied, "Just a soda," as he slipped her coat from her shoulders, hung it up in the closet, laced his fingers with hers, and drew her out of the entryway. Simply by his gentle touch and unwavering attention, she was calming. When she was not in the mood for anything, he was here, wanting to make everything better—and already the weight she had on her shoulders from the afternoon lifted. Until his next words.

"Josh, Effie, I'd like to introduce you to my Mystery Woman," he laughed, "although now it seems maybe more appropriate to be using our names, I guess?" Smiling encouragingly down at his Mystery Woman, he saw her mouth drop open, while a flush colored her ivory cheeks pink. She seemed rooted in place, not saying a word, staring instead across the room at his cousin, who had an equally strange expression on his face that slightly mirrored his Mystery Woman's. Suddenly, Josh erupted in a fit of laughter.

"Oh my god," Josh gasped between his bouts of mirth, "this is too unreal. Is this a set-up?" Liam watched as his cousin looked around the room. "Am I being pranked here?"

"What the hell are you talking about? Pranked? Dude, have you gone mental?" Liam asked his cousin, now growing annoyed by Josh's response.

Laughing was the farthest thing from Lana's mind as she stared at Josh in horror. How had this happened? She could not fault him from assuming that this was some kind of prank—unless that's what it was, she thought, as the pit in her stomach grew. After all, it had happened to her before, in another lifetime, when her feelings for a man had made her the butt of someone's sick joke. "I don't understand," she admitted softly, glancing at her Hook Up. To his credit, he not only looked as confused as she felt, but his mouth was frowning, and the hand still holding hers had tightened into a clench. Forcing her gaze over to the one man whose name she *did* know, she asked him, "Josh? What are you doing here?"

"Josh?" Liam questioned, looking from his cousin to his Mystery Woman. "How do you know Josh?"

Josh raised his hand and said, "I think the bigger question is: how do you know Lana, Cousin?"

"Lana? As in Lana, your former office mate?" Liam questioned, never having been more dumbfounded in his life.

"I'd say, more accurately, as in Lana—doctor, already having done one rotation of residency in internal medicine, now in her second rotation in surgery, and I believe going on to her third rotation in…pediatrics, isn't it, Lana?" Josh corrected Liam and questioned Lana in almost the same breath, rising from the sofa.

"Umm, pediatric surgery, specifically, but the rest is correct." Lana trained her blue eyes on the silvery eyes of the man still holding her hand, realizing that she now knew where she had seen those eyes before, and he was standing now in front of her. Although not the same color, since Josh's were the blue of a summer sky, her Hook Up's eyes had the same shape and depth of feeling. Looking back to him, she asked in disbelief, "Josh said you were his cousin?" She knew Josh had several male cousins—one was a chef named Daniel, one an architect she believed was called Felix, and if memory served her, the other one was a car salesman whose name was L—

"Lana, this is my cousin Liam. I mean, if you didn't already know. Your 'Hook Up', I believe, is what you call him, right? And you are the 'Mystery Woman. I mean, I can't even believe any of this is real. How the hell did you two even meet?" Josh's voice kept getting louder and louder, as if he, too, had cause to be upset.

Effie spoke up then, "Josh, I think maybe the two of us should leave —they clearly have enough to discuss without us here."

"No, I don't think so," he told Effie, who was also now standing next to him, and burned Liam then with his heated gaze. "What the hell is going on, Liam? Was this some kind of game? Especially after what we talked about in the car?" No…Liam thought. His Mystery Woman could not be Josh's office mate, the woman who they had joked about being in love with Josh. She couldn't be Lana, the brilliant surgeon, the head of her class, the woman who had earned a fellowship instead of Josh. If she was better than his perfect cousin, what chance did Liam have with her?

The car, Lana thought, what car? What had they talked about? Why would Josh think her Hook Up…Liam…would be playing a game? They hadn't known who the other one was the night all those months ago when they met in the bar…had they? Lana recalled the moment so clearly—she had been standing with her back to him when he had approached her, buying her shots of tequila and another beer. Oh god, she realized with humiliation washing over her. It had been all a game, hadn't it? Regardless of if he had known who she was or not—his move with the salt and the lime and her wrist. His words, so seductive, so practiced. Every single story Josh had told her about his cousin Liam had involved some exploit of his, some conquest that Josh had always sounded half annoyed by and half envious of. Liam the playboy, Liam the rake, Liam the forever single. Wrenching her hand, finally, from his, Lana stared at Liam, shaking her head when he took a step toward her.

Witnessing the betrayal cross his Mystery Woman's face…Lana's face…punched him in the gut. None of this was going as he had planned. Josh was meant to be *happy* for him, *excited* to meet his Mystery Woman, not telling him hotly, "You just couldn't stand it, could you? You knew she had feelings for me so, what, you thought you'd make a play for her? I called it the morning after you met her—you ran your game on her. You went to meet me in the bar, saw her instead, and thought it would be hilarious to bag Lana. Buddy, you're punching way above your league with this one."

"Josh!" Effie cried. "That's enough! What has gotten into you?" Liam watched as she tugged on Josh's hand. None of what his cousin was saying was true, of course, except the last bit: he was punching above his league with her. Lana. His Mystery Woman.

Eventually, all the color drained from Josh's face, and he sat down. Lana cleared her throat, telling Josh, "Actually, it was me—I was the one who made the play. He may have started the ball rolling, but I'm the one that ratcheted up everything. I'm the one who suggested going back to his hotel room." Not exactly the truth, since she remembered him explicitly telling her, a mere minute after their first shot, that he had a hotel room in the area. She simply could not remain silent a moment longer while Josh was behaving so cruelly to his cousin. Her Hook Up. Liam.

Josh said, "I stand corrected, then. Effie is right," he announced, getting up again from the sofa. "We should leave you both alone. Liam, I should say I'm sorry for what I said, and Lana, I should excuse this outburst. Oddly enough, I can't bring myself to do either, and for that, I am sorry. This is the last thing I was expecting tonight—my cousin and my friend." Josh gave a little laugh that sounded anything but happy, and told them, "The last time it was my fiancée and my friend, so I guess things are improving, huh?" Josh held Effie's hand as she stood beside him, kissing her on the temple as she did so.

Lana's emotions were all over the place, but when Effie, who had not even officially been introduced to Lana, came to her and hugged her, she almost broke down entirely. "I'm here for you whenever you need. I'll get your number and call you, okay? We could all use one more friend," Effie told her, and she was so generous and kind, Lana let a few tears escape, hoping to wash this day away.

Josh embraced Lana briefly. "I hope we see you sometime, Lana. Look," he sighed, "I'm sorry about everything I said."

When Effie embraced him, Liam held on to her, absorbing her graciousness as she told him in his ear, "Give him grace—I think we were all surprised today." He nodded in agreement, because what else could he do? Part of him felt as if he had betrayed his cousin, however unintentionally. Humiliation didn't describe what Liam was experiencing. For his Mystery Woman to be Lana (the woman who last year had written his cousin what was essentially a love letter), was not what he had been expecting. How was he, Liam (of the car selling trade), supposed to stack up against Josh (a brilliant surgeon), to Lana? Josh raved about her when they shared an office—how she was the only other surgical resident potentially better than him. All Liam offered her was hot sex and freely spent money. Now as he surveyed this hotel room, he saw it as over-the-top, verging on tacky. Frivolous. All "flash and flair" just as his sister had accused him just hours earlier. He imagined Cait witnessing all of this, gleeful that her brother was getting his come-uppance.

"Love you, Cuz," Josh told him, as he hugged Liam's stiff form.

He accepted the hug his cousin gave him, telling him, "Love you, too."

"Be careful here." And then Josh grabbed Effie's hand, who glanced back at Lana and Liam with a worried smile before leaving the room.

The door shut, and with Josh and Effie gone, heartbreaking silence remained. "You have Christmas music playing," Lana said, noting "Last Christmas" in the background, unsure of what else to say. What could she say? Standing in this glamorous hotel room, she knew she must look ridiculous, wearing her second-hand dress, with her hair falling out of its sloppy braid. Her Hook Up was a fantasy at this point, and Liam was the reality. God, he was the one out of her league, she mused when her eyes finally had the strength to look his way. What she needed now was to be taken into his arms—she could go for some sex up against the wall, definitely the antidote for this dismal day, but he stood there, a foot or so apart from her, staring at the door. Why would he want to touch her, look at her, be with her? Knowing she had foolishly believed herself to be in love with his cousin? It was beyond humiliating. She must seem so shallow, able to transfer her affections from one man to the next so easily. Not that he had been looking for anything more than a hook up...but what about what he had told her at the beginning of this week? That he had wanted them to be "them" this week. Well, this was "them".

"I can't wrap my head around the fact that you are 'Lana'," he hoarsely told her. "Do you know how many times I asked Josh to introduce us when I came to the city?" Liam glanced over at her, wanting those blue eyes on him, but she was staring at the Christmas tree. He let out a rueful laugh. "He refused every time, and now I know why." At last, he allowed himself to reach out and smooth a wisp of her honeyed locks behind her ear, gratified when she stepped closer to him. At least their magnetic draw to each other was real, but would that be enough? Enough for her to overlook everything he was lacking? Enough for her to realize that, whatever she may have heard from Josh about his romantic past, he was different with her? From that moment with the tequila shots upon their first meeting, it may have been "a bit" he had performed, but her reaction to it, and his response to her, had been completely genuine.

Lana closed her eyes, finding staring into Liam's light blue eyes, so bright yet haunting, seared too painfully, too sharply, into her heart. What do they do now? Pretend that their lives weren't interwoven in a way neither had suspected. What would everyone think...people like Cal, who had surmised that she had a crush on Josh, because she brought him coffee even though she loathed spending money on it, or hung on his every word as he told her about the lectures he attended, or invited him to dinner in her shabby studio apartment, begging him silently to kiss her at the end of their evening? The men weren't interchangeable, but how many people would mistakenly believe she thought so? Dear god, what did Effie think? Pathetic Lana couldn't get Josh, so she hooked up with the first man who crossed her path that night in the bar. Another moment to regret, now that she was aware of just how much information about her Josh had been privy to. Had Liam been filling his cousin in with personal, intimate details the way she had told her sisters? How she had described him to Ava and Greer, what had he said about her to Josh? At least Liam *was* sexy and exciting, gorgeous and thrilling, words that could never be said about her.

Liam was close to losing her—despite being cognizant of the fact that he wasn't good enough for her, he wanted to try. He could show everybody that he had changed—show her he was worthy of being with her. He heard her trembling sigh, almost predicting what her words were going to be, and he was desperate to keep her in this room. His mom always told him, "Liam, you could talk anyone into anything." Let him prove it with her. "Lana," he began, "none of this has to mean anything —the fact that we now know the truth about us. We can still finish our week together. We still have time together. We don't have to go anywhere."

Was he crazy? Surely, he had to know this ended everything for them! "You can't be serious, Liam. I've been humiliated today too many times. Do you know that I was supposed to meet with Josh and Effie in the hospital cafeteria earlier, but I overheard Cal talking about me to them?" She turned from him and headed to the closet to take out her suitcase. "I was so mortified that I left to hide out in my office and then sent Josh a text *lying* about why I couldn't meet them." Lana gave a rueful laugh and, bracing herself for more embarrassment, told him, "Then I hid from Josh and Effie again, when they came to my office. How pathetic I am, huh?"

"Baby, they know Cal was being an ass—trust me, I don't know why Josh puts up with him sometimes," he told her. "And you are anything but pathetic. You're beautiful-" but she cut him off.

Taking her clothes off the hangers, Lana said, "Of course you would already know—I must seem so pitiful to you," she cried. This was why she preferred to remain free of entanglements. Effie had claimed to want to be her friend, but only because she felt sorry for her. Now Effie and Josh were headed back to Brooklyn, and Sam and Tess would find out about how stupid and naïve she was. She groaned. "How am I supposed to move now? I was going to rent an apartment from Tess and Sam, but I can't face them." Lana threw her dress in carelessly to her suitcase—the one she had worn to the ballet, the one he had so carefully arranged to have pressed for her. The one she had bought in the thrift store—not simply because she loved vintage clothes, as she often explained to people, but because it was where she had been shopping since she was young, whenever she hadn't been wearing her sisters' hand-me-downs. "I can't face anyone." Lana chanced a look at Liam, noting his chestnut hair, carefully held in place by the products sitting on the bathroom counter, expensive products available for purchase primarily at hair salons. This hotel, this room in particular…she shuddered to think what it cost him. How many houses would her mom have to clean to afford a single night? How many cabinets would her brother have to build for his wealthy customers out on Long Island? Furthermore, what would Montgomery think about any of this? Lana's high school regret, sleeping with the rich kid, had taken ages to move past, and yet she had just repeated the past. Yes, she had known from the first night with Liam that he had to have money, but it was different when he had been anonymous. Now it was messy, with too many entanglements, and she needed, more than anything, to breathe, and she could not do that here. Not with him looking devastated, defeated, and still so, so desirable.

In a panic, Liam watched her, helpless to do anything to stop her from throwing her clothes into her suitcase. "What are you doing?" he asked in a panic, somehow sure that if she left him now, he would not see her again. And he would do anything he could to prevent that—she just needed to slow down and listen to him.

Lana finished closing her suitcase and replied, "I can't stay here anymore. Not now. Not with everyone knowing." Blindly wrenching her coat out of the closet, she put it on, refusing to look at him, knowing if she did, she would buckle.

"Everyone knowing what?" Liam asked her desperately. "Knowing who you are? Knowing who I am?" Please, he silently begged, please let her deny it. He needed reassurances from her that she felt for him everything he felt for her.

"Yes," she exclaimed. "All of that." Tugging her case out of the closet, she had to stop because his arms were around her. "Please, let me go," she cried, unable to prevent herself from melting into him, still finding him irresistible.

Liam breathed in the scent of her, getting drunk from her heady aroma. "What difference does any of this make? None of it changes how I feel for you—how I think you feel for me." Slowly, she turned in his arms. "Lana, Lana, Lana. Your name has haunted me from the moment my cousin first talked about you. I wanted, more than anything, to meet you, but he refused, never introducing us. Yet somehow, we found our way to each other." He ran his thumb over her lips—the lips that gave him the most delectable kisses of his life. The lips that had kissed a sensual path over his body, night after night. The lips that now formed his name with them.

"Liam—this has all been a fantasy; one that I will forever be grateful to have had with you, but it's not reality." Unprepared to let the fantasy end, though, resistance was futile as his hands made their way from her face to her breasts, and she moaned in response, until they moved on to her waist, her hips, and then he cupped her bottom and pulled her body flush with his, as he had done too many times to count over the past few days. Her own hands clutched his biceps, and her mouth descended on his chest, through the top two buttons of his shirt. The hairs tickled her nose, and she wanted more. Ripping the rest of his shirt open, buttons pinged off the floor as they scattered. Dropping her coat to the floor, she pulled him down, laying back under the glow of the Christmas lights, watching, as their ornaments danced above them.

# CHAPTER
## Twenty-Nine

### Lana and Liam

TEXT TO MYSTERY WOMAN

Hey, Darlin', where are you? Our bed is too empty.

TEXT TO MYSTERY WOMAN

I guess you must have gone out to get breakfast. Get me something tasty. Nothing could be more delicious than you, though. You should've waken me up to go with you…

TEXT TO MYSTERY WOMAN

Okay, Baby, been awake for half an hour now— where are you? Should I be worried?

TEXT TO MYSTERY WOMAN

Thinking maybe you had to go in to work? Thanks to my cousin, I know all about that surgery life.

TEXT TO MYSTERY WOMAN

Lana, please answer me—it's been over an hour. Normally I like to play it cool, but have to admit you have me stressing, especially since you're not answering me..

TEXT TO MYSTERY WOMAN

Lana—just checked the closet and all Your stuff is gone. Where are you? I thought everything between us was good, that we settled it all last night. Please tell me you just ran home to get different clothes.

TEXT TO LANA

Really going nuts here. It's been two hours.

Why won't you at least respond to my messages? Any one of them—you pick! I just need to see that you're okay.

Please, Lana

TEXT TO JOSH

Josh, you have to help me.

Woke up to find Lana gone this morning.

I need to find her—she's not answering any of my calls or texting back.

TEXT FROM JOSH

God, sorry about that, Liam. I don't know what to do, though.

TEXT TO JOSH

Maybe you could just text her to make sure she's okay?

TEXT FROM JOSH

Ok, texted her but doesn't even say that it's been read.

TEXT FROM EFFIE

Josh told me about Lana, and I tried texting her, too, just in case she would talk to me, but nothing. Sorry, Sweetie.

TEXT TO JOSH

Josh, tell me her address. Maybe she will let me in to talk to her?

I know if she saw me in person, we could work everything out.

TEXT FROM JOSH

Umm, I'm not good with that. Hope you understand.

TEXT TO JOSH

Actually, no, I don't understand. What the hell, dude?

Not to blame anyone, but you're partly responsible for this mess.

TEXT FROM JOSH

Liam, please calm down, think about it.

Giving you her address, when she didn't even tell you her name, is a huge violation of trust. I'm sorry, I don't feel right about it.

TEXT TO JOSH

What the fuck, Josh?

Are you fucking kidding me?

Violation of trust?

You mean all of those times you probably told her all kinds of shit about me? That's the reason she won't talk to me now, because I'm THAT Liam!

Dude, you owe me!!!

TEXT FROM JOSH,

Liam, please, I'm begging you to understand.

This isn't about me being your cousin, but about giving personal information away.

TEXT TO JOSH

You do realize that 20 years ago I could have just looked her up in the phone book?

I just want her to listen to me.

TEXT TO EFFIE

Effie, please help me. Please have Josh tell me Lana's address. I need to see her. She's gone, Effie.

TEXT FROM EFFIE

Liam, I'm sorry, I can't be in the middle. You know how Josh can be when he thinks he's right. I don't know how I'd feel if I were Lana.

Just FYI, she hasn't read my text, either.

TEXT FROM JOSH

Liam, I know you're stressed, but please don't put Effie in the middle. I'm sorry, I don't know how else to say it. You're right. I never should have told her anything about your dating history, but I'm not the one who made those choices, am I?

TEXT TO JOSH

Wow—throwing my past at me?

Way to skate over your own reaction to finding out we were together.

Maybe if you'd been more supportive, she'd still be with me.

TEXT FROM JOSH

Together? Liam, I know you felt something for Lana, but you were not, in truth, in a relationship. I'm not throwing your past at you.

I knew if she met you, though, she'd get hurt.

Even if it wasn't intentional.

TEXT TO LANA

Lana, please. I'm trying to give you space and time, but we don't have that luxury. I only have a few days left in New York.

Can't we at least go back to meaningless sex?

TEXT TO LANA

Ok, ok, that was a joke.

The truth is, Lana, I'm desperate. I have spent the day walking around the Upper East Side, hoping to glimpse your hair shimmering in the winter sunlight.

I went to Whistling Dixie, thinking maybe you might be there. I went to the hospital, walked the floors, hoping for you to come around any corner, with your white doctor's coat on, your hair in that braid like yesterday. You were gorgeous, the woman of my dreams.

TEXT TO LANA

Remember the first night we met? I told you I'd wait forever.

I don't want to do that, but if you need time to get your mind around me being "Liam", I will give you whatever you need. Just don't give up on us.

Also, perfectly happy to go back to being your "Hook Up". I'll be anything for you, because you are my everything.

TEXT TO LANA

Every night since you left, I lay under our Christmas tree and remember how you felt under me, beside me, on top of me, on our last night together. I look up at the lights, which once gave me such hope. I watch our ornaments hang from the branches and remember how we put them up there. I bought a new one today, but couldn't bring myself to hang it up.

How could you leave your heart here?

TEXT TO LANA

Is this really how it ends?

I'm going home the day after tomorrow, two days early. I guess you know where home is now. One word from you and I will stay.

I've never had anything close to this with anyone else. You are everything, and I am here, for you.

TEXT TO JOSH

Going home tomorrow. You guys are on your own.

Thanks for nothing, cousin.

TEXT FROM JOSH

Liam, please. Why don't you stay in Brooklyn with us? We can talk this through.

TEXT TO LANA

I guess this is it. Finally had to take down the tree.

I'll be honest and admit that I was tempted to throw it all out, including the ornaments. I have never been in so much pain. I feel like my heart is being ripped out of my chest, and there's no one to help me. You were the only woman who has ever seen me. Part of me wants to just let it go, but I believe what we have is real.

TEXT TO LANA

Here at the airport, but one word from you and I can still stay.

TEXT TO LANA

Boarding now. I may be leaving, but my heart stays with you.

TEXT FROM JOSH

Lana, please give Liam a chance. Don't close the door on him.

I hope nothing I have said in the past about him is what is driving you to not respond to his messages. He is really hurting.

TEXT FROM UNKNOWN

Lana, this is Effie. I know what went down in the hotel must have been painful. Josh is your friend, but you can have a relationship if you want with Liam. The way he talked about you made it clear to me that he cares for you.

TEXT TO HOOK UP

Hi, Liam. I could not respond while you were still in New York. What we shared this week was beautiful, but you have to admit it was not reality. The two of us could never be together, for so many reasons, none that have to do with Josh. I told you before that I have goals in my life. I can't get sidetracked with a relationship. That's not what I want. If you truly knew me, you'd understand.

TEXT FROM HOOK UP

What more do I need to understand? I understand that you shivered whenever I touched you. I understand that you told me you loved me with your body. I understand that you are serious, and smart, and sweet, and funny. I understand that I love you.

TEXT TO HOOK UP

Please don't tell me these things.

I am serious—I'm serious about my career.

I am smart—too smart to fall in love.

I am sweet—but so are a million other women.

I am funny—but nothing is funny about continuing this.

I'm sorry if I hurt you, Liam. I think the only way forward is to cut off all communication.

I'm hurting, too.

TEXT FROM HOOK UP

Baby, if you're hurting, let me help you. You don't have to be alone. I get that this was all confusing, but we can move past it. We can be happy together. I love you.

TEXT FROM HOOK UP

It's been a month now, and the wanting I feel for you has not gone away. If anything, every emotion I had is stronger. I never got the chance to tell you how stubborn I am, did I? Well, I am. Hardheaded, too. And I am terrible at following orders, so even though you said we should cut our ties, I can't do that. I won't. I can't see if you are reading any of my messages, but I will know that I tried to reach you.

To tell you I love you.

TEXT FROM HOOK UP

It's been 40 days without you.

Now that you know my name and who I am, you already know some things about me. Things that might make me less appealing, like that I manage a car dealership. My family's car dealership. I am fully aware of how much nepotism this carries, but do you know hard it is to get a job in a company that your family doesn't own? Going for humor, here, Lana—is it working?

Here's something else that will make you laugh.

It took me 5 years to get my business degree. Funny, huh? Graduated from NYU, I didn't appreciate any of it until last year. Then I started getting serious about my career. It may not seem like much to you, and I know I'm not a surgeon, but I do my best to help people, too.

You might not know this, but competing with Josh is hard.

Loving you is easy.

TEXT FROM HOOK UP

It's been 52 days without you, but loving you gets me through every day.

A woman, a single mom, came into my shop today for a car. Not a new one, which is, of course, what my family would prefer to sell, but a used one. Her husband died last year. Right after they married, they bought a car together. They drove to the hospital in that car both times their kids were born. She drove to the hospital in that car every time her husband had chemotherapy. Then when he died, she drove to the funeral home in that same car. Finally, the car's engine gave up. She sat in my office, unable to get a loan because she didn't have a job. Today she got a job. And a car.

TEXT FROM HOOK UP

It's been 66 days without you.

Today Josh came by the dealership, asking me to go to Shorty's with him after work. Not sure if I ever mentioned that place? It's a little pool hall in Beverley that Josh and I went to shortly after he moved back to South Dakota. Notice I didn't say when he came back, but when he moved back. I knew the moment he was here that he was staying. Of course, that night, he also reconnected with Effie, and it was game over for him. Like how I knew from the moment I met you that you were my end game. Except I'm sitting alone in my house. All I want is you. All I need is you. I still haven't forgiven Josh for the things he said that day in the hotel. Not that he was wrong about any of it. I always knew you were out of my league, just never realized how much. Doesn't stop me from loving you.

TEXT FROM HOOK UP

It's been 85 days without you.

I never told you, but I have a sister, one year younger. She went to college down south, and stayed there, rarely even coming home for the holidays. About killed my mom every year. Now she's back, but no one knows why, and she won't tell anyone. Something has changed her over the years. We used to be really close but grew apart as teenagers. Even then, she wasn't like now—hard, stiff, almost like she is about ready to crack. I don't know how to reach her. I have to admit, I'm beginning to feel the same way with you. Darlin', tell me what to do to make everything go back to what it was.

I could feel your love, and I know you felt mine.

TEXT FROM HOOK UP

It's been 100 days without you.

Every day, I look at that picture we took on the tram, and I see two people falling in love. Hell, if I'm being honest, I look at it every hour, at least. If I'm really honest, I was already in love.

Tell me what to do here, Lana. If you are completely out, I can leave you alone, but I don't know if you want that. Every text I send I can now see that you read it. Sometimes while I'm typing, I can feel your breath on the other end. I imagine your beautiful dark blue eyes looking up at me our last night together. I can't sleep at night because I miss you in my arms.

TEXT FROM HOOK UP

It's been 125 days without you.

Spring has finally arrived in South Dakota. I considered going to New York last month, to see the trees when they start blossoming. What I really wanted was to see you.

I remember when I was a student and spring felt so promising. Everything coming back to life. Lana, I feel my life slipping away. I have lost interest in anything that used to bring me joy, because the world is dark without you. Still no word. Just tell me to move on. It won't be easy, because my love for you still lives. You remaining silent is clearly not dissuading me, because I convince myself that you are just too busy, but you want to reach out.

Or I just think that you still just need time? My love for you will wait, however long you need.

TEXT FROM HOOK UP

It's been 130 days without you.

I ashamed to admit that part of me was wondering if the reason you didn't want to be with me was because I'm not brilliant—not like you or Josh. That's why I told you that I went to NYU. A cheap shot to get your attention, but even that failed.

What hasn't failed is my love for you.

But I get it if I am not enough for you.

The idea of me taking 5 years to graduate must seem pathetic when you finished in three years. Lana, you are incredible, and I know you're too good for me.

TEXT FROM LIAM

It's been 151 days without you.

I never told you that when Josh and I drove to New York last year, before he formally moved back and when he was all hung up on Effie, for some reason he was stuck on REO Speedwagon. Dad music, I know. Still, somehow it got into my brain and then I started listening to them on my own. They have a song called "In My Dreams", and I have been listening to it over and over. So, I am going to sign off with it: "Let the world go on below us, we are lost in time. All I know is I love you, in my dreams."

This is it. I finally got the hint. Goodbye, my love.

# CHAPTER
## Thirty

## Cait



Caitriona, please drive over to Beverley to check on your brother. We haven't heard from him in a week. Your Dad and I are having a wonderful time at Lake Tahoe, but are worried sick about Liam. Let me know how he is.

Love you.



Mom, I'm sure he's fine, but I'll go over there. Give Dad a kiss from me.

Love you, too.

Cait resisted the impulse to roll her eyes over her mom's text, because she, too, was worried about her brother, a feeling unfamiliar to her. Gone was the Liam who had not a care in the world—now he walked around with his shoulders slumped, visibly weighted down by what had transpired last winter in New York. Also missing was the glint in his eyes that made them sparkle silver in the sunlight. Come to think of it, she had trouble recalling when she had last seen him out in the sun, and that wasn't her brother. Whether he was playing amateur baseball in Beverley, coaching middle school softball over in Clover Lake, golfing with his endless supply of friends, or swimming at Lake Shelley, he spent every minute he could outdoors in the summer. Her brother had changed, and not for the better. Cait only knew the barest of bones about Liam's love life, with Effie supplying information deemed "non-personal". Cait and her cousin's girlfriend had become friends over the past year, and Effie had filled in enough gaps that Cait understood whatever had happened between Liam and Lana, his "Mystery Woman", had left a scar on her brother, and she was worried he may never heal. Cait admitted to herself that some of the fall-out from the Mystery Woman rendezvous was justified because it was about time her brother was due some heartbreak. Hadn't every other person in their mid-thirties experienced the pain at some point? She undoubtedly had. It was why she was here now.

Pulling up to the dealership, Cait parked her Toyota Prius in the furthest spot from the doors. Her Grandpa Kinsale hated she drove a car that they didn't sell, so she parked far enough away from the vehicles for sale in the Kinsale Motors lot. Her car, a compact hybrid, was the last thing she had purchased before fleeing Mobile, Alabama, and was meant to represent her new life. Maybe "fleeing" was slightly dramatic, especially after hearing Effie's story about how she left her husband, her career, and her life in Denver to move back to South Dakota. Compared to that, Cait's own story fell somewhat flat—welcome to her life, by the way: flat, uninteresting, definitely *not* "Mystery Woman" material.

Pulling down the black skirt to her modest suit ensemble, she checked her reflection in the doors before pulling them open, fully aware that she had an image to uphold, one that differed greatly from her brother's more flamboyant one. Since they had been kids, he had outshined her in almost every way; by the time they were adolescents and growing apart, she had figured out that instead of competing with him, she would be his opposite: serious where he was funny, punctual where he was late, and plain where he was gorgeous. Both siblings were intelligent, but Liam was more naturally so, never having to study all that much, yet getting excellent grades anyway. Look at his track record at NYU, Cait often pointed out. He had screwed around for four years, and then his last year (who takes five years earning a business degree, anyway), his grades landed him a spot on the Dean's List. Cait, on the other hand, had to have a tutor in math and science in high school; fortunately, after her first year in the debate club cemented her belief that she could out-argue anyone, she focused her sights on becoming a lawyer, spending hours at the library poring over law journals, relieved she wouldn't need math or science, anyway.

Pulling off her prescription sunglasses, she traded them in for her regular glasses once she was out of the blistering South Dakota summer sun. Having lived in the Gulf area for the last ten years, one would think she would be immune to the heat, but not in her case, evidenced by the reflection she had seen in the glass door of the frizzy mess her brown hair had become in the humid air that was prevalent in South Dakota on the eastern side of the Missouri River. Another thing to compare to her brother only to come up lacking: her very brown, very blah hair, unlike his own reddish-brown hair her mom insisted on calling "chestnut", and combined with his striking silvery eyes, so light blue, her own plain hazel ones couldn't even decide if they were brown or green…yuck.

"Oh, hi, Miss Livingston," greeted the receptionist at the Beverley branch of Kinsale Motors, the only location to have such an employee. Elsewhere, the salespeople were required to fulfill multiple jobs, including answering their own phones.

"Ms., actually," Cait looked at the name tag the woman at the desk wore, "Lillian."

"Excuse me?" Lillian's eyebrows raised with her question.

"It's Ms. Livingston. Mizz, not Miss," Cait corrected her, heavily pronouncing Ms. in the hope the other woman understood the distinction, and Lillian blushed in response.

Quickly, the woman came out from behind her reception window, apologizing. "I'm so sorry, Ms. Livingston. Of course, you told me that last time you were here. I'll remember next time." Once Liam had assumed management of the location, he had hired the woman, insisting that since Beverley was the largest location, they needed more of a "business" atmosphere. What probably furthered her case, Cait assumed, was her blond hair and brown eyes. Of course, her brother had given her a sob story about how the young woman was a widow whose husband had died last year from cancer, leaving a mountain of medical debt and two children under the age of six. Originally, Lillian had come to the dealership to buy a used car. After the bank turned her away, Liam (true to form), contacted a buddy at the Beverley Credit Union who gave her some kind of extended loan, based on Liam's word. Or so he said. Cait wouldn't put it past him to have put forward some kind of down payment with his own money, because that was what one did who had no financial burdens. Cait, meanwhile, was still paying off the law school loans she had stubbornly insisted on taking out instead of letting her parents pay. So, now Lillian had a car *and* a job, thanks to Liam's "generosity".

"Are you here to see Liam?" Lillian asked.

"Mr. Livingston, you mean," Cait corrected her, just as the man himself stepped out of his office, and Cait was stunned to see he was wearing a navy suit with a white and purple striped shirt and a purple paisley tie, carrying a cup of some sort of hot beverage, based on the steam. True to form, the suit fit his frame gorgeously, emphasizing her brother's broad shoulders, and the colors only highlighted his eyes. She ran a hand down her skirt, hoping it hadn't become too wrinkled in the car ride over, and silently acknowledged that her brother had once again one-upped her, even if unintentionally.

"Well, if it isn't my sister, come down from her high horse to check on us peasants. Tsk, tsk, tsk, Cait—are you scaring the employees again?" Liam frowned at her, his words teasing, but his tone resigned, as it had been since his return from New York City the past winter. She had always viewed their verbal sparring as a kind of sport, but it wasn't much fun anymore when her brother looked so morose every time she saw him.

"Well, what a relief—the favored son *is* alive! At least I can report back to Mom and Dad the joyful news." Cait watched as he fidgeted with his tie. "What's up with your outfit? Career day at the high school or something?"

Liam turned to Lillian. "You can go for the day, Lillian."

"Are you sure? I know you have that appointment with—" she started, but Liam cut her off.

"No, it's fine. Didn't you say your daycare was closing early?" Lillian bit her lip and studied her boss, and Cait could see the hero worship on the woman's face, which is why she had warned her brother repeatedly to not get too personal with his employees, especially the females. He was well known in at least ten counties for his charm alone, and those were the women who hadn't even seen her brother. Cait wondered just how personal things could have become in this workplace between the two of them. No wonder they were on such an informal, first-name basis, Cait pondered suspiciously.

"Okay, thanks, Liam…I mean, Mr. Livingston," she said, shooting a glance at Cait, and she rounded the window to pick up her purse. "See you tomorrow," she said with a wave as she skittered away.

"Don't even start," he warned Cait. "I can tell by that slight curl at the right side of your mouth that you are about to deliver a lecture and I don't need to hear it. Yes, I realize Lillian may be too informal according to your standards, but she is a phenomenal employee. Nothing more than that, which I have made crystal clear previously."

Cait held her hands up in a sign of deference and said, "Okay, fine." Drawing in a breath to let the moment pass, she wondered how to move forward with her brother. Despite what he probably thought, she did not enjoy constantly being at odds with him. "On another topic, why are you dodging Mom and Dad? Mom texted me in a panic this morning," she informed her brother as they entered his office. Cait followed her nose to the coffeemaker in the corner, smelling the luscious brew appreciatively. "MMM, is this Uncle Henry's special blend?" At Liam's nod, she picked up a cup that read "I Don't Give a Sip" from the little stand. "Wow—classy," she said as she filled it with the delicious-smelling drink. "When did he get so good at making coffee?"

Liam shrugged. "I don't know, but he dropped some off here yesterday. Made a big point to mention that Josh is working in Beverley today. Like I care," he muttered.

Cait's eyebrow raised upon hearing this. After witnessing, for her entire life, Liam and Josh being closer than some brothers, she found it difficult seeing the rift between them. Liam had been acting like this since getting back from New York two days earlier than expected. He had arrived home on the day of New Year's Eve: sullen, silent, and much to the dismay of the family, sad.

A sigh from her brother precluded his next question. "Why are you here, Cait?"

Why *was* she here? She had asked herself this with every mile marker she passed driving the forty miles from Clover Lake, where she was currently staying. Cait's grandparents had accompanied her parents to the family property in Lake Tahoe, but Grandma Catherine had been nervous leaving her house unattended, her mail ungathered, and her plants unwatered, so Cait had volunteered to house sit. Regretfully so. Last night, only meaning to pick up a few things at the grocery store, she had run into Boyd Timmons. Somehow, he proceeded to sweet talk her into cooking dinner for him at her grandparents' house. Boyd managed the grocery store owned by his father, and any time she ran into him in Clover Lake, he always flirted with her. Since she had been experiencing a dry spell where men were concerned, she had been flattered and began flirting back, and one thing led to another. Compelled to share her mistake with someone this morning, she wrote:

TEXT TO EFFIE

May have made an error in judgment last night. Cooked dinner for Boyd at grandma and grandpa's. You were right warning me away from him.

TEXT FROM EFFIE

WHAT. THE. HELL

Girl, I told you—NO!!!

He is a barn fire waiting to happen.

TEXT TO EFFIE

I know, but he was so persistent.

And charming. Until he wasn't.

By then it was too late. I'm a mess.

TEXT FROM EFFIE

Oh no—Cait, what happened?

Please tell me you didn't…

TEXT TO EFFIE

My shame prevents me from admitting any
more. Are you around?

Heading to Beverley to see Liam. He's been
radio silent for the past month. Things any better
with him?

TEXT FROM EFFIE

You mean with him and Josh? No.

I had lunch with him yesterday, but he still won't
talk to Josh, or to me about Josh. Come to the
house when you're done.

As she pushed her glasses up the bridge of her nose, she told Liam, "Look, I realize things have been rough for you since Christmas, but—"

"Don't even start acting like you have any understanding of what I've been going through this year. You've never once seemed interested in my personal life, other than to ridicule me about it." Cait opened her mouth to deny his accusation when he continued hotly, "Every comment on how many women I date, or the kind of women I date, or why I can't commit to anyone—I've taken the ridicule. Then, when I *do* find someone…someone who I genuinely have feelings for…it's treated as a joke. Not just by you, by everybody, but it doesn't help that my own sister can't even have my back. What do I expect, though? I'm an idiot, right?" His eyes were flashing silver as he studied her, and Cait was taken aback by the pain in them. "When you moved home, I truly believed that we could forge a new relationship as adults, maybe put whatever this animosity is between us aside. But you don't want that." Her brother took a deep breath, smoothed his tie down as he stood up, ran a hand through his chestnut hair, then said, "Now, if we are done here, I have a meeting at the college."

"Wait," she called as he started to leave his office. "Effie is worried about you, too. So is Josh."

269

"So I've heard. Now, if you'll excuse me, I need to leave. Florence," he called to the saleswoman in the showroom, "I am leaving for the day, but call if you need anything."

"Will do, boss," responded the employee, and Cait followed as Liam left the building, stupefied about what meeting he could have at the college. And wondering how she could fix everything with her brother.

## Thirty-One

*Lana*

> Just landed. Flight was hell. Is it okay that we are staying with Sam and Tess tonight?

> We can find somewhere else to stay.



> It's fine—completely over it.

> Besides, I will need to see Josh eventually at the wedding.

> So heartwarming (hahaha) glad you're looking forward to it.



> I'm looking forward to seeing you, but still worried things will be awkward with Josh.

> Sweetie, things are always awkward with Josh. I just deal with it.

L ana had been comfortably ensconced in her new apartment, living on the top floor of the house owned by Tess and Sam for seven months. After adopting two cats from her mom, Cannoli and Stromboli, she had then gotten a membership for the city's bicycle rental program. Since there were docks for the bikes at each end of her block, Lana usually had no problem getting a bike to ride, commuting (if the weather cooperated) from her apartment in Greenwood Heights to the hospital in Park Slope. Lana began going to Tess's bakery on an almost-daily schedule, and Tess would sit with her for coffee and a muffin or tea and a scone, and the women talked about what books they were reading or recommended British television shows to each other. With so much in common, they had become fast friends. Through frequent texts and ever-increasing phone calls, Lana had also grown close to Effie. For the first time in her life, Lana had close female friends, all made possible by the man who had at one point been her only friend, yet who now Lana dreaded seeing again. Josh and Effie would be back in New York to attend the wedding of Cal and his former wife. Or was it a re-wedding under those circumstances? Lana wasn't sure but had received what she viewed as a pity invite, which she had accepted, under the pressure of Tess and Effie, who were both going with their significant others. To give Cal credit, a few days after she had overheard him in the cafeteria, he had stopped in to her office when she was back at work to apologize for his thoughtless comments, telling her that he had always admired her dedication and work ethic, not to mention how caring and considerate she was with her patients, a rarity at times with surgeons, in his opinion. Deciding to be the bigger person, Lana had forgiven him. Accepting the invitation to the wedding had been more difficult, especially considering its location out in Montauk, of all places, but Lana had made the decision to confront her demons, figuring the relative safety within a group of friends would prove less traumatic. A bonus was the potential for her to even maybe have fun with her group of friends. The wedding was tomorrow, and Sam was driving all of them out for the day. After the wedding, Effie and Josh were staying a few days out there for a beach vacation, but Sam, Tess, and Lana would head back after the wedding. Now if only she could stop thinking about Liam, a task that would not be made easier by seeing his cousin today.

Leaving Liam back in that hotel room last winter had been excruciating, but Lana had been certain it was her only option. No way could they have moved forward as a couple—that had been a non-starter, despite whatever her heart had been telling her during those few blissful days with him. Spending days and nights cocooned with him had been magical, but not real, and she would rather have those precious memories to live in her mind than deal with anything marring them and based on Josh's reaction to discovering that she was Liam's "Mystery Woman", that would have happened eventually. Lana had known deep down that men like Liam didn't want someone like her, long-term—she was too serious, too focused, and yes, too smart, and while those qualities may have intrigued him for a while, he would have lost interest in her, eventually. From what Josh had told her about his cousin in the past, Liam always lost interest eventually.

After breaking things off with Liam, Lana had almost texted Tess to tell her that she would not be renting their apartment after all. How could she face Tess and Sam when she was convinced the world was laughing at her for having made such a fool of herself? Instead, she had taken out her phone to find:

TEXT FROM TESS

Lana, I know what happened with Liam. I am probably the only one to truly understand what you're going through now. You can move on from this, if that's what you want.

And you can do that here.

Please don't change your mind about the apartment. We are here for you.

Of course, that was what she wanted—to move on, put Liam in the past, and start her new life, and she had done so, thanks to Sam and Tess and a fresh start in Brooklyn. And surprisingly, with the help of her family, all of whom had shown up to help her move in to her new apartment in January. Although her lease for the studio apartment had another month left, Lana had wanted a more immediate fresh start, even if that meant a longer commute from Brooklyn to the Upper East Side for a couple of months, until she started at the hospital in Park Slope. On moving day, while Monty, both brothers-in-law, her nieces (Julia, Amelia, and Allie), and her teenage nephews (Arthur and Max) carried boxes down four flights of stairs on the Lower East Side, Lana, her sisters, and her mom had arranged everything to be moved in the back of Monty's pickup and the trailer he had borrowed from a friend. Everyone had been working silently until her sisters started questioning her.

"Lana," Ava had begun hesitantly, "it's fine if you don't want to talk about it, but whatever happened with your Hook Up?"

"Liam," Lana quietly corrected her, then inwardly cursed herself for doing so. Now her sisters wouldn't stop until they had all the information.

"What?"

"His name is Liam," she sighed. "The whole 'Hook Up' thing is over. We're over, if there ever really *was* a thing." Lana had turned her focus to stacking some smaller boxes in her mom's cleaning van.

"Ooookay," Ava answered, and Lana didn't miss the look that passed between her sisters.

Greer had picked up then where Ava had left off. "But what about all that time you spent together? Wasn't he here, like, a week?"

"Girls, if your sister doesn't want to talk about it, just leave her be," Fiona had admonished her older daughters. Lana had felt a bit of relief for about five seconds before her mom asked, "Did he do something, Lana? Did he leave and you haven't heard from him?"

Ava had gasped. "What an ass! Based on your description of him, I kind of thought he would be a jerk."

"Totally," Greer had agreed. "Real hot men are always pricks."

"You mean really hot men," Lana had corrected her sister, who stared at her in confusion. "You said 'real hot men', but you need an adverb, not an adjective."

"Umm, okay, college girl, calm down. I don't think grammar is the point of this conversation, anyway," Greer had told her.

"You want answers? Fine—**Liam** turned out to be Josh's cousin, who was-"

"Josh…as in…*your* Josh?" Ava had appeared dumbfounded.

"Well, not *my Josh*, but if you mean the Josh who I shared an office with, yes." Lana had flushed then, as the mortification began anew.

Luckily, she had never confessed her misguided attraction to her office mate to her family, sparing herself that particular humiliation.

"You know, I always kind of thought maybe you had a crush on him," Ava had said. Or not, she thought, now bracing for further impact.

"Totally, A," agreed Greer. "I mean, who wouldn't? Remember that day we surprised her at the hospital? He was in the office, looking so fine-"

"Girls, enough!" cried their mother. "Someone please get in the back of Montgomery's truck to arrange those boxes. Honestly, this is why I prefer to work alone. No arguing, no chatty coworkers. No meddling daughters," Fiona had shot her oldest two a warning look, which they each had taken the liberty of ignoring.

"Oh, there's Amelia," Ava had pointed out, as her own daughter carried a smaller box to put in the van. "Do Mommy a favor and get in the back of your uncle's truck to fix those boxes. I'm too old to climb up there," she had pouted to her daughter, who had rolled her eyes in response, yet had done her mother's bidding.

"Anyway," Ava had turned back to Lana, "I'm sorry about...*Liam*... that sucks to be ghosted."

"Totally," Greer had agreed.

Lana had shaken her head, feeling the need to correct her sister. "He didn't ghost me."

"What do you mean? You said that he left-" Ava had responded.

"No, *you* said that he left." Lana had argued.

Greer had put her arm around Lana's shoulders then, telling her, "Look, L, it's fine to admit it. No harm, no foul. You had fun, right?"

Unable to keep herself from proving that she had not been the wronged party, Lana told them, "Look, read these if you don't believe me," pulling up the text messages from Liam, beginning with when she had left the hotel room.

"Wow—this is pretty harsh, L," Ava had told her with a frown, after reading for several minutes.

"Totally. He is pouring his guts out to you, and you said nothing," Greer had agreed, then had added hesitantly, "Lana, he told you he loved you."

Ava unnecessarily added, "He counted the days after he left you. Lana, what did you do?

Thankfully, at that point, her movers had been bringing down a string of smaller boxes, so her sisters' inquisition had ended. Lana had dropped the matter of Liam all together, never bothering to explain her side of things, but it hadn't really mattered. They wouldn't understand—her sisters had never been single, not really, and had never had any focus except for their relationships and their half-baked careers. And Lana's mom? Forget it—Lana had always been certain that if their dad walked back into her life at any point and time, Fiona would take him back.

Lana pulled up to the bike docking station and slid her bike in to lock it into place. Since she had showered after her shift at the hospital, she decided to take a walk in Green-Wood to clear her mind, so she was prepared to see Josh upon his arrival. As she chose a path to walk, she followed it up the side of a hill that overlooked one of the ponds in the cemetery. A squirrel darted in front of her, and in the silence, she could hear a woodpecker in the distance. Choosing to walk the stone paths instead of the roads allowed Lana to be surrounded more fully by the beauty the cemetery offered, and she stopped to look at a hydrangea bush bursting with color thanks to the blue and purple flowers. Suddenly, a shadow passed overhead, and Lana tipped her head back in time to see a red-tailed hawk soaring above, and she gasped in awe. Taking out her phone to take a picture, she saw that Josh and Effie were due to arrive in half an hour, so she began her journey back.

Walking up to the gate of the house, the front door underneath the outside set of stairs opened, and Sam's dark head popped out. "Hey, Lana, home for the day?"

She answered, "Yes, at last! I just took a quick a walk in Green-Wood before Josh and Effie get here."

"They should be here pretty soon, I think. Oh, Tess wanted me to tell you that she made your favorite lemon cake today, and you are to report to the bakery immediately for a slice." Lana's stomach rumbled at the mention of the lemon cake. Tess made a delicious lemon curd as the filling, and topped it with fluffy lemon buttercream, and it was divine. "I just came from there myself. I wanted to be here when Josh and Effie arrived. Oh, this must be them now," Sam said, as a yellow taxi pulled up in front of the house.

Effie sprang out of the back of the vehicle squealing, "Lana," as she ran to her, hugging her tightly. "Josh is really nervous," she whispered in her ear.

Her friendship with Josh had been on a tight rope since they were here at Christmas, mostly because she knew Josh regretted much of what he had said that day. Obviously, if Josh and Effie had not been there, the identities of Hook Up and Mystery Woman could have remained hidden for longer and Lana and Liam would have been able to stay in their blissful love nest, remaining free of the outside world, for at least the rest of the time Liam was in New York. However, Lana couldn't help but think that Josh had done her a favor by inserting reality sooner than expected. Harsh reality was more her scene, anyway—it suited her. No more fantasy. Having been in the front seat witnessing what pinning your hopes and dreams on romance did to someone's life, how it wrecked them, tortured them—she just didn't need that.

Lana turned to Josh, unable to mistake the tension around his mouth for anything else and said, "Hey, Josh, good to see you," and, hoping to put them both at ease more quickly, opened her arms to hug him.

"Lana, I'm sorry," he began as he returned her hug, and she saw behind him that Effie and Sam had stepped into the house with the luggage. He put his hands in his pockets and took a deep breath. "I don't know what else to say except that it was a shock to find out that you were the woman my cousin had been communicating with for so many months. That you were the woman Liam met in the bar that night? You were his Mystery Woman all along? It seemed too unbelievable to be true; but, I mean, in retrospect, it makes sense. Effie has reminded me more than once that the whole thing was my doing, anyway, since I not only arranged for the gathering, but pressured you into meeting up, and then cancelled at the last minute, which left you two alone. Even if I had shown up, though, you two still would have met. Some people would consider it fate."

Fate? Josh could not be serious right now, could he? Josh was a man who dealt with reality, so it surprised Lana to hear him speaking about fate. "Josh, it's fine—I understand," she told him, wanting to move on from the topic of Liam.

Josh shook his head. "It's not fine, though. I deeply regret the things I said about Liam that day. He didn't speak to me for months, and that was something I can never forgive myself for. Over the years, I know I told you some anecdotes about him—which were all true, by the way—but may have been exaggerated for effect."

"Please, stop, Josh," she pleaded. "It's fine," she insisted again. "I'm fine. I've moved on. I'm good."

"What do you mean, you've moved on? Are you seeing someone?" Josh's eyes widened and his brows furrowed. Why was he looking so concerned?

"No, just that I realize I need to have one focus, and that's my career. I was never looking for anything else, and do not need to get sidetracked now. Besides, how ridiculous would it have been? He lives in South Dakota, and I live here." She shook her head again. "Stupid, really, to have imagined anything else."

Josh laughed, "Well, Effie and I are proof that distance is surmountable. And Tess and Sam are proof that fate can deal a pretty heavy hand of cards. But I need you to understand that I was wrong over the years to emphasize only Liam's outrageous qualities, without balancing it out with his good qualities. He is the funniest person I know, not to mention the joy he brings to the world. He has been there for me, throughout my entire life, with never a question. Whatever I've needed, he has given me. And last, I want to say that I have never heard him talk about any other woman the way he talked about you. And trust me, there have been plenty of opportunities. But he has never been as serious about them as he was with you."

Lana's heart raced as Josh talked about Liam, remembering the way he looked at her with those luminous light blue eyes. The tender way he held her in his arms. How she fit so perfectly against him when they watched a movie on the sofa in their hotel room. His thoughtfulness in the way he had made their room so beautifully festive. All moments of a certain time and a certain place, she reminded herself, to be treasured in her memories for eternity.

"Thanks for telling me all of that about him, but I already knew it.

Our time together was magic, and it was all because of him." Josh smiled at her words, until she said, "It makes no difference now, though. As you said, he has had a lot of…experience…and I don't doubt he will again." Josh's frown was back in place. "It's fine, Josh. Please, can we move on? Let's get Effie and go down to the bakery. I hear there's some lemon cake Tess made today." Josh then smiled at her and Lana saw him briefly check his phone before he went to the house to collect Effie and Sam.

Lana heard her phone ping with an incoming message. Assuming Tess was tired of waiting for them at the bakery, she opened her phone to reply to her but saw instead a photo. In awe, she stared at herself and Liam, and the expressions on their faces stole all breath away. Instead of facing the camera, their photographer that day on the tram had instead captured them looking at each other, and while Lana studied the expressions on both of their faces, she now did not know how she was supposed to live up to the expectations she had set for herself to move on…

# CHAPTER
## Thirty-Two

*Liam*

TEXT FROM JOSH

Thanks for trusting me.

Phase one accomplished.

TEXT TO JOSH

Thanks, Cousin.

See you tomorrow.

L iam had been miserable in the months since his trip, finally understanding that his disinterest in maintaining a relationship had been due to him fearing he lacked the capacity to care for someone deeply. All he had needed was the right person, and from the minute he looked into Lana's eyes, he knew she was the one. How long did it take other people to fall in love? Was there a timeline? Josh had seemed to think so when he listed every reason Liam could not actually have fallen in love with Lana the very first night he met her. What did his cousin know, after all? He had been engaged to Tess for five years, not reading the obvious signs that they were each just settling. Instead,

Josh had buried himself in his career trying to ignore the truth. When Josh had accused Liam of using Lana, that had stung, especially considering the fact that in Liam's view, his cousin had been the one who had used her—letting her cook dinner for him when he had to have known damn well her intentions (misguided, clearly) and then kissing her to stroke his own ego after being told the truth about Tess and Sam.

Leaving New York (and Lana) back in December had been the most difficult thing he had ever done, but what choice had Liam had? To this day, he was still raw when he considered the fact that she had never responded to any of his texts, other than pleading with him to stop, and that was an impossible demand. While it was true they didn't know everything about each other, what more could he find out that would make him change his mind about her? Nothing, just as there was nothing he could learn that would make him love her more. Even his sister had backed him on this, telling him to follow his heart. Where his relationship with Josh had splintered in parts, the one with his sister had become stronger, oddly enough. Liam had struggled with forgiving Josh for the things he had said back in that hotel room until his uncle Henry had paid him a visit two weeks ago.

Liam had just gotten home from having a meeting at the college and was shrugging out of the suit jacket he had worn, pondering how Josh wore such formal clothing every day. Not only that, but he seemed to enjoy it? Liam was more at home in a t-shirt and jeans, sometimes a pair of khakis at the dealership, occasionally donning a sports jacket if meeting one of his more formal customers. A soft knock at his door startled him; since his rift with Josh, he hadn't had many visitors to his house, unless his mom was stopping in Beverley, or Effie was popping by, trying to plead Josh's case for forgiveness. Opening the door, Liam was surprised to see the face of his uncle on the other side.

"Uncle Henry! Hey, I'm sorry, I keep meaning to stop in at the shop when I'm downtown, but-"

"It's okay, Liam, I know you've been busy." His uncle peered at him knowingly from underneath the brim of his ball cap, with the Livingston eyes that always seemed to understand what wasn't being said. "Can I come in?"

"Of course. Sorry, I just got home, and I'm in a daze, kind of." Liam held open the door for Henry, closing it quickly to keep the central air conditioning from escaping into the blistering heat outside. "Can I get you something to drink? I have some iced tea in the fridge."

Henry sighed with relief. "Yes, that would be quite welcome right about now. It's been so hot this week that I've been forced to drink my coffee iced, and you know that goes against everything I used to believe in." Liam nodded, fully aware of his uncle's feelings on diluting his carefully roasted coffee blends with ice.

As Liam walked to his kitchen to grab the pitcher of tea, he was curious about what brought his uncle to his house. Before Liam had moved to Beverley, it was quite common for him to stop in and visit his uncle at the shop whenever he was in town for anything. Sometimes he would pick up a little treat, like ice cream or pastries, but he would also bring lunch if he timed it just right. Once Josh had moved back, Liam wanted to give them more time together, since he knew how much Henry had missed his son while he lived in New York. Henry was so much like Josh, yet even quieter, if that was possible. His calming effect on everyone was probably because he was the middle child among his siblings—George was the oldest, and their sister, Beatrice, was the youngest.

"You said you just got home?" Henry asked. At Liam's nod, Henry continued, "The dealership's been closed for a couple of hours now, hasn't it?"

"Yeah. I was, believe it or not, at a meeting at the college." Beverley Community College, which had once boasted one of the highest enrollment rates among the state's smaller colleges, had been through a tough decade in the 90s, with many high school graduates attending large universities or even going out of state. Now, though, it had seen a resurgence the past fifteen years and was thriving. Paul Larsen, a close friend from high school and captain of the amateur baseball team, had reached out to him when he hadn't signed up to play this summer. Paul also happened to be vice president of enrollment services at the college, and over drinks at Shorty's, incidentally a block from the college, Paul had asked him about his future now that he was living in Beverley.

"What do you mean—my future?" Liam had laughed. "My future is selling cars for my family."

"Dude, stop! Why do you always do that?" Paul had chastised him.

"Do what?" What else did he have going on in his life since his Mystery Woman stopped communicating with him? Nothing.

"That thing where you downplay shit about yourself. I happen to have heard the talk around town, and it seems you have increased sales at the Beverley dealership in less than a year and did the same over in Carlisle."

Liam had shrugged. "Not too hard to do when some of my customers are hot little housewives. You know how it is." May as well lean back into his stereotype, Liam thought glumly.

Paul had laughed and responded, "There you go again. I honestly don't know how it is having women throw themselves at me—that's why I have always lived vicariously through you!" Paul grew serious as he continued, "Anyway, the college is going through a rebuilding phase, and a couple of areas we want to expand are our math and science departments."

Studying his friend's face over the bottle of beer in front of him, not sure what he really wanted or what anything concerning the college could possibly have to do with him, Liam had asked for clarification, "So, what, you want me to ask Josh? I don't know—he has a lot on his plate with working at the hospital here and then a couple of days a week in Sioux Falls."

Paul had widened his dark brown eyes and looked at Liam as if confused. "No, why would I ask you to do that? If I wanted to talk to Josh, he'd be here now instead of you; although considering how thick you're being, maybe it is Josh I should be speaking to. Let me be clearer —do you remember in high school who helped me get through every single math class? Geometry, Calculus, all the algebras-"

"That was a million years ago," Liam had interrupted.

"And? Current confusion aside, I doubt you got dumber over the years, dude. Uglier, yes, but dumber?" Paul had sipped his beer and chuckled.

"Well, I'm sure that is a matter up for debate, but what is this about? I doubt you asked me here to talk about my brain power." The truth was, Liam had shown an affinity for both science and math back in high school, and perhaps if Josh and Felix hadn't overshadowed him in both areas, his family would have taken more notice of his capabilities back then.

"Now that is where you are wrong, my friend," Paul had corrected Liam.

Now Liam told his uncle about drinks with Paul, and how Paul had encouraged him to apply for an open math instructor position.

"Evidently," he told Henry, "they already have two instructors, but with the class sizes getting larger, the college wants to keep up with demand and is looking to add a third."

"Wow, Liam—that's incredible!" Liam felt his uncle squeeze his shoulder.

"Yeah, they are clearly desperate, right?" Liam studied his uncle's face, trying to read what he was truly thinking. Henry, usually a man of few words, had liberally lavished praise on his only child for his good grades, his intelligence, his natural way with school. Liam, meanwhile, had gotten none of that same praise from his parents. He supposed it had been difficult, with Josh being damn near a genius, and his sister Cait studiously hitting the books every night, for either of his parents to take him seriously when it came to his schoolwork. Had he dicked around when he was in school, blowing off a test to party or to hang out with a girl instead? Yes, but he had always managed to sweet talk a teacher into extending a date on a paper, or letting him retake an exam, which he always then passed with flying colors. Until he got to college, that is, where he had been a small fish in a big pond. Where nobody knew the Livingston name, good or bad. Despite finally making the Dean's List his final year, all talk focused on how long it had taken him finally to graduate with his bachelor's degree.

"Liam, why would you say that?" Henry had asked.

"No one has ever looked to me for academics, Uncle Henry. Josh and Cait have always been the studious ones. Hell, Felix, too," he reminded his uncle. "Daniel may not have gone to a fancy university, but he graduated from one of the most prestigious culinary schools in the country. Every one of them has been a success but me."

After a pause, Henry said, "I assume you know I was supposed to go to college—that I wanted to be a doctor, right?" Liam nodded, because that was part of Josh's lore—he picked up his dad's dream of being a doctor but had gone one step further by becoming a surgeon. No one really ever discussed it, but the story went that the summer before going away to college, Henry had been working at the Grand Canyon, and it was there he had met Josh's mom. The two had fallen head over heels in love, moving back to South Dakota to get married and start a family. "But when I came back home instead, to work in the family's auto shop, I felt like an absolute failure. No one needed to say anything, but I could read the disappointment on everyone's face, including your dad's. I put so much pressure on Josh to become a surgeon that sometimes I wonder if he did it to fulfill my dream or his."

Liam shook his head, "No, that was all Josh—I remember when we were kittle kids. Josh always talked about being a doctor."

Henry waved his hand. "My point is that your parents have given you the space to become whatever it is that *you* want to become. I think they always saw me as being too intense with Josh, especially after his mom left, that maybe they leaned too much the opposite way with you. But you need to know, Liam, that everyone has always seen you as special: someone who can walk into a room and light the place up. You have such an easy demeanor with everyone, whether it is someone you just met or a long-time friend. You are capable and trustworthy, and if Paul sought you out for this position, I think that is an honor and worth considering it." His uncle's words touched a nerve in him that he desperately needed. Aware that his own dad could have told him the same thing, hearing it from his uncle hit differently, mostly because of Henry's sincerity.

"You know, I actually thought Paul wanted to talk to me about Josh doing something at the college," Liam confessed ruefully.

"Josh?" Henry looked astonished. "My son may be capable of many things, but I cannot begin to wrap my head around him teaching kids at the community college—remember how hard he worked to convince himself that being a surgeon in South Dakota *wasn't* a step down on his career ladder?" The two men laughed, and Henry said hesitantly, "Josh is actually why I stopped over today to see you."

Liam felt a pit in his stomach, as he often did when he thought about Josh any time over the past six months. It was the longest he had ever gone with not speaking to his cousin—in fact, the two of them had never had a falling out on this level before. Slight squabbles and minor miscommunications, sure, but that coincided with two cousins being as close as brothers. Liam's pain was still so raw when he thought about Josh's reaction to finding out that Lana was his Mystery Woman, and in fact, he blamed Josh for Lana's refusal to continue with their relationship. Perhaps if Josh had been more encouraging and less disparaging, Lana would now be with him, in some way, instead of seemingly ignoring every attempt he made to communicate with her.

"You know he hates himself for whatever happened in New York between the two of you?" Liam hung his head, unable to look at his uncle, because he wasn't proud that he seemed to be choosing a woman over his cousin. "I don't know every detail, but from what I understand, the woman you have feelings for is the same woman who Josh worked with in New York, right?"

"Right," Liam confirmed. "A woman who Josh has sworn up and down to not have had any feelings for—except when he tried to kiss her, which I only found out about last December, but it seems everyone else already knew. You know I had asked him to introduce me to Lana on several occasions over the years whenever I visited him in New York. He never took me seriously, though. I wasn't good enough for a surgeon, I guess."

"Liam, what would you have done if he had? You feel strongly for her now, but just imagine the position that would have put Josh in if it hadn't worked out with you and Lana—his friend, his co-worker...his office mate? I seem to recall a string of young women over the years, who you brought to family reunions, or holidays, or long vacations at Lake Tahoe, but I don't recall ever meeting the same woman twice."

Liam blustered, "But that doesn't mean that's how it would have gone with Lana! She's been different from any woman I have ever met, since the beginning!"

Henry sighed then, "And how was Josh to know the difference?"

"It just would have been nice for him to have my back—treat me the way he has always treated Sam, maybe." Here was Liam's old wound concerning Sam, reopening.

"Sam, as in Sam who fell in love with Josh's fiancée? As much as he has forgiven Sam, Josh is still recovering from all of that—you know how much he hates change. Effie told me the other day that she wants to take out the wallpaper in one of the bathrooms in their house, but Josh keeps trying to talk her out of it." Henry poured himself another glass of iced tea.

Liam told his uncle, "But that doesn't make any sense—Effie bought that house before she even was with Josh. How could he have any emotional ties to it?"

Henry shrugged. "That's your cousin. Let me know when half of what he does makes sense. He keeps bringing me a coffee from Mr. Beans when he knows I prefer my own blends, but what can I do?"

"I know you're right, Uncle Henry. Effie sends me a text every other day, trying to get me to talk to Josh, but it's just gone on so long now that I guess I don't know where to start."

"Just call him. You know he will be thrilled to hear about this opportunity at the college, and it'll make a good icebreaker."

Heeding his uncle's words, Liam had called Josh that night, and the two met for breakfast at Betsy's Diner the following morning, after months of ignoring texts, calls, and drop-ins. Drop-ins were the hardest because Josh could be extremely annoying and persistent. Fully encouraging Liam to take the job at the college, Josh then told him he'd be stupid not to, which was very on brand for his cousin. The two did not speak of Lana during breakfast, with both men leery of upsetting their newly found peace. The cousins picked up where they had left off in the world: completely at odds, yet absolutely in sync. When Liam had arrived home from work that day, an invitation from Cal for his second wedding to his ex-wife was in his mailbox. Assuming it was Josh's doing, Liam had texted his cousin.

TEXT TO JOSH

Why is there an invitation to Cal's wedding in my mailbox? You know I can't really stand the guy, especially after what he said about Lana.
Besides, how many times does one man have to marry the same woman? You'd think his wife would have learned her lesson...

TEXT FROM JOSH

Don't be an idiot—Lana got one, too, and she has forgiven Cal. I know he can be…trying…but he has been there for me. Anyway, you and Effie can rag on him together at the wedding. When you're not making up with Lana, that is.

TEXT TO EFFIE

Am I really going to this dick's wedding?

TEXT FROM EFFIE

Lana still talks about you.

TEXT TO EFFIE

Flight booked.

Now here he was, back in New York, after half of a year gone and spent alone. He turned up the volume on the speaker as the radio connected with his Bluetooth, thinking of Lana as he listened to Judy Garland sing "Get Happy". Having landed at LaGuardia two hours ago, and with an invitation to Cal's wedding on the seat next to him, Liam was in his rental car headed east—as far east as one could go on this island, with his mind on Lana and Lana only.

# CHAPTER
## Thirty-Three

*Lana*

TEXT FROM MOM

Oh, Honey, that is a beautiful photo.

It makes me emotional seeing how happy you look.

TEXT TO MOM

Happy—that's what the woman who took the photo said, also. Mom, have I made a mistake, pushing him away all of these months?

TEXT FROM MOM

Maybe not—there must a reason he sent the photo now, I would imagine. Did you respond?

TEXT TO MOM

Not yet—I don't know what to say.

Take your time, then, but just remember to keep your heart open. I know how my mistakes with your father affected you, and I will always regret it. I can never regret loving him, because I have you kids, but I can regret the years I spent wasting energy in the hopes he would come back to me.

I love you my sweet baby girl.

Traffic had been standard heading out on the Long Island Expressway (which meant bumper-to-bumper), giving Lana plenty of time to consider the photo she had immediately saved to her phone. While the two couples she was traveling with bantered, at times bickering playfully, all Lana could do was pretend to be sleeping while she ruminated about the seven months she had wasted attempting, and failing, to ignore the depth of her feelings for Liam. How much had her mom and dad's history affected how she had processed her feelings for Liam? How much had her dad shaped the way she viewed herself and her place in the world?

When she had moved in with her dad and stepmom, Lana had adapted to the new lifestyle seamlessly. Slightly surprising, considering she had spent her childhood on the sidelines watching as people like her stepmom talked down to her mom as she cleaned their homes, or worse, treated her disdainfully if they saw her in public and out of uniform. After all, what if their friends caught them talking to the hired help cordially? To her shame, Lana had lived in fear of her mom showing up unexpectedly in her work van to the private school deemed to be worthy of the high scores Lana had earned on her placement tests. Since Oyster Bay and Riverhead were not close to each other, Lana's separate lives had been relatively easy to handle. Until they weren't.

"Lana," she heard a voice calling her, "we're here." Lana opened her eyes to find Effie smiling down at her, her tantalizing tawny eyes shining in the sunlight from the moon roof opening at the top of the SUV. "You feeling okay?" Effie asked with a knowing look. The two traded texts frequently, and Lana was drawing on the strength of her friendship with both Effie and Tess to face the Montauk country club.

"Yeah," she responded with a yawn, "just tired."

"Didn't you tell me once that you're from out here, Lana?" Josh questioned.

"Umm, kind of. Not this far out, though," Lana responded evasively. She then clarified reluctantly, "Riverhead." Lana had never confided in anyone about her family, but not because she was ashamed—it was just too messy to explain. God, even now, this place was overtaking her, like a vampire sucking its victims dry. She just hoped she could return to Brooklyn tonight unscathed, but her track record in Montauk told a different story.

Opening the door to the vehicle, Lana stepped out into the searing sunlight and snapped on a pair of sunglasses. Effie followed her and gasped, "Oh my god—have I stepped onto a movie set?"

No, not a movie set—the Montauk Marina Beach Club. Possibly the last place in the entire world Lana wanted to be. Ever. Again. Why was she here?

Tess whistled, "Wow—Josh, I didn't know Cal was so loaded. I mean, this is posh, even by a doctor's standards." Tess laughed then and said to Sam, "Hey, Babe, when you get your next advance, maybe we can get a membership out here."

Sam took her hand and reeled her into him. "Anything for you, but is this how you want to spend your time away from the bakery? Locked in a car on the expressway for three hours in traffic?"

"If it puts anything into perspective, the price of our hotel room alone is costing us a pretty penny for the evening," Josh informed the group as he pointed across the beach to the hotel. "But in response to your question, Tess, this isn't Cal's money, despite his dad being a plastic surgeon. Sadie's family owns some real estate out here, I guess. Despite the grandeur of the place, Cal told me that the guest list isn't that extensive —just friends and family. Unlike their previous wedding, which was huge."

"Oh, my god—remember how drunk Cal's sister got at that wedding, Josh?" Tess chimed in.

"Oh, yeah, she was a mess. Cal says she's been sober for a couple of years now but has been divorced twice already due to her issues." Josh answered.

"Well, I am ready to enjoy some of the ocean experience while we're here," Effie announced, winking at Josh, who blushed in response.

"And some cocktails, I hope," Tess said, linking her arm through Effie's, and then through Lana's.

The group made their way to the clubhouse patio, which was adorned with small lightbulbs strung overhead. Lana remarked nervously, "I hope I'm dressed okay."

Effie looked at her and responded, "Girl, you are gorgeous. That dress is a stunner on you," she commented on the navy-blue dress with gold buttons down the front, cinched at her waist and then flared at her hips. Effie had raided Lana's closet last night after she had shown Effie and Tess the dress she had originally planned on wearing.

"Nope—too boring," Tess had declared.

"Seriously, Lana, you're not going to a funeral. This is supposed to be a happy event. Let me have a look," insisted Effie, who had immediately shrieked when she found the navy dress at the back of the closet. "God, this is gorgeous."

"And way too tight. I don't even know why I have it. I bought it when I graduated from med school and have gained at least twenty pounds since then," Lana had told her friends once she tried on the dress.

"Bull," declared Tess, "it fits beautifully. Everything just needed to be redistributed differently." And redistributed, the women had done, making Lana blush as she looked in the mirror.

"Absolutely not," Lana shook her head.

"Oh, wait, I have the perfect accessory," Tess announced, and she had raced out of Lana's apartment down to her house. Returning, Tess had said, "Look, here's a lightweight pashmina you can borrow that looks like it was made to go with this dress."

Walking across the parking lot, Lana tugged the pashmina tighter around her with her free arm, despite the heat, wondering if she looked as out of place as she felt. This whole place was making her a mess of nerves. When she had told her sisters she was coming out to Montauk for the wedding, she could sense their trepidation through their texts:

Group text with Ava and Greer

TEXT FROM AVA

L, are you sure you want to do that?

I mean, you barely know this Cal, right?

TEXT FROM GREER

And wasn't he, like, a dick the last time you saw Josh?

TEXT TO AVA AND GREER

Maybe he was, but it wasn't like he was wrong. Not his fault he knew I had, or thought I had, feelings for Josh. Anyway, he apologized profusely.

Plus, his wife is super nice. Or ex-wife? Bride-to-be?

TEXT FROM GREER

Whatever. You swore you would never go back there.

TEXT TO AVA AND GREER

Right—I was 16. A stupid kid. Besides, no one knows me out here anymore. I'll be fine.

TEXT FROM AVA

I think we are all in agreement to not tell Monty, though, right?

TEXT FROM GREER

Totally.

Once the group arrived at the clubhouse, Josh opened the doors to usher them into the air-conditioned room. "What a relief—it feels so much nicer in here. I think I will find a nice spot near the bar and-"

"Absolutely not!" exclaimed Effie. "Please, let's go out to the patio? This South Dakota girl needs an ocean view!" With that, Effie grabbed his hand, and he kissed her fingers, allowing himself to be steered outside.

Tess remarked, "My word, that woman can get him to do anything. Josh absolutely hates the heat, but he barely put up a fight."

Sam laughed, "Well, he is a man in love, and I know from personal experience what it means to be putty in the hands of the woman you love. Nothing I wouldn't do for you, Theresa. Just say the word." Sam bent his head down to nuzzle Tess's neck, and she wrapped her arms around him in response.

What was she doing here with two madly in-love couples? To give them credit, they seemed to be doing their best to make sure she wasn't having a third-wheel experience, but times like these, when their affections toward their partners overwhelmed them, Lana couldn't help but feel the pang of loss in her heart, knowing Liam's affection towards her would have rivaled them all.

Needing a moment alone, Lana told Tess and Sam, "Hey, I need to use the restroom, okay? You two go on and see where Josh and Effie are and I'll find you guys when I'm done."

Tess and Sam exchanged a look, and Lana saw him give a small nod toward the far corner of the room. Trying to track his gaze, Lana failed to see above the taller crowd. Suddenly, Tess broke out in a grin, telling Lana, "Okay, Lana. Come find us soon, though, okay?"

Lana made her way to the ladies' room, humming along to Frank Sinatra singing "The Way You Look Tonight". Behind her she heard, "Lana?" Lana turned around and saw the voice belonged to Dr. Scanlon, head of the surgical department from Lenox Hill Hospital on the Upper East Side. Though Lana had been at the hospital in Brooklyn for most of the year, she still felt gratitude toward Dr. Scanlon, who had hand-picked Lana for her department when she was in her last semester of medical school at Stony Brook University. Lana already had a rotation in internal medicine lined up first but had been honored and eager to follow that up at Lenox Hill, because she held the other woman in high esteem. Dr. Scanlon's parents had immigrated from the Dominican Republic, making their home in the Bronx when she was a newborn, and she was the first female, regardless of race, to hold the position of Head of Surgery at the prestigious hospital.

"Dr. Scanlon, hi. It's so good to see you," she told her, as Dr. Scanlon drew her into a hug. "I'm surprised to see you here." Lana relaxed a bit, knowing there was one more person here she could draw comfort from, should the location become overwhelming.

"I could say the same to you, I think. My husband and I went to med school with Cal's dad, so I've known Cal since he was a young boy." Dr. Scanlon accepted a glass of champagne from the waiter passing by, but Lana shook her head no at the offer. In a hushed voice, she told Lana, "Between you and me, he's had a lot of maturing to do over the years, but I think he might get there." Shocked, Lana stared at Dr. Scanlon in awe, while the woman took a sip of champagne, and then chuckled as she winked at Lana. "So, Dr. Miller, I am hearing nothing but rave reviews from Park Slope Presbyterian about you."

Lana blushed at the compliment, somewhat surprised her name had come up under any circumstance. "I am learning so much there, and I just hope I can continue to grow as a doctor and surgeon."

"I know you will. Oh, there's my husband, looking lost without me. Take care, Lana, and please let me know if you ever need anything."

"You, too, thank you." Lana watched as Dr. Scanlon walked over and offered her champagne to her husband. What must it be like—to be so successful, having had so many barriers in your path, but now have everything you've ever worked for, Lana wondered?

In the restroom, Lana was washing her hands at the sink when she saw two women enter the lounge area, separate from the toilet stalls. "I mean, can you even believe it? That she would have the audacity to show her face here?" Lana overheard one of them say as the other one applied more lipstick.

"Cecily, who the hell cares? You said yourself you didn't even recognize her. It's been fifteen years since high school—get over it!" Cecily? Lana had known a Cecily in high school, but that must be a coincidence. Not exactly a common name, though, she reminded herself, as a sense of unease came over her.

"Get over it? Mindy, that little bitch slept with my boyfriend at the senior party! I can still see her little white trash face following him around all the time." Now Lana ducked back into a stall, recalling that Mindy's best friend from high school was not only the most popular girl in the senior class but also one of the richest, with her dad being…oh god no, Lana thought. Mindy's best friend was Cecily, whose dad was a plastic surgeon. Could it be? She closed her eyes, computing the reality that Cecily could very well be the younger sister of Cal, whose dad was a plastic surgeon. Cal, who also grew up on Long Island. Cal, who was around Josh's age, so at least five years older than Lana, so even though she had started high school at thirteen, he would have already graduated.

She heard the woman who she was fairly certain was Cecily say, "Stupid bitch didn't even realize he was only using her to get a good grade in biology—what's that they say about supposedly smart people actually being stupid in real life? You know she's the reason we broke up that summer? Tony felt so guilty for that night. He said he was only trying to make her feel special, and didn't mean for anything to happen, especially after he found out she was a virgin," Cecily cackled madly. "Virgin my ass—you know those white trash girls are always giving it away for free, anyway."

Lana heard Mindy's voice respond, "Oh my god, Cecily, chill. Just forget about her and enjoy your brother's wedding."

Cecily said, "You know her mom cleaned our house, right? Can you imagine how pathetic you have to be to clean other people's bathrooms?" Lana sat on the closed toilet lid with her head in her hands, steeped in humiliation, but more for her dear, sweet mother, knowing she herself had felt the same derision for her during her troubled teenage years.

"Didn't you ever feel sorry for her, though? I mean, she was so much younger than us."

"Give me a break, Mindy—she knew what she was doing, trust me. Desperate for her daddy's love, that's what my mom always said. She was friends with her stepmom. Her dad abandoned that family not just once, but *twice*. No wonder she was always wearing those stupid dresses around. 'Oh, look at me, I'm *vintage*'," Cecily screeched, howling with laughter. Lana wanted to tear her stupid dress off now and not leave this bathroom until everyone was gone for the night.

She heard the footsteps walk to the door of the restroom, and the soft swish as it closed behind them. How was she going to leave this room and face everyone out there?

Anthony Russo—her biggest regret. How could she ever have trusted him? But she had. When she had been such an odd duck in high school, not fitting in anywhere, Anthony had been the one person in that private school to give her the time of day, with a nod of his head or a small smile when he passed her in the hall. No one was sure where she had gone to school before, yet everyone had somehow known her dad had been the construction worker to marry the recently widowed heiress. For the shame she felt toward her old life in Riverhead, she had paid the penance with loneliness every single day for three grueling years. Lana had loved that school, though, in a warped way, with the highly pedigreed instructors, and the experiences it offered with the range of science classes. She had excelled in ways that would have not been possible at her public school, but only academically. Until her senior year.

And then out of the blue one day, Anthony did more than just smile or nod at her. Underneath the tree she had considered hers, in the sunniest spot on the campus quad, he had sat next to her during lunch. Eating the turkey and Swiss on rye her stepmother insisted on having prepared for her every day (despite Lana telling her repeatedly she hated rye, and preferred cheddar over Swiss) and reading *Moby Dick* for her literature assignment, she had heard a voice from above ask, "Is this seat taken?" Looking up, she found him standing with the sun at his back, with a halo of black curls framing his perfect features. The star football player and captain of the lacrosse team, the leading man in the high school's production of *The Music Man*, he was the boy she had pined for since her first day of school, and the only one to show her any kindness —he was Anthony Russo.

Of course, she had mumbled, "Sure," at his plea to sit, keeping her eyes on her book as she did so, stupefied by what could have brought him to her tree. Oblivious to the whispers fluttering around the court-yard, unmindful of the stares from his table of friends, Lana heard him ask, "So you're, like, really smart, right?"

"Ummm…I guess?" How was she to communicate with this perfect creature? Lana had regretted not listening to her sisters when they had tried to teach her the finer art of flirting.

Anthony had inched closer to her until his large hand was resting within a breath away from her smaller one, and she watched, with her heart fluttering, as his pinky finger slowly reached out to graze hers. "So, I have to take physics this year, and word on the street is you aced all your other science courses. I could really use your help…Tara, is it?" His brown eyes then looked directly into hers, and she had trouble swallowing.

"L-Lana," she whispered to him.

Anthony leaned in closer, so close his nose grazed her cheek. "I'm sorry, Lana. I should have known a sexy girl like you would have a sexy name. You know my name, don't you?"

Breaking off eye contact, Lana glanced down at her novel. Sexy? No one had ever called her that...no one had ever even flirted with her...no one had ever wanted to be her friend, at the very least. She had no rung on any social ladder in her high school—too young for the other kids in her classes, and not enough time around teens her own age. Repeatedly, she had begged her dad to let her join an after-school activity, but neither her dad nor stepmom were willing to pick her up afterwards. Her dad was fond of pointing out to her that if she didn't want to end up like her mom or her sisters, she needed to just concentrate on her schoolwork.

"Well," Anthony prodded her, "do you know my name or not, sexy girl?"

She softly responded, "Anthony."

"Hey," he huskily told her, "we're friends now—you can call me Tony." Again, his finger slid across her hand, and he asked, "So do you think you can help me?"

Not taking her eyes from her book, Lana questioned, "You mean like be your tutor?" Her sisters had been trying to convince her to tutor some of the "Richies" so she could make some money for college next year.

"Naw...friends don't tutor friends, Lana. Friends help each other out —and we're friends, right?" Then Anthony lifted her chin with his finger, staring into her eyes with those deep, dark brown eyes of his.

"I guess so," she agreed quietly, with no understanding what she had been signing herself up for, nor how deeply it would become one of her biggest regrets in life, or how she would end up here, in this same country club, the night of her senior year graduation party.

Shaking her head, Lana brought herself back into the present, still not entirely sure how she had ended up in this place for a second time in her life—a place that held so much torment for her she had cried herself to sleep almost the entire summer after graduating, until she started college at Stony Brook University that fall. Lana had applied to (and gotten accepted at Princeton, Yale, Cornell, and NYU), but her dad, who was paying for what the scholarships didn't, said it was a waste to go to an Ivy League school, when the state school was as acceptable, pointing out that she could move back in with her mom and not need to live in a dorm room at an extra cost.

For comfort, Lana brought out her phone, staring at the picture of herself and Liam that he had sent. Remembering the warmth of his embrace, the strength of his arms as he wrapped them around her, she regretted, once more, her decision to leave him that day. Had she made the right call then? A future together had seemed impossible, and the obstacles they faced were insurmountable. Now she wasn't sure.

TEXT TO LIAM

Thank you for sending the picture of us. It was one of the happiest times of my life.

Sending the text had roused the courage she needed to leave the comforting confines of the toilet stall. Lana cautiously opened the door and, once finding the coast completely clear, approached the sink to wash her hands for a second time. Just as she shut off the water, the door opened from the outside, and Lana clenched in horror that Mindy and Cecily were returning, but to her sagging relief, a friendly voice instead greeted her, "Lana! There you are! We have a cosmopolitan with your name on it, or a Heineken—your choice!" Tess laughingly informed her.

Effie chimed in, "We had a big ol' debate about what you would want to drink, and Tess thought cosmo, but I said-".

Tess interrupted, "Lana, what's the matter? You look like you've seen a ghost. Are you okay?"

Lana chided herself to pull herself together—she had been through worse before, and as long as she kept a low profile, she could avoid anyone from her high school years and make it through the wedding. Maybe she'd just say she got sick and then take the train back early? Yes! Perfect! She applauded herself, beginning to lay the groundwork. "Actually, I'm not feeling well—maybe I should just find a quiet place to sit until the ceremony starts...somewhere out of the way."

"Aww, sweetie, of course. Our table is in the shade and off to the side, so just follow us, okay?" Tess told her and held the door open for Lana and Effie to pass through. As Lana walked through the door, Effie whispered, "We have a surprise waiting for you."

What? Lana wondered. What could they have? Now that she thought about it, Tess and Effie had been acting somewhat secretively since last night, exchanging furtive glances and knowing smiles.

She had almost made it out onto the patio when she heard a male voice behind her. "Lana?"

# CHAPTER
## Thirty-Four

*Liam*



That week with you was, without a doubt, the happiest time of my life.

Desperate to see Lana again, Liam tried to compose himself after getting her text. Even though he had been anxiously awaiting it, he'd been worried it had taken her a day to send her response.



All set over here—at table on the east corner of patio!



Walking over from hotel now

Where the hell is the east corner???

Damn, Liam thought, his cousin was the only person in their age group to use east/west as opposed to left/right. How in the hell was he supposed to know where the east corner was? Check for the location of the sun once he stepped out onto the patio? He had meant to be at the country club already; in fact, had intended to be there before his friends arrived, but a call from his mom concerning a donation Liam had made to the local food pantry had detained him. Following her son's lead, Nora had decided that every dealership would contribute the same dollar amount in every town where they had a dealership, with Cait looking into other towns with similar needs. Liam was flying high, finally convinced he was part of something bigger than simply making money—he was hopefully making a difference. Soon, his professional life would also expand once he started teaching at Beverley Community College. All he needed to make every aspect of his life complete now was Lana, desperately. Coming back from the feeling of complete devastation when he had written his last text to her months ago had been incredibly difficult. When he had said goodbye to her in that final text, he had done his best to mean it.

Striding into the club, Liam surveyed the room, and the old-money atmosphere of the place intimidated even him, a man not easily cowed. His family's money was not new money, but this was East Coast Money, and by the looks of the majority of people in here, their noses were so far up in the air, he wondered if they were dizzy. His understanding had been that this second wedding for Cal and his wife was going to be small, but there had to be a hundred bodies in the room, making him a touch claustrophobic. He couldn't wait to get out of here with Lana and take her back to his hotel room.

Deciding to get a beer before finding his cousin's table, in the hopes it would settle his nerves slightly, Liam weaved his way up to the bar in the center of the room, where he wedged in between two bottle-blondes. "I'll take a Guinness," he told the bartender. Nothing like a stout to provide some strength, Liam mused.

"Aren't you a tall drink of water," came a voice in his left ear (see, Josh, he mentally teased his cousin, his *left* ear, not his *east* or *west* ear). "I'd like to climb right up and get a taste of you."

Wow. Liam had been subject to many pick-up lines in his life, and had probably provided even more, but at a wedding, they usually came *after* the bride and groom had said their vows, perhaps at the wedding dance. Now, a frighteningly long fingernail slowly dragged its way up his arm, stopping at his bicep, only to then have an entire hand of the same terrifying fingernails wrap around and squeeze, like the owner was checking a grapefruit at the grocery store.

"You must work out a lot." His eyes tracked to the speaker's face, who had at one point probably looked like she was around his own age (maybe even a couple of years younger), but now had that indistinct, artificial look that came from too much makeup—or was it surgery? Or maybe it was because of facial implants, something he had seen on some rendition of *The Real Housewives*.

Liam smiled thinly at her—not enough to show any interest, but also enough to not appear rude. Holding his gaze with her own, she dropped whatever the gauzy wrap was around her shoulders, and he could see from the corner of his eye that her face hadn't been the only thing to have been worked on. "Like anything you see?" She fluttered her thick black eyelashes at him, raising a glass of champagne to her lips, evidently not caring that her wedding ring winked at him from her finger.

Spared having to reply, as the blonde out of touching distance gasped, "Oh my god, Mindy—I see her again! Guess who just came out of the restroom? The little bitch must have been spying on us in there."

Mindy responded, "Cecily, let it go." Her friend stormed off, and Mindy sighed, turning back to Liam. "I'll come back for you," she promised him. *Please, no,* he taught to himself.

Finally getting his beer (thank you, open bar), Liam accepted a bao bun from the waiter as he emerged from the throng at the bar. The patio doors were on the far side of the clubhouse, so Liam began making his way over to them when a movement caught his attention. Turning his head to the right, Liam saw a small woman, with honey-blonde waves tumbling down her back, and immediately he recognized every glinting strand. From across the room, he could recall how fragrant her hair was, how her skin tasted on his tongue, how her curves filled his hands. Drawn to her by their magnetic pull, as he started toward her, she turned enough so that he saw her delicate brows pulled down, distress clearly marking her beautiful, but pale, face. Now that he was closer, and other guests had fallen away, he could see a hand restraining her, and he guessed that explained her distress. Like two birds of prey descending on something more fragile, he spotted the blondes from the bar circling Lana as well. What the hell was going on?

"You really think a slut from the sticks belongs here?" Liam overhead one of them say, and looking at them next to each other, he found them indistinguishable.

A dark-haired man wearing a tuxedo gripped Lana's arm, then said, "Cecily, please—we were kids then. I'm just trying to explain to her-"

"Explain what, Tony? How your high school side-piece ended up at my brother's wedding?" one of the women shrieked.

"Really, Tony, we presumed you got your rocks off years ago with a one-and-done with our little ragamuffin here. But here she is, showing up at Cal's wedding? You and Cecily are finally in a good place, but now she has to stand here and watch you fondle another woman in front of everyone?"

"I just wanted to apologize to her for being such an ass in high school —that's it. Lana, I'm sorry-"

"You think I believe this is a coincidence, Tony? You said you were done messing around, and that you and I would make this marriage work for each of us—that's why I finally forgave you."

"Cecily, please, just give me a minute. Lana, I never meant to hurt you that night. Your dad said you needed a friend, and I tried-"

What was keeping him from reaching Lana more quickly? Liam thought frustratedly, as he darted around the wedding guests. A crowd had formed around Lana and the people she was talking to, making the circle difficult to break through. Who the fuck were those people? Why was this "Tony" holding Lana as if he had a right to do so, and who were these vicious women?

"Please, just let me go," Lana begged her captors. "I never wanted any of this-"

"'*Please let me go*'," Liam heard one of the women mocking Lana, which made his blood boil. "You are as pathetic now as you were back then. Little mouse scared of her own shadow."

At last Liam tore through the onlookers, "Enough—I don't know what the hell is going on here, but she is with me. You all should be ashamed of yourselves." He cast a damning glance at the man *still holding on to Lana* and the two women, whose eyes widened as they looked from Lana to Liam.

Fright glazed Lana's eyes as they met Liam's. "Liam?" Her bottom lip quivered, and she strained against the hands holding her.

"Is this how civilized society works here on the East Coast, because I have to be honest: from my neck of the woods, this isn't how we act at a wedding. And you," he lashed out at the women, "calling someone a *slut* when mere minutes ago, you were coming on to me up by the bar, despite your wedding ring. You're all disgusting, as far as I can tell." Liam took a deep breath, knowing he could say so much more, knowing he wanted to say more, but also taken aback by the rage coursing through him for these strangers.

"Lana," he said softly and offered her his hand. Finally, the other man ended his grip on her, and with a small sob, she clutched his hand in hers.

Tightly lacing his fingers with Lana's, Liam turned to lead her outside, when suddenly something yanked her from his side—or almost, at any rate, because Liam was either stronger or more determined (or both) than this idiot Tony, who couldn't seem to keep his hands to himself. While still holding Lana's hand, Liam separated the idiot from her with his own body. By standing in front of Lana, he shuffled the idiot back six inches to the wall. Leaning down several inches to put himself in this bastard's face and through gritted teeth, Liam warned him, "You touch her again, and you will regret it. Those women say one more word to her, and you will regret it. You follow us out of here, and you will regret it. Am I making myself clear?"

Ignoring Liam, this Tony looked over Liam's shoulder, saying, "Lana, please—I only want to talk to you." In return, Liam took his finger and flicked the man's nose, much as his own mother had done to him as a child when he wouldn't listen. He knew from experience that it stung like hell, but more from embarrassment than pain, and Liam found more satisfaction in humiliating a man as stupid as Tony clearly was than physically hurting him.

With no more words to anyone, Liam led Lana out the front door and around to the side of the building. Since the ceremony was starting in a few minutes, he was satisfied all wedding guests were inside, leaving the two of them alone. Liam's heart was racing, more from his proximity to Lana than from successfully ignoring the urge to beat Tony to a pulp, and he gathered her in his arms, smiling at the color beginning to resume in her face. His hands stroked up her back, and he cradled the back of her head as he bent to kiss with every ounce of affection he held for her. No—more than that. It was love.

Liam swallowed her moans into his open mouth, tasting her as if she were the only thing on the menu and he hadn't eaten for days…months. Wait, he calmed himself. This wasn't how their reunion was supposed to go, and as he reluctantly let go of her mouth, she whispered, "Liam."

"Baby, I know." Kissing the top of her head while she pressed her ear to his heart, he held her while the sobs she had visibly been holding back wracked her body. "Shh," he comforted her, "let it out". His own mother was a world champion crier, and she cried at everything: happy or sad, and had told him that most times, it was about the cathartic effect, and Liam hoped these tears would help Lana heal from whatever had gone on back at the clubhouse. At last, the shaking subsided in her shoulders, and he linked his fingers with hers. As if by some mutual understanding, the two of them just began walking, following a narrow sandy path carved out between the blades of seagrass, almost taller than Lana. After about five minutes, they came to the lighthouse; its red-and-white-striped body loomed over them as they sat in its shadow.

Finally, in the low light of the late summer evening, his eyes feasted on her. Perhaps because their last season together had been winter, and heavy coats and sweaters had swathed her, she was more glorious than he remembered. Overflowing with love for her, his hands cradled her face as he kissed her gently. "God, you're gorgeous—this dress is something out of my dreams," he confessed as his finger traced the tops of her breasts, and she shivered in response. Gently, he lowered them down to sit on the beach.

While the waves crashed with the tide coming in, Lana asked, "Liam, what are you doing here? I couldn't believe it when I looked up, and you were there. I thought I was hallucinating." Her fingertips traced his cheek, and he shivered in response to her touch.

"Lana, I have done nothing but think of you from the time I left in

December. I have no memory of anything from before we met—all I have is after you, like that's when my life started." She raised herself up on her knees, put her cool hands on his fiery cheeks, and hiked up her dress to straddle his lap. "I came back for you." Watching as the pupils of her dark blue eyes dilated, he gripped her hips tightly.

"I want you, Liam," she whispered in a raspy voice. Lana licked the line of his lips and unbuttoned the vest of his three-piece suit, making her way to the buttons of his shirt next. What was she doing? He was all for hot sex, but out here, only a short distance from the wedding, and right next to the lighthouse? A quickie was not how he had imagined his reunion with the love of his life. Liam had taken as much care with his hotel room, adjacent to the country club, as he had with the one they had shared last winter, setting it up for the romance he had expected to follow tonight after the wedding.

"Lana, Lana…baby…hey," gently he stilled her wrists in his hands, the fluttering pulse a reminder of the trauma she had experienced only a short time ago. "Slow down, baby. We have all night." With the rush of her adrenaline fading, she collapsed on his lap, curling against his chest. "Want to talk about what happened back there?" Liam was absolutely flabbergasted about what could have happened, causing Lana to be attacked in that way. She shook her head no, almost violently. "Okay, okay, we don't have to," he reassured her, not wanting to cause her any more stress.

"Liam, please, I don't want to talk about it—I just want to forget." She raised herself up on her knees again, sinking her hands into his hair, and he moaned in response, ready to give himself over to her, but then this "new" Liam, the one he was training to think more carefully and logically, encompassed her small form in a hug instead, choosing safety over sensuality.

"Look, I don't know about any of this," he told her, sweeping his arm out to encompass the golf resort, the ocean, the beach, "but I ran into those women at the bar, and I could tell they were nasty pieces of work. What they were saying must have been incredibly painful for you, and I want you to know that you don't have to hide that from me." He paused, stroking her back as they sat on the sand, watching waves breaking on the Atlantic through the path of the seagrass. "Let me take on your pain —just talk to me." He waited patiently while her breathing evened out, then tried again, "You mentioned once that your mom cleaned houses out here—is that how you know them?" Still, she remained silent, and he wrapped a few waves of her dark blonde hair around his finger, willing her to confide in him.

Deciding to try and explain why he acted poorly in response to Josh in that Manhattan hotel room, he began, "I never told you this, but I spent my entire life knowing I don't quite measure up." Time to confess his own doubts, he supposed. "My younger sister—she's a lawyer, just two years younger, and we were close when we were young, until puberty, I guess, and then she hated me. Not entirely sure why, because she got all the attention from our parents. She had problems with her eyes when she was a kid, so she had trouble learning how to read at first, and school was a bit more difficult, so my parents would spend our evenings helping her with her schoolwork. I was smart and school was relatively easy for me, but it's not like I was brilliant—not like Josh or our cousin Felix, who's an architect. I have no special skills, like our cousin Daniel, who you probably know is a chef." Liam drew a deep breath, then told her, "What I'm trying to explain is that when I first found out you were Lana, back in that hotel room, I was ashamed."

Lana still said nothing but shot him a surprised look. He continued, "All I had, really, were my looks and party-boy attitude that set me apart from my family. There you were...still are...practically genius-level doctor. Josh used to talk about you all the time when you shared an office. About how you graduated high school early, and college early, and then when you earned the fellowship? Even Josh is in your dust, so I was terrified where that left me. Where it left us. But these months alone, without you, I realized that none of that mattered." Taking another deep breath, Liam realized that now was maybe the perfect time. He hadn't planned on doing it here, out on the beach, but maybe it was better if it was spontaneous? Reaching into his pocket, he felt the small box he had carried around with him every day for seven months, touching it to keep himself grounded in the love he knew she felt for him.

"Lana, you are the most fantastic, incredible, desirable woman I have ever met." He stared deeply into her dark-blue eyes, so like the sky just after the sun sets. In her eyes, he could read their future—the kids they would have, the love they would share, the life they would build. "I love you with everything in me. Will you-"

# CHAPTER
## Thirty-Five

*Lana*

TEXT FROM EFFIE

Hey, Lana—you still talking to that friend of yours?

Ceremony starting soon.

TEXT FROM TESS

Lana, send the signal and we will come out to rescue you. That guy seemed like trouble.

TEXT FROM JOSH

Lana, are you okay?

Tess and Effie said some guy wanted to talk to you?

We have someone else joining our table, and should be here soon.

What was happening right now? What was he doing? Lana's stomach clenched with dread, watching Liam's hand reach into his pocket. Stunned could not begin to describe her reaction to seeing him *here* in the first place, since this was the *last* place she could have ever imagined wanting to see him. All this country club had ever held for her was misery, a symbol of misplaced hope and damaged dreams. Hearing a masculine voice call her name as she had exited the restroom with Effie and Tess had so startled her, the first person she thought of (the only man she ever thought of anymore) was Liam. Adrenaline had rushed through her, assuming that he had come here to surprise her, with the help of the friends she had come to the wedding with. That was so Liam, she had thought to herself, but upon turning then, Lana had been immensely disappointed, for it had not been Liam's smiling, handsome face staring at her. Not entirely sure who it was, at first, until he said her name again, in the same way he had said it when she was fifteen years old, under that tree .

Anthony Russo hadn't changed, really, in the sixteen years since she had last seen him—he still had the same sly grin, as if he could tell exactly what she was thinking. Still the same devilish glint in his brown eyes, the same dark hair flopping down into his face when he dipped his head. And the same darkly attractive face that had half of the girls in high school in love with him. Lana had been mystified when he had singled her out that day under the tree. Other than nodding and occasionally smiling at her, he had never said a word to her in the two years she had attended high school. Two agonizing years of just putting her head down, focusing on her classes, and trying to be grateful that her father had given her the opportunity to attend the elite academy.

The last night she had seen Anthony, she had finally discovered why he had approached her that fateful day under the tree. Her dad. Thomas Miller had always had a gift of drawing people in, getting them comfortable, regardless of economic status—it was how he had charmed his second wife, after all, while her first husband was still alive and kicking (the first time he left his family). Once he had finally committed himself to the Merry Widow, he had effortlessly and swiftly ensconced himself in her world, complete with joining the country club out in Montauk. The summer before Lana's senior year, while Thomas was enjoying a couple of drinks at the bar, Anthony's dad had also been at the bar, and Thomas had struck up a conversation with the other man, who had been frustrated that the Old Westbury Beacon Academy was enforcing their policy ensuring each student had a 3.7 GPA to graduate. Poor Anthony Jr. only had a 3.5, and he had to take physics that year, but the boy had no mind for science. What a small world, Thomas must have mused to Anthony Sr., that these two men would happen to meet out on the east end of Long Island, at that particular golf course, only to find out that both men had children attending the same high school back in Old Westbury. Thomas had assured Anthony Sr. that his brilliant, studious daughter would be more than happy to help his attractive, popular son raise his grades—after all, she needed help with her social connections, anyway (Thomas had been constantly after Lana concerning her lack of friends and why she always stayed home, with her nose buried in a book, when the other kids must be out doing whatever it was that the rich kids did).

Even while not knowing her father's arrangement with Anthony Sr., Lana had agreed to help Anthony, of course, for how could she resist his charming plea? After several months of tutoring, he had, indeed, showed her what rich kids did for fun, beginning with an occasional invite to a party, where Anthony took Lana discreetly by the hand, drawing her away from the crowd, then slipping away to a private area of the house for a few tender moments together. Lana knew well that he didn't invite her to every party; he explained to her that he had to make it look like he was still dating Cecily, to keep up appearances for his senior year. Believing herself to be in love with one of the most sought-after boys in school, content with whatever crumbs of attention he threw her when they were alone, she had not been worldly enough to understand that Anthony was stringing her along. Until Spring Break came, and she was back at her mom's house. March and April were two of Fiona's busiest months, prepping the summer homes in the Hamptons for the month of May, when most clients started heading out east for the weekends. Lana had begrudgingly agreed to assist her mom for the week since she needed the money—her dad had put an end to her allowance after

Christmas, telling her she needed to learn how to stand on her own two feet, especially if she wanted him to pay her tuition for college. During the week, Lana had been paranoid that someone from her school would see her working with her mom. When they had cleaned the last house for the week, Lana had been relieved to have encountered no familiar faces. Or so she had thought, until the night of the graduation party.

Since most of them were members of the private club, the parents of the senior class had chosen The Montauk Marina Beach Club as the location for their senior party. Limousines would escort the students out to and home from the party, an extravagance that most of them were familiar with already, except for Lana. So enamored was she for the privilege, she hadn't minded having to ride in separately from Anthony, because he had promised her that he had a special surprise planned for the two of them later that evening. Lana had convinced herself that he was going to ask her to spend the month of June with him at his family's home out in Montauk, after overhearing him on the phone one afternoon when she had arrived early to their tutoring session, telling whoever was on the other end about his plan for him and "his girl" to have the house to themselves the following month; ever since, Lana had been giddy with anticipation, unbothered that she had barely seen Anthony alone in the month before the party.

The night of the senior party had been hot and steamy, unusual for a Montauk May evening, as the temperature tended to cool down once the sun set. Lana had worn her hair down for the evening, because Anthony had told her how nice it would look loose, underneath the stars on the beach. For the first time in her life, Lana had also spent some of her own hard-earned money on a new dress, one she had purchased in a second-hand shop while thrifting with her mom and sisters one weekend. Once she stepped into the restroom at the clubhouse, however, she could see how ill-advised wearing her hair down had been, as the fine waves had instead formed a halo of frizz around her face due to the humidity and salt air that had found its way inside, despite the air-conditioning and closed doors. Meanwhile, other girls from the senior class streamed in to freshen up after the two-hour ride. Lana dipped into a stall to avoid comparing her reflection to that of the more polished, older girls in the mirror, when beside her, in the largest stall, she heard whisperings. "Can you even believe she would wear that? Like excuse me, didn't they have anything from this century?"

Another voice answered, "God, I know. I can't help but feel sorry for her, though."

"What? Why? Bitch needs to learn to stay in her lane."

"No, I know, but she's younger than the rest of us. I just think she's clueless."

"Clueless? She's done nothing but make moon eyes at him since day one, and he has had to smile and take it."

"No, I know, but why does he spend all that time with her? I mean, that's a little suspicious, right?" Lana desperately wanted to flee but was terrified of someone seeing her.

One girl let out a huge sigh in response. "Look," the voice said, "I guess his dad asked her dad if she could tutor him, so he's been paying her back. I told him he can have his little flirtations if he was getting his rocks off with it, whatever—just don't spread any trailer trash disease to me. Oh my god, and you'll never believe this! You know her mom cleans our toilets, right?"

A giggle made Lana freeze with her hand on the door. "What? What do you mean?"

A gasp this time. "You mean you haven't heard? Oh my god, this is the best—last month we were chilling by the pool at his house, and we saw the cleaning lady's van pull up. Guess who got out of the passenger side, wearing those hideous yellow gloves and carrying a vacuum! Like excuse me, I knew there was something off about her." The voices left, and Lana stayed in the stall until she was sure almost everyone had gone.

She had ducked out of the restroom, and then immediately out the front doors, blindly following the narrow beach lane leading down to the boathouse. Somehow, Anthony had found her down there sometime later, drawing her into his arms. She didn't know then if he knew the things that were said about her, nor did she want to believe what she had heard, but the way he held her so tenderly convinced her that he didn't feel the way everyone else did. He had touched her in a way that no one had before, and she had never felt more loved than she had that night. Until after, when she had confessed her love for him. Immediately, he had sat up, pulled on his pants, and clarified that he was still dating Cecily—had always been dating Cecily. Their time together tonight was a "thank you" to her for helping him. "What do you mean?" Lana had asked Anthony. "What about all of those other nights—all those parties?" Then, Anthony had explained about Lana's dad volunteering her to help him with physics if he helped her socially. Sick inside, she realized everything those girls had said in the bathroom had been true. Complete mortification had made it impossible to hear anything else he had to say. Once her tears had begun (for the second time that night), Anthony had hurriedly finished dressing, trying to explain that he never wanted to hurt her, that he did like her, but just not like *that*. Lana had run from his pitiful excuses and lame attempts at an apology. She had ended up at the lighthouse, only knowing one person who could help her. Montgomery had answered his phone after one ring, almost as if knowing he would need to rescue his baby sister that night.

To be confronted by Anthony tonight, sixteen years after that disastrous evening, once again overhearing malicious talk about her in the same damn bathroom, had been too much. "God, you look gorgeous," he had the audacity to tell her. She had sent away Effie and Tess, not wanting them to pity her even more than they probably already did, preferring to deal with Anthony in private.

"I always knew you would bloom, but, wow, Lana—you have defied my expectations." Lana hadn't managed to say one word to him, longing to tell him to get lost, leave her alone, or something similar, before Mindy and Cecily had swooped down on her, also, clearly having spent every year since high school sharpening their claws to prepare for their next attack on her.

Then, to her utter astonishment, Liam had swept through the crowd, like her own personal avenging angel, giving her some relief, but too late. The old scars had sliced open, leaving her reeling in pain once again, pulling back the thin facade she had in place, hiding her insecurities behind her surgical scrubs. Having Liam in the place of her teenage humiliation kindled conflicting emotions for her—she had been elated to see him (worrying at first she was only hallucinating him), but at the same time mortified he had witnessed the terrible words being said to and about her.

Now, on this beach, she whispered to Liam, "Don't," even though she wasn't sure what he was about to do but had a sense of foreboding. Nothing good ever came from being on this beach.

His silvery eyes, made even shinier in the dimming sunlight, locked with hers in surprise. He shook his gorgeous head of tumbling chestnut locks, and she had a feeling that no woman had ever stopped him from doing anything before. "Lana," he began again, "I have spent this past year thinking of only you. No time existed before you, for me, and no woman meant anything to me until you." This time he was successful in pulling out a small, teal-colored box from his jacket pocket, making Lana terrified that her heart was going to beat out of her chest.

"Liam, no—please," her voice cracked as she spoke, and she read the bewilderment on his face. Whatever he had planned could not be done here—not in Montauk, not on this beach, and not mere yards from the boathouse where she had given herself to the wrong boy. Lana rose on shaking legs, sure her knees were going to collapse, as Liam kneeled before her. What was he doing? she asked herself, wanting desperately to be wrong about his intentions.

Liam gave a small laugh, and for the first time she saw a crack in his confident veneer; yes, he had been earnest with her before, certainly sincere, but always with his swagger, secure in the knowledge of his own boldness. Now she saw a glimmer of hesitation, a lack of assuredness, and the only way she could get him to stop what he was doing was to lean on that. She could not have something as beautiful as the possibility of a proposal from him be sullied by this location.

"Surely you're not planning on asking me to marry you?" Lana threw in an exaggerated guffaw to make her point. "We have had some incredible sex, no doubt, but I don't think that qualifies us for marriage, Liam."

Watching some of the light dim from his electrifying eyes killed her as he sat back on his heels. "Lana, I love you," he reiterated, more passionately than he had before. "I know this seems fast, maybe too soon, but I will feel this way no matter how much time passes, even if it is another year."

"You're not getting it, Liam—there is no 'another year'. I was surprised to see you today...pleasantly so, but there is no future for us."

"Why? We can have whatever we want, Baby—you and me. You can finish up your internship in Brooklyn, and maybe after that Josh could hook you up at his hospital? He's happy in South Dakota, Lana, and we could be, too," Liam pleaded with her, his magnetism causing her to sway on her feet.

"Liam, please, you don't understand that this place holds nothing but terrible memories for me. Please don't make another one for me. I'm begging you." Lana barely held on to the panic threatening to overtake her.

He reached for her, but Lana quickly side-stepped him. "Whatever happened here is in the past, but *we aren't*. Let me help you erase whatever happened here, create a new memory, with you and for you. We can do that, if only you'll let me." There was nothing she wanted more than to do that. But not here. Not now.

Close to losing the little control she had over her emotions, Lana needed to get away from him or she would give in to him. "Nothing is in the past!" she cried. "You saw them back there, Liam—those were people I knew in high school. People who never thought I was good enough— and I'm not! I'm not like them…and I'm not like you. I can't afford extravagant hotel rooms. I couldn't afford to almost not graduate from college. I don't have an inheritance or a wealthy family to give me whatever I need. In the end, you and I are nothing alike, and we would never last."

Liam's face contorted with pain, and he said, "Lana, those things mean nothing to me-"

"That's the problem, Liam," she yelled, "because they mean everything to me! And you not getting that proves my point!"

"Lana, where is this coming from? I told you how hard I worked so my family would see me in a new light, and I'm still working on it! There's stuff that has happened since we were last together—stuff I haven't gotten the chance to tell you, but that can wait." Finally, she had stilled enough for him to catch her hand in his. In his eyes, she could see every emotion she had for him, as if his eyes were mirrors, not windows. "This is all new for me, too, but we can figure it out together." His husky voice cracked, and Liam's emotions were almost her undoing. She believed he meant what he said, but for how long? How long until he left her the first time? Ten years? That was how long Lana's parents had been together before her dad had left the first time, and it was the amount of time he stuck around the second time before leaving again.

"I'm sorry, Liam, but I can't. I just don't feel the way you do. I need to go. Please." With that, Lana turned and fled, her only desire to escape the destruction she had just caused to the only man she had ever loved.

# CHAPTER
## Thirty-Six

*Ruth*

*Eight Months Later*

TEXT TO EFFIE

Heading to pick up Tess and then off to look at cars. Meet for lunch after? I can't wait to talk about the book you wrote!

TEXT FROM EFFIE

Sounds good—library quiet today so time is flexible. Let me know how Liam seems. We saw him last week, but he has a new "girlfriend"— this month, anyway.

Regarding my book, I am still a bit stunned I did it!

TEXT TO EFFIE

Oh no—I thought I saw him at the movies a couple of weeks ago with the same woman we saw him with on St. Patrick's Day.

Tess said that according to Sam, your book is
amazing!!!

TEXT FROM EFFIE

Nope—new girl. His new dating rule is nothing
longer than a month. Poor Liam—just seems so
miserable. Sam has been an angel, helping me
self-publish..

TEXT TO TESS

Leaving the house now, heading to Mom's

TEXT FROM TESS

Hurry—Mom is trying to foist all these doilies
on me!

Where did they all come from?

TEXT TO TESS

Whatever you do, do not take any doilies!

She says once anything leaves her threshold, it's
not her property anymore!

TEXT FROM TESS

Sis, I can't anymore with her! I thought they
downsized when they moved into town two
years ago!!!

TEXT TO TESS

They did! Until they brought in everything from
the farm then, months later. Poor Sean was
humping boxes for months after we moved here.

Tess opened up the door of the apartment complex where their parents, John and Ellen Lefferts, had moved into over two years ago. Tess and Ruth had grown up on a farm ten miles out of Beverley, where their dad had run a very successful veterinary practice specializing in large animals. Their mom, Ellen, had been a nurse practitioner at Beverley General Hospital for thirty years before retiring. Both women had grown up under the glow of their parents' love, until Ellen had what she liked to call now a "midlife crisis" (but her husband, John, referred to as "her lost five years"), when she had separated from John after Tess had gone off to college in California. Not long after the separation, the couple had gotten divorced but then reunited at Ruth's wedding to her devoted husband, Sean. John and Ellen were still in their second honeymoon phase, seven years later. Two years ago, they sold the farm and vet practice to a young family and bought an apartment in Beverley to live out their retirement years. Although the way Ruth was having babies, Ellen joked, they would need to upsize from their cozy two-bedroom to something with enough rooms for their grandchildren. "Ruthie!" her little sister squealed, racing over to grab the stroller from her.

"You're just in time—Arielle needs a diaper change, I'm guessing, from the smells coming out of this thing. Mom, thanks for helping me potty train Eloisa last fall, because if I had both girls in diapers, I would have lost my damn mind by now!" Ruth declared, wondering how in the world she had let Sean talk her into having babies in such quick succession. Their first-born daughter, Eloisa, was two and a half years old, with fiery red hair the exact shade of Sean's. Her green eyes were replicas of Ruth's, and her independent spirit? Ruth liked to take credit for that, but only when her darling daughter was being simply independent and *not* bordering on stubborn or willful. Arielle, her second-born daughter, was a true Irish twin to her sister, born eleven months after Eloisa. Arielle's hair was also red, but more like Ruth's, who was a strawberry blonde; she had her father's blue eyes, and, luckily, Sean's easy-going attitude. And now here Ruth was, pregnant again, and four months away from having three daughters under the age of three.

Having put off finding a larger vehicle for as long as she could, Sean had informed Ruth that today was the day that she had to go shopping for a minivan. Her husband rarely "laid down the law", but Ruth could tell he was becoming frustrated with ducking into and out of the family's sedan when putting his daughters into their car seats. Growing up in Philadelphia, Sean had taken public transportation everywhere, with no need for a car, making Ruth the decision-maker for their family vehicle. Even now, the hospital where Sean worked was only a few blocks from their house, so he walked to work every day. Despite his complete disinterest in automobiles, Ruth considered him to be the most perfect man, and every morning she woke up next to her husband, she congratulated herself for choosing him. At least her sister was here to help her adjust to the changes, Ruth thought, shuddering at the thought of having to take her dad instead. Bless him, her dad always meant well, but often ended up getting sidetracked instead: every time John Lefferts stepped onto a car lot, he ended up trading in his current vehicle for a new one.

The sisters kissed the babies goodbye, and Ruth gave her mom a kiss on the cheek. One thing Ruth never regretted was moving back to South Dakota after starting her family. Sean had taken to Midwestern small-town living so naturally, and his pediatric practice was thriving at the hospital here in Beverley. "Do you want to walk over to the dealership, Tessie? Take advantage of this beautiful weather?" Although it was late March, the winds were non-existent and the temperature an enjoyable fifty degrees (almost tropical for South Dakota).

"Oh, I'd love that," Tess responded eagerly. "I love how Mom and Dad's apartment is so convenient to everything here. We walked over to the diner this morning for breakfast."

"Oh, nice! Knowing you, I'm sure you were up bright and early, right?"

Tess laughed, "Too early for the retirees, I think, since not only am I on New York time, but I'm so used to waking up before dawn to start baking. I've been up since five."

"Good lord, Tessie! You were up even before the girls were." The sisters walked past the hospital and Ruth waved at a few nurses she knew who were smoking outside. When they got to the diner, Ruth saw Paul, the deputy sheriff, coming out of the diner with his husband Adam, and she called out, "Hey, you two—how were the cinnamon rolls this morning?"

"Haha, you know us too well, Ruth! Where are those gorgeous babies of yours?" asked Adam.

"Back at Mom's," she answered, stopping to introduce Tess. "This is my little sister, Tess."

"Oh, *Tess*," Paul said, "so nice to finally meet you. We have missed you the last couple of times you've been back."

"Ruth says you make the best cookies," Adam said, shaking Tess's hand.

"And she tells me that you guys are some serious pool players!

Maybe we can get together some night this week?" Tess was visiting for ten days, and Ruth nodded eagerly at the thought of going out with her sister to shoot some pool at Shorty's, while she could still reach the table, despite her ever-expanding belly.

"I'll be in touch," Ruth promised Adam and Paul as they got into their car and drove off.

Once they got to the lot of Kinsale Autos, Tess asked Ruth, "So, have you seen Liam recently?"

Ruth sighed, "I was just texting with Effie before I got to Mom's—I guess he has a new girlfriend. He's not doing well. Sean had an emergency call during the night a couple of weeks ago at the hospital, and when he finally was on the way home, he saw Liam's car in the parking lot of Shorty's. Imagine how he acted in high school and multiply that by a million. He's being very reckless. Effie told me that Josh is worried about him for the wedding."

Josh and Effie's wedding was in the beginning of September, an event that it seemed the entire town was looking forward to, since Effie had become not just a favorite librarian at the Beverley Carnegie Library, but she also was an assistant track coach at the high school, and she helped the English teacher put on theatre productions every fall and spring.

Tess asked, "Oh, because of L-" but the sisters both fell silent as the door to the dealership opened, with Liam there seemingly to usher them in.

"Hello, ladies," Liam greeted them exuberantly, and he was polished, wearing a three-piece suit that had become standard for him at the dealership. Ruth had to admit that he still looked as fit as ever, despite his heartbreak.

"Hi, Liam," Tess answered, and Ruth caught the worried glance her sister shot her way. Tess had called Ruth the night of Cal's wedding as she and Sam were driving home from the Hamptons, telling her what little they knew about the reunion of Liam and Lana. Poor Lana had been so distraught, Tess had reported, that she had gotten a taxi to the train station without telling anyone. After an hour of both Effie and Tess frantically calling and texting her, not knowing where she had disappeared to, Lana had finally replied, stating only that she was on her way back to Brooklyn.

Once Effie and Josh had gotten home to Beverley from the trip, Effie and Ruth had met for coffee, and Effie had been unable to keep her emotions under check when she told Ruth about Liam being so soundly rejected by Lana. Effie informed Ruth that she had never seen Liam, usually so smooth, so polished, so unruffled, be so completely lost, mired in his own misery.

"Tess, good to see you again." Liam hugged her and kissed both her cheeks. Then he turned to Ruth and gave her the same treatment, telling her, "Sean texted you were on the way." He led them around the corner to his office. "Why don't you both have a seat in here while I get you each a coffee? Ruth—decaf for the little one? Tess—light and sweet, right? Uncle Henry has been perfecting this light roast blend that will be perfect for car shopping," and then Liam buzzed out of the office, rounding a corner somewhere, making it impossible for either woman to see him.

"Umm, okay, that's not strange at all," Tess commented. "Why didn't he just pour us some coffee from the coffeemaker over there?" Tess pointed across the room to the machine with a full pot of coffee.

"Good question. And who the hell is this Liam-bot? Like he *seems* like the old Liam, but just so…" Ruth was at a loss for words. Liam never just went right to work. He liked to chat people up, usually wanting to know how Ruth's girls were when she saw him, how her parents were. He was always personal before business.

"Empty," Tess responded. "He seems empty. I was expecting him to look…I don't know—bedraggled? Maybe have a beard? He was so despondent the last time I saw him. But he looks like the same hot Liam. But super hyper."

Ruth laughed lightly, telling her sister, "I love how bedraggled to you means having a beard. Correct me if I'm wrong, but doesn't your own husband have a beard now?"

Tess chuckled. "Well, yes, but that's Sam, and a beard fits him, you know, because he's a writer."

Ruth lifted her eyebrows. "He's a writer but not bedraggled. Got it."

Tess smiled and told her sister, "Only under certain situations, if you know what I mean." Ruth laughed.

"Whoa, I must have missed something good while I was out." Liam breezed back into his office carrying two coffees as a young woman followed him. After he gave Tess and Ruth their respective drinks, he told them, "I think Lillian will be a better fit to help you find a car, Ruth. She has a couple of kids, so can understand your needs better."

"Lillian? Oh my god, it's been years," Tess exclaimed as Ruth smiled at Lillian.

"Tess, I thought I recognized you! I see your sister around town, of course, but I can't remember the last time I saw you!" Lillian and Tess hugged, and Lillian then said, "Wait! I remember when we last saw each other—I think it was the summer we were both finally twenty-one-"

Tess interjected, "Yes! It was at the street dance! We had so much fun that night!"

"Wait—you two know each other?" Liam questioned, not sounding that surprised. Yes, Beverley was a larger town than most within a fifty-mile range, but by no means had it achieved "city" status.

Tess laughed, "Yeah, we were in the same class in school, and we were partners in oral interp two years in a row!" Oral interpretation, part of the drama club, was an extracurricular activity that students performed readings, either poetry, dramatic soliloquies, or even comedic routines, and Ruth remembered that Tess and Lillian had gone to the state championships with their comic duets.

The women left Liam in his office and Tess became more somber as she told Lillian, "I was so sorry to hear about Ross. He was such a sweet guy. Josh told me when he passed away."

Lillian nodded. "I can't believe it's been almost two years already. It was a blessing when Josh moved back here, because he was so great with Ross, and me, at the end."

Lillian led Tess and Ruth across the showroom, and as her sister and Lillian made small talk, Ruth wondered why Liam had pawned them off on his employee—not that she had anything against Lillian, because she quite enjoyed talking to her whenever they saw each other around town, but the Liam Ruth knew would have taken this time to charm her, working the magic that only he did so well. Watching Tess lift her coffee to take a sip, it dawned on her that she had left hers back in Liam's office, making it the perfect excuse to double back and try to get some answers.

"Hey, you two, I left my coffee in the office. I'll meet you guys outside by the minivans?" Tess gave her a thumb-up as she heard Lillian ask her sister about the new book Sam was writing.

As briskly as possible in her condition, Ruth walked back to Liam's office, halting in her tracks in the doorway. Liam was standing facing his desk with his back to her, holding his phone. His head was bent almost as if he were studying the picture on the screen. Ruth took two small steps toward him and saw that he was looking at a picture of himself and a woman who with the most gorgeous shade of honey blonde hair. Ruth had only met Lana once, when she and Tess had gone to Josh's hospital to meet him for lunch one day before the sisters headed further uptown to go to the Metropolitan Museum of Art. The younger woman had been almost silent after being introduced, but Ruth had noted the way her eyes tracked Josh's movement, and the hero-worship in them. Ruth had commented to Tess about it, but Tess had brushed her off, declaring Lana as harmless, with Josh viewing her as more of a little sister.

Ruth cleared her throat to announce her presence, watching as Liam's face flushed, and he quickly put his phone in his pocket. "It's okay, you know," Ruth told him softly.

His eyes flashed to hers, and he asked, "What are you talking about?"

Ruth pointed to his hip. "It's okay to miss her. Or forgive her. Or want her back."

Liam shook his head. "You don't understand. I have nothing to forgive. I rushed her, moved too fast." He shrugged then, and said, "Or maybe she didn't feel the same way I did. Maybe I wasn't good enough for her." He gave a sad laugh then, and the expressions on his face almost brought Ruth to her knees. "What would a brilliant woman like Lana want to do with me, after all? She's too good for me, Ruth." Rubbing his hand over his face, he said, "There was a reason Josh never introduced me to her, you know."

"Maybe there was, but not because you're not good enough or smart enough." Ruth cocked her head, admitting to Liam, "You realize that you intimidated the hell out of me in high school, right?"

"What? No way," he denied, shaking his head again. "You were always such a ball buster, obliterating anyone who got in your way. You didn't take any crap. If anything, the opposite was true—*you* intimidated *me*."

Ruth chuckled, "Oh, please. You were, still are, entirely too good-looking for your own good, and you're always so at ease in every environment." Picking her coffee up from his desk, she sipped it as he gave a quick shake of his head. "And you can deny it, but you are just as smart as Josh—you're just not as obsessed with anything like he is with surgery, and that's not bad. You're good at this, Liam. You may try to hide everything under the banner of Kinsale Motors, but I know the good you have done for the community, the time you have given to different organizations, not to mention your personal contributions—they make a difference. And Effie told me that her brother, Hamilton, could not get his math credit at the college until you started teaching the class."

Liam shrugged. "I never even got to explain any of that to Lana. I had an entire speech planned for that night, a romantic setting back at the hotel. She shut me down, Ruth, before I could share any of that with her. Threw my family's money in my face...insinuated I didn't think she was good enough." Ruth hugged his broad shoulders as he slumped over in his chair.

"Look, Tess told me that it seems like Lana has always been very concerned about money, even in the little things she does, like furnishing her apartment or buying new clothes. We have the feeling that maybe she didn't grow up with much, and despite now being a doctor, she still views the world through that lens. Where Lana was raised, out on Long Island, the difference between the wealthy and non-wealthy is much more dramatic than it is around here. Sometimes there's a huge chasm." Ruth hoped she was getting through to Liam, convincing him to reach out to Lana, who, according to Tess, was just as miserable.

Liam, clearly overwhelmed emotionally, said, "I don't know what to do anymore. If she wanted to be with me, she could have explained all of this herself. I've been so open with her about everything, but I guess she just didn't trust me as much, and that hurts."

"What's the plan, then? Keep her picture on your phone while you're dating other women?" Ruth watched as his hand went to his pocket, almost as if to assure himself Lana was still with him.

Liam sighed, "You better get out there to look at minivans, or Sean will have my ass for distracting you." He then turned from Ruth, who recognized her cue to leave. Just before she left his office, he told her quietly, "Thanks, Ruth."

Ruth found her sister and Lillian outside among the minivans, and after looking at a few, Ruth settled on two of the least offensive-looking models, taking plenty of photos of them to show Sean later. She thanked Lillian for her time and told her she'd be in touch.

Linking her arm through her sister's, Ruth told her, "Let's go get Effie —I'm starving."

TEXT TO EFFIE

On our way—Mexican or coffeeshop?

TEXT FROM EFFIE

Coffeeshop—need one of their warm chicken salad sandwiches!

Once the three women settled around a table at Mr. Beans, the coffeeshop at the other end of Main Street, Ruth focused on Effie, asking her about the young adult book she had been working on for the last six months.

"How did you find the time to write a book while also planning the wedding of the year?" Ruth queried. "All I manage to do is get knocked up every year."

Tess and Effie laughed, and Effie said, "Since I became the head of the children's section at the library, I could see there was a gap in books about Indigenous People, and I've had this story in my head for a while now. Getting back in touch with the Lakota side of my family has made me see that, as a culture, we need that representation. I know I needed it, desperately, when I was growing up."

Tess nodded. "Sam says he wouldn't be surprised if a publisher picks it up after the second one."

"Oh, come on, now you're just showing off—you've written a second book already?" Ruth exclaimed.

Effie chuckled and replied, "You know, those long winter nights, when Josh was commuting to Sioux Falls, it was just me and the cats—I needed something to do so I didn't worry about him driving when the weather was crappy."

Ruth laughed. "Girl, what do you mean if the 'weather was crappy'? This is South Dakota, and we are still in March! You know damn well it could snow tonight without any warning!"

"Too true, too true! But at least he's not working in Sioux Falls quite as regularly."

Tess said with some shock in her voice, "I still can't believe you and Josh have two cats now—I had to beg him to let me keep Rapunzel when she followed me home."

Effie smiled slyly. "I do have my ways of convincing Josh to see things my way..."

"I don't know whether to be impressed or appalled right now—you know my sister almost married the man, right?" As they shared a laugh, Ruth waved her hand at her companions, announcing, "Okay, enough. We need to make a plan."

"What plan?" Effie asked.

Tess sighed, knowing what was coming, "A plan for Liam—am I right?"

Ruth nodded, "And for Lana. You know if there's anything I hate, it's letting people manage their own lives when they are clearly not doing it up to my standards."

Tess and Effie nodded in agreement, because without Ruth, the two of them would not be with the men of their dreams.

# CHAPTER
## Thirty-Seven

## Lana



Paging Dr. Miller—where are you?



Hey, Lana, not sure of your schedule, but can we grab coffee some time this week at the bakery?



Earth to Lana! Entering our orbit soon? We miss you!



I'm off tmrw. Should I come over in the morning?



Sounds great!



Hi, baby sis, in case you missed my other hints, we haven't seen you in forever—Mom is worried about her baby chick.

TEXT FROM GREER

Please answer Ava—she's driving me nuts.

TEXT FROM AVA

Don't make me send Monty!!!

The past nine months had been the longest year in Lana's life—and yes, though she was well-aware that there were more than nine months in a year, it didn't make her feel any differently. Waking up to her phone playing "Ain't Goin' Down ('Til the Sun Comes Up)" was intended to motivate Lana to rise from slumber and get her day started, but lately, all she wanted was to pull the covers back over her head. She still loved her walks in Green-Wood every day. She still loved connecting with her young patients before their procedures at the hospital. She still loved living in the apartment at the top of the house owned by Tess and Sam. But was she happy? Groaning, Lana realized she had better text her oldest sister back before she took drastic measures.

TEXT TO AVA

Sorry, I know I've been silent.

The truth is I messed up with Liam and nothing has been right ever since. I made a huge mistake. I'll call Mom, maybe come out this weekend.

TEXT FROM AVA

I'm sorry—why haven't you said anything? We know how much you cared about him. It was obvious.

Ever since that moment on the beach with Liam, each day dragged her further away from the happiness she was meant to be working towards. How would things have gone if Mindy, Cecily, and Anthony hadn't accosted her? Would the reunion with Liam have ended with them being engaged, assuming that was a ring box he had pulled out of his pocket? Even now, she could imagine him placing his ring on her finger, and the vision never failed to cause a shiver to run through her or to bring tears to her eyes. One day last month, she took the train into the city, getting off the D at Bryant Park, and walked the seven blocks uptown and two avenues east to the Midtown location of Tiffany's, where she gathered up the courage to enter the posh jewelry store. Ignoring the voice in her head telling her she didn't belong in a place like that, she looked at case after case, trying to guess which ring Liam would have chosen for her. Sparing no tears during her window shopping, she was a complete wreck once she came across the beautiful crystal heart ornament—the same heart Liam had gifted to her almost two years ago, and one she feared was lost forever, after leaving it on the Christmas tree when she had fled from him for the first time.

Each time she took out her phone, staring at the picture of them together, regrets and "what-ifs" besieged her. What if her dad had been fully present in her life, instead of vanishing twice, the last time seemingly for good, right before med school? What if her mom had let go of her dad, once and for all, moving on with her life, either alone or giving her children a stepfather capable of putting them all first? What if Lana had never had feelings for Anthony? Or Josh? What if Liam had been the first one she had given her heart to? What if she could forgive herself, finally entrusting her heart to the right man? What if she had been braver, instead of so damn timid all the time? What if she never saw Liam again?

More than anything, she wanted to be the version of herself he had met initially—the woman from the bar who licked salt from his wrist, telling him to take her back to his hotel room—that's the woman she longed to be, and even though Lana had only met her once, she missed that version of herself. That woman would have called Liam, telling him she had made a grievous mistake by insisting he leave her alone. That woman would have told Liam she was lying when she said she didn't feel the same way he did. That woman would have asked *him* to marry *her*.

Now she was in Brooklyn, alone—well, not alone, necessarily, for she had the two adorable kitties she had adopted from her mom. She had her family—though she had not been out to Long Island since Cal's wedding. Much to the consternation of everyone, and in an effort to forget the anticipation from Liam's visit the year before, Lana had chosen to work during the holidays. And she had Tess and Sam, who had her down to their house for dinner at least once a month since she had moved in last year. Aware that Tess had gone back to South Dakota last month, Lana had to fight the urge to ask Tess about Liam every time she saw her, terrified that Liam was moving on without her. In the months that followed that dreadful night on the beach with Liam, her heart skipped a beat with every text notification, always hoping it was him. Unlike after they had separated after that Christmas together, nothing came from him this time—no constant stream of texts, no reminders of how many days it had been since she had abandoned him on the beach, no professions of love. What had she expected, though? To walk away from him a second time, leaving him to beg for a crumb of acknowledgment from her? Lana longed to reach out to Liam, but what would she say? Profess her own love? Apologize for not giving them a chance? Plead with him to return to New York? If she had any sense or the tiniest amount of courage, she would do all of them.

Knowing from experience that the morning rush at Tess's bakery, The Cookie Jar, didn't die down until after ten, Lana had a couple of hours to kill before meeting Tess, so she took a hot shower, blasting Garth Brooks the entire time. Lana thought of her brother, who loved Garth Brooks; when she was young, right after their dad left, she would sit with Montgomery in his room as he strummed along on an acoustic guitar, learning every song with him. Lana guessed he had been trying to comfort her— to ease her pain as much as he could. Monty was the one who had no tears of his own, instead drying every one of hers. He was, truly, the only man she could ever count on, and she wondered why he had no one in his life. His long-term girlfriend had broken up with him a few months ago, he had mentioned to her when they had dinner at Junior's last week. Over a slice of cheesecake, he nonchalantly mentioned his newly single status, shutting down when Lana had asked too many questions. Was she like her brother—destined to be alone?

After her shower, she chose a yellow skirt and a bright blue top to wear and slipped on a pair of flip-flops. One luxury Lana had begun to allow herself was drop-off laundry service every couple of weeks, so she bundled her laundry up to take to the laundromat down on the avenue a few doors down from the bakery.

While Lana ate her breakfast (a mushroom and spinach omelet and a toasted and buttered bialy), she thought about the meeting she had yesterday with the head of surgery at Park Slope Presbyterian. Her fellowship was ending next month, coinciding with finishing her residency, but she was unsure what she wanted to do next with her career. The hospital had offered her a position in the surgical department, either in pediatric or emergency surgery, but something in her wasn't feeling the satisfaction she had once gotten from performing surgeries. When she had worked with Josh, so much of her own gratification had come from his love of surgery enveloping her, convincing her to forget about how much she had loved working previously in internal medicine.

Deciding now was a good time to head to the bakery, Lana opened her apartment door, tossing her bag of laundry down the stairway. Shoving her arms through a gray cardigan, Lana grabbed her keys from the hook next to her door, descended a flight of stairs, and took her folded grocery cart from her hall closet. She made her way down the exterior flight of stairs with her laundry in the cart. Breathing in air that smelled like spring, Lana greeted the neighbors on the block she had become familiar with over the last year, people who had lived on this street anywhere from thirty to fifty years: the Polish couple who lived in the house closest to Fourth Avenue, the older couple originally from Puerto Rico, who owned two of the houses in the center of the block, the Russian immigrant whose parents had both been Holocaust survivors and had moved to Brooklyn right after the Second World War. Of course, there were people like herself on the block who had lived in the area for a shorter period of time, and it was this mix of people and cultures that made New York such a magical place to live.

After Lana dropped off her laundry, she was craving one of Tess's specialty bacon and Swiss muffins she had recently started offering. Opening the door to the best-smelling business in Brooklyn, Lana found Tess wiping down tables to the beat of Taylor Swift. "I wish I had this much fun while I'm at work," Lana said as a greeting, eager to start the conversation lightly.

Tess startled and put her hand on her chest. "Oh, my goodness, you scared the hell out of me! I haven't had a customer in ten minutes, so I was entrenched in my cleaning zone," she laughed. "Coffee?"

"Yes, please," Lana paused, wondering if perhaps Tess's motive for asking her to come to the bakery had nothing at all to do with her trip to South Dakota. Stop being so self-centered, Lana lectured herself, and just relax. Taking a breath, she asked Tess, "How about one of those brunch muffins? I've been dreaming about them for a week." Lana took a seat by the front windows, where Tess had put two well-used armchairs that had come from Sam's apartment in Boston, which he had sold once he moved to Brooklyn. Now that Lana thought about it, if there had been news about Liam, Tess would almost certainly have told her by now, considering she had seen her a few times since her return.

"Ooh, I think I'll have the same, although in full disclosure, this is my second breakfast," Tess admitted, handing her a coffee while she warmed up the muffins.

"Haha, mine, too!" Lana sipped her coffee, which Tess had doctored perfectly with cream and sugar.

"Is that amazing smell some of those brunch muffins warming up?" Sam asked, as he came into the bakery, probably having been upstairs where the small bookstore, The Book Nook, was located. "Or is it just the tantalizing aroma of my gorgeous wife?" Sam put his arms around Tess, nuzzling her neck, while Lana looked away from their public display of affection. After living above them for over a year now, Lana was used to witnessing the palpable love between the couple. Sam routinely could not keep his hands off Tess if she was within two feet of him, and Tess blushed like they were still newlyweds; Lana guessed they actually were, considering they had not even been married two years yet.

Tess answered her husband, "I'm warming up some for us—don't worry. I knew you would want a few, as well." She kissed him and then asked, "Sam, I'm going to take a break with Lana for a bit—could you ask Marisol to come up front when she's done? She's in the kitchen finishing up some orders."

"Anything for the love of my life," and with a final kiss, Sam poured himself a cup of coffee and headed to the kitchen.

Tess smiled at Lana, her green eyes warm and soft. "It seems like forever since we've had a chance to have a good talk, Lana. I know we've seen each other in passing, but it's not the same. How have you been?"

How had she been? A question she asked herself daily yet could never provide an answer. Deciding to give a sightly evasive answer, she responded, "I'm okay—you know, working, finishing my fellowship."

Tess's eyes probed Lana's. "Well, that's good, right? I remember when Josh just had the one year left of being a surgical intern…he was so close to being done, and then he told me he was applying for that fellowship, which I knew meant two more years of training. You know, he announced it a week before I left to take the train to my bachelorette weekend. Our wedding was six months away, we had so much left to plan, and he made a choice without even consulting me. I was furious."

Lana had known this, but not from Tess's perspective. At the time, Josh had confided to Lana that he thought he should have a rotation in pediatric surgery before finishing the surgical internship program. When he had floated the idea with Lana, she had encouraged him, of course, because he was a brilliant surgeon. Lana had thought Tess was being short-sighted and not supporting her fiancée (based on the information from Josh). She flushed with shame now at her involvement in any aspect of Josh's personal life. Of course, Josh hadn't received the fellowship in the end—Lana had, after she had applied for it, as well. Never expecting to get it instead of Josh, it had almost ruined their friendship. Marisol approached their table with a plate of bacon and Swiss muffins, and Lana's mouth watered as she breathed in the tantalizingly delicious aroma.

Lana shook her head, "No, I didn't know. I mean, obviously I knew he was applying, but not all the details pertaining to you." Lana sighed, realizing this was a perfect place to be a "new" Lana. "Tess, I have to apologize for anything that I may have done or said that caused any strife between you and Josh. I was so naïve, about everything—relationships, careers…life, I guess."

"What? No, Lana, I'm sorry. I didn't say that to make you feel bad, and you certainly have nothing to apologize for. It's a well-accepted truth now that Josh and I were never going to last, and I shudder to imagine if we had gotten married. We had known each other for too long, been together for too long, that it was just safer to be together than end the relationship. Which he did, once, you know, years ago."

Now Lana was stunned. "I had no idea…I thought you guys had always been together."

Tess nodded. "Oh, yeah, when Josh was first graduating from college here in New York. I was on my way to come here for his ceremony, when he told me not to come. Claimed I needed my freedom since I was two years younger. We got back together four years later, but nothing was the same."

"How did you know?" Lana questioned Tess.

"Know what? I just covered a lot of territory," Tess answered with a chuckle.

"How did you know to move on with Sam? How did you know to let go of your past with Josh?" God, she sounded so inexperienced to her own ears, she couldn't imagine what Tess was thinking.

"Honestly, it was hard to move on to something new—even when it's as appealing and persuasive as Sam. When we met on the train, we were both just swept up, like two magnets always finding each other over and over. I couldn't have stopped anything with him even if I had wanted to." Tess took a muffin off the plate and split it in two, then took a bite of one half. "I always forget how good these are." Lana nodded in agreement, already having eaten one. "Anyway, life intervened, and that was when a choice had to be made—when Sam and I made our way back to each other. But Lana, so many factors came into play, with my sister being a huge part of everything to bring us together." Tess ate the other half of her muffin, then pierced Lana with her deep-green eyes. "Do you believe in fate?"

Did she? Lana wasn't entirely sure, only having been able to rely on science and facts most of her life. The times she had trusted anything else, she had ended up crushed. "I don't know, honestly."

"Okay, that's fair. But Lana, consider this: how else do you explain meeting Liam in that bar that first night? Out of all the people who could have bought you a drink, or just been in the place, it was *Liam* who approached you. Just like with Sam and me on the train—something brought us together. I have seen Liam work his magic in a bar...hell, anywhere, for that matter. He doesn't lack attention. But he chose you. And you chose him—the cousin of the man you had worked beside for two years. Completely the opposite of Josh in many ways, except in ways that matter—his integrity. His heart. His spirit."

Lana's eyes filled with tears at Tess's words. Maybe a part of her had been afraid that he was trying to use her, like Anthony had all those years ago. The notion was ridiculous, she knew, but her self-doubt was always there, telling her she was never good enough…always the daughter searching for her father's love, coming up empty-handed every time.

Tess touched Lana on her arm, took a deep breath, and then said, "I wasn't sure how this was going to go, but I have something for you," She rose from their table to glide behind her counter, returning with a small bag she handed to Lana. "It's not from me, but I was asked to give it to you. Take your time," she said, disappearing into the kitchen.

Once she held the bag in her hands, Lana knew, with her own heart sinking, what was inside. She'd been hopeful that Liam was keeping it, a symbol of his feelings for her. Opening the bag, Lana drew out a folded sheet of paper that had her name written on the outside. Running her fingers over it, she imagined what he must have felt writing her name— the name of the woman he had held so tenderly in his arms…the woman who had willingly walked away from him when he was down on one knee.

Unfolding the note, Lana read:

Dearest Lana,

I'm returning this heart to you, after more than a year of holding on to it, realizing that the hope I had that you and I would hang it up again on another Christmas tree is misguided. I have waited for you to contact me. To let me know, in some way, that you cared even a fraction of the way I cared about you. I am an idiot, because I am still waiting. Like last year, I wanted to give you space and time, hoping that you would realize that you can't live without me, but I guess you can. Each time I talk to Effie or Josh, I hope they will give me some indication that you have asked about me, but your name is never mentioned.

I don't know what I did to make you turn away from me, but if you had only looked back, at any point, you

WOULD HAVE SEEN ME WATCHING YOU THE ENTIRE TIME, MY HEART BREAKING WITH EVERY STEP YOU TOOK. I UNDERSTAND THAT WHOEVER IT WAS THAT I RESCUED YOU FROM (MY WORDS, NOT YOURS—YOU ARE STRONG ENOUGH TO STAND ON YOUR OWN, I KNOW THAT) AT THE COUNTRY CLUB THAT NIGHT SAID TERRIBLE THINGS TO YOU—THINGS THAT AREN'T TRUE, UNDER ANY CIRCUMSTANCE. I DON'T KNOW IF YOU NEEDED TO HEAR THAT, BUT I NEEDED TO SAY IT. YOU ARE KIND AND COURAGEOUS, BEAUTIFUL AND SEXY, THOUGHTFUL AND FUNNY.

MAYBE I WASN'T ENOUGH FOR YOU? OR WHO YOU THOUGHT I WAS WASN'T ENOUGH? THERE WERE SO MANY THINGS I WANTED TO TELL YOU THAT NIGHT. I NEVER GOT TO TELL YOU THAT I AM TEACHING A FEW CLASSES AT THE COMMUNITY COLLEGE. I'M NO COLUMBIA PROFESSOR, BUT I AM MAKING A DIFFERENCE FOR THE STUDENTS TAKING MY CLASSES. OR SO THEY TELL ME. I NEVER GOT AN OPPORTUNITY TO TELL YOU THAT I COACH SOFTBALL EVERY YEAR TO SCREAMING PRETEEN GIRLS. ORIGINALLY, I STARTED DOING IT MANY YEARS AGO AS A WAY TO MEET WOMEN, BECAUSE SINGLE MOMS LOVE ME, BUT IT HAS GROWN INTO SOMETHING BIGGER, AN EXPERIENCE FOR ME TO MEAN SOMETHING TO A BUNCH OF LITTLE SOMEONES, EVEN IF THEY MAKE ME DEAF AFTER A GAME. I NEVER GOT TO TELL YOU THAT I TRY TO HELP ANYONE I CAN GET A RELIABLE MODE OF TRANSPORTATION, IN A PLACE THAT HAS NO BUS OR SUBWAY. YOU NEED A CAR FOR EVERYTHING HERE, AND I DO MY BEST TO WORK WITH ANYONE TO MAKE THAT HAPPEN.

MOST REGRETTABLY, I NEVER GOT THE CHANCE TO TELL YOU THAT YOU HAD MY HEART, FULLY AND COMPLETELY, IN A WAY THAT NO ONE HAS EVER HAD IT BEFORE. NOW YOU WILL ALWAYS HAVE IT.

ALL MY LOVE,
LIAM

# CHAPTER
## Thirty-Eight

*Liam*

TEXT FROM LANA

I hung up our heart ornament in my kitchen, where it catches the light just so, as the sun streams in. Often, I get nothing done, too enchanted am I with memories of us. Of what I let go. Of how I miss you. Of where I long to feel your touch again.

Liam stared at the messages on his screen—the first communication he had received from Lana in almost a year—eleven months, to be exact. Eleven months that he had spent mourning Lana, in the only way he knew how—celebrating the lifestyle he had known before he had ever met her: spending every other weekend in Sioux Falls with friends he had known since middle school. Some were married and getting away for a "boy's weekend", some divorced now and ready to be out on the town, and some were still single and waiting to meet "the one". Liam accepted every invitation, attending every bachelor party of the men *not* already married (after all, wasn't he well-known among his circle of friends as the consummate party-boy?), heading west to Deadwood every few weeks to gamble (in an attempt to spend the extra money he was earning teaching at the college, coaching softball, and now being an assistant track coach Effie had roped him into), and finally, dating as many women in the last year as he could, trying to forget Lana (only dating, much to the consternation of several women who left extremely disappointed after their attempted seductions had gone unfulfilled).

Seeing Tess at the dealership three months ago had dredged up the raw emotions he experienced the day on the beach with Lana after she had walked away from him—after he had failed in asking her to marry him. How depressing was that? He had known a couple of men who had gotten turned down with their proposals, but no one had ever been denied the opportunity to at least *ask* the question, to his knowledge. After work the day Ruth had been car shopping, the only thing on his mind was drowning his sorrows, and the perfect place in Beverley for that happened to be Shorty's. He had been two Heinekens and three tequila shots deep when Tess and Ruth entered the establishment with Adam and Paul. Groaning when he noticed them, he hoped the dark corner he had squirreled himself away in would keep him out of sight from two of the most meddlesome females Liam had ever known. To ensure that he would remain unseen, he even pulled down the brim of the baseball cap he was wearing. Liam had never been one to sport a cap, but this year, he felt the softball team he coached needed more than just some t-shirts with their team's name, the Lady Leopards, so he had purchased caps for the girls and their parents. From his corner, he watched as the sisters schooled the men in two rounds of pool, laughing to himself as Ruth, even pregnant, bested everyone. Liam breathed a sigh of relief when the game ended. Good, he thought, maybe they would leave, and he could get back to drinking, which had slowed down once the others arrived. No table service at Shorty's during the week meant he had to go to the bar himself to get another round, and he refused to take the chance of being detected by the Lefferts sisters. As the pool players all headed for the door, Liam rose from his seat and ambled to the bar; much to his chagrin, Ruth tossed a look over her shoulder at the same time. Damn, how did that woman know everything?

"Liam," Ruth called out, while pulling Tess away from the door and over to him. "Hey, I'm so glad we ran into you. I wanted to thank you for today—Lillian was terrific!" Ruth looked over his shoulder at the table holding his empty drinks, and then remarked, "Wild night for a party for one?" She held his gaze with both of her eyebrows raised.

Inwardly groaning, Liam answered, "Something like that. Nice to see you again, but I'm sure you have to get home to your family," Liam told her, looking pointedly at the door.

"Actually, Sean is meeting us here—he had to run home to shower and change. Tessie and I were going to run to the diner to get a bite to eat, but we can do that here, also—right, Tess?"

Tess flashed her sister a look of surprise, nodded in response, and added, "Umm…sure. I mean, I had my heart set on that chicken sandwich, with the Canadian bacon and melted Swiss on top. Ruthie, you know the one." Liam watched Ruth covertly step on her sister's toe, which had to have hurt, because Tess then winced. Grimacing, Tess then said, "but yes, one of Shorty's famous burger baskets sounds yummy."

Ruth nodded at her sister, clearly pleased her subterfuge had been successful. "I have an idea—Liam, why don't you join us?"

No, he absolutely did not want to join them, but it looked like he would have no choice in the matter, so he sighed and said, "I guess." From experience, Liam knew it was better to concede where Ruth was concerned than to resist. Liam grabbed the empty glassware from his earlier table and carried it to the bar, got himself another beer, and then slid into the crescent-shaped booth that Tess and Ruth had just sat in, sitting next to Tess. "So, what's up?" He asked Tess and Ruth.

The sisters exchanged a glance, and Tess said to Liam, "Ruth told me about the picture on your phone."

"Okay, and?" Great, now everyone would know how obsessed he still was with Lana, when he'd been doing his damndest to convince them all otherwise.

"And...it's clear that you miss Lana, Liam. Otherwise, why would you still be looking at the photo of the two of you?" asked Tess.

"Especially since I've seen you date almost every eligible female in the city limits of Beverley," noted Ruth.

"Why don't you just reach out to her? I've seen the same picture on her phone, too. I know she regrets whatever happened in Montauk that day," Tess said.

Liam's head whipped up to stare at Tess. "Why? Has she said something?" Liam was unable to keep the hope out of his voice.

Tess hesitated. "No, but she's very lonely, Liam. You know, Josh told me once that she never really talked about her family, or about her past. He said that he was pretty sure he was her only friend at the hospital. Now he's been gone for two years, and in the year-plus she's been in Brooklyn, she never has any visitors. Unless you count her family, but they don't come in that often. As far as I can tell, she goes to work, comes home, eats with Sam and me occasionally. She also spends most of her free time walking in the cemetery, and I join her when I can, but she is living a pretty lonely life."

Hearing about Lana being alone broke his heart. When he was with her, she had taken the empty space in his heart that had gone unfulfilled by his rambling ways: meaningless relationships, shallow friendships, a career that had meant little to him. Somewhere deep within himself his lonely heart had recognized hers—beneath her tremulous smiles lived a woman with a life in need of sharing, a woman with exceedingly large amounts of love to give, a woman with too much sadness experienced already in her relatively young life. That's why he had wanted to propose that night on the beach—who cared if they had only known each other a short amount of time? He had already wasted years being only moderately happy (on a good day). Each day spent with Lana had showed him what true contentment and joy were.

Sensing he was close to breaking down in front of Tess and Ruth, he whispered, "I tried so hard, before that day on Long Island. I texted her every day for weeks, months, with no answer. Then I backed off, because I didn't know what she wanted. So, I started texting less frequently. Each one I could see she had read, but never a response. Then when I finally saw her at Cal's wedding, standing in the middle of those assholes saying such fucked up things—I know they humiliated her, even more so, I'm guessing, by having me witness it. I began to understand why she was shut off."

Tess had tears in her eyes when she told him, "She admitted to me, finally, a few months ago, that she knew those people from high school. That they were older, but in her class, and she had been the subject of their teasing back then. I guess the guy was someone she had a crush on or something like that—she didn't go into any details about him, but both Effie and I got a bad vibe from him."

Liam put his head in his hands, feeling as if he were being tortured as he remembered the look of pain on her beautiful face that night. He had swept in, his only mission to protect her and make her smile again. Was it possible he had taken the wrong approach by rushing into a proposal? He was so ignorant—he should have asked her about those people... convinced her to confide in him, as he had in her.

"I failed her," he muttered. "I was so fixated on trying to make things better for her that I didn't ask her what was wrong in the first place."

"Stop, Liam," Ruth advised, reaching over to give his hand a reassuring squeeze. "Don't beat yourself up. If you still want her, you need to focus now on how to move forward—how to reach her now."

"That's all I want!" Liam exclaimed. "But honestly, I'm scared of getting rejected. There's only so much one man can take, you know."

"Especially you, though," Tess stated. "I'm guessing, unlike the rest of us mere mortals, you have not been subjected to the finer art of rejection."

Liam blushed, fully cognizant that he had lived a charmed life with the opposite sex—a fact that Josh used to tease him about in college after Josh and Tess had broken up. Dating soon after the break-up, Josh found himself unable to emulate his cousin's continual string of girlfriends. Instead of playing the field to sow his wild oats, Josh instead ended up having two short-term (for Josh) relationships in the four years he and Tess were apart. "What do I do?"

"You need to think big—like really shock her out of her head. A big declaration," Ruth suggested.

Liam nodded. "Like when Josh showed Effie how he really felt."

Ruth snapped her fingers. "Exactly! You remember how Effie—hell, everyone in town—swooned over him for it. And that was *Josh*. Imagine what you could do with your years of seduction and sexy moves." Ruth wriggled her eyebrows suggestively.

"Sexy moves?" Everyone at the table turned to look at who was standing behind Ruth, interrupting their conversation.

"Sean, thank god you're here," Ruth said as her husband slid into the booth beside her.

"I don't know how I feel about my pregnant wife and sister-in-law taking to Beverley's most eligible bachelor about his 'sexy moves'." Sean laughed, and finally the bartender came to their table carrying a Dr. Pepper for Ruth, a Squirt for Tess, and two Heinekens for Liam and Sean.

"Well, Babe, if we have our way, he won't be eligible for much longer," Ruth informed her husband.

Tess added, "Let's be honest with each other—this man is the furthest thing from eligible there is."

That night, Liam had gone back to his house, filled with some optimism but also trepidation, and written his letter to Lana, in which he had done his best to convey his own longing and deep-seated self-doubts, making himself vulnerable, hoping she would do the same. Returning the heart ornament to her had been the most difficult thing to do, but he wanted her to have it, even if he never heard from her again. And he hadn't. Until today.

Although Lana was the first woman to maintain his interest, in the dark of night, Liam questioned himself if their romance had been heightened to such dizzying levels because of their secrecy with one another, their explosive sexual chemistry, and when together, they closed out the rest of the world a little too well. Over the past many weeks, Liam began to convince himself that was, indeed, the case. Until today.

After months of restraining himself from reaching out to Lana, desperate for her to make the first move to communicate, attempting (unsuccessfully) to move on, he finally opened himself up again with his heartfelt letter, which had evidently not affected her in the least. Or so he had thought. Until today.

Should he respond? Yes, Lana had reached out, finally, but she still wasn't saying anything. A knock on his front door turned his attention away from his phone. "Come in," he hollered from his kitchen, where he was putting the finishing touches on the shrimp and grits he had made for himself and his dinner guest.

"My god, Liam, it smells divine in here," his sister declared, pushing her glasses up her nose as her brown hair fell over her shoulders. She had always complained about the shade of her hair compared to his, saying hers was too ordinary, but Liam always thought she was too hard on herself. "What are you making?" Cait asked after she threw her purse on his sofa and placed a bottle of white wine on the table. "Want a glass —it's pinot Grigio?"

Liam groaned. "You know, when you said you would bring some adult beverages over, I was thinking some beers or whisky. Doesn't Dad still have that Irish whisky he brought back from Ireland that they still haven't opened? And to answer your questions, I am making shrimp and grits." After a brief pause, he added, "And yes, I would like a glass."

"You certainly bitched about it long enough before giving me your answer. Just FYI: when someone volunteers to bring something to drink, you should always clarify what they are bringing, in case you want something particular. I happen to love Grigio and hate whisky. And yes, Dad still has the bottle unopened, but good luck getting it from him— he's, like, emotionally attached to it." Cait rolled her eyes at this.

"Haha, I know—I made a joke about it the last time I was at their place, and he was so offended by it. I get the vibe that Mom and Dad drank too much when they were over there the last time. They got down and dirty in the sheets, and they brought a bottle home to get their freak on again."

Cait stared open-mouthed at her brother. "Oh, my god—I got that same vibe! And eww, by the way." Cait clinked her glass of wine to the one she just handed to Liam and said, "Cheers." She took a long drink, then remarked, "So shrimp and grits, huh? You know, when I was in the Gulf, I ate this at least once a week. Every place makes it differently, but I never disagreed with any of them. Didn't know you knew how to make it, though."

"Well, there's a lot about me you don't know. And there's a lot about you I don't know, either." Cait had begun to thaw, gradually, over the past year, after she returned from a trip to Mobile, Alabama, the past spring. Since then, she seemed to let go of whatever anger had been driving her upon her initial return to South Dakota, and Liam was more than happy to make amends with his sister. At least once a week, the siblings got together either for a movie or a meal (sometimes both). Now, as his sister turned away from him, he pondered the idea that Cait had many secrets about her time in the Gulf she wasn't ready to share, and Liam didn't feel like prying, so instead he asked, "Can you get the salad out of the fridge?"

"Your place is really starting to feel like a home now, Liam," Cait told him as she pulled a wooden bowl out containing spinach, chopped apples, and candied walnuts that Liam planned on dressing with a simple balsamic vinaigrette.

"Yeah, thanks—it took a while-" he was interrupted by a loud guffaw.

"'Took a while'? Big brother, you've been living here for almost two years with only a couch and coffee table in here. Those end tables are a nice touch, though—they look familiar." Cait snapped her fingers. "Weren't those great-grandma Livingston's?"

"Those old things? I'm not sure…I had them in storage." Liam had to reroute this conversation before she remembered-

"And didn't Josh take them when we were cleaning out her house before he went back to New York for med school?" Her hazel eyes shot a look at him, and he busied himself tossing the salad with the dressing.

"He did, I remember. You took the bedroom furniture, I got the dining table, Daniel got the-"

"Can we please stop listing every item pilfered before the estate sale? You know I always loved those end tables! Suddenly, though, Josh wanted them? Letting Grandpa referee between us was a huge mistake on my part, so I got the bedroom stuff instead. You know, I offered to swap the dressing table and bureau for those tables, but the little shit said he didn't want to cart the bigger stuff back to New York," Liam proclaimed hotly.

"Yes, but he keeps asking if anyone has seen them—hey hasn't he been over here since you've had them out?" Cait inquired.

"Nah, I just brought them down last week. They've been safely tucked away in my bedroom," he smugly replied.

"You mean along with the other things you *also* got? Man, Josh will lose it when he finds out," Cait told him.

Liam waved his wineglass at his sister, which she refilled with a laugh. "Besides, Effie has their house furnished with some of that mid-century modern stuff she likes. These things would stick out like a couple of sore thumbs."

"Didn't you once-" Cait ducked under one of the end tables and came back up grinning. "Yep...still there. 'Liam loves mom'. How adorable: you carved your undying love into the bottom of the tables."

Liam flushed. How was he to deny that this was the actual reason he wanted those tables? "I was only seven! Besides, what was anyone doing letting me have a blade in the first place?"

"A blade—like you were a prisoner in a high-security prison?" Cait laughed while shaking her brown head. "But you do have a point. My lips are sealed about this, because you will never hear the end of this from Josh." Taking another sip of her wine, Cait practically slammed the glass down on the table. "Speaking of Josh, you will never guess who he and Effie asked to officiate their ceremony!"

Liam responded, "The last I heard, Ruth wanted to do it."

Cait chuckled. "Along with being the maid of honor, head of the planning committee, having three kids..." The siblings laughed. "Anyway, Josh and Effie took me out for dinner the other night and asked me to do it-"

"Wow—thanks for asking me to go out for dinner. I just sat here alone. I'm only the best man and everything, don't mind me." Liam interrupted.

"Right—like you are ever alone. You've been dating like you're in a reality show. Anyway," she drawled out, "they said there was no one more officious than me, and I said, 'Why—because I'm a lawyer?' And I got ordained that night on the internet."

"Pretty cool, Sis, pretty cool. Supper is almost done," he told her, as Cait told him she needed to use the toilet. "Use the one upstairs—I'm having work done on the one down here."

As Cait padded up the stairs, Liam heard his phone ping.

TEXT FROM LANA

> It's hard for me to know what to say sometimes.

> I've never been good with personal relationships, but with you it was easy (when I wasn't messing it up) and that scared me.

> Liam, I have trusted the wrong men before and gotten my heart broken.

What was she talking about—trusting the wrong men? Who had broken her heart? Why did he feel like his was breaking, as well?

"What's up with that tree in your room?" Cait's voice brought his attention away from his phone.

"What? Why were you in my room?" What the hell had she been doing snooping around his bedroom? "I said to use the bathroom upstairs."

"Yeah, and your bedroom door was open with the light on in the ensuite bathroom there, so I assumed you meant for me to use that one. "So, are you going to answer me? What is with the Christmas tree in your room? It's August."

"It's not a Christmas tree," he snapped.

"Okay, but it has all of those ornaments on it. Why are you so touchy about this? Some of them are really nice, Liam." Cait poured more wine for herself and topped off his glass. He was going to need the entire bottle tonight, it seemed, if his sister continued to ask questions.

"Look, that tree up there is personal, as are the things on it, which is why it's in my room and not on display down here."

"Alright, alright, I just never took you as a collector. I mean, you barely have any decor of any kind down here."

Liam took the pot of grits from the stove and placed it on the table and then walked back to get the bowl of shrimp with its spicy Cajun sauce, announcing, "Dinner is ready." He waited for his sister to sit before sitting across from her. Even though he was studiously ignoring her gaze, Liam could tell she was studying him over the rim of her wine-glass as she took another drink.

Cait sighed and said quietly, "I'm sorry about using the wrong bathroom. I wasn't trying to snoop or anything."

Liam dished out grits for himself and Cait, ladling a hefty portion of shrimp over each bowl of grits, and then handed a bowl to Cait. "Look, I'm sorry for freaking out. Those ornaments are from that trip I took to New York after Christmas."

Cait raised an eyebrow. "Christmas…you mean the one that was a year and a half ago? When you met up with…Lana…right?" He nodded. "There are a lot of ornaments on that tree, Liam," she said softly. "And not all of them are from New York."

What had she done up there—taken an inventory? Talking over the lump that had formed in his throat, he said, "Since we bought ornaments together every place we went, I kept doing it when I got home." Liam took a big drink of his wine and confided, "Wherever I go, I am always thinking of Lana."

"Oh, Liam."

"I know—it's stupid and pathetic. I just…I can't…it's like she's always with me."

Cait shook her head. "It's not stupid and certainly not pathetic—I think it's romantic, actually, if that doesn't sound creepy coming from your sister. But what about all the other women?"

Liam paused, his forkful of shrimp halfway to his mouth. "What other women?"

"The ones you've been dating like a horny frat boy. Don't they ask about the tree when you bring them here?"

"Caity-kins, there have been no other women in my bedroom, nor have I been in theirs. Not since Lana." Chewing his food, he wondered how long his bedroom would remain free of any company, but he had absolutely no interest in or desire for anyone else. Once he swallowed his delicious dinner, he admitted, "But there is someone I am considering bringing to the wedding."

"But what about Lana?"

"What about her?"

"You do know she's coming to the wedding, right?" Cait clarified, and no, he didn't know. Hadn't even considered the possibility.

TEXT FROM LANA

Until you, Liam, I never imagined someone would love me. Until you, I didn't realize I could put my heart in their hands. Until you, I never knew what it was to trust someone so implicitly. I know all of this now. Am I too late?

# CHAPTER
## Thirty-Nine

## Effie and Josh

TEXT FROM LANA

I just don't think I will feel comfortable at the wedding. I'm sorry but I hope you and Josh understand.

TEXT TO RUTH

Well, just got another message from Lana about not coming to the wedding. You were right.

TEXT FROM RUTH

And this is news how???

Stick with me, kid.

"I can't believe you have dragged me to New York City when we have a wedding in two months—won't our honeymoon be enough for you?" Josh half-heartedly questioned his fiancée, knowing full-well that he would do whatever this woman in his arms wanted him to do. Forever. Always.

"Haha—not even close." Effie whispered in his ear, "Nothing

357

concerning you is ever enough for me," and her teeth tugged on his earlobe, intending to show him how eternally grateful she was that he accompanied her on this four-day trip. Effie wanted to come back to New York to talk to Lana in person about coming to the wedding. Although Liam was still floundering, he had dated a few perfectly nice women over the past few weeks, and Effie and Ruth both feared he could eventually develop feelings for one of them—but nothing that would ever match what both women were positive he still felt for Lana.

Helpless to deny his longing for Effie, Josh turned her so her back was against the wall of the spare bedroom in Sam and Tess's basement. Ever so slowly, he unbuttoned her blouse while his mouth devoured hers. Her hands thrust on his shoulders as her long legs curled around his hips, and he savored the weight of her as his hands moved from her breasts to her bottom.

Effie released a long, heavy moan, deeply appreciating the particular way his tongue always paid special attention to her collarbone. With her hands in his hair, she brought his mouth back up to hers, and sent a silent thank you up to Tess for putting them in their basement this time, where they could make as much noise as possible. Effie loved the way she could make Josh lose himself in her.

Later, as Effie caught her breath in the sweaty embrace of her soon-to-be husband, she stroked his arm that draped across her stomach. Normally seen by many as staid, stiff, and unyielding, he was the complete opposite with her, and it drove her wild knowing that she was the only one privileged enough to experience his most tender, loving side. Not that he treated his friends or family without any warmth—the opposite was true: he had his best friend, Sam, who he had been friends with now for eighteen years; his cousin Liam, who thankfully had forgiven Josh for his part in anything that had blown up his romance with Lana; and most importantly, he had his father, Henry, who had sacrificed so much for his only child, had been his only parent after his mother had left both him and his father when Josh was twelve, never to be heard from again, as far as Josh was concerned. A couple of years ago, Henry had admitted that Melanie had, indeed, been keeping tabs on Josh intermittently through Henry's dad, unbeknownst to even Henry.

Now, Effie considered the DNA ancestry test that she and Josh had submitted a few months ago, on a lark. A gift from Tess before the couple separated, Josh had kept the kit in his briefcase, until one day Effie had questioned him about why he had never finished it. Curious what her ancestry results would show, also, she had ordered a test for herself; she was especially interested in how much of her DNA was Native blood. Prior to taking the test, her cousin, Abigail, had informed her that their great-great-great-grandfather LeBeau had been a French trapper, but had no other details. A drawer at home in Beverley contained all the secrets that both Effie's and Josh's DNA test had revealed. Truthfully, Effie's results hadn't been that surprising, other than finding out that her mother's side of the family, the Fullers, had come to America on the Mayflower. Her French trapper bloodline had been confirmed, much to the relief of Abigail. Josh's results hadn't exactly been Earth-shattering, but the message in Effie's inbox certainly had been, and Effie was now harboring the secret until *after* she and Josh were blissfully married. So much devastation had followed his almost-marriage to Tess two and a half years ago that Effie wanted everything for their own ceremony and honeymoon to be as blissful (and stress-free) as possible.

"Hey, you're awfully quiet," Josh commented as his fingers slid across her stomach and the way he heard her breath catch made him smile. Effie made him smile; she lifted him up; she made him believe that every day was magical. "Everything okay? I get nervous when you're quiet for too long."

Effie laughed and turned in his arms, lifting her hands to stroke his face. "Everything is perfect. I love you so much," she told him, staring into his crystal-blue eyes. With wonder, Effie remarked, "I can't believe that Tess and Sam are having a baby—is that weird for you?"

Josh chuckled, "Why? Because Tess and I would quite possibly be married right now if she hadn't done all of us a favor and run into Sam on that train?"

Effie grew quiet, "Yeah." Effie hated imagining everything that could have stood in the way of her and Josh falling in love. "Do you regret I made us wait to get married?"

"Effie, you didn't make us wait to do anything. I would have married you the night I came back to South Dakota, with our friends and family at that gazebo, no doubt. And I would have married you every day since then. But I'm glad we waited—you were just out of your crappy marriage, and I had just made my peace with Tess and Sam." Josh brought up her left hand to his mouth, kissing her ring finger. "We have spent that past two years building a life together. I love you more today than I did yesterday, or the day before." Their wedding in two months was a mere formality at this point, but it gave them a reason to gather their nearest and dearest together for a celebration. They had pledged their love and loyalty to each other the moment Josh moved into the house Effie had bought shortly after moving back to South Dakota from Denver two years ago—a house that now had both of their names on the title. "And don't forget—Sam and Tess aren't just having 'a baby'."

Effie laughed, "God, I know—twins! They're so happy. I can't believe that Ruth never said a word to me. Actually, I never thought Ruth could keep a secret."

Josh put his forehead against Effie's, letting their breaths mingle. Originally, Effie had planned to make the trip by herself, but then she suggested it might be better for Lana if he was there as well, helping her plead the case for Lana to come to their wedding. "Speaking of Ruth, I still don't know how comfortable I am with the plan you have concocted with Ruth and Tess, trying to strong-arm Lana into all of this," he admitted to Effie just before he kissed her again.

"'All of this' being what, Sweetie? We want her to be there, right? I mean, she and I have grown quite close." Effie sat up and began to redress.

Josh groaned, knowing he would also need to put his clothes back on. He had been hoping to convince her to stay in bed just a bit longer but was fully aware they had not traveled halfway across the country to spend the day naked together. Unfortunately.

"Plus, you want to talk to her about her future, right? I mean, Tess told us that Lana wasn't happy staying in surgery. You said that Beverley General is hiring more general physicians," Effie reminded Josh—as if he needed it. He just didn't find the idea of meddling in someone's life as agreeable as his future wife clearly did. "Then there's the issue that you kind of helped split them apart...not that I'm blaming you, or anything..."

"Wow, and here I thought everyone had forgotten my outburst in the hotel room *a year and a half ago*," Josh said emphatically. He made one tiny error, and no one would let him forget it. By the way both Liam and Lana were acting, caught up in their own hurt but unable to vocalize it to the other, he could see now how right they were for each other. All he wanted was for everyone to be as happy as he was, so if intervening in personal love lives was the way to do it, then he would get the job done. The business with Lana's professional life, however, was entirely trickier. Momentarily distracted by the sight of Effie covering up her glistening, golden skin with her clothing, Josh considered trying to lure her back into bed, but a text alert pinged on his phone.

TEXT FROM LANA

Hey, everyone, if you guys are available tonight, would you all like to come up to my place for dinner?

A loud gasp brought him to his feet. "What? What's the matter?" he asked his fiancée.

Effie laughed, "Did you see this text? See, Josh, it was meant to be. Our plan is coming together already. Let me text her back. I am sure Tess and Sam will be up for it, since we were going to go out with them, anyway."

TEXT TO LANA

Would love to! Just let us know what time.

"Honey, I hate to point it out, but we haven't even begun our 'plan' yet. We haven't seen Lana," Josh pointed out.

Effie sputtered, "Well, maybe not, but at least she's not laying low or avoiding us, which is what Tess said she's been doing to them for a while."

Josh drew her into his arms. "I love you and I love that you are so concerned about Lana and Liam, but I don't want you to be disappointed if things don't go how you want them to. I'm willing to talk up Beverley General, but asking Lana to consider taking a job there is questionable—

she's got no ties to the area. She's from New York, and it would be a huge adjustment. It was for me, and I'm from South Dakota. Plus, didn't you say that she has a big family here?"

Effie nodded, knowing she had a hill to climb here, but as far as she could see, Josh was putting unnecessary obstacles in the path. She was growing frustrated with him and with her own unending optimism. Optimism, it must be noted, she had lacked *until* she had fallen in love with Josh. Before Josh, Effie liked to consider herself as a badass woman —granted, one with occasional mommy issues and a fractured family. Happily reuniting with her father's side of the family (who she hadn't seen since her biological father had died when she was five) a couple of years ago, she had even chosen to forgive her maternal grandparents. Their racist comments to her when she was a child had caused enough self-doubt to almost earn her a lifetime supply of therapy, until that life became sunshine and rainbows, courtesy of the man she would soon wed. "Josh, I am fully aware that I can't fix everything with Lana and Liam, but I want her to at least be at the wedding, so that the potential is there for them to work everything out and just be in love." Standing in the circle of Josh's arms, Effie put her own arms around his shoulders. "You know, she's texted him, but he's never responded?"

"I didn't, but how long was that *after* he sent that letter back with Tess? He couldn't wait around forever, you know. I've never known him to go this long without a girlfriend, but that can't last." He watched Effie type on her phone, then told her, "Lana will have to make a move with Liam this time—he's put himself on the line for her, and I think he feels burned."

TEXT FROM TESS

Sam and I are done working by five.

TEXT FROM LANA

So is seven good for everyone?

TEXT TO LANA

Perfect for us!

Effie tossed her phone down onto the bed. "Glad that's settled. I agree with what you're saying about Lana, and she's ready to take some chances—I can feel it. Now, do you want to go out for a walk?" Josh shook his head. "What about heading over to-" Silencing Effie with his mouth, Josh considered his own genius in not having put his own clothes back on as he relished the feel of her nails scraping his chest. "I wondered how long you were going to stand there naked before I could lure you back to bed," Effie said sultrily.

"As always, Effie, your wish is my command."

# 

## Forty

*Lana*



I know I messed up. I know I waited too long, but as long as I know you are reading my texts, I will keep writing.

Until you tell me not to.

And she did. Lana wrote to Liam every day once she started, as if the dam holding back her trust, her care, her love, her insecurities had broken inside of her. She told him about her days and how mentally and emotionally exhausting she found pediatric surgery.



I had this three-year-old patient today, being treated for bone cancer. I don't know how much longer I can perform these procedures without a piece of my heart breaking.

Lana told him about her family, hoping he could understand her better, without having to make herself too raw, and she found she took comfort in talking to him through her messages.

TEXT TO LIAM

My niece, Julia, came to stay with me this weekend. She's 22, only 10 years younger than me, but I can already see how much better she is at every aspect of life. I watch her with her boyfriend, and I marvel that she has more of a life than I do.

TEXT TO LIAM

I've always come up short making friends.

Something in me pushes people away, like I did with you. I'm sorry for that. I know you deserve answers for my erratic behavior, and I'm trying to work it out. To explain it to you. Honestly, part of me wishes we could just move forward and not have to talk about it. I am doing better, though, making friends, trusting people. Because of you.

Then there were the long, sleepless nights where her legs tangled in her sheets, and her hands reached out, only finding the other side of her bed empty and cold. Liam had awakened in her the longing for someone to wake up next to, or someone who was there in the middle of the night to turn to when she awoke feeling anxious, maybe someone who could help her as she tried to figure out what to do with her life.

TEXT TO LIAM

The time has come for me to make a decision about my career. The hospital I'm at now, Park Slope Presbyterian, has asked me to join their surgical staff, but I just can't imagine even one more year of this.

TEXT TO LIAM

> More news: Lenox Hill Hospital has a position for me as an attending physician, but I'm not sure I want to be in charge. God, Josh would be so good in that role. I looked up to him so much. He reminds me of my brother, Monty, sometimes, because he could just put his head down and do the work—not constantly question if he is doing the right thing. Not like I do.

Was this how life was supposed to work? Absolutely unsure of your future, yet expected to make decisions concerning the next ten years of your life? She couldn't even make up her mind about going to Josh and Effie's wedding. When Effie had first asked her a few months ago, she had held the heart from Liam in her hands, freshly returned to her. Wanting nothing more than to see him again, she had told Effie that she would absolutely be at the wedding. However, as the weeks rolled on and there was no response from Liam to any of her text messages, Lana wavered, reconsidering the trip to South Dakota. After all, it wasn't like it was a short plane ride away. Both of her sisters encouraged her to go, assuring her that Liam just needed to see her and everything would be fixed between them—how could that be, though, when Lana hadn't even acknowledged to him what had truly made her walk away from him on the beach? Neither Ava nor Greer knew the truth about what happened on that beach so many years ago with Anthony—only Monty and her mom had dried her tears. And none of them were aware of the extent of her humiliation as far as her dad was concerned when he refused to pay for any college but Stony Brook University. Ironic, really, since it had been Thomas who had encouraged Lana in the first place to apply to Ivy League schools, only then to yank them away when she had gotten accepted. Instead, Lana had told her family that she was the one who had chosen to stay on Long Island to attend college. Nothing wrong with Stony Brook—it was a fantastic school, but she had been left feeling undeserving or unworthy of anything more, eerily similar to her feelings concerning her father's love.

With the smells of coq au vin filling her homey apartment, Lana put a pan of potatoes on to boil for the mashed potatoes she was also making for her dinner party. This was what real grown-ups did, right—have their friends over for dinner? Flushing slightly at the memory of the last time she made a meal for someone other than a member of her family, Lana had done her best to move past the awkwardness of that evening. Poor Josh, so distraught after his break-up with Tess that Lana had only wanted to make him feel better with a home-cooked meal. That had been the night she truly had hoped there could be more for the two of them than simply "friends", especially once he had shown up with a bouquet of flowers. Chuckling now at how surprised she had been then, Lana shook her head, thinking of the almost-full circle moment tonight would be, with both Tess *and* Josh at her apartment for dinner.

A knock on the door sounded, and Lana looked at the time. She still had half an hour yet until everyone was due to arrive, but knowing her guests, she wasn't surprised when she opened the door. "Effie! Oh, and Tess!"

"Surprise!" Effie announced, holding a bunch of flowers tied together beautifully with a blue bow. "Don't go getting any ideas now," Effie told her laughingly as she hugged Lana with one arm.

Lana blushed and laughed, "Oh my god—I can't believe Josh told you about that. I still get embarrassed when I think of how I misunderstood his gesture."

"If anything, it's my fault," Tess, who was holding a gorgeous blue and green vase, proclaimed. "I always made it a point to take flowers when someone invited us to their house for dinner, but I would have thought Josh would use better judgment than to take them to a dinner with a female co-worker. Alone. At her apartment. When I heard about that, all I could do was shake my head."

"Let's place the blame where it truly belongs—with Josh. That being said, Tess, maybe if you hadn't dumped my fiancé the night before your wedding, he would never have gotten himself in that situation," Effie sarcastically informed Tess, winking at her as she filled the vase Tess had handed her with water.

Feigning shock, Tess saucily replied, "Hey, I thought we were still at the point that you were thanking me for giving you your chance with him?" Tess shook her finger at Effie. Watching the two of them reminded Lana of how her sisters had their unique way of communicating with each other, somehow always making Lana feel like a third wheel in her own family. A growing unease built up in Lana, and she wondered if this was a mistake—two couples and single Lana on her own. What was it like to be part of something? To have a built-in best friend, someone to be your plus-one?

Tess sniffed the air and then sighed. "Whatever you are cooking smells positively divine."

"That's why we came up early—the smells drifting down were driving us crazy," Effie said, lifting the lid of the Dutch oven on the stovetop. "Ooh, what is this glorious concoction?"

"It's coq au vin, but with white wine instead of red." Lana took a plate of cheese and crackers out of the refrigerator, putting it down on the countertop near Tess. "Actually, I'm glad you two came early. I'd like to talk to you before Sam and Josh show up." Lana hadn't planned on bringing it up, but now that Effie and Tess were here, the opportunity seemed right.

Lana heard cooing noises from her living area, so she figured Tess had found Cannoli and Stromboli, who were likely curled up at the front windows, birdwatching.

"Wait," Effie interrupted. "Tess, where'd you put that bag?" Tess trotted back to the kitchen and handed a white canvas bag to Effie, who pulled out two bottles. One appeared to be a bottle of Chardonnay, and the other a bottle of *sparkling cider?*

Tess grinned. "No wonder that dang bag was so heavy—it contained a bottle of guilt-juice."

"Guilt-juice? What's that?" Lana had never heard the expression until tonight.

"It's what someone who's drinking alcohol offers to someone who isn't, so they don't have to feel guilty," Effie explained. "I've heard about it from Ruth now for her last two pregnancies," she said with a smile.

"But who's pregnant?" Lana asked and then gasped, "Oh my god— Effie? Congratulations!" Lana squealed, preceding to hug her friend, who backed away looking appalled.

"Good god, no! Can I please get to the altar first?" Effie took Tess by the shoulders and announced, "This woman right here is having not just one but two babies!"

Lana teared up as she looked in Tess's eyes, knowing what this must mean for Tess and Sam. Last fall, over a cup of tea and a plate of cookies, Tess had confessed to Lana that she and Sam had been trying to conceive since they had opened up the bookstore. Tess admitted that the timing hadn't been the best at first, since they each had a new business, and Sam also writing his fifth book. A year later, though, and they still had had no luck. Tess had been beside herself, having wanted to be a mother for so much of her life, and watching her sister conceive so easily. "Oh, Tess," she told her now, "I'm so happy for you," and embraced her in a warm hug. "And twins? Really?"

Tess nodded, telling her friends, "Of course, Sam is over the moon—we both are! Took a lot of trying, but-"

Effie interrupted, "Yeah, I'm sure that part was a struggle—we've seen how your husband looks at you! Like he can't wait to remove every item of clothing." Effie opened both bottles while Lana took her cue to get some glasses. "Kind of the way I've seen someone look at you, Lana."

Okay, so it was starting. Lana wasn't exactly *not* prepared for this conversation—it was, after all, one reason she had asked them over for dinner. She had just expected to be the one to bring it up.

"About that-" Lana began. Now she could explain to Effie why she could not possibly attend her wedding to Josh.

"Here we go," pronounced Effie.

"Yep, exactly as predicted," agreed Tess, who raised her glass of guilt juice to toast with Effie.

"Wait," cried Lana, "what's going on?" Had they been discussing her behind her back?

"We knew you were going to back out of coming to the wedding. At first, you were definitely coming," Effie reminded Lana. "Then you got that letter from Liam-"

Lana cut her off, "Which also included a returned gift." Lana shouldn't have to point that out to Effie or Tess, both of whom knew how hurt she had been.

"Umm, not really, though." Lana's gaze shot to Tess, who continued, "He was returning *your* gift to *you*, babe. Not returning a gift *from* you *to* him."

"Exactly! If anything, it was a signal for you to make your move," declared Effie.

Lana replied indignantly, "Which I did! And he still hasn't replied to any of my texts."

Tess hesitated and then added, "Not yet. But he will. Eventually. You didn't respond right away, Lana. Imagine how that must have made him feel."

Effie explained, "He waited for you to let him know how you were feeling for months."

"So, if he's acting out now, that's why," Tess said.

"'Acting out'? What do you mean 'acting out'?" Lana looked from Tess to Effie, sure that they were keeping something from her concerning Liam. "Is he okay?"

Effie shot a look to Tess. "What Tess means is that Liam has been, umm…" Effie paused to finish off her glass of wine, poured another for herself, and then picked up the glass intended for Lana that still sat on the counter, pouring the contents into her own glass. Tess began eating some of the cheese and crackers, probably in an attempt to not have to answer any questions. Lana's stomach clenched, dreading whatever Effie was trying to tell her. Finally, Effie sighed and continued, "Liam has been seeing someone. Just a few dates. *Very casually*, and I need you to understand that I am stressing the *casually* part-"

"And the *very* part, according to Ruth," Tess interjected.

Effie nodded in agreement, "Yes, and the very. She teaches some classes at the college, that's how they met. And to my knowledge, all they have done is have a couple of coffee dates." Effie refilled Lana's wineglass, handed it to her and motioned for her to drink. "Full disclosure, he has taken many women out on dates the past few months, but nothing has stuck."

"Until now, you mean." Lana drank her wine and refilled her glass, tossing the wine to the back of her throat in a huge gulp, trying to dull the pain that was worse than she had imagined. So, it was over…Liam had moved on. Not exactly shocking, when she recalled the stories Josh used to regale her with about Liam's dating history: ultimate playboy, impossible to tie down, never committing himself to any woman, and some ridiculous two-month dating limit. Who was she to judge, though, never having had any kind of relationship? As hard as she had tried over the past couple of years to build friendships, particularly with these two women in her kitchen, but also with her sisters and her adult nieces, and to be more well-balanced and "normal", Lana still found herself lacking when it came to romance. Closing her eyes to her own pain, Lana was surprised when two pairs of arms encircled her.

Tess whispered, "Hey, we just wanted to make sure you had all the details, not for you to give up."

"If Liam is worth fighting for, you at least have to put on your suit of armor," Effie told her. "Let me tell you something I haven't admitted, out loud, to anyone. My ex-husband was a scoundrel, like lower than a snake's belly-"

"You've absolutely said that before, Effie," Tess broke in. "You have at least ten versions of this soliloquy."

"Yes, dear, but if you'd let me finish before pouncing on me, you would have heard the rest. I'm chalking this up to your hormones, but I have to tell you, you are acting more like your sister now," Effie admonished Tess. "No, scratch that, you *are* your sister now, because she has chilled out since the baby was born. I'm beginning to think it's a pregnant Lefferts-sister thing."

Tess erupted in laughter. "Oh my god, you're right! Sorry! Continue on." Lana couldn't help but smile at their banter—unintended or not, her spirits were lifting somewhat. She sank down into a kitchen chair in utter defeat, and Effie and Tess followed her lead.

"Anyway, Damon was a complete bastard who betrayed me in almost every possible way during our marriage. Even so, I fought for him...for us. And while it humiliates me when I think about how I let him manipulate me and my emotions, I can't feel degraded for fighting for what I thought was right at the time. But you and Liam are not me and Damon. Liam is at least a thousand times the man Damon could *ever* aspire to be. And if you haven't done everything you can to let him know, then you are cheating him out of this, also, not just yourself." Effie reached over and took Lana's hand into her own. "Remember, Liam fought for you, more than once, but you walked away from him. Twice. I'm sure you had your reasons, but you have to tell him."

"I've tried," Lana told Effie, but was that the truth? Even with all of her texts to him, she hadn't addressed leaving him on the beach. Then there was the issue of moving forward with her career. Part of her knew the reason she held back from accepting a permanent position anywhere was because of him, dreaming about "what ifs". What if he loved her still? What if he wanted her enough to ask her to move to South Dakota? What if she gave up her life here? What if no man ever made her feel the way Liam had from their first night in that bar…in that hotel…in that bed?

Tess took Lana's other hand. "I know it's scary to be vulnerable. I walked away from Josh on the day before our wedding, to take a chance on a man I met on a train, for crying out loud. A man I only spent a few days with. I didn't know his favorite color, or what meal he liked to eat on his birthday, or if he leaves the seat up on the toilet after he uses it in the middle of the night. Hell, I didn't even know about our past history. What I was certain about was how he made me feel when we were together, and how, after months apart, he made me feel when I finally saw him again."

Was it too late to reignite a relationship with Liam? What about this woman he was seeing? Would he want her if he saw her at Josh and Effie's wedding? Would he respond if she reached out to him? Could she live with herself if she didn't try?

TEXT TO LIAM

I have spent this past year mired in regret for how I left you on that beach. It was never my intention to hurt you, because I am well aware of how much being in that place can hurt. Something terrible happened to me there, as a teenager. I trusted the wrong boy, who used my feelings for him to get what he wanted from me. Spoiler alert—he got what he wanted, and I was left with whatever belief I had in myself tarnished. Top that off with my father failing me over the course of my life, leaving my brother to be the only man I could ever count on. Until you, Liam. You have never let me down. You opened my eyes, enabling me to look in a mirror and see what you see. You gave me the world, and all I needed was your love. Do I still have your heart? I can assure you that you still have mine.

# CHAPTER
## Forty-One

*Liam*



When I was 8, I watched my dad leave. I was too young to understand it at the time, but this wasn't new for him. He had done it years ago, before I was born, but he came back.

I was the product of his homecoming. After he left, I would see him sporadically. None of my siblings wanted anything to do with him, but he was still my hero.



When I was in 6th grade, the guidance counselor suggested I test out of my classes for middle school and moving me to high school the following year. I had no choice but to leave behind any friends I had already struggled to make. Just as I had done when I skipped 2nd grade. That's what my life has been.

Meeting people and leaving them. Or having them leave me.

L iam rubbed his thumb over Lana's texts, letting her childhood pain wash over him. Confusion was new for him—he had spent the last thirty-six years trying not to let anything affect him... until Lana. Trying to get over her had been hell, but he had moved on. Sort of. He wanted to. Didn't he? And then Lana began laying her heart bare for him in her texts, a web of mixed messages for him to get caught up in. She said one thing and then did another, in his experience—she wanted him, but eventually pushed him away. Even for Josh's wedding, no one seemed sure if she was attending or not, and it was next month. How much more of her indecisiveness was Liam's own heart to take? And why, now, was she talking to him about her career?

Considering the glow each had exuded upon their return home, Josh and Effie's trip to New York last month had to have been a pre-honeymoon for the couple. Josh had called Liam the morning after they got back, asking him if he could meet him at Beverley General for lunch that day. Knowing that the hospital cafeteria offered some mighty tempting daily specials, he enthusiastically agreed. Before heading to the hospital, Liam texted a woman he had dated several years ago who worked in the billing department, asking if she knew the menu for the day. Immediately, he received a response, and she had circled one of his favorite dishes before sending him a photo of the menu—chicken and dumplings. He texted her a thank you in response, and sent greetings to the woman's husband, an anesthesiologist. By the time Liam plopped down onto his seat across from his cousin, his lunch tray piled high with not only the special, but two dinner rolls, a dish of cherry Jello (topped with copious amounts of whipped cream, after winking at the cafeteria lady on the other side of the serving line), and a whoopie pie. Josh's tray, meanwhile, depressed him upon sight, appearing to have come from some kind of sad lunch jail, with a few wilted-looking lettuce leaves topped with yesterday's chicken and a watery vinaigrette.

"I can't do this," he complained to Josh.

"Do what?" Josh asked, after finally spearing a shriveled cherry tomato to bring it to his mouth, which Liam slapped away before he could eat it.

"Did you make your plate two weeks ago and ask them to hold it in the walk-in for you? Seriously, that is the most depressing collection of food I've seen in a long time, and I once dated a woman who served me 'pink chicken' because it was close enough to being done. Or is it so close to your wedding that you are on a starvation diet? Does Effie know about this? God, please don't," he warned his cousin as he put a piece of the haggard chicken into his mouth.

"You know, Cuz, you will not have that body forever. Eventually you, too, will have to change your eating habits because age and metabolism will catch up to you," Josh lectured Liam, while also grabbing the whoopie pie from Liam's plate, breaking it in half, then practically swooning as he shoved part of it in his mouth. "God, this is good," Josh mumbled around bits of chocolate cake. "No," he finally addressed Liam's inquiry into his lunch, "Effie doesn't know, but you know how I bought my suit for the wedding six months ago?"

Liam nodded, having bought a complementary suit that day as well, since he was the best man.

In a whisper, Josh told him, "Well, I tried it on yesterday, and it was… snug."

"Look, why don't you come work out with me? I was going to go tomorrow morning but am flexible timewise," Liam suggested.

"Tomorrow morning? Haven't you and Sabrina had a standing breakfast date on Saturdays for the last month?" Josh looked at Liam while he ate the other half of the whoopie pie.

Not anymore, they didn't. Things had been going pretty well for him and Sabrina, or so he had thought. Getting to know each other slowly was new for him, and Sabrina had tried more than once to speed up the process by inviting him back to her place after a night out, even once popping in at his house with a bottle of wine and a trench coat (the sexy lingerie underneath should have brought him to his knees), but he had remained steadfast, telling her he had to wake up early the next morning as an excuse to turn her away. However, a few nights ago, they had been out to dinner when a text from Lana had arrived, along with a selfie she had taken that he had stared at for far too long. "What are you looking at?" Sabrina had queried from across the table at the Italian restaurant in nearby Carlisle that night.

"Oh, nothing," Liam had quickly assured her, putting his phone upside down on the table next to his plate.

"Lana, huh?" Liam's eyes shot up to meet Sabrina's.

How did she know? "What?"

Sabrina nodded to his phone and, following the direction of her brown eyes, he saw the picture of Lana, breathtaking under the shade of a Japanese maple tree, taking up his phone screen. Her honey-blonde hair glinting where the sun streamed in through various branches, the smile on her face one he recognized as being solely reserved for him. Damn, he thought, chastising himself for being careless enough to not ensure that he had, indeed, put the phone face down.

"So that's the Lana who has been texting you?" This was a first. Before Lana, Liam had never had a different woman on his mind while on a date with another, and now that he had been so blatantly obvious about it, he wasn't entirely sure how to handle it. He remained speechless, having no words to either deny it or defend himself. "It's okay, Liam," she informed him softly. "I knew there had to be a reason we were not moving more with this relationship."

"I'm sorry, I didn't mean-" he began.

Sabrina cut in, "I know. You have been incredibly sweet and attentive, mostly, but I could feel you holding yourself back." She gave him a melancholic smile, then told him, "The night I showed up at your house wearing a coat and a smile, and little else, pretty much told me everything I needed to know, but I wasn't ready yet to admit defeat." Sabrina leaned across the table to squeeze his fingers with her own. "No man would turn down what I was offering without having a good reason, and at least now I know what it is."

Josh's eyes widened as Liam told him of the break-up. If what had happened could, indeed, be categorized as such. "To quote the great John Mellencamp: 'The walls came tumbling down', huh?"

"Yep, and now here I am, one month away from your wedding, and I have no date," Liam informed Josh.

"Okay, why do you need one? Lana is coming for the wedding." Oh, was she? This was new information, and Liam tried to play it off by not responding. His cousin continued, "Maybe you two could reconnect? Obviously, she's been communicating with you." Josh reached over and grabbed one of Liam's uneaten dinner rolls and two pats of butter. "Look, it takes a lot to match your energy: you're the 'cool' guy, the one everybody wants to be around. The one all women seem to want to date —some men, too, not to discriminate. You know how to have a good time; you've always had plenty of money to burn, and although I am clearly the best looking of the Livingston grandsons, you're not too bad on the eyes. Just from the experience of being your cousin and best friend, though, you can be a lot."

"Is this a pep talk or are you putting me in my place?" Now that Josh had eaten almost all of Liam's lunch, except for the Jell-O and one dinner roll, his cousin had certainly perked up.

"What I'm trying to explain is that for the two years I worked with Lana, she never confided in me about her personal life; meanwhile I was bombarding her with my personal issues, but I essentially knew nothing about her or her family. I knew she had a mom, but she always made it seem like she was an only child."

Liam shook his head. "No, she's got an older brother, two older sisters, four nieces, three nephews-"

"See? You know more than I do. She is letting you in, Liam. It may have started slowly, but she has been hurt, from what I understand. Effie has told me some of it-"

"And I can't imagine going through what she has...I just wish she had opened up to me before now," Liam's chest was tightening uncomfortably, as it did whenever he considered where he and Lana could be right now, at this point in their lives—in their relationship. Now, he feared, it was too late.

"Why is it too late?" Josh demanded from across the table, using a sterner voice than Liam had heard from his cousin in quite a while.

"What?" Liam rubbed his chest, waiting for Josh to finish the Jell-O he had just taken.

"You just said that you feared it was too late," Josh explained.

He had? "I did?" Liam shook his head and said, "I didn't mean to say it out loud." Buttering his remaining dinner roll before Josh could eat that as well, he said, "I just think we have moved on."

"You haven't, though. You cycled through enough women to find out you're not interested in any of them, and then semi-seriously dated a wonderful woman for a month, who broke up with you because you are clearly not over Lana yet."

Sighing heavily, Liam rubbed his hands across his face. "So, what do I do?"

Josh twirled the straw in his glass of Diet Pepsi before answering, "This may be completely off base, but have you tried texting back? Remember how it felt for you last year, when you sent her those messages but she never replied? I would imagine Lana is feeling much the same way…only you haven't gone through what she has."

"Yeah, I know. She told me about problems with her dad. I have no idea how that must have felt for her," Liam replied.

"No, you don't. You've had your loving, devoted parents for every stage of your life. Some of us aren't that lucky. When my mom left, she took with her half of my life. Don't get me wrong, my dad was fantastic, but having a parent just leave you makes you wonder what it is about you that isn't good enough or lovable enough. And then there's the other crap," Josh stated.

"What other crap? Like her brother having to step in as a replacement dad?" Liam watched the shocked look cross Josh's face—either he hadn't known that fact, or he was surprised that Lana had told Liam about it. Montgomery sounded like an unbelievable brother, but Liam believed that if Lana's brother got within ten feet of him, he'd probably want to punch him for hurting his little sister, much like Liam would want to do to anyone who hurt his sister.

"No, that stuff with that guy from Cal's wedding." As Liam remained silent, Josh must have realized that he had said something Liam hadn't known and, glancing at the watch on his wrist, he got up from the table. His cousin announced, "Oh, I forgot I'm meeting Effie at my office. She's dropping by to pick up the RSVPs for the wedding."

"Oh no, dude, you're not getting away from this conversation," he warned Josh. "What about the guy from Cal's wedding?"

"I've said too much. Effie told me I need to let Lana explain it all in her own time." With that proclamation, Josh hastily pushed in his chair, grabbed his tray, and said, "Talk later, Cuz," over his shoulder.

"What the hell?" Liam exclaimed, while he picked up various bits of garbage from the table: paper straw wrappers, napkins, sugar packets from his coffee, and the multiple small plates that had contained his random lunch items. "Damn, why didn't I use one big plate?" he scolded himself, figuring if he had, he would have been able to bird dog Josh while he headed back to his office instead of picking up so much trash.

Liam finally deposited his tray and garbage in the appropriate locations and then sprinted down the hall—or tried to, anyway, until he met the clearly starving medical staff on their way to the cafeteria. He even dodged a few women he had dated over the past twelve years—a nurse, an anesthesiologist, a laundress, and a receptionist. "Goddamn, is there some convention for ex-girlfriends taking place today?" he muttered to himself when he finally reached the end of the hallway, after exchanging pleasantries with the various women, and turned the corner to the elevator bank. "Shit!" All the elevators were at higher floors, so Liam strode to the stairway door and flung it open, bounding up the four flights to Josh's floor. He had to reach Josh before Effie showed up, so he could get the full story about Lana and the dick from Long Island. Liam had a feeling that Josh, being completely under his bride-to-be's spell, would not tell him one more detail unless Effie gave him her approval, and he had the feeling his soon-to-be-cousin-in-law was in the "it's her story to tell" camp. Frankly, Liam didn't give two shits about *whose* story it was—if it concerned Lana, then didn't it concern him, as well? After all, isn't that what this was all about? Reconciling him and Lana? How could that happen unless he knew *everything*?

Collapsing once he reached the fourth floor (he clearly needed to add stair-climbing to his workout routine), he allowed himself about ten seconds to get his breath back. Wrenching the stairwell door open, he surged through, a man on a mission. Passing the nurse's station, it was his reflex to smile broadly when he encountered anyone, especially a woman, but he had worked over the past couple of years to tone it down —he knew how it could unintentionally affect someone without him meaning to. At last reaching Josh's office, Liam flung the door open and charged in, coincidentally as Josh was handing a stack of postcards to Effie, who he had *not* managed to beat to the office. Unfortunately, Liam's kinetic energy caused him to crash into his cousin, sending the cards flying around the room.

"Oh my god—what the hell, Liam?" he heard Effie shout.

"What is wrong with you?" Josh exclaimed at the same time.

"I just...I needed to..." Liam faltered.

"You needed to *what*? I've got to get my stuff together and go to Sioux Falls for a consultation this afternoon, Liam, not spend an hour playing fifty-two card pick up!" Josh fumed, clearly unamused.

Effie laughed, "And seriously, I need to get back to work. I only stopped to pick up these RSVPs. Not all of us have the leisure of a three-hour lunch, Buddy."

"Look, I'm sorry. Let me clean this up and then I'll run them over to you at the library. Josh, you can be on your way." He bent over and started picking up the cards. "Why did everyone have to send them back at the same time?"

Effie answered, "They didn't—your cousin just hasn't brought them home after picking them up at the post office over the past week." For some reason unfathomable to Josh, his fiancée had insisted on renting a post office box for all things concerning their wedding, which somehow made it Josh's job then to collect the mail from the post office every couple of days. Effie's logic hadn't made sense to Liam, either, when Josh had explained it to him.

"Okay, I do need to get going—you're good here, Liam?" asked Josh.

"Yes, both of you get outta here. Effie, I'll be over in a few minutes," and he waved the couple out the door, leaving him in silence to gather the cards. Swooping as many together as he could, he shuffled them into one big pile, congratulating himself on a job well-done. "That didn't take too long," he said to himself. After surveying the room one last time before walking out the door, a lone card under the desk caught his eye. Liam walked back to the desk and picked up the card, noticing the postmark was from New York. Turning it over, he saw Lana's name written, in a delicate, lovely script that encapsulated her perfectly. His breath stilled, though, upon seeing that she had marked "2" for the number of guests. 2? If, as everyone had been speculating, Lana was planning or hoping to reunite with him at the wedding, why would she be bringing a date? And why would she be wasting time texting him? Confiding in him? More confused about her now than he had ever been, all sense of hope drained from his body. The energy with which he had conquered four flights of stairs was lost as Liam dejectedly pressed the "down" button for the elevator.

# CHAPTER

## Forty-Two

*Lana*

*Wedding Day*

**Text to Tess**

I'm so nervous about seeing Liam. I poured my heart out to him, but he never answered any of my messages. Tess, how can I see him today, thinking he might not care anymore? Maybe I shouldn't have come…

TEXT FROM TESS

Lana, I hope this isn't your way of saying you're not coming to the wedding! You seemed fine yesterday. Everything will be okay once you get here, I promise.

TEXT TO TESS

No, the flight was delayed.

We are on the way.

I texted Effie, but could you make sure she knows?

TEXT FROM TESS

BTW, I talked to Liam last night and he knows you're coming.

It is strange that he hasn't said anything to Effie or Josh about you, though.

TEXT TO TESS

Exactly! According to Effie, Liam stopped asking her last month if I was coming to the wedding. I really thought he was going to answer me at one point. I saw those little gray dots, but then he didn't send anything.

TEXT FROM TESS

Unless…Lana, somehow he knows you have a date.

Lana groaned. Of course, Liam knew she had a date—but what was she supposed to do? Come to this strange new place by herself? Especially when it looked like he would be bringing a new girlfriend. And then she had gotten the news.

TEXT FROM EFFIE

Liam is single again!

Josh is pretty sure it's because of you.

Lana had been elated, of course, but her travel plans had already been in motion. Besides, men like Liam did not attend a family wedding solo, she had told herself. And then she had gotten confirmation a few days ago.

TEXT FROM TESS

Liam has a date for the wedding.

Fair enough. Now they both had dates for Josh and Effie's wedding. But it wasn't like she had a "real" date. Lana, always the sad imposter, likely to be laughed at if she ever managed to get to Beverley for the wedding. Especially after last night's news:

TEXT FROM EFFIE

I know you heard about Liam's date.

You have nothing to worry about, and that's why I never mentioned it.

Of all the days to be late for something, it had to be today? Josh and Effie's wedding day! Given the fact that she had been on the verge of not attending at all, and had actually changed her mind more than once, it could be considered a minor miracle that she was even here. Technically, on the way "there". Wherever "there" was, Lana considered, gazing out the window of her rental car at the foreign landscape as they cruised down the highway. She'd never seen so much open space before. Where were all the towns that spilled over into each other, like on Long Island? And all this farmland…Long Island had farms, too, but nothing like this. Not miles and miles of green crops as far as her eyes could see. And the sky? After several years of working and living in Manhattan, where skyscrapers hid the sun for most of the day, this sky went on forever, nothing breaking up the pillowy clouds except the brilliant azure. Only trips to the ocean offered a sky as vast as this.

"Hey, earth to Lana," she heard a deep voice saying and turned her head toward her handsome brother sitting in the driver's seat. No matter the situation, Monty always remained calm and clear-headed, and when she had waffled about whether or not to go to the wedding of the year, he had been the one to suggest traveling with her. As always, her safety blanket. When she found herself in times of trouble, her brother Monty always came to her, always with words of wisdom and advice. Never mind that he consistently refused to talk about his own love life or any personal issues. Only now, though, was she considering how embarrassing it was going to be to have to explain that her "date" was her brother.

Lana groaned again. "Sorry, in my own thoughts—what were you saying?" Why couldn't Montgomery just give her these two hours (according to Josh, but Effie had told her it was more like an hour and a half) of driving to get herself settled? He was not usually so loquacious (thank you, word of the day calendar), but today he needed to be chatty Cathy?

He laughed as though completely unbothered, which, in all fairness, he probably was. Nothing about this day meant anything to him, even being here, or "there", with her. She shook her head at her own thoughts now, knowing that wasn't true. God, Lana, get over yourself, she lectured internally. Her brother was speaking, "I just asked if it was going to be weird for you, since you had a 'thing' for the groom? Right? Didn't you have the hots for the hotshot doctor?" Oh my god, not this.

Lana groaned for the third time. "Surgeon," Lana corrected him, as her face burned from embarrassment. "Josh is a surgeon, and what we had was more meaningful—to me, anyway, than 'the hots'." Over the last two years, she had done her best to put her past feelings for Josh behind her and loathed being reminded of them, especially since she had become quite close with Effie, his bride-to-be. Besides, what she had shared with Liam taught her any feelings she had felt for anyone before him had been questionable, paling in comparison. Nothing had ever or would ever even come close to the level of intensity that she had experienced with Liam. "Please don't bring anything up about Josh. Or anyone else," she warned Monty.

"Sorry, sorry, I know it's a sensitive subject. I guess I was trying to lighten the mood." Monty ate the candy bar, a Nut Roll, he had bought at a truck stop outside of Sioux Falls. "Pretty good—why don't they sell these back in New York? I mean, I enjoy a Payday as much as anyone, but this has a certain something that makes it better, you know?"

"Oh my god—enough about the candy bar. I told you to get two of them. Anyway, can't you go any faster? I'm afraid we're going to be late." Damn flight. Unfortunately, the only way to fly into Sioux Falls from New York required a connecting flight. An inexperienced air traveler, Lana had naively booked the two legs of their journey with only a thirty-minute layover; however, the flight from New York to Minneapolis had been delayed taking off by almost an hour, making them miss the connecting flight from Minneapolis to Sioux Falls. Then the siblings had to wait two hours for the next flight to Sioux Falls. Originally, they should have landed at 11:30 this morning, but it was now after three, and the ceremony was starting at five this afternoon. At least she wasn't in the wedding—she just hoped they could discreetly find their seats once they got there. "The speed limit says 80."

He grunted as he stepped on the gas pedal. "If you were so worried about it, why didn't we fly in yesterday? And are you sure I look okay? Will I have time to change clothes before we go to the venue?" King of casual over there, wearing jeans that, as far as Lana could tell, at least had no oil stains on them, so she figured he must have at least worn his best pair. The Willie Nelson t-shirt under the unbuttoned flannel was, admittedly, the part of his outfit that gave her pause. Who wears a flannel shirt in September? Or a Willie Nelson shirt to a wedding? So not only was her brother her date, but he looked like he should be attending Farm Aid, not a wedding.

And what had he said? Fly in yesterday? Now he's all full of suggestions! Why didn't they fly in yesterday? Because she was nervous enough about seeing Liam the day *of* the wedding—the last thing she wanted was to be wandering around town and bump into him. Not that she was looking to avoid him—the opposite, actually, but that was for *after* the ceremony. Instead of admitting the truth to Monty, though, she simply told him, "Do you know how expensive tickets were to fly in yesterday? I could barely afford these. You look fine, and anyway, I'm not sure how much of a 'venue' there is…I think it's in the city park or something like that." Smoothing down the skirt to her best dress, Lana regretted her decision to wear it for traveling today, but it had made the most sense. However, two plane flights later, plus rushing for their connection and then standing around for hours, had given her a less-than-fresh appearance.

Lana lowered the visor to study herself in the mirror. She hadn't seen Liam since last year…had she changed? Even on her best day, she had never considered herself to be the most attractive woman, but he had seen something in her that had told him otherwise, and her only hope was his vision remained unchanged. She put her ear buds in, knowing her companion would prefer the silence, closed her eyes, and let the sounds of Judy Garland sing her to sleep.

Waking up to a slamming door, just as Judy was belting out "The Man That Got Away", Lana glanced at the clock on the dashboard, stunned to see that she had been asleep for almost an hour. "The winds grow colder, suddenly you're older. All because of the man that got away." Never had lyrics been more meaningful than at this particular moment in her life.

Pulling open her car door, Monty informed her, "Well, Sleeping Beauty, it's about time you woke up. According to the invitation you gave me, we are here. Wherever 'here' is. Middle of nowhere, if you ask me." As he took her hand in his to draw her out of the car, she felt his calloused fingers, and guilt consumed her as she considered what it cost him to take this time off from work to be her date. No one worked harder than her brother, and part of her hoped that the week they were spending here after the wedding would find him well-rested at the end of it. Effie and Josh weren't leaving for their honeymoon until next weekend and had promised all kinds of post-wedding fun for family and friends.

Monty said to her, "Let me know who this Liam is…or should I call him your Hook Up? I still don't know if I need to punch him in the face for putting that frown on my baby sister's face." And to Lana's astonishment, he rubbed his hands together as if savoring the moment he could inflict violence on Liam.

"Stop, please," she pleaded with her brother. "No punching or threatening to punch anyone. Unless you call him my Hook Up, that is—then I will punch you." Lana blamed her nerves on the fact that she was warning her brother off with the threat of violence, something she had never done before in her life.

Lana breathed deeply, trying to recall the joy she had first felt when the wedding invitation arrived in the mail. Now that they were finally here, though, all she felt was dread and anxiety. Yesterday she had been teeming with excitement and the anticipation of seeing Liam again had nearly driven her mad. Now, all she could think was, why had she come? This was a mistake, she told herself, just as a voice screeched out, "OH MY GOD!!! You're finally here!"

Lana looked to the edge of the open park, and a relieved smile took over her face. Almost side-swiping a red-haired man pushing a double baby stroller, Lana saw Tess making a beeline for her. Maybe this wouldn't be so bad after all, she thought, before responding with a laugh, "Tess! I come all this way and the first person I see is someone I run into on an almost-daily basis." Tess had promised to show Lana around the town she had grown up in, and a quick glance around proved that Tess had not been exaggerating the charms of Beverley.

Holding Lana by her shoulders, Tess exclaimed, "Let me look at you—wow, Lana, you look gorgeous! Love this dress. Is it vintage?" If by vintage Tess meant Lana found it in the back of her mother's closet, then yes, it most definitely was vintage. Fit her perfectly, almost as if it had been made for her exclusively, and Lana planned to use her assets, currently hidden under the light wrap covering the bodice, to full advantage later this evening. Lana took a deep breath to answer when Tess quickly fired off a follow-up question. "And who is your date? I don't believe we've met." Tess laughed then, because although she had met Monty several times, Lana had not confided in her that he would be the one accompanying her to the wedding.

With Tess's deep green eyes loaded with insinuations, Lana suddenly felt foolish bringing her brother here under the ruse of being her date, no matter how much stronger she felt with Monty by her side. Tess's eyes searched her own dark-blue ones for answers, and Lana impulsively decided to introduce Monty to Tess, playing it like she was in on her own joke, and started, "Oh, meet--"and then, as a motion from across the park lawn caught her attention, Lana simply had no more words, for there he was.

Tall in his finely pressed jacket she was sure was new for the wedding, standing up near the gazebo (of which Lana had heard endless stories from both Josh and Effie, as much a starring role in their romance as either of them), he was at least half a head taller than the man to whom he was speaking. Chestnut-colored hair glinted in the afternoon sun, with warm highlights taking on a rusty hue that was all too attractive on him, and she remembered what it felt like under her fingertips, so silky and sexy. Knowing it would be unavoidable seeing him, months ago she had made the decision to come anyway, even if he never spoke to her again, despite the yearning she knew she would feel. But the yearning had led to the overwhelming feeling of loss, and that was why she had changed her mind multiple times. Of course, then the yearning became more powerful once again, causing her finally to make her mind up to attend the wedding of her treasured friends. Indeed, she felt it all now—the yearning, the loss, the desire, and the intense loneliness—as his face turned toward her. The handsome, unforgettable face she had spent the past two years dreaming about: the man that got away. More than that—he was the man that *she* had allowed to get away. He had been hers, back on the beach as the sun faded from view. He had been hers, back in that hotel room, with the lights of the city in the near distance. He had been hers, back on that tram, suspended in midair. He had been hers, that night in the bar…two strangers in a room full of strangers, drawn together by an undeniable force. *He* was the reason she had now ventured farther from home than ever before. Tired of the mixed messages from her heart and her head, Lana intended to push everything else aside and accomplish one thing tonight—getting back the man that got away. As Judy sang, "A one-man woman, looking for the man that got away."

# CHAPTER
## Forty-Three

## Liam



> I remember the feel of your hands on my thighs, just before you…

Holy hell, Liam thought, ripping his eyes away from the text before he could read anymore. He didn't need to be reminded of any of their intimate moments, for he recalled them as if they had happened this morning, not a year and a half ago. Depositing his phone back in his pocket after he had silenced it, Liam scanned the guests gathering for Josh and Effie's wedding. Was she here? A mild breeze carried with it the scent of vanilla and jasmine, delicate and floral, and he knew without a doubt that she was here, somewhere in the state of South Dakota, perhaps in the city of Beverley—maybe even tucked away in the city park, the site of the main event for today.

"Hey, how are you doing?" Turning to the voice behind him, he smiled at his date, Vanessa, whom he had met when she came into the dealership last week to trade in her car. New to Beverley, she informed

Liam that she had recently moved from San Jose, California, to join her brother, who had bought the veterinary practice that John Lefferts had established almost forty years before his retirement. As Beverley continued to grow, so did the need for more veterinarians in the town. While her brother, Colton, specialized in large animals and livestock, Vanessa primarily cared for small animals and house pets. Rain and high winds were lashing outside the day Vanessa had strolled into Kinsale Motors. Since car shopping tended to be heavily influenced by inclement weather, Liam had sent Lillian home early (still paying her for the entire day) to pick up her kids from daycare. With the smell of a fresh pot of Uncle Henry's coffee brewing (flavor of the month was macadamia nut/white chocolate chip cookie), Liam had pondered how his uncle managed to make it taste almost the same as the cookies Tess used to bake for Josh back in the day.

"Hello?" Liam had been pouring a cup of the delicious-smelling coffee when the voice from across the showroom startled him, causing him to splash the hot beverage onto the hand holding the cup.

"Damn it," he had exclaimed, using his shirttails to dry his hand. Normally he would never be at the dealership so bedraggled, but once Lillian had left, Liam had cranked up his office stereo, singing along with "Take It on the Run". Damn his cousin, who had ensured REO Speedwagon left an indelible impression on his brain since their road trip to New York City two years ago. Suddenly, a head had popped into his office. Needless to say, one did not jam out while remaining primly tucked, so the shirttails had found their way out of the waistband of his jeans. He had no classes at the college that day, so instead of the suit he wore when teaching, he was dressed "business on top, party on the bottom".

"Anyone working around here?" asked an incredibly attractive woman with the smoothest chocolate-colored skin, broken only by her beaming smile. "Oh, are you okay?"

"I'm fine. Just spilled some coffee," he explained. After fully wiping his java-hands on a paper towel, he extended one to the woman. "Hi, I'm Liam."

She had smiled a knowing smile. "Well, you're just the man I want. I'm Vanessa."

Taken aback, Liam said, "Excuse me?" He had been hit on before while at work, but it usually took at least one trip around the car lot before that happened.

Laughing, she had responded, "Okay, that came out wrong—don't worry, you're not my type. John Lefferts told me that you were the man to see about getting a truck. My brother took over his practice, and I need something to haul around animal crates and carriers."

"Oh, you're Colton's sister," Liam exclaimed, realization dawning. "He told me you were moving here. Sorry, my mind has been elsewhere these days. Of course, let me pull up the inventory on my computer—it's too nasty to go outside." The two of them had then spent the better part of two hours discussing cars, coffee, and relationships. Unsure of quite how it happened, Liam had somehow ended up talking about Lana, his almost-proposal, and the upcoming wedding of his cousin.

"Josh is your cousin? Wow—I mean, I don't know him personally, but I've heard a lot about him." Liam flashed her a quizzical look, and she explained, "Since I moved here last month, I have been a frequent visitor to the Beverley Carnegie Library. Developed a teensy crush on one of the librarians there, but it turns out that, evidently, your cousin is more her type than I am." Her frankness caused Liam to laugh, and Vanessa promptly added, "Her loss, I know." Vanessa then snapped her fingers, declaring, "I have an idea."

"What's that?" Liam had been intrigued, because the stranger he'd known less than a day had spent the entire afternoon assuring him that he was more than worthy of Lana.

"Take me as your date to the wedding. Clearly, I would not be a threat to her, but I am quite charming, so I can sidle up to whatever date she's bringing, and you can get her alone."

"I don't know…I hate to say this, but the idea of her having a date to the wedding intimidates the hell out of me. I've never been in this position before and don't get why she would bring a date if she still has feelings for me."

"How else is she supposed to face you? She's traveling halfway across the country, and from my understanding, to a place she's never been. Her date is probably some gay friend of hers who works with her —haven't you ever seen a rom-com? This is the way they work. I mean, this is classic—she will bring her gay best friend, and you'll take me—your new lesbian friend!" Liam laughed, but hesitated to agree, still reeling from the pain he experienced seeing Lana's RSVP. Could it be as simple as Vanessa was assuming? "Liam, people make rash decisions in a split second, and those consequences can reverberate for years," Vanessa softly told him.

"This is new for me—this uneasiness and wondering if I've made an ass of myself. She hurt me when she left me on the beach, but I'm worried I waited too long to reply to her texts. Now it may be too late." Liam's chest had tightened, as it did when he considered how much regret he had with the way he handled himself after Cal's wedding.

"Okay, I want to assure you that you *have* been an idiot for not replying to any of the texts from Lana. The woman is pouring her heart out to you, and you'd have to be a cold-hearted snake to ignore her as long as you have." At his blank stare, Vanessa asked, "Do you not know any Paula Abdul?" Liam had shaken his head, "No," to which she had responded, "Wow. Just wow. That's what's wrong with our generation—we've lost the true classics. I mean, I come in here and you're blasting music from two generations ago, but you don't even know the lyrics to one of the greatest songs from the eighties?"

"It's not that I haven't *heard* of Paula Abdul—I just don't know that exact song. Did it occur to *you* that maybe it's a lesbian reference I'm just not getting?" Liam hated having his ignorance being called out.

"'Lesbian reference'? I'm not talking Brandi Carlile here, son, so you can quit right there. Anyway, we are digressing way too much. You need to get your love eyes back on for this Lana," Vanessa had insisted.

Liam had sputtered, "For your information, I never lost my 'love eyes' for Lana!"

"Exactly! Only took me two hours for you to admit it! Now quit moping around about it and take action! Dude, you're clearly hot, for a guy, but that picture you showed me of Lana? She is smoking, and if you do not beg her to be with you the night of this wedding, I may have to give you a run for your money."

Liam still couldn't quite believe that he had brought his new best friend as his date to his cousin's wedding, but admittedly, this situation was certainly preferable to bringing an actual "date". Liam smiled at

Vanessa, shaking his head as he tried to convince both of them that nothing was wrong, he was perfectly fine, and he hadn't spent the entire morning with his stomach in knots as he kept a watchful eye first on Josh while he got ready for his impending nuptials, and then on the guests as they arrived leisurely in the park for the wedding. Still no sign of Lana—only her tantalizing text from this morning. Effie had informed him last week that Lana was flying in this morning, and then Tess had shown up a few hours ago with the news that Lana's flight had been delayed, but she would be here before the ceremony began, which a quick glance at his Apple Watch told him should be in fifteen minutes. Knowing his cousin, fifteen minutes *meant* fifteen minutes, and coupled with the fact that Cait was running the show, only solidified the timeline.

"I'm going to go get a seat," Vanessa told him, right before his cousin Felix approached him.

"Okay, Cousin, who is that? You know, I've never understood why you always have the most insanely beautiful women surrounding you." Felix poked Liam in the ribs. "Woah, must be nice to have so much free time to spend at the gym."

"First of all—Vanessa's not your type, and not just because she has class. Second—I am willing to bet that you have more free time than I do, considering I am picking up yet another class to teach at the college this semester. Third—you're just jealous that I'm Josh's best man. Twice in a row, I might add."

Felix sniffed. "You'd think he would have changed up things considering the way his last attempt at a wedding ended. I mean—wasn't Ruth *also* maid-of-honor then, too? Like, don't they know anyone else?"

Liam laughed, and Felix asked, "You doing okay?"

He responded breezily, "Sure, why wouldn't I be?" Then felt a tap on his shoulder. Turning, he looked into the worried face of his sister, who asked, "How are you doing?"

With a groan, he answered, "Why does everyone keep asking me that? I'm fine," he assured her, but she continued to frown at him.

"I just want you to know that I am prepared to do whatever it takes to make today wonderful for Josh and Effie," Cait responded.

"Okay, good—me, too," Liam said.

Cait nodded. "That includes keeping you from doing anything even remotely impetuous."

"Impetuous? ME? Like what?" Why did everyone constantly remind him about his mistakes, his failures, especially those involving his heart? Furthermore, why was everyone all up in his business?

Raising an eyebrow, Cait said, "Well, I know how the last wedding went down, and you-"

"If you're talking about Josh's first wedding, I had nothing to do with that. However, if you are talking about Cal's wedding, the only people who know what happened that day are Lana and me. Admittedly, I may have tried to move things too fast for her, but I can say with certainty that I will remain the epitome of calm today." His eyes scanned the crowd again, which was growing in size. "Besides, she's not even here yet." Where was she? Was it possible she decided at the last moment to not come after all?

Cait took his hand, telling him, "Maybe that's for the best. Hey, look over to the western part of the park. Do you recognize that woman?"

"You know I don't know directions—what am I? Lewis and Clark?" Here we go, thought Liam, buckling himself up for a navigational lesson.

"Timely reference, really. No, I don't think that you are two separate people, but not for nothing, it was Sacagawea who did most of their navigating. Not only that, but the western part of the park is clearly where the tree line begins."

"So why didn't you just tell me to look over to the trees?" Liam asked Cait, who sighed in annoyance.

"Fine—look over to the trees! Do you know who that woman is over there?"

Liam looked to his right and saw a young woman, probably in her mid-twenties, standing alone with her arms crossed in front of her. Light blond hair, medium build, but nothing too significant about her overall. "No idea—why?"

"Well, I don't recognize her, and I asked Effie if she was maybe one of her relatives, and she said no."

"Okay, so what? Chances are, we won't know everyone at the wedding," he told his sister.

"No, I know that. I just thought there was something familiar about her. But she's kind of young to be at a wedding and no one knows her, don't you think?" Cait chewed on a fingernail while she studied the younger woman across the park. For someone who complained when anyone asked her a personal question, Caitriona never seemed to have a problem nosing in where she didn't belong.

"Not too worried about it. Hey, I know—maybe she followed you from down south, and she's finally going to tell us all what you're avoiding down there?" He needed to get away from his sister's paranoia and the quickest way to do that was to bring up whatever secret she was keeping from her past.

"Whatever," Cait said dismissively. "I'm going to go and check on the bride and groom. Ceremony starts in five minutes," she warned her brother, which he ignored. He was in place, or nearly so, since he just had to walk up the steps of the gazebo.

"Liam, you certainly look dashing today," Diadema, Effie's mother, complimented him. He had known Diadema his entire life, since she was the best friend of his own mother. Despite being twice his age, she was a stunning woman, exuding class and wealth.

"Diadema—you definitely do not look old enough to be mother-of-the-bride," he charmingly told her as he kissed her on the cheek. "Burnside, pleasure to see you, as always," he greeted the older man, offering his hand for a handshake. Nora, Liam's mom, had confided to him that despite Diadema implementing a new diet for her husband to follow after his second heart attack, Burnside was still being quite cavalier about his health. Effie's stepdad had been in to the dealership a few months ago for a new vehicle, and he had not looked the best, so Liam agreed there was some cause for concern.

"Liam, you have really built up that dealership here in town, I have to say. When I was there to buy my truck, I was impressed by how modern everything was," Burnside declared.

"Yes, Burnside did nothing but rave about it for weeks on end. I don't know where you find the time," Diadema added, "considering you are also teaching at the college. You know, Hamilton simply loved taking your class there—he said you were a fantastic instructor. Your mom always knew you'd find your calling, Liam. You're making her very proud."

A lump in Liam's throat grew—both of his parents consistently told him how proud they were, but it was different hearing it from a third party. To know that his accomplishments were worthy enough of being spoken about by his parents to their friends and colleagues brought Liam a renewed sense of purpose.

His sister's voice suddenly rang out over the park, and Liam looked up to find her standing in the center of the park's gazebo. "Hello, everyone," Cait said into the microphone. "If you all could please take their seats, the wedding will begin momentarily."

Liam bade farewell to Effie's parents, trotting up the stairs to the gazebo to stand next to Josh. Josh—his best friend, his cousin, his partner-in-crime while they were growing up. Only a few months separated them, and they often thought of each other as brothers rather than cousins. He was certain that until they were twelve, he and Josh had seen each other every single day. They fought, argued, and annoyed the hell out of one another, but in the end, no one had his back the way Josh did. Eyes welling with tears, Liam was proud to be standing next to him on one of the most significant days of his life.

As they waited for Effie to make her grand and gorgeous appearance, Liam cast his eyes to the family members and friends in attendance, where nearly every seat had filled. Interestingly enough, he found the young woman who had caught his sister's attention sitting in the back row on the "groom's" side of the aisle. A movement flickered in the corner of his eye, and based on the amount of lace he glimpsed, Liam assumed Effie was ready to at last meet her groom under the gazebo. Fixing a broad smile to ward off his own burgeoning disappointment over not seeing Lana, he began to turn his head to the stairs of the gazebo, when his nose once more picked up the scent of vanilla and jasmine in the air. A blur of green drew his eyes to the back row again, only this time the only sight filling his vision was that of the most luscious, desirable, and devastatingly perfect woman he could ever know. Forcing his breathing to return to normal once he got his breath back, this time his smile was genuine and not for appearances. She was here. Lana was here.

# CHAPTER
## Forty-Four

*Lana*



Montgomery texted that you made it safely to South Dakota. I love you, my youngest daughter, and I know without a shadow of a doubt that everything will work out as you want it to, because you have always been a gift to the world, and from what you have told me about Liam, he recognized that the first time he saw you.

Lana pulled Montgomery into the last row of chairs in the park after spotting two still empty in the center. How did Josh and Effie know this many people? Sliding into her chair, Lana looked to the young woman on the other side, who smiled brightly at her in return. Probably in her mid-twenties, she had light blonde hair that shimmered in the late afternoon sunlight and sky-blue eyes that seemed familiar somehow to Lana. Now firmly ensconced in her chair, Lana gathered up every ounce of courage and looked to the front, finding Liam immediately.

No one else existed while Lana and Liam locked eyes, hungrily devouring each other from across the park. Over the heads of the other guests, while the bride made her way up the stairs to the gazebo (gleaming brightly on this late summer day), with the groom undoubtedly eager, waiting for the moment in which he would profess his ever-growing and never-ending love to his bride, Lana and Liam were doing the same with a mere shared look. Honestly unaware of how much time had passed since she had taken her seat, Lana feasted her eyes on Liam. Her fingers clenched, itching to touch him, and she found herself eager to explain (or try to explain) her past odd behavior so the two of them could rekindle their romance, or relationship, or whatever anyone wanted to label it. She was willing to call it anything as long as they were together.

How had she let an entire year pass without explaining everything to Liam? He had not deserved her silence, and she doubted that she deserved his forgiveness now. Well, not forgiveness, necessarily…more like understanding. But holy hell, he was divine up there under that historical gazebo, his hair slightly longer than it had been a year ago, when she had last driven her hands into it. Aching to touch the silky warmth under her fingertips, Lana smoothed down the skirt of her green dress, borrowed from her mother's closet. As she was planning her trip to Beverley for the wedding, finding nothing in her own closet adequate enough to wear for the occasion, she had been on the phone with her mom. Fiona had implored Lana to make the trek out to Riverhead to see some dresses that she hadn't worn in years: "They're too young for me now, and I think they'd fit you beautifully." More than her sisters, who were each taller and thinner, Lana had inherited her mom's fuller, shorter figure. On her next day off, Lana had taken the Long Island Railroad from Brooklyn to Riverhead to see her mom, who had picked her up at the train station, greeting her baby girl tightly in a long hug. Returning the hug, Lana felt a twinge of guilt: unbeknownst to her mom, when Lana had to change trains in Queens at Jamaica station, there had been a split second that she had almost turned around to go back to Brooklyn, but she had remained steadfast. Rarely did Lana have her mom alone to herself, and they had spent the day combing through Fiona's closet, with Lana gasping when Fiona pulled out the green dress.

Although similar in color to the one she had worn to the ballet with Liam, the fabric and cut were different.

"I've never worn this, you know," her mom had confessed, stroking the silky fabric of the iridescent jade-green dress.

"Why not?" Lana had asked, curious why her mom would have bought something that had to have been slightly expensive decades ago, only to stuff it into the back of her closet, unworn and unappreciated.

Fiona had smiled ruefully at her daughter, "Honestly, I bought it when I thought your dad was coming back, when you were ten. He wanted to reconcile, he claimed."

Lana was stunned—this would have been two years after he had left the family that second time. "What? Dad never came back, though."

Fiona shook her head, "No, he didn't. Ava had just gotten married and had baby Julia, Greer and her friends had gotten into trouble selling those pills, and you were with Montgomery all the time—his little shadow. Your dad had tracked me down at a job one day, told me he wanted come home, so as soon as I finished my job for the day, I stopped at Macy's, bought the dress, and drove over to the North Fork to meet him at what used to be our favorite Italian restaurant in Mattituck." Her mom pushed a lock of silver hair behind her ear and sighed. "I was so excited he wanted to come home, but the closer I got, the more I thought about how much he had missed—the family he had walked away from. How your brother had to fill your father's role, your poor sisters and their terrible choices, with no dad beside me like he should have been to help me guide them. Your grandpa tried, of course, but he had already been a dad." Fiona paused, taking Lana's chin in her hand. "In the end, I just couldn't do it. So, I turned around and came back home. Put this dress in the back of my closet and never saw your dad again until I went to him and asked him to enroll you in that fancy school. Killed me to have to see him, but I did it for you. You deserved so much more. All of you did. Your brother could have been an engineer, you know." Lana gaped at her mom in surprise. None of her siblings had ever expressed any interest in college that she could remember. Her mom amended, "Would have been, had he gone to college. But Montgomery refused to be away from home. Long Island was my home growing up, and I've been happy here, but I never intended for my children to stay here, too."

Lana sobbed in her mom's arms, feeling her mother's tears on her own shoulders. How could Lana have been judging her mom for so many years, for what she had seen as Fiona waiting for Thomas to come back, only to find out now that she had, finally, rejected him??? How could she have never asked her brother or her sisters what dreams of theirs had gone unfulfilled, while they had all given her the space, time, and money for her to follow her dreams?

Fiona told Lana quietly, "Now I want you to take this dress, go to South Dakota, and live your life however you want. You deserve love, you deserve companionship, but most of all you deserve to live life on your own terms. Lana, I have always believed that you somehow felt you had to stay here, in New York, as some kind of familial payment, but you are free, my darling girl, to spread your wings."

In the park, Lana listened as her dear friends Effie and Josh pledged a lifetime of love and devotion, but all she did was listen, because her eyes had not left Liam's since she had taken her seat next to her brother. The brother who was now poking her in the leg to get her attention. Ignoring him, she studied as a look of panic crossed Liam's face before he turned his head to Josh, who looked slightly annoyed at his cousin. Immediately, Liam patted his breast pocket, pulling out a little bag and put something in Josh's hand. Lana felt her brother prodding her again. Why had she brought him along? she asked herself. Yes, she had been dreading seeing Liam again, but even across their distance in the park, she could read the emotions on his face that mirrored her own. Desire. Lust. Empathy. Joy. Fear. Love. Everyone under the gazebo smiled as Effie and Josh made their vows to one another, and Lana noted Liam wiping at his eyes, clearly feeling the emotion emanating from the couple. Effie had told her that Liam's sister, Cait, was officiating their ceremony, and after Lana opened up her wedding program to verify it, the sibling resemblance between the two was easy to see. Yet, where Liam was always smiling, Cait conducted the ceremony with such solemnity, giving Lana a sense that she was much more serious, and she recalled Liam making some comments to that effect.

The crowd stood as Cait pronounced the couple husband and wife, and after a long and intensely passionate kiss between Effie and Josh that caused some people attending to whistle in appreciation, the couple turned to the crowd arm in arm. Everyone began rising from their seats then, and Lana attempted to stand up, but her wrap stopped her from doing so. Looking behind her, she saw her brother's meaty arm draped on top of it.

"Why is your arm on the back of my seat?" Lana hissed at Montgomery as she wiped away her own tears. "You know, you're not *actually* supposed to be my date—you're my brother."

"Maybe because I am penned in with these ridiculously tiny chairs they have squeezed us all into, trying to fit the entire state into this park. There have to be a hundred people here," Monty complained. "And don't worry, I noticed you making googly eyes at the best man, who I'm assuming is your Hook Up? Either that, or the guy has some competition, especially based on the way he couldn't keep his eyes off of you for the entire ceremony." Since when had her brother ever been this observant? Too bad he hadn't paid this much attention to his ex-girlfriend and her needs, who Lana suspected had broken things off with him months ago because she had finally had enough of Monty dragging his feet. The fact that they had been together for eight years without at least living together as *some* form of commitment, Lana thought it was typical Monty hadn't seemed all that bothered by it, and in fact rarely mentioned Megan anymore.

"I swear to god, Montgomery, if you refer to him as my Hook Up one more time, I will hurt you." Lana inhaled and then held her breath, until at last she released it slowly. "Were you serious, though, when you said he was watching me?" If so, did that mean, then, that Liam hadn't stopped loving her? That he felt the same way she did? At her brother's nod, she scanned the crowd for him. Overcome with the irrepressible need to find Liam, Lana told her brother, "I'll be back."

Lana turned, only to find Cal and his wife Sadie standing behind her, a reminder of last year that was most certainly unwelcome at this point in her life. Obviously, she mused, they would be attending Josh's wedding to Effie, but Lana was still taken aback. All Lana wanted to do, however, was move forward, figuratively and literally, and she smiled broadly at the pair. Having no idea if Cal knew about the events at his wedding, she decided to act as if nothing had happened back then and greeted them warmly. "Hi, Cal…hi, Sadie. It's nice to see you both."

Cal grabbed Lana's hands in his, telling her, "Lana, I am so happy to see you. I wanted to reach out so many times, but never knew what to say-" Well, there goes the idea that Cal was unaware of her humiliation, Lana thought.

Cutting him off, she said, "It's fine…I'm fine." Looking over his shoulder, she panicked at not being able to see Liam anymore. "Sorry, I really need to-"

"What he's trying to say, Lana, is that his sister was completely out of line," Sadie told her, with dark eyes filled with sympathy. "Cecily imbibed too heavily due to the open bar before our wedding even started and ended up offending more than one of our guests. Not a great track record for her, since your sister also was a train wreck at our first wedding," Sadie reminded Cal with a frown. Lana debated the quickest way to end this conversation without offending anyone. She needed to get to Liam!

Cal nodded, adding, "She actually had to be escorted out of the club before the dinner. Lana, when I heard how she accosted you, I was appalled. She's had…umm…a drinking problem since high school, and we all thought she had gotten better, since her marriage to Tony."

"But that doesn't excuse her actions that night," Sadie shot Cal an exasperated look, making Lana wonder how often Cal had to apologize for his sister.

"I appreciate you telling me this," Lana assured them. "Cecily was out of control and out of line that night…to be honest, I've never had a good interaction with her." Lana watched as surprise crossed Cal's face, clearly shocked that Lana spoke so openly. "I assure both of you, though, that I don't hold any of that against either of you." Looking into the distance again, Lana said, "Sorry, but I need to go. It was good to see both of you." With that, Lana was off.

Desperate to speak to Liam before he was swept up in his duties as best man for the reception, she grabbed her wrap and her purse from her chair before anyone else could stop her. Because they had gotten two of the last seats in the last row, Lana was heading upstream to the gazebo and forced to dodge around the other guests who were streaming down the aisle, attempting to make it over to the receiving line for the bride and groom on the edge of the park. When she neared the first couple of rows, a man suddenly walked out in front of her, with his phone to his ear, whispering angrily to whomever was on the other end.

Lana heard him say, "I told you not to call me anymore. It's not my problem you were not invited." A brief pause, and then the man continued, "Then maybe you shouldn't have left him."

Lana was now close enough to hear the other person, a female, respond, "No—you don't understand. I'm trying to tell you-" but the man ended the call with a seemingly frustrated sigh. Lana had no choice but to wait for the gentleman to move, because he was standing next to a hydrangea bush, and more wedding guests were still making their way from their seats to the back of the park on his other side. Looking up from his phone, the man flashed a beleaguered look to Lana, who smiled awkwardly back at him. With his dark blond hair highlighted with bits of grey, and his eyes the color of a summer sky, there was something familiar about the man.

"Would it be ironic to say, 'Never get married' at a wedding?" He smiled ruefully at Lana, adding, "Especially when it's my son's wedding?" Of course! Now that he said it, she could tell that this man was clearly Josh's father. "I'm only kidding, of course, about marriage. It will undoubtedly suit Josh and Effie, but some people just aren't cut out for it." Now an attractive woman in her late forties with shiny brown hair and friendly brown eyes came over, putting her hand on the man's arm.

"Henry, they're waiting for you on the reception line," she softly told him. "Hi, I'm Charlotte," the woman announced to Lana, and she held out her hand to Lana's.

"I'm sorry," he said to Lana, "I never introduced myself. Henry Livingston, father of the groom, of course. Are you a friend of Effie's? That woman is a genuine gift to the world. So spirited and loving. I'm honored to have her as my daughter-in-law, officially now," he added with a chuckle.

"I am a friend of Effie's, but started as a friend of Josh's, actually. I'm Lana, we shared-"

"Lana! Say no more! I feel like I know you already," and then he opened his arms, and Lana, with no hesitation, walked into them. She closed her eyes, letting Henry's warmth envelop her. "He is anxious to see you," he said into her ear before releasing her.

In response, Lana said, "I can't wait to see Josh and wish them well."

Holding her by the shoulders, Henry shook his head. "Not Josh. Liam." Henry looked at Charlotte, and with a wave, the couple departed. Now her path was clear, with everyone having gone to greet the newlyweds, but there was no Liam. Had she missed her chance?

## Forty-Five

## Liam

MESSAGE TO LANA

> All I have done since meeting you is think about you. No time existed before you, and that is the difficult part for me, because I am finding no time exists after you either. Every night is spent wishing you were in my arms, in my bed, in my life. Every morning is hell when I wake up alone. I have tried to go back to the man I was, before I met you but finding that to be impossible. I've changed…you changed me. Rather, I should say that loving you changed me.

Locking eyes, no one else existed while Lana and Liam hungrily devoured each other from across the park. Over the heads of the other guests, while the bride made her way up the stairs to the gazebo (gleaming brightly on this late summer day), with the groom eagerly waiting for the moment in which he would be able to finally profess his ever-growing and never-ending love to said bride, Lana and Liam were doing the same with a mere shared look.

Never had Liam wanted anything more than he wanted to race over to Lana, sweep her off her feet, and carry her the distance to his house. Longing to explain to her that all he cared about was the present, that whatever terrible thing that had happened on that beach (or ever in her life) was of no consequence now, as long as they were together.

Up under the gazebo, someone was clearing a throat. "Liam," came a frantic whisper from beside him. Forcefully pulling his gaze from Lana's, Liam looked around and found four pairs of eyes staring at him: Ruth's, whose eyes were laughing; Effie's, whose eyes were understanding; Josh's, whose eyes were annoyed; and Cait's, who eyes were perplexed.

At his blank stare, Cait prompted him with some exasperation, "The rings."

Josh had insinuated misgivings last week concerning Liam holding on to his and Effie's wedding bands, something that had grievously offended Liam. Now, however, he wished it had been someone else's responsibility. All he wanted to do was stare at Lana. Was it wrong to wish the ceremony was over? Feeling selfish now, Liam reached into the breast pocket of his shirt, pulling out a small velvet bag that held the two rings, and placed one in his cousin's hand. As he watched Josh slide the platinum band onto Effie's elegant finger, he pondered how significant this was for his cousin, and for him. From the moment Josh had reconnected with Effie over two years ago, Liam had proudly witnessed how Josh developed into a better man—a more well-rounded man—with the warmth and generosity of Effie's love. In Effie's hand, he placed the ring meant for Josh. Liam took a moment to reflect that Effie, also had changed, becoming more trusting and less cynical when it came to affairs of her heart. Her first marriage had burned her, but Effie had taken a huge chance allowing herself to love Josh. Liam wiped away tears as the couple kissed for the first time as newlyweds.

Finally able to look somewhere other than at the bride and groom, Liam's eyes flashed directly back to Lana's. Unfortunately, Liam also crashed back down to harsh reality, noticing an arm on top of the back of her chair, which seemed to belong to the rugged gentleman sitting beside her. Black-haired with a thick black beard and wearing glasses, the man he assumed was Lana's "date" to the wedding was not what he would have imagined being her type. Then again, as he thought back to their first night together two years ago, when she had drunkenly assumed the two of them had been more intimate than they had *actually* been, did Lana have a type? According to Josh, she never discussed her personal life, devoting herself to her studies and then work, therefore not leaving herself much time to date. Now here she was with *him*, after he had stupidly not replied to her messages. Was it too late?

"Liam…LIAM!" Tearing his eyes from Lana and her bedraggled mountain man (what was with the flannel shirt when it was mid-seventies outside? Had he not gotten the memo he was attending a wedding, for the love of god?), Liam looked to find Cait clearly awaiting some kind of response from him.

"What?" he snapped at his sister. Couldn't she understand he was in the middle of something here?

"I *said* that I will pick up everything here, but you need to go to my car and grab the marriage license—it's on the front seat, in a manila folder with the words 'Effie and Josh' written in blue marker on the front. Here—take my keys because the doors are locked," Cait instructed.

"You locked your doors at a *wedding*-" he began mocking her.

"Liam, now is not the time for one of your 'bits'," Cait said, using air quotes. "I need to keep track of the newly married couple and get them to sign their license before they get carried away with the rest of the festivities. GO!"

Damn, his sister was bossy. One of his "bits"—seriously? More than bits, they were off-the-cuff amusing observations—like *Seinfeld*, not some well-honed pieces of comedy, he thought defensively. Walking away from Cait, it occurred to Liam that maybe he could also keep an eye out for Lana and her date while he made his way to Cait's car. Oh, crap, he thought, she never said where she had parked it, and he studied the cars that seemingly lined every street bordering the park. What the hell? Did every single person in attendance drive here separately? Liam made a snap decision to just press the "door lock" button, and he heard a faint honking from the opposite side of the park, closer to Bits and Bobs Hardware store, and began to jog over there.

At his sister's car, he expeditiously opened the passenger door. As promised, the manila folder was sitting on the seat. He bent his tall form to reach into his sister's compact car (how in the world did she drive this thing, anyway?) and grabbed the folder. As he did so, a note from inside the folder slipped out and drifted down, landing on the floor mat. "Damn," he muttered, now needing to bend himself further. Deciding to step down off the curb to make the job of contortionist easier, he did so, and ended up slipping on a patch of grass, landing on his ass. "Goddamn it!" Now his pants were going to look like he had made a mess of himself, and the last thing he wanted was to be the laughingstock at the wedding reception, especially in front of Lana. Or anyone else, for that matter. Too many people already knew about her, and the news of her arrival was sure to spread like wildfire now that the ceremony was over. Liam braced himself on one hand to push himself off the ground when he spied another piece of paper underneath the seat of the car.

"Now, what is this?" His sister usually kept her car immaculate, so Liam wasn't sure if this was garbage that had made its way down to the footwell or if it could be something Cait herself had shoved under the seat, attempting to either hide it or forget about it. Curiosity nearly overwhelmed him, but was he overstepping the bonds of their sibling relationship if he read it? Maybe it was something she thought she had lost —then he would be helping her, right? Would that make it any less offensive to his sister, who was certainly the most private person Liam knew? Even though Lana had not talked to him about every aspect of her life, she had been honest in every way that counted, from her affection for him to her openness in viewing the world when they had been together. Cait, however, held even her emotions closely in check. Had she even shed a tear today watching their cousin marry his true love? That's probably why they asked her to officiate, Liam thought to himself—not because she was a lawyer, but because she had no problem appearing severe and staid.

"Oh, screw it," Liam muttered, as he opened up the piece of paper, and his jaw dropped when he read the contents. "Holy shit," he said, just as his phone buzzed in his pocket. Hastily, he folded the paper back up and shoved it under the seat where he had found it, retrieving his phone then to read his message. Speak of the devil.

TEXT FROM CAIT

Hello??

Where the hell are you?

Get your ass back to the gazebo!

Correction: his sister only held her good emotions in check; she clearly had no problem letting anyone know when she was pissed or annoyed. Wrenching himself off the ground, he closed the car door, locked it, and then dusted off his ass, jogging back across the park.

Once the newlyweds had finished signing their marriage license, and Liam and Ruth signed as witnesses, the couple was swept away by Cait back to the receiving line that had formed since the wedding had ended.

"You okay?" asked Ruth, who was gathering up flowers from the gazebo. At Liam's questioning look, she explained, "Effie wants these over at the Cattlemen's Club to use at the reception."

"Yeah, I just slid on my ass getting the marriage license from Cait's car. I like how she was annoyed at me for taking too long in fetching it, when she was the one who forgot it in the first place," he told Ruth, motioning for her to have a seat on the bench while he grabbed the rest of the flowers for her. Her youngest daughter was only a few months old, so he was sure she had to be exhausted.

Ruth chuckled, "Yeah, she's always so intense, isn't she?"

"That's one word for her," Liam laughed, turning to take down the arch of flowers at the gazebo entrance.

"You weren't kidding when you said you slid on your ass, Liam. Your pants are a mess!" Ruth unnecessarily announced.

Liam groaned, "Ugh—I was afraid they were bad."

"Jeez, Liam, what's up with your pants?" Turning he saw Tess climbing up the stairs of the gazebo.

"He fell getting the marriage license," Ruth told her sister. "Liam, you must have another pair of dress pants at your house, right?"

"Of course—I have a closet full of them." His wardrobe had gained suits since he had begun teaching at the college—granted, it was only a community college, but he wanted to do his best to convey an air of authority and wearing a suit certainly helped. Ironically, he had to stop wearing them at the dealership, because he sold fewer cars on the days he wore one, discovering that his customers there wanted a more relaxed-looking salesperson.

"So go home and change," Tess suggested. "I'll finish here with

Ruthie, and since you're only a couple of blocks away, you'll be back by the time we go over to the reception. People are milling around, anyway. Have you seen that receiving line? That thing is never-ending!"

Liam eyed her pregnant figure, uneasy about leaving the sisters to do the work, but then Sam bounded up the steps, wrapping his wife in his arms. "Absolutely not. You go get decent, Liam, and I will do this while these two sit and watch me work."

"What's this about work?" Now Sean, Ruth's husband, had joined the party, with his three daughters in some kind of UFO-looking contraption that held all three sleeping girls. Sean left the wheeled conveyance at the bottom of the stairs before he, too, joined his wife under the gazebo. Ruth quickly got to her feet and grabbed her husband to her in an intimate embrace.

"Clearly I am not needed or wanted here," he told the couples sarcastically, "so I am going to head home to freshen up." Not that either couple even noticed his departure, consumed as they were with each other.

Liam strode over to Dakota Avenue, turning south when he got to Fourth Street, then headed east on Plum Avenue for two blocks until he arrived at his gray Cape Cod-style house. After unlocking his yellow front door, he tossed his keys on the small table, flying up the stairs that were only a few steps from the door. Heading down the hallway to his bedroom, he took out his phone to start up some music. Shortly after he had moved in, he had speakers installed in the garage, living area, kitchen, hallways, and his primary suite, and while he could manage the system if he only wanted music in one area, like the kitchen, Liam enjoyed hearing music playing through the entire house. As Garth Brooks "The River" played, he took a minute in the solitude to gather his thoughts. Stripping off his suit jacket and pulling out the tails of his shirt, Liam lay down on the bed, thinking of Lana. Wanting nothing more than to take her in his arms the minute he saw her again (the same way that Sam had done with Tess, and then Sean with Ruth), he knew he needed to play it cool, so he didn't scare her away being overzealous. Not too cool, though, that she would think he wasn't interested. Now that she was here, he wanted their past mistakes firmly behind them. Taking out his phone, he went to her text, wanting to see if she had responded to the message he had sent her before the wedding had started. She must have, based on the intensity of her stare during the ceremony, despite the lumberjack sitting next to her.

"Fuck!" He had failed to hit the blue arrow to send the message, which he immediately did now before he thought twice about it. "It's fine," he assured himself. Maybe even better than fine, since his lack of response had not diminished her depth of feeling, if those stares were any indication. Heaving himself off his bed, Liam ambled to his closet, finding a pair of pants that matched his jacket.

After unbuckling his belt, his fingers then unbuttoned his stained pants, but his hands stilled when he heard a soft voice behind him say, "I knocked, but there was no answer." The one voice guaranteed to make his blood hot, his heart pound, and his head dizzy.

# CHAPTER
## Forty-Six

## Henry



How could you hang up on me, Henry? After the life we shared, and the love I thought we shared, I would think that my existence as the mother of your son would rate an invitation to the wedding. I have apologized so many times that I have run out of ways to say "I'm sorry". But I am, and I will be forever. Haven't you ever made a mistake? All I'm trying to do is be in his life. Please.

On what should have been one of the happiest days of his life —the day of his only child's wedding—Henry shook his head as he silenced his ex-wife. Already having had to endure a phone call from her that had immediately followed Josh and Effie's wedding (which he had answered mistakenly trying to access the camera on his phone), he now did not need to be bombarded with angry, hurt texts from his son's mother. The mother that had abandoned both of them twenty-five years ago, when Josh was twelve. The mother whose absence Henry and Josh had to try and explain to their friends and family…sometimes even strangers. The mother who was now claiming to be the injured party after not being invited to her son's wedding. Henry was clueless how Melanie had even found out about the wedding. Henry searched the crowd for his own father, wondering if William could have told Melanie about the wedding. After all, his dad had kept Melanie informed about Josh in the past. Typical Melanie—knowing the date of the wedding, not bothering to come, but then calling to chew him out for slighting her. Melanie excelled at playing the injured party, under any circumstance.

"Henry? They're looking for you to take pictures," his date told him, placing her warm hand on his arm.

Henry smiled down at Charlotte, who was proving to be a safe harbor when his seas were stormy. Charlotte had brought her Jeep Wrangler into his auto shop almost two years ago, but he hadn't had the courage to ask her out until about five months ago, despite her palpable interest in him whenever he ran into her around Beverley. Then one day the two of them were on line at the same time at Mr. Beans, the coffee shop. Henry rarely went there for coffee since he brewed his own blends, but he did love their smoothies. Upon ordering his blueberry/kale/banana concoction, along with one of the warm chicken salad sandwiches Effie was always raving about, he had stepped aside to wait for his order. "That's my favorite, too," a female voice behind him had commented. Henry had looked over his shoulder to see Charlotte standing there. It had been spring, but South Dakota spring, so still snowy and cold. The brisk weather had caused her cheeks to flush an attractive shade of pink. She had been wearing a wool hat with a jaunty pompom on top, and snowflakes had clung to the ends of her brown hair. It had been years since he had experienced a visceral physical attraction to a woman, but something within him had flared to life that afternoon as she smiled so broadly at him that dimples appeared in her cheeks. Having had his heart broken twice before in his fifty-eight years, Henry had been reticent about ever allowing himself to be that vulnerable again, which explained why (or so he assured himself) he had never asked her out. Many women had tried to raise his interest, of course, after Melanie, but he had kept his heart locked away, instead focusing on raising his son and growing his auto repair business.

Charlotte, however, was not a woman he could easily ignore, he had discovered. After she had placed her lunch order of warm chicken salad sandwich on a croissant and an English toffee breve, she had pointed to an empty table nearby, inviting him to sit with her. Unable and unwilling to refuse her, Henry had held her chair for her, sliding it in slowly after she had sat down. In doing so, her light scent brushed over him, one that smelled like lemons and warm sunshine, so welcome after a harsh winter. Nervously, Henry had wracked his brain for a topic of conversation, when he remembered Effie pointing out that Charlotte was the English teacher who visited her in the library, so he asked her about her career, proud of himself as he kept the quiver of nervousness out of his voice. Two hours had quickly passed on that blustery afternoon, with Henry so immersed in his conversation with Charlotte that it had taken a text from one of the guys at the auto shop to make him aware of the passing time.

Text from Phil

Hey, Boss—do I need to send out the sheriff for you?

Feeling rather foolish, Henry had risen so abruptly from the table that Charlotte's glass of water had tipped over. Thankfully, only the sleeve of her heavy parka had gotten damp from it, but she had informed him that if he wanted to make it up to her, he could take her out for dinner at La Hacienda later that night. Henry and Charlotte had gone on their first date, which had left him wanting another date immediately. Henry, however, had never been a "dater" and had made the mistake of consulting his son, his nephews, his brother, and the guys at the auto shop—all of whom had given him conflicting advice about asking Charlotte out again immediately, waiting a few days to ask her, or even allowing enough time to pass for Charlotte to ask *Henry* out. Befuddled, Henry had done nothing, then, instead of doing the wrong thing.

Shaking his head now, Henry was aware that it had been a miracle that Charlotte had still been available this summer; after running into her at a street dance here in Beverley, when one dance had turned into two, and then three, Henry had then walked her home, kissing her on the cheek before swiftly departing. Again, Henry had been unsure of how quickly to progress things with Charlotte, with his body telling him one thing and his brain another. The two of them had started seeing each other regularly over the past couple of months, and now here she was, his date to the wedding. Taking her hand, he followed her back to the gazebo, where Josh and Effie, along with Diadema and Burnside, and Hamilton, Effie's brother, stood with the photographer. Henry kissed Charlotte's hand before releasing it so he could join the others. Looking up as he ascended the stairs, he caught Diadema's gaze on him before she quickly averted her glance. Henry's history with Diadema went further back than becoming in-laws today, but one he no longer permitted himself to dwell on.

"Okay, now how about one with just dad and the happy couple?" suggested the photographer.

Henry stood on the other side of Effie, smiling happily for the photo, prouder today of his son than he ever recalled being, including Josh's graduation from medical school. Not because he had gotten married, but because Josh was truly happy with his life, and he had moved on from so many things that could have brought him down. Instead, though, his son had gained wisdom and experience, and he seemed to get stronger and wiser with every challenge he faced. Henry had a front-row seat after Josh's relationship with Tess had ended, and after his career had taken a turn; likewise, Henry had been there when Josh had reconnected with Effie after so many years, witnessing Josh falling in love again, taking a chance again, having the kind of tenacity that Henry himself had lacked when faced with his own heartbreak.

"Now maybe just the parents of the couple?" The photographer took a moment to take a drink of water as Diadema and Burnside began walking up the steps.

"Sorry, but maybe I can sit this one out?" Burnside asked, with his hand on his chest.

"Burnie, are you okay?" Effie asked her stepdad.

"I'm fine, just feeling a little winded. Thinking I do need to catch my breath, though," Burnside said, before taking a seat in the front row of chairs. Hamilton jogged over to a cooler behind the gazebo, pulling out an icy bottle of water for his dad.

As the photographer called for more members of the bride's extended family to be added to the photos, Henry watched as Effie's Lakota family came forward, most of whom had dressed in brightly colored garments, with intricate beading and traditional patterns. Henry hugged Aurora, Effie's paternal grandmother, and shook the hand of her grandfather, Chaske, as he passed them on the stairs. Charlotte smiled at Henry as he walked over to her, and her entire face lit up as she did so. He had never known a more animated woman than her—she was so open and positive. "You look like you need a refreshment," she told him when he was standing in front of her.

Taking his hand once again, she kissed his cheek and then led him around the back of the gazebo to where Hamilton had stowed the cooler. Bending over, she pulled out two bottles of Amstel Light, freezing cold from being at the bottom of the cooler. "I hid these for us," she told him with a laugh.

"You know what I need more than this?" Henry asked her, as he took her beer from her and placed both bottles on top of the cooler.

"I have an idea, but I hope you're going to show me," she responded with a throaty chuckle, fanning herself with a wedding program.

Henry pulled her to him, groaning as her lush form melted into his solid frame. "I don't think I have told you enough times today that, with the exception of my new daughter-in-law, you are the most beautiful woman here." He kissed the underside of her jaw and then her neck, which were exposed to him thanks to the intricate braid she had pulled her hair into that morning in his house. His hands settled on her hips, slowly stroking a path following her curves, and her mouth opened under his. Charlotte's fingers slid into his jacket, and her nails scored his back through his dress shirt.

"I would hope I haven't outshined the bride on her big day. You, on the other hand, are by far the sexiest man here," Charlotte whispered in his ear, sending a shiver down him on this warm day. "Why don't we run back to your house? I'm sure no one would miss us for half an hour."

On the verge of agreeing with her, his phone pinged in the pocket of his trousers and brought him crashing back to reality. He didn't want to look at it, let alone respond, but he worried that if it was

Melanie again, left unanswered, she would escalate things, as she had earlier.

"Sorry," he apologized to Charlotte, "let me just see who this is in case it's about the reception." He loathed having to fabricate a story to her, but he had not told her that his ex had been trying to reach him multiple times.

Charlotte reached up and straightened his tie, smoothing down his jacket when she was done. "Why don't I take these back to the seats with me? I'm sure they will be ready for the Livingston family photos soon." After one last deep kiss, Charlotte pulled back, rubbing her thumb over Henry's mouth. "I want you to remember, later tonight, when you're making your speech to the bride and groom, how I almost lured you away so I could have my hands all over you…how desperate I was for you." Henry stared gaping at her, watching as she grabbed the beers from the cooler lid before rounding the gazebo, hips swaying as she walked to the front. Taking a minute to himself, he leaned against the back of the gazebo and closed his eyes, willing his pulse to stop throbbing. As his breathing leveled, Henry pulled out his phone and saw, to his relief, that it was his niece who had texted:

TEXT FROM CAIT

> Everything looking good over at the restaurant! Our family photos scheduled to start in 5 minutes.

Have you seen my brother?

After the photo sessions, Henry was in charge of making sure that people began heading across the park and to the Cattleman's Club, so the reception could begin on time. So detail-oriented was his niece, that not only had she officiated the wedding ceremony (it was a matter of family debate if the couple had asked her to do it, or if Cait had insisted on it), she had also taken it upon herself to organize most of the events for today. She did, however, have a reputation for being a bit *too* rigid at times, and he wondered if the Van Holland/LeBeau family was aware they only had five minutes left with the photographer before Cait bulldozed in with the Livingston crew.

"Excuse me?" Henry heard a quiet voice say behind him. Turning, he found a young woman, probably in her mid-twenties, with blonde hair. Who was she? he wondered, as he recalled seeing her early this afternoon, before any other guests had arrived. Maybe a cousin of Effie's that he had never met? Then again, if that was the case, why wasn't she taking pictures with the rest of her family? Perhaps she worked with Effie at the library? Or even with Josh at the hospital?

"Yes? How can I help you?" Her bright blue eyes were a few inches below his, and for some inexplicable reason, something in the pit of Henry's stomach began expanding. "I'm sorry—do I know you?"

"You're Henry Livingston, right?" Henry nodded his head in confirmation, and the young woman held out a hand and said, "I'm Sophie."

Henry looked down at her hand, perplexed about what was happening; then before he could respond, someone yelled from above, "Has anyone seen Liam?" Looking up, he saw Ruth hanging over the edge of the gazebo. "Henry, please tell me you've seen Liam?"

"No, I'm sorry—not since the ceremony. Cait just texted me, looking for him as well. Is something wrong?"

"We're gathering everyone to take pictures of the wedding party, and no one has seen him since he went home to change his pants," Ruth explained, then added "don't ask," at the quizzical look Henry gave her. "Just know that he's been gone for longer than he needs to in order to change a pair of pants."

Henry turned back to Sophie to ask her who she was, but she, too, had disappeared—as quickly as she had appeared, it seemed.

# CHAPTER
## Forty-Seven

## Lana and Liam

TEXT FROM CAIT

Liam, where the hell are you???

TEXT FROM RUTH

Liam—hello? Your sister is going apeshit over here!

How long does it take to change a pair of pants???

TEXT FROM MONTGOMERY

Lana? Where are you?

No one has seen you and I am worried sick!

"Lana?" Liam croaked in disbelief, unable to compute the fact that she was here—not just in his house, but in his bedroom. "What are you doing here? How did you find me?"

"How did I find you?" Lana's words mirrored Liam's own, as she sauntered through the doorway of his bedroom, using every ounce of audacity she possessed. While he stood there, looking so delicious it should be against the law, with his shirt untucked and his belt hanging to the sides of his waist. On the inside, she was a quivering mass of nerves, but that was not the image she wanted to project. She was **bold**. She was **fierce**. She was **confident**. Gathering her courage, she told him, "Well, one night I was in a bar, minding my own business, when a stranger came up to me and said-"

Liam interrupted, finishing for her in a choked voice, "You're just what I had been hoping would walk into this place tonight." No truer words had ever been spoken than those he had told her then, two years ago, and what he had just repeated to her now. Despite wanting to sweep her into his arms, however, he found himself unable to move, not yet ready to believe she was almost within reach.

Lana tossed her purse on a nightstand beside the bed, walked over to the closet where Liam was still standing, still as a statue, then ran her hands up to his chest. Sighing as he cupped her face in his, she asked, "Really? How long have you been waiting?"

Breathlessly, she awaited his response, and he did not disappoint, telling her, "For you, I'd wait forever." As the opening chords of "Shameless" started over the sound system, Lana dropped the wrap that had covered her shoulders until now, watching as Liam's pupils dilated, taking over the silver color of his eyes, and it was exactly the reaction from him she had imagined, hoped, dreamed.

Fuck, she was a goddess, with her glowing skin, her dewy lips, her honey hair cascading over her shoulders. And then she was in his arms, and his lips were devouring hers, with his mouth feasting on them. Lana's hands were on the waistband of his trousers, and she smiled against his lips when she found his pants already opened. Liam rotated them so her back was against his closet door, and then his hands were holding her weight up on his thighs, bracing them both.

Lana slid her hands across the bunched muscles of his chest, unbuttoning his shirt as quickly as she could, desperate to feel his hot flesh under her fingers. "Liam," she moaned and dropped her head back, allowing him full access to her tender throat and heaving chest.

Somehow, they made it to his bed, where he gently unzipped her beautiful dress, pulling it from her trembling body, before placing it carefully on the end of the bed. Lana's eyes watered at his tenderness, yet all she wanted was to tear off her clothes, so his bare flesh was on hers. As if reading her mind, off flew the rest of their clothing, and Lana pulled him down to her, gazing into his endless silver eyes, the late-afternoon sun making his hair shine as if it were on fire. Lana and Liam linked their fingers, vowing their complete devotion to each other with their bodies.

Afterwards, as they faced each other, unable to let the other out of their sight, Lana began to giggle. "What's so funny?" Liam whispered softly, stroking her cheek, fully enjoying the sight of her so carefree and calm.

"Josh is going to be so annoyed when we show up to the reception-"

"If we show up," Liam interrupted her. "I'd be happy if we stayed here all night long." Liam heard his phone ping, knowing his family was more than likely looking for him, having no idea how much time had passed since he had been away from the wedding festivities. "God, that's probably my sister, wondering where I am." Josh he could handle, but he was certain his sister was more than likely spitting nails right now, possibly burning an image in his likeness for ruining her carefully constructed schedule for today.

Lana laughed and then told Liam sincerely, "Anywhere I am, I will be happy, as long as we are together." Stroking his chest, she found it impossible to not touch him constantly, almost as if she were making up for every moment they had been apart. Growing somber now, she told him, "I need you to know how sorry I am…how wrong I was to walk away from you-"

"Shh," Liam stopped her, not caring about anything that had taken place in the past and placed a gentle kiss on her pillowy lips. "What matters…the only thing that matters… is that you're here now. Whatever magic brought you back to me, I will be forever grateful. I don't care about the past," he assured her. "If I'm honest, I have been able to glean some of it from the little that Josh and Effie have said, which wasn't much. I never knew my cousin could keep a secret before this. He kept your confidence, though. Or I guess he protected Effie so she could keep your confidence." Liam ran a finger down between Lana's breasts, luxuriating in her soft skin and ample beauty.

Raising herself up on one elbow, Lana declared, "That's just it—I want to talk about it. I don't want any of my past to hold us back. I need to explain, okay?"

Liam nodded, remaining silent so she could tell him whatever she wanted, at her own pace. Lana began again. "When I was a teenager, I thought I loved a boy, but it turned out that he was just using me." Staring into Liam's sincere eyes, she said, "I didn't figure it out, though, until after we were…intimate. It was my first time…my only time…until you. Needless to say, I was humiliated, crushed, devastated. Last year at Cal's wedding, he was the man trying to talk to me. I have no idea why—he said he wanted to 'explain', and one of the women was his girlfriend from high school, or his wife now, I don't know, or care, really. After running into them, everything I had tried so hard to escape from that time just came rushing back, and I freaked out on the beach." Lana rested her head on Liam's strong, sturdy chest, letting the solid beat of his heart soothe her. Her fingers rubbed his chest hair, and she whispered, "I hate that you were part of any of it, and I wish I had handled it all differently. Liam, you make everything in my life so much better, in every way—I need you to know that."

Rubbing her bare back, Liam recalled the nastiness of the crowd gathered around her that day and remembered the asshole trying to get Lana's attention. No wonder she had been so distraught and emotional. He found himself relieved that she had cut off his proposal back then, not allowing him to continue. He would never have wanted a memory of theirs to be marred or associated with anything in her past that caused her pain.

"I also need you to know that when everything happened in high school, it was my dad who let me down the most. I couldn't even rely on him to help me after. He betrayed me, too. Instead, I called my brother, who has had to take the place of my dad so many times."

Suddenly a lightbulb came on in Liam's head. "So…is that your brother with you today?"

Lana nodded, drawing a heart with her fingernail through his chest hair. "I was so terrified that you wouldn't understand or…I don't know…forgive me, that I couldn't face coming here alone."

Softly, he assured her, "There is nothing, in this entire world, that would ever make me turn from you." As he caressed her soft cheek,

Liam chuckled then. God, was it any clearer that the two of them belonged together? "Don't be surprised when my date demands an introduction later on," and he told her about Vanessa.

Lana laughed, pulling Liam to her again, and she ran her hand down his body, underneath the light sheet covering them both. "Let me show you something I've been dreaming about," she murmured, when an annoyed voice broke through the sound of their lovemaking and Garth Brooks's singing.

"Liam! I swear to god, you had better be lying unconscious or I am going to kill you!" Astonished, Liam watched while Cait's eyes grew wide as she stood in the doorway to his bedroom. "What in the hell, Liam? This is so you, I swear. You are the best man, for the love of god, but no, here you are, on some afternoon delight, with, I am assuming… Lana? I hope it is, or the real Lana is going to be pretty pissed when she finds out about this later from her bro-"

"Lana?" What? Why was she hearing a voice that sounded suspiciously like her brother? Lana thought. He wasn't in Liam's bedroom, was he? This had not been part of her plan! Montgomery should be back in the park, where she had left him. After speaking with Josh's dad, Lana had lost sight of Liam after the ceremony, becoming almost frantic and worrying that she may have missed her chance to fix everything between them. Judging from the timeline on the wedding program, she had roughly thirty minutes to be alone with Liam before the photos started. According to the schedule, fifteen minutes after the ceremony were family photos, with the reception an hour after that, and then the wedding dance. Where was the cocktail hour? Lana had asked her brother. And why was the dance listed separately from the reception? Monty had merely shrugged, responding that maybe they did weddings differently here in the middle of nowhere. Lana, both panicked and impatient, had told her brother she needed to talk to Tess, who had been standing off to the side of the gazebo with Sam.

"Hey, Tess," she had greeted the other woman, "any chance you know where Liam is? I just want to talk to him before it gets too late."

"Ruth said he fell getting something out of his sister's car, so he ran home to change. He should be back soon, though, because he only lives a couple of blocks from here." Tess had looked at Sam, who gave a small shrug of his shoulders.

Sam snapped his fingers then. "Tess, remember, I was going to run over to the coffee shop and get you a drink, right?" Tess had simply just stared at her husband, who had raised an eyebrow in response. "You wanted that special drink? I could give Lana a lift over to Liam's on the way." Sam turned his brown eyes to Lana and told her, "Our car is right here, and then you'll get to his house faster."

Tess had blinked rapidly, then answered just as quickly, "Oh, right—that drink! I would love one." Grabbing Lana by her shoulders, Tess pulled her in for a hug, telling her, "You look beautiful—now go and get your man."

Lana had heard the stories about Ruth intervening in Sam and Tess's romance, and how family and friends had come together to make Josh's return to Effie a magical surprise, so she was grateful to enlist aid from Sam and Tess, knowing they had deemed the relationship between herself and Liam to be just as special.

After Sam had dropped her off at Liam's charming house, everything had gone better than Lana had hoped. Until now. Monty continued, "Christ, do you know how worried I've been? No word on where you went, you just disappeared from the wedding, leaving me-"

"If everyone is done swearing and invoking the name of your lord and savior, can we please get some privacy?" yelled Liam, who had rolled over to hide Lana from view the moment he heard his sister's voice. "I had to come home and change my pants after getting the certificate out of your car, Cait," he attempted to both explain and defuse the current situation, wondering if he should lean into his reputation as a carefree idiot or that of a ladies' man?

"Sure, I can see how that made you end up in bed with my sister. Lana, this isn't why you came here-"

"Speak for yourself," Lana told her brother, from behind Liam's back, bewildered as to why neither her brother nor Liam's sister had left the room yet—how were they supposed to get dressed with an audience of annoyed siblings? Lana peeked around Liam's broad shoulders and noticed her brother's flushed face. "Monty, please leave this room immediately. I am fine, but I am certainly not going to get out of this bed with you standing there!"

Cait then spoke, "The least you could have done was stick around for the the family photos, Liam. Mom is simply beside herself now, and she is threatening to Photoshop you into the family Christmas card this year."

"Oh, my god—Mom will be fine! I'm sure there will be plenty of opportunities for another photo as soon as we get there, but you both **NEED TO LEAVE!!!**" At last, with copious amounts of grumbling and mumbling, Cait and Montgomery exited the room.

"So that was your sister, huh? She seems nice," Lana said with a giggle, and then both she and Liam were laughing hysterically. "I probably should be mortified, but I'm not. My brother and your sister found us naked, in bed. We're going to walk into the reception, and everyone will know where we've been and what we've been doing."

"Let them know! Half of them already know that you are my 'Mystery Woman' and I was your 'Hook Up'," Liam told her.

"*Was* my 'Hook Up'? I think our certain state of affairs would prove otherwise," she corrected him, playing with the curls at the nape of his neck. "Now, where were we before being interrupted?" Lana asked, leaning over him, kissing him passionately.

With a groan, Liam took her hand to show her where they had been. What was another fifteen minutes? A glance at his watch told him that they had plenty of time before the reception began…

"So, how did you find me?" Liam asked her, once they were both completely out of breath (but too love-drunk to care), pushing a strand of hair behind her ear, unwilling to move too quickly to disrupt their current state of bliss. Liam wasn't truly all that curious about how she had wound up at his house, but more in awe of her determination to find him alone, so they could move forward together. Finally.

Lana brought his face to hers. "I'll always find you, no matter what." She took a deep breath, then released it shakily. Doing her best to hold her emotions at bay, she told him, "More than anything in my life, I regret the first time I walked away from you, in that hotel room in New York. I hate that I let so much time pass, but you need to know that reading your messages got me through those months afterwards. When I saw you again at Cal's wedding, it was all too much for me—I wasn't expecting to see you there, and I certainly wasn't expecting to see those people from my past." Lana shuddered in Liam's arms, and he pulled her close, winding her hair around his fist, then dusting her forehead with kisses. "I should have explained it to you, though. You need to know now," she promised him, "that I will never leave you again."

Liam remained still, afraid that any movement from him would snap Lana back to reality, breaking their reverie. "What are you saying?" Liam held his breath, hoping she meant what he wanted her to mean.

Now was the time, Lana decided, so she rolled over to reach for her purse on the nightstand. Liam, scared that she was trying to get out of bed, held on to her tightly, nuzzling her neck, which made her chuckle.

"I'm saying," she informed him, with tears threatening to fall, as she rolled on to her back, "that my heart is yours," and above their heads she held the crystal heart ornament that he had given her two years ago. "Although from the looks of that tree on your dresser, I don't know if there will be room for it." Lana began crying in earnest then, remarking, "I can't believe you have a tree in your bedroom filled with our ornaments. Almost like you've been waiting for me."

"Darlin', rest assured that I have been waiting for you for my entire life, and there is more than enough room on that tree, and in my life, for your heart. Your gorgeous body," Liam kissed her brow, "your generous heart," now he kissed her cheek, "your brilliant mind," then he kissed her mouth. "I want all of you," he told her. Now it was his turn to roll over, reaching for the pants he had been wearing earlier. Pulling out a small, aquamarine box, Liam turned back to Lana, asking her, "Lana Miller, will you marry me?"

In response, Lana flung herself into his arms. Liam managed to slip the ring on her finger as she replied, "Yes! Yes! A million times, yes!"

TEXT FROM CAIT

Liam! Where are you? You do know you have the first toast at the reception?

TEXT FROM MONTGOMERY

I'm going to assume you will show up eventually…Interestingly enough, I have been talking with Felix, Liam's cousin. He's an architect, and it seems that his company is looking for a reliable contractor for some of their jobs. Wouldn't that be weird if…no, never mind. Too weird.

What is with his sister, though? She is really high strung.

TEXT FROM TESS

Lana, thanks to your brother and Liam's sister, everyone knows you guys have reunited. Which we are all super happy about, don't get me wrong, but it would be nice if Liam made it here by the time dinner started.

TEXT FROM GREER

OMG!!! Monty says you are totally getting lucky!

TEXT FROM AVA

I cannot believe our brother caught you in the sack with your hook up!!!

TEXT FROM CAIT

Lana's brother is kind of intense.

What's his deal?

You better not finally show up here engaged or anything!

That would be so tacky!

# EPILOGUE

*Eight Months Later*

TEXT FROM JOSH

Hope we make it to the wedding.

Might not be able to leave the bedroom.

We are still newlyweds.

TEXT TO JOSH

Dude, how many times do I have to say I'm sorry???

I mean, we made it to the reception. Almost.

TEXT FROM EFFIE

And then to have you show up to our wedding ENGAGED???

So Liam-coded…

TEXT TO EFFIE

Wow, you, too, huh?

With the May sun bleaching the sands of the beach, Lana looked over at her groom, who was rarely more than an arm's length away if they were in the same vicinity as each other. Getting married on the beach had been Lana's idea, convincing Liam that she should reclaim her own past, rewrite her story. Because she was extremely skilled at getting her own way, he had agreed, as he usually did, since she let him get his own way often enough, too. Besides, Lana reminded Liam that it was the bride's prerogative to choose the wedding location.

Liam stood in the shadow of the lighthouse in Montauk, where he had once watched the woman of his dreams walk away from him. Believing that she would, eventually, come back to him, he had waited for her, and now here she was, stealing his breath, his sense, and the pieces of his heart she hadn't already claimed.

The couple had asked Josh and Effie to be their "best people", and serving as bridesmaids were Greer and Ava (though the two were as far from maids as women could get, Lana liked to tell them). Liam and Monty had grown close since his move to South Dakota, so he was one of Liam's groomsmen, as was his cousin Felix. Cait, having done the best with what she had to work with for Josh and Effie's wedding (the comment mostly concerned her own brother), had commandeered most of the planning for her brother's wedding to ensure that he and Lana would make it to the altar (such that it was) on time.

The bride was wearing a vintage (of course) tea-length wedding gown that had to have been modeled after the one Grace Kelly had worn to her own wedding to her Prince. Lana's niece, Amelia, had discovered it when she was thrifting in Boston, calling her up late one night to tell her about it. Almost as if the dress had been tailored for her own body, it had fit perfectly, despite Lana's hesitation immediately before trying on the garment. The expression on Liam's face upon seeing her in it, when he had unexpectedly come home for lunch that day, had told her everything she needed to know. Effie had been on hand to help Lana into the dress that day (as she was today), but it had been Liam who had helped her out of it, swiftly, after Effie's hasty departure.

Montgomery was playing double duty today, as he was also walking his sister down the "aisle", a beach path that had been lined with seashells collected by Lana's nieces and nephews. Lana's father had been invited, after much deliberation, but in true Thomas-fashion, Lana had heard no reply. Just as well, since Lana preferred Monty to do the honor, anyway.

Liam's mom had not stopped crying since he had announced his engagement to Lana at Josh and Effie's wedding dance—not because she was upset that her son was going to be married, but because, after so many years, he had finally met someone he loved enough to make a commitment to, and that woman was someone who clearly and unabashedly adored and treasured her son as much as he deserved. Despite talk to the contrary, Liam *had* arrived at the reception in time for his toast to the bride and groom, albeit looking somewhat more rumpled than he had at the ceremony, but he explained that away, blaming his fall at his sister's car. Only two people knew the truth, and neither one of them had said a word, and two others were certain they also knew the truth, and there had been plenty of speculation by several people about why Liam came back to the reception wearing the same pair of pants he had gone home to change. As Effie remarked repeatedly about the sudden appearance of Lana and Liam arriving together, arm-in-arm, to the reception, it was so Liam-coded.

Lana had gone to South Dakota with every intention of never leaving Liam's side, should everything go the way she had planned. And hoped. And wished. And it had. Her scheming had begun about two months before Josh and Effie's wedding, when she had reached out to Josh about any possible openings at Beverley General. Lana was done with surgery, wanting to focus instead on general practice. Liam was thriving at both the college and the dealership, but knew he would scale back at some point, especially with the news that Lana had whispered in his ear last night, as they lay side by side under the moon glow, hands entwined, watching the beaming light from the lighthouse skim over the ocean, searching for ships in need of guidance.

Just as this lighthouse had allowed captains to land safely, so had

Liam done for Lana—he had proven to her countless times since they had met that he would always be there. Lana, in turn, had seen Liam as no one else ever had—someone that could be counted on and believed in, for despite having been disappointed before, she had trusted in her heart, and in Liam. All of this was why, at the suggestion of Monty, they had chosen "When You Come Back to Me Again" for their wedding. Garth Brooks sang, "It's been tossed about, lost and broken, wandering aimlessly…that someone out there still believes in me."

# SERIES NOTE

*Mixed Messages* is Book Three in the series "Love, South Dakota Style". If you loved this book, be sure to read the other titles: *Excess Baggage* (Book One) and *Cutting Losses* (Book Two). You will get to read in full how Tess and Sam fell in love, and how Josh and Effie found their way back to each other.

The love never ends, so scan the QR code below to go to my website JodiCulliney.com to enter my world of books. Stay tuned for announcements concerning my book currently in progress.

# Acknowledgments

The past sixteen months have been a whirlwind, and it is unbelievable to me that I wrote three books in that time! The outpouring of support and encouragement from my family and friends has been incredible, as always, yet it is important to recognize people I had not automatically thought would be my cheerleaders and readers. Thank you to everyone in my hometown of Wessington Springs (of which the tiny town of Clover Hill is *loosely* based) for showing up to book signings and book talks, for buying my books and reading them, and for promoting them in even the smallest ways. Thank you to the Springs Inn for hosting my events (so far), to the Springs Area Council for the Arts, to the Huron Public Library, and a special thanks to Lou Ann for always getting the word out. Thank you to anyone who bought my books, read my books, and especially those who attended any book signings or book events. I appreciate your support.

My books are always works of fiction, but I do take some inspiration from my own life and from people I've known throughout the years, so thank you to anyone who has implanted a memory in my brain I can then draw upon later. I honestly never thought I would enjoy the process of writing as much as I do, and I always have my husband to thank for helping me discover that. Special thanks to my sisters: Kris, Candi, Laci, and Chelsea for reading, promoting, and supporting, and also to my mom, one again.

My books would not look as beautiful without the work of some very talented artists themselves, who can be found on fiverr.com:

Katarina @nskvsky for designing my gorgeous covers

Brady Moller @bradymoller for the page layout, interior art, and design.

I always welcome hearing from readers, new and old, and can be reached at jodi@jodiculliney.com.

# ABOUT THE AUTHOR

Jodi Culliney, former bookstore clerk and lifelong lover of books, grew up in South Dakota, where she lived a peaceful existence until she met the love of her life and made the move to Brooklyn, NY. She has a Bachelor's degree in English from Black Hills State University and is working on her next novel.

Scan this QR code for a link to my Substack - It's called Reader Becomes Writer and it is where I write about how I started my journey and talk about my books!

https://jodiculliney.substack.com/

Thanks for reading!